The Arcangineers

AN ECHOES OF THE END NOVEL

Cover Artwork by: Martin Hulka

Cover Design by: Erica Lynn Evans

Edited by: Lily Ingersoll

ISBN: 978-1-963266-00-9

Visit the author on the internet
http://www.therunespring.com

FOREWORD

A little information for all you readers. This book, being set on an alien planet, has a few terms and words that are used differently than they are in English. To help everyone understand the language usage, I have included a glossary at the end of the novel. I hope it helps you all on your journey across Ahlysim!

~ CM

PROLOGUE

"Awake"

She opened her new eyes for the first time. Her eyes slid around the blank chamber. There were no windows. Everything was painted a uniform dull grey. The only source of color in the darkened room was a garment hanging from a hook on one of the blank walls. She could see that there had once been a light overhead, but the element had burned out long ago. How long had she been asleep? She touched her fingers to her head and looked at them, but there was no blood.

"What happened to me?" She wondered aloud. She received no answer.

She got to her feet and realized her Constraints were gone. She sent a probe down into her mind and found the psychic blocks. They had all been thrown open. She closed each of the five blocks. Strangely, she still felt too strong and fast for her Constraints to be closed. What could have caused her to push her body all the way to the breaking point?

She took the garment down off the wall. It was a blue sundress - a plain one with a wide blue ribbon around the waist tied in a bow at the small of the back. There were purple flowers embroidered high on the left breast. She frowned. Whoever had left this here had not known her very well. She only wore dresses on those few special occasions when she felt she could afford to truly relax and enjoy herself. Still, she had little choice in the matter, so she pulled the dress over her head. There was a small pocket on the front of her dress, one that she had not noticed until she had put it on. A square of paper peaked from the lip of the pocket. She pulled it out. It turned out to be an entire page folded over many times. Perfect letters flowed across the page in a script she recognized, though she was unable to remember whose hand had penned it.

She could feel the pieces of her mind going through the finalization of some sort of repair process. Long ago, she had taken a shot to the head after jumping off a cliff. When her Cellstructs had finished repairing her damaged brain, she had felt this sensation. She shook her head once to clear it, and then looked down to the note again.

It read:

"My Dear Alessandra, I do not know when you will wake, or even if you will. You appeared at my door covered in the blood of a foe that I know now to have been another member of the Corps -- the one they called "The Traitor." Your body was nearly destroyed as you released all of your Constraints. Whoever The Traitor was, he must have been quite powerful for you to need to push yourself past your inborn limits. We found his body torn nearly apart, his face a ruin. He was entirely impossible to identify, as his body disintegrated not long after it was discovered. However, many believed him to have been Alizar.

There was nothing to dispute this fact as there were no others with your skill and strength. There were two witnesses to your fight with The Traitor, though they did not see much. They said you moved with such speed and power that you destroyed the temple around you. Only by the shattering stone floors, were they able to follow the fight between you. When it was done, and you stood over the broken body of your foe, they had to escape as the temple was collapsing around you.

I didn't know any of this until days after you lay unconscious in my operating room. Your body had begun to repair itself even as you made your way to me, but even once you were healthy again you would not wake. I have no idea why your mind has lain dormant all these cycles, but I have poured my craft into you in my attempts to wake you. Everything I know of Tieran Structures I have imbued into your body. I have used materials of which I have no further supply and experimental processes that I cannot properly repeat. I hope that you do not find my gift to you a curse. You shall live throughout the ages, until you wake once again. Your body will not age, at least not until you wake and break your stasis. Even then, I am not sure how the combined technologies I have given you will affect the aging process. It may cease entirely.

Your body has been enhanced by these processes even beyond the five levels of Constraints you knew in our time. You must place two further mental blocks in your mind to compensate for these further levels of physical enhancement. Much like when your physical enhancement was limited to five separate levels, if you go into the sixth, and especially the seventh level, it will damage your body with prolonged use. Know this, my daughter: you saved our world that day, and the changes you wrought echo on into the future - a future I hope that you will live to see. I love you, my daughter, and I hope you find happiness when you wake. Good Luck.

Father."

Alessandra tried to recall the events her Father was speaking about in the letter. She had no viable memory beyond waking just a few minutes earlier. The last thing she remembered was a conversation with one of her best friends at the Corps. She could not even see a door to the room. She closed her eyes and concentrated. She remembered her abilities well enough. Those had been written down to her very soul, ingrained in her bones - the abilities of the Vision.

She realized that her Vision was already open, but it was pulled back to the weakest level. That was how she was able to see in the pitch black room. She concentrated and instantly her sight was overlaid with a thousand small details about the room. She could see it right down to the molecular level and beyond. She could see the minute particles as well, right down to the tiniest portions of the universe, and the strings vibrating inside of those particles. Her Vision showed her how it all fit together - how everything affected everything else and how it was all connected. She didn't drill down to that level, however. It was unnecessary.

It took her only a moment to locate the invisible door. She pushed against it, and it slid aside of its own accord. There was a hiss of escaping air as the seal was broken. She made her way down the hallway beyond the door. There were no doors except one at the opposite end of the hall. She reached the end of the hall, and went through. There, she found an empty circular room with three doors leading out. The first, on the far right, was marked with the symbol for a bathhouse. The second, in the middle, was marked with a symbol of valuable possessions, and the third was the exit... but the exit to where?

"Hello?" She called in the dim light of the chamber. There was no response. She suddenly felt a powerful need to get clean, and went to the bathhouse door. Inside was a beautifully tiled room. There were two pools of still water, and as soon as she opened the door, illumination filled them from below. They were clean, and looked to have Tieran filtration systems. She let the door swing closed, and that was when she saw it. Next to the wash basin was a Tieran display panel. The small screen would have been used to control the various functions of a home. It would control the climate, the lighting, and things of the like. This one, however, displayed a Tieran counter. It showed the current date and time.

"This place should be controlled by a Mind." Ales mumbled to herself. Then recognition hit her mind like a sledgehammer. She slid down to her knees as she stared at the cool blue numbers slowly counting each passing tick of the clock. Tears began to leak from the corners of her eyes. She could not cope with what the display made clear to her. It simply was not possible.

She had been asleep for over thirty-one hundred cycles.

PART 1

1

By the count of the Tieran timepiece it had been an entire span since she had woken from her sleep. Her memories of what had happened to cause her long sleep were slowly reemerging from the dark corners of her mind. It had taken that entire span for her to come to terms with the idea that she had been asleep for twenty two generations of the Tier. All her friends, all her family would be gone. Her sister would be long dead. Her soul returned to The Core to be reborn again and again. Bann was gone before they ever really had a chance to be together.

When she got to the top of the stairwell, she found that a massive slab of rock blocked the exit. It only took a moment with her Vision open to find the switch to move the slab aside. It slid silently open. She stopped, unsure of what she might find when she set foot outside of this bunker. She looked back down into the bunker. Her Structures told her that the bunker had to have been run by a Tieran Mind. A Mind was an artificial intelligence that could be incredibly useful. They were able to decode and understand any language no matter how complex, or indecipherable it may seem. It was a feat her Cellstructs could perform, but only with speed if the language was close to her own. But she couldn't bring it with her.

Without The Core, she couldn't connect to the mind without taking it with her. Not to mention that she had not been able to find it. She had no idea how it was possible that she could not connect to The Core. It was entirely impervious to any sort of damage. She had to find out what had happened in the past thirty-one hundred cycles. She finished the climb to the outside, and stopped in her tracks. There standing not ten marks away was a goddess.

"Mother." She gasped. She fell to her knees, but before she could prostrate herself the Mother was there taking her hands pulling her back to her feet.

"Please my child, please, you know me better than that. Avaara will do just fine." She said, and her voice was a sigh on the wind. Ales looked up into the face of beauty. Avaara had pale porcelain skin with a slight blue tint too it. Her eyes were pupiless cobalt orbs the color of dusk sky. They seemed to have stars floating through their deep blue depths. Her hair was a carpet of cerulean trefoil leaves. Two soft triangular ears peeked up through the top of the carpet of leaves. Unlike Ales Avaara's arms got wider as they approached her hands, and her fingers seemed to sprout directly from the end of the softly rounded arms. She wore a dress made of a violet moss that fit a very shapely figure and fell to below her feet. It appeared as if it had grown from her skin. She had seen that moss take deadly poison from a child that was far too sick to be treated any other way. That child had been her younger sister. She did not walk, but hovered a mere tick off the ground. She did this out of necessity as any part of Ahlysim she touched would explode with flora in reaction to her presence. It had been an effort of will simply to touch Ales without doing harm.

"I looked for you. I remember I did. I didn't want to kill another of the Tier. I di..." Avaara shook her head, and pressed a delicate finger to Ales' lips to quiet her.

"Child I know you looked for me, but I was not to be found for a reason. Zezzhz and I are limited in what we can do. We have great power, but the sort of power we have makes it necessary for us to move slowly. It is like a great old Griog my child. Slow, and ponderous because were they to move to quickly they could do great damage. This is why we could not interfere in your fight with our child Alizar." Avaara's voice was like her power. Slow, and lovely beyond all description.

"What happened here Avaara? Where is The Core? I cannot sense your presence through it."

"Much happened. When you stopped Alizar you were gravely injured. Your Father did what he could, and when he could not wake you he came to the Temple. He asked Zezzhz, and I to help. We spent some time investigating your condition for your father as his Vision was not strong enough to breech the subatomic level. It is still a mystery why you have lain dormant so long though we have theories." Avaara tilted her head curiously.

"How is anything a mystery to you Mother?" Avaara frowned at the question. Ales realized a moment later why.

"Avaara, I'm sorry it is just the last time I saw you I was very young, and you are very..." Ales trailed off unsure how to describe the goddess in a single simple word. It was impossible. Avaara's smile returned like a sunrise.

"Ah child, that is the rub of power such as ours. Everyone expects that we should simply know everything. Unfortunately it is not so. There are many things that we know instinctively because of our connection to each of you, but while we created all that lives here on Ahlysim you have all evolved far beyond our ability to understand everything. This was the purpose of The Core. To help us to understand more about how the world was changing. But we are getting off the topic. The point of this statement is that we understand most of the intricacies of how the universe functions. However the mind is an ever changing matricie of energetic atomic states, as complex a thing as Zezzhz has ever designed. Once set into motion, even we cannot predict completely how it will function. Hence we have theories concerning why you would not wake. Theories that could not be proven until now." Avaara grinned, and Ales thought she might weep from the beauty of it.

"What happened?" Ales asked.

"Yes. Your brain was damaged quite severely by your fight with Alizar. Your Cellstructs were attempting to recreate your synaptic structure from the last snapshot they had of your complete mind. This process is normally something that could be completed in a few rotations. But whatever Alizar had done to you had severely scrambled the atomic structure of the memory units of your Structures. Presumably it took this long for them to rebuild their own memory before they could go to work on the damage you experienced. I am sure if you requested their status they would tell you as much." Avaara's face took on a very somber look.

"That look tells me that you are preparing to tell me something that may be more than I am able to cope with." Ales said. Avaara bowed her head slightly.

"Apologiesm, my Daughter. I am not familiar with facial expressions, and so I act on instinct. I know that you have just woken to something already devastating, but you did ask what happened. I wish to tell you, but before we go any further I have brought a friend who has been a great comfort to me these long cycles. I hope that she can do the same for you."

Avaara turned slightly, and held out her hand making a beckoning gesture. There was some movement in the violet scrub brush behind her, and then a sleek form slipped out of the trees. It was a katali. She had baby blue fur with a peppering of white spots across her face and down her back. She had puffy white tufts at the end of her ears, and unlike most of the species she had round pupils. Ales's eyes went wide. This katali was one of the Wild, but not just any one of the Wild.

"Lia!" Ales came to her feet, and ran in a way she had not since she was a child. She slid to her knees, and wrapped her arms around the massive feline's neck. Tears streamed down her face.

"How is this possible?!" Ales asked.

"The letter your father left for you. He was unable to repeat the processes that created your very special Cellstructs. I on the other hand was able to use his data from The Core to reproduce the effect. When your sister learned of your predicament. She asked to undergo the procedure. She wished to be here when you woke. I advised her that it could be a lonely existence. She told me, quite bluntly, that if I did not do this thing she would never speak to myself or Zezzhz again. How could I refuse?" Avaara smiled fondly at Liassa. Ales felt the mental handshake that was a hallmark of Tieran telepathic communication.

{It is about time you rolled out of bed. You sleep like a balath after the rut!} Liassa's mindvoice was filled with so much joy that it couldn't be expressed in any language. Ales burst out laughing, and clutched her sister's neck so tightly that Liassa made a choking sound.

{Glurk! Need breathing!} She said into Ales' mind. Alessandra loosened her grip, but did not let go.

"Not like I had a choice in the matter. I see your tail is still attached, Spook. I guess you learned to keep it down."

Ales let go of her sister, and looked back up to Avaara. Her smile was radiant in ways Ales had no words to describe. Liassa laid down and arranged her six legs for comfort.

"Would you like to tell it Liassa or shall I?" Avaara asked.

{I think that it would be best if you told the story. My time among the Wild has made my memories dormant. It will take time for me to reestablish my bonds with those memories.} Liassa replied.

Avaara nodded graciously. She folded her legs up from the ground, and took a sitting position where she floated in the air.

"As you wish. Ales, you were able to stop Alizar, but regrettably, your interception was not entirely successful. Had Alizar been allowed to continue his activities, he may very well have achieved a reaction that would have devastated all of Ahlysim. But as it was, the device he built became unstable in the cycles after his death. So well was it hidden and protected that we had no sense of it until it was too late.

The Core detected the danger and alerted all of the Tier, for only those with the Vision would be able to manipulate the energies coursing through the device. The effort was too late. The device was not a simple bomb. It was some form of anti-matter reaction that I would have dearly liked to study. That, however, is neither here nor there. The Tier used their Vision to examine the reaction, and inject ariation devices at strategically chosen points at the heart of the reaction to bleed off the heat and stall the reaction. However, it could not be done quickly enough.

The Tier saved Ahlysim that day, as Zezzhz calculated that uninhibited the reaction would have breached the planetary core. However all of Ahal was destroyed, and the Tier with it. Only a few of the Wild were unable to make it back to Ahal. Among them was dear Liassa. Though only she, and you, remain of the Tier as she did not find a mate before the Cataclysm."

Ales watched in awe as two tears of azure liquid rolled down Avaara's cheeks. Avaara produced a small square of some soft white gauzy substance and daubed at her face. She folded over the cloth twice, and held it out to Ales.

"I do not often find a reason to shed tears, but so many of my children died that day. I do not think I could do any less. In that cloth, they will stay fresh indefinitely and you can use them to heal any one wound, even a dire one. I entrust them to you."

Ales took it and tucked it into her dress' single pocket.

"Mother, I do not wish to be impertinent, but could these have sped my recovery?"

Avaara smiled. "You carried no wound, daughter. These heal hurts, but the damage you received was different. We simply had to wait and hope that you would recover. Zezzhz and I believe that somehow The Core was displaced by the explosion that vaporized Ahal. We do not believe it destroyed, but Zezzhz believes that its energetic structure was somehow altered by the blast. We have been unable to locate it in the subsequent three thousand cycles.

I come to you now with a task. Alessandra, Liassa, the world has become a very dangerous place. Uncontrolled Tieran technology has been spread by the Cataclysm. To bring peace, you must find The Core and return the stability of Tieran protection to this world."

Wind blew into the clearing rustling through the tangle of leaves serving as Avaara's hair, and then she was gone.

2

Liassa looked up as Ales got to her feet. She watched Ales for a long moment, and then arranged her six legs beneath her. She stood up and padded towards the bunker entrance behind Ales.

{I'm sorry about the dress.} Liassa said into Ales' mind.

"You brought it?" Ales asked.

{You've been asleep thirty one hundred cycles. I've brought at least half a hundred garments, if not more. Only the paper survived, as it was infused with Bondstructs by our father. It is not easy for a katali to get clothing in this age. The dress was the only thing I could find I could be sure would fit you. There are dangers in the world, even for Arcangineers. We are the only two left, and no one recognizes one of the Wild anymore. They do not realize my eyes are not the eyes of a katali, nor do they want to get close enough to see my collar. They have taken the remnants of our technology and perverted everything we stood for, Ales. And the machines they have made are powerful. Too powerful for me to take them all on alone.}

"What is the currency of the land these days?" Ales asked.

{Gemstones and precious metals are still accepted in many places. Some of the Centers have a structured elementary currency system, though.}

"Centers?"

{It's just the word used for large settlements like Ahal. It is not the same, Ales. This isn't our world anymore. When the Cataclysm happened I was racing back towards Ahal. I had just made the border when Luan stopped me. He said it was too late, and that I should run as fast as I could. Then I lost contact with him. I ran, Ales. I ran like I had never run before in my life. I had never felt such finality in anyone's mindvoice.

That was when the blast came. It blew me across the Ahlyn Divide, and I landed about six lengths into the Black Wilds. When I finally came to my senses, Ahal was gone. The Tier were gone. Zezzhz found me nearly dead, and despite my foolish protests, nursed me back to health. He told me that you were still alive, but you were not the only one who needed my help. He gave me a purpose in a time when I needed it desperately. He made me collect and take care of the handful of Tier who were far enough away to have survived the Cataclysm. In my debilitating depression over the loss of all of our people, I would have lost myself to the wilderness. That, it seems, will never be my fate.}

Liassa let out a breath. The process of becoming one of the Wild was not dangerous in itself. But as they aged, many of the Wild could mentally lose their connection to the rest of the world. Once that happened, their mind would quickly degrade until they were just another of the animals of nature. Losing yourself to the wilderness was a touchy subject for all of the Wild. It was considered a great tragedy, and a great sin.

"You have been alone for all these cycles," Ales said apologetically.

{No, not alone. For the first few hundred cycles, it was not so bad.}

They made their way down into the bunker, leaving the door open behind them as they descended into Alessandra's sleeping place.

"You had the others. How many did survive the blast?"

{Six total. I didn't know any of them personally, but all of them were injured in the discharge from whatever it was Alizar had left behind. It was terrible. Two of them had severely damaged over ninety percent of their Cellstructs. One of them died within days. Zezzhz and I were able to save the other one. We are getting off track, Ales. I have things to tell you, and we cannot stay here long. They will be tracking me, and I've only been able to stay off their radar for this long with The Mother's help.}

Ales stopped at the bottom of the stairs.

"Who is tracking you?"

{They are called The Three. You have a lot to learn, and they are not the only ones that are after me. But they are the primary threat as far as I know.} Liassa sat on her haunches at the bottom of the stairs.

"Threat? You should be able to handle nearly anything." Ales tilted her head questioningly.

{No, not anymore. At least not on my own. Their armor is nearly impervious to my abilities, and it is self-repairing. They have had a lot of time to research how to use our Bondstructs in very dangerous ways. They have increased strength and speed from their armor. I am stronger by far, and I doubt they will catch me on their own. However I have taken injuries from them. We left things here for you that will help us, but I can't use them. No thumbs, you see.}

Liassa lifted one of her forepaws and wiggled the digits. Then she pressed it against the wall. A square section of the wall slid aside, revealing a space the size of a gym locker.

{We thought you might need these when you woke up.}

Ales went to the hidden space. Inside was a long flat bar of metal with rounded edges. Along one side, for about three quarters the length, was a slot cut into the metal. Ales reached for the end without the slot cut into it. She gripped it like a sword and drew it out.

{It's impossible for me to swing a Windblade anymore, but you can use it to cut through their armor. Your Sparks are in there too.}

Ales set aside the Windblade and reached in to take out the hide pouch that held her Sparks. Unlike the Windblade, the Sparks could down an opponent without doing permanent damage. The Windblade was a far more useful tool overall, but it was difficult to use it without hurting someone. Ales noticed there was a small square box of black wood in the back. She leaned into the locker and picked up the box, staring at the symbol on the top. The crest was one that she recognized. It was a symbol that every one of the Tier would recognize. It stood for memories.

"This isn't what I think it is?" Ales asked.

{It is the only sample of The Core we could recover. It contains father's research, and some of mother's memories. I don't want to touch it again. I got to see how mother felt about me becoming one of the Wild. I always thought that everyone was unhappy that I made the change, but she only wanted to see me happy. It didn't matter that I had six legs and a tail to her. I was still her daughter. But how many other things didn't I know? How many of them were good?}

Ales began to laugh, quietly at first. "Oh, Lia. Mother was always so proud of you. She thought that it took a lot of strength to understand that you had to distance yourself from what you had to do to protect others. I doubt she had many bad thoughts about you."

{All of us have flaws, Ales. I just don't know if I want to find out if she knew what mine were.}

Liassa laid down on the floor, resting her chin on her front paws. Ales took a couple of practice swings with the bar of flat metal. Air rushed away from the blade in a soft wave that blew back Liassa's fur. Her tufted ears twitched.

"You know I've always meant to ask you. Aren't female katali supposed to be a single color? You have spots."

{I... liked my freckles, alright?} Her mindvoice was a shy mumble.

"It must have sent mixed signals to other katali all these cycles," Ales teased her.

{I never found a companion, Ales, and I spent a lot of time with Avaara. As you well know, the Tier were the closest to them. They created all life on Ahlysim, and many still worship Avaara and Zezzhz, but we were the ones who knew them. It hurt them a great deal when all of the Tier were lost. We can talk about this later. The Three will be here soon.}

"How far behind you are they?" Ales asked.

{Not far.}

Liassa lifted her head and took a long deep breath through her nose.

{I can't smell them yet, but they have some sort of tracker on me that I haven't been able to get out of my fur. Something that bonded itself to me. If I focus my Vision on my forepaws I can see them. They are like Bondstructs but I can't connect to them to shut them down,} Liassa explained.

Her Vision was strong, but not as strong as Ales'. Her Vision stopped at the molecular level. She could see no further down than that. That would mean she couldn't see energetic particles. Ales opened her Vision. Suddenly, the world snapped into absolute focus. She could see beyond any average sight. Understand everything she saw. The connections in the world. How everything fit together. Why everything was the way it was. It was both simple and profound, the way opening that sixth sense made her see the world. She concentrated, and the world narrowed in her sight. The rocks, the trees, the world went away as she focused on just seeing the building blocks of reality. The atoms and particles that made up everything. And that was when she saw waves of elementary energy coming off of Liassa's body. More specifically, she saw how they effected the particles around her.

"The Mother couldn't help you with this?" Ales asked.

Lia looked away, ashamed.

{I never asked her. I was careless. It is my problem to fix,} Lia said her mindvoice slightly ashamed.

"I see it. You're right, it's a dusting of Bondstructs, or at least they are like Bondstructs. They are less sophisticated than what we used for building. They are not designed to be able to be released. But I might be able to..."

{Too late, Ales. They are here.}

She turned, and then her eyes adjusted back to normal levels of vision. Ales put her things down except for the Windblade. She strode outside, resting the blade on her shoulder. She continued to walk until three people came out of the trees. They were covered head to toe in black garments. As Ales examined it more closely, she could see it was a skin tight layer of interlocking Structures. Microscopic machines that covered their bodies completely. But the men inside were just men. It was possible that one of them was a woman, but she couldn't be sure without getting closer. She did not intend to do that.

"I can see why these are giving you trouble. You never got past the molecular level with your Vision. The armor interlocks at the atomic level. Against someone without deeper Vision or the Circle of Breaking, they would be difficult to damage. I assume there are only these three?"

{Not really. They call them The Three because they are the only three who are allowed to advertise the power of their armor. There are many others, but they are either military or part of the royal family. They don't advertise the armor's abilities. It grows the rumors without putting too many facts behind them. Any action within the city by others using Bondarmor is just attributed to The Three.}

"This will only take a minute."

Ales swung the Windblade out to her side and held it there at the ready.

{I didn't expect it would take any more.} Liassa said.

There was a reason Lia had confidence in what Ales said. Ales was the most powerful of the Tier that anyone had ever seen besides the Traitor. Unlike the Traitor, she was a true protector of those weaker than her. She had gone to fight Alizar knowing full well that it would likely cost her life to stop him. Liassa sat down on her haunches. There was no need for her to get in the way.

"There is no need for you to be hurt. We only want the katali. It has killed people. It must be put down." One of the three spoke loudly to cover the distance.

"If my sister has killed, then she must have done so to defend herself or others. You will not harm her. Withdraw."

The men exchanged a look, and then drew strange weapons from holsters at their belts. They pointed them at Ales.

"Drop the weapon!" The man in the middle shouted.

Ales did not hesitate. She swung her Windblade in a blur, and there was a roaring sound. The men were blasted back off their feet by a high pressure wave of air generated by the device.

"That was a warning. There will not be another. Withdraw." Ales said from between clenched teeth. She did not want to kill these men. She wanted them to leave. She waited until they got to their feet.

"We will not." The men lifted their strange weapons again.

Ales sighed. "You were warned."

She swung the blade but this time, the sound was different. It was a high pitched whistle that made Liassa fold her ears back. It actually physically hurt her ears. Ales swung the blade three times so quickly it looked like one movement. Each of their weapons were sheared perfectly in half. The crackling sound of the gauntlets of their armor sounded like breaking bones. The armor exploded away from their hands. Yet so precise were the strikes that their hands were left undamaged. One of them let out a startled yelp. It was indeed a woman.

"This is your last chance to withdraw. Your weapons are destroyed. If you insist on pursuing this course of action to its last idiotic step, I will destroy you. Choose."

They exchanged another look, then turned and fled. Ales sagged as soon as they were gone.

{You were bluffing?} Liassa asked into her mind.

"Not really. I would have killed them if I had to, but I am exhausted. My body has been dormant for three millennia. While my Cellstructs have kept my body from serious atrophy I am certainly not one hundred percent." She grimaced.

"My body needs food, water, real rest," Ales finished.

{Do you know where we are?} Liassa asked as Ales rested her Windblade on her shoulder.

"It looks like the Nasmath Forest, but the topography is all wrong." Ales turned her head this way and that.

{The Cataclysm caused a number of tectonic shifts. If you open our mental link fully, I can give you a better sense of Ahlysim as it is now.}

Ales did as she asked, and her mind was momentarily bombarded. Images of maps, topographical charts, and settlements filled her head for a moment before her Structures were able to process it all.

"So where do we go from here?" Ales asked, and Liassa looked up to her.

{We hoped, that you might know where to start looking for The Core.}

3

"So Vilhena is where these three came from?" Ales asked. They were headed towards the Center at that very moment. Liassa walked next to her, slinking between trees and bushes as if there were nothing in her way. Thousands of cycles as an animal on her own in the forest had clearly honed her ability to move through it.

{Vilhena is where Kiltik came down after the Cataclysm. It was the least damaged of the Minds that survived the explosion. At least among the ones I was able to contact,} Liassa replied.

It had been two days since their encounter with the Three Knights of Vilhena. Apparently they were not always the same men inside of the armor.

"Kiltik was very close to The Core. It lived in the same complex where The Core resided. The building possessed extremely heavy fortifications so it makes sense that it was the least damaged."

Kiltik, like the other Tieran Minds, was an artificial intelligence, each designed for a purpose. Kiltik had been the engineer of all of the Bondstructs.

"If Kiltik was damaged, that could explain why their Bondstructs were so crude. But this isn't all of it, is it, Liassa?"

Liassa looked down at the ground as she walked. Her ears twitched this way and that as she used them instead of her eyes to navigate around trees and other obstacles.

{There is a lot more, but Vilhena is as good a place as any to start.}

"Did you kill their friends?" Ales asked it quietly. There was no accusation in her voice. It was simply a question.

{It wasn't my intention. I needed some things from the Center. I took what I needed but I left ample payment behind for what I took. They chased me like I was a common animal, and even when I displayed obvious intelligence beyond what a normal katali would have, they would not stop. I even wrote messages, Ales, right in front of them. I only killed one of them because he shot me with his lancer. It was a reflex. He shot me, I reacted on instinct and caved in his chest. He was dead before he hit the ground. I'm not proud of it.}

Lia tried to hide the haunted look in her eyes, but Ales could see it. One of the Tier never forgot having to kill to defend themselves or others. It was both memory and pain, that did not fade.

"I never thought you would be, Lia. I just had to know what happened, that's all. I didn't mean to make you dredge it up."

{It was two cycles ago. I give them credit. They don't give up. I probably could have killed them if I was forced to. Their armor is great for sharp force trauma. Not so much against blunt impact. Your awakening made it easier. I appreciate it.}

"I know, Lia. It was always hard for you, even after your transformation. How far away are we?"

{About two lengths out at this point. Want to run?}

There was barely hidden hope in Lia's mindvoice. Ever since she had been changed from a human into a six legged feline big enough to be mistaken for a small boulder, she had loved to run. It was definitely an effect of the change, as she had never had much interest in it before, even when she was a child. Ales chuckled at the way she tried to hide that barely contained enthusiasm.

"Are we just running, or are we going to make it a race?" Ales grinned.

{If I get to the wall first, you have to brush my fur. All of it. I haven't had a brush run through my fur in hundreds of cycles.}
Lia's mindvoice practically vibrated with joy.

"And if I win, you use those magic paws of yours on the sore muscles I'll wind up with for running after you like a fool after laying on a slab of stone for three thousand cycles."

{Come on, a run will do you good!} Lia shouted inside of Ales' head like a child. Then she bolted through the forest like a shot.

Ales shook her head and crouched. She released her first three levels of Constraints. The ground exploded from beneath her feet as she bolted into the woods. Leaves were torn from branches to be pulled along in their wake as they blurred through the forest. At that speed, a run of two lengths lasted just under minute. Ales decided that they should both get what they wanted, so she touched the Center wall at exactly the same time as Liassa. She could have won, she thought, but this was better.

"Looks like a tie to me," she panted.

{You did that on purpose!} Lia groused as she took her paw away from the wall. She looked towards the gate, but it was out of sight from where they stood around the wall.

"And if I did? I want my massage, you want a brushing. We both win." Ales grinned, and Lia eyed her with annoyance. It was hard to tell. Her feline face did not show emotions the same way a human one did, but Ales could see it in her eyes.

"So where are we going to stay tonight? You said they take gold here. What do they have for accommodations? I'm sure nothing as luxurious as a true Tieran wayhouse."

{No, nothing so good as that, but they have places to rent. I'm not sure how you will get me in, though. It's not as if I can pass for a pet.}

"You have a collar, you are well behaved, and house broken." Ales smirked and Lia swatted at her with a massive paw. Ales slipped aside.

"Well, maybe not that well behaved."

{Oh, ha ha.} Lia replied, sarcasm thick in her mindvoice. Then her mindvoice turned serious.

{I am glad we had a couple of days to get caught up, but this is serious, Ales. I know that the Three Knights were fairly easy for you to beat, but there are far stronger threats here in the Center. The Knights are so successful here because the royal family is very careful about who gets access to the Bondstructs Kiltik manufactures. But the royal family is smart, and they have much more powerful armors.} Lia explained as they made their way along the wall towards the gate.

"We aren't here to start a war, Lia. We are here to look for The Core."

{Even with help from the god and goddess, we haven't been able to find it. What are we going to find here?}

"Kiltik. If we can access its memories, we can get telemetry on the explosion." Ales said it casually, guessing how Lia would react. She made a choking sound.

{What?!} Her mindvoice had the same choking sound. *{You do know we can't access it remotely, right? You have to physically find Kiltik and connect to it directly. Ales, I don't know where to even start looking for Kiltik in this place. I have never been able to move around freely,}* Lia said, almost desperately.

"Well you are with me now. If you really can play pet for me for a time, we can find Kiltik, get the information we need, and then I can get back to having a breakdown over the fact that, you know... Everyone I know besides you is dead." Ales' voice was barely on the near side of that breakdown.

{Ales, we don't need to do this right now. We can wait if you need time to pull yourself together. You were the one who wanted...} Lia trailed off when Ales shook her head sharply. She swiped at her eyes.

"It's alright, Lia. This was the life I chose when I went into the Corps. I always wanted to be an Arcangineer. I wanted to know how to use my Vision to help people. To protect people. It's still hard, but I'll be alright. I knew it would be hard." Ales sniffed back the tears.

"I'm sorry. I am being selfish. You experienced it firsthand."

{Yes, but I have had three thousand cycles and the help of a goddess to deal with this pain. I had six others of the Tier for several hundred cycles to help me cope. I mean it when I say we can wait. I know many quiet places where we can go until you can process all of this,} Lia offered, her ears perked forward tentatively.

"To be honest, Lia, I would rather just be with you. I would rather get back to work. I have to move to think. You know that better than anyone."

{Alright, Sister, but if you need a quiet place, The Mother has provided. I still don't know how you are going to pass me off as a pet. I weigh three hundred and fifty sphere. Might as well put a leash on one of the Defenders and call it your pet.}

"Just, don't roar at anyone, don't bite anyone, and I should be able to get us through."

{You know I can play pet, Ales. We have done this before.}

"You said you weren't very connected to those memories. I didn't think you would remember." Ales got a faraway look in her eyes as she remembered.

{You were always so worried that I would be upset playing that little role, but I always got the biggest kick out of it.} Liassa's mindvoice had a nostalgic tone to it. A mindvoice only got that tone when the person speaking was remembering something fondly.

"I just thought it was demeaning. Sit, stay, beg, roll over. I mean, you did tricks just to get people to believe us."

{Ales, it is just like play acting when we were little. It is fun!}

"Alright, Spook, as long as you don't mind."

The two days spent trying to learn as much of the currently widespread language as Ales could were about to pay off. Thankfully, it was a derivative of Tieran. It was a far derivative, but it made it easier for her to learn. They approached the open gate into the bloomward section of the city. There were two guards at the gate, and they stopped her. Lia stopped obediently at her side.

"Where do you think you are going with that wild animal?" The guard growled.

Ales looked around, affecting confusion.

"What wild animal?" she said innocently. Lia had always admired her ability to affect any emotion she wanted, no matter the circumstances. Her acting ability was amazing.

"Katali are not pets. We cannot let you into the city with that monster."

"Dear boy, did you not see the Menagerie pass through here earlier? I am one of the performers, and this Katali is indeed my companion."

{*This is never going to work. What menagerie?*} Lia said into her mind.

{*A little faith?*} Ales replied purely mentally.

Lia rolled her eyes very deliberately at the guard. Ales thought the guard's eyes might roll too, when he saw that. Roll right out of his head. She grinned, and said in a stage whisper to the guard.

"She's very sensitive about being called a pet," Ales said, hiding her mouth from Lia with her hand.

"She is a *performer*. But if you are truly in need of proof, would a simple wild animal wear a collar and follow me of her own accord?"

"What collar?" the guard asked.

Ales stroked her fingers beneath Lia's chin and Lia leaned her head back. Ales stuck two fingers underneath the collar. It looked like tanned hide, the same color as her fur. There was a brass colored nameplate that appeared to be riveted to the collar. Liassa's name was there, in Tieran Script.

"This collar," Ales said confidently.

The guard bent over and attempted to read the collar. He was unsuccessful, but he covered very well.

"It's a pretty name. Does she do any tricks?"

Lia did not move, but she turned her head and growled at him. Ales spoke with an air of eccentric insanity.

"She does not do *tricks*. She *performs!*" Ales grinned lopsidedly and punctuated her point with a raised finger as the guard eyed her askance. Ales looked down towards Lia with a raised brow. Anyone who saw her expression would have no doubt her peculiar madness was genuine.

"Lia, up!" Ales said, snapping her fingers.

Lia got her balance and pushed off with her back legs. She balanced perfectly on her front two paws. This put two pairs of her feet in the air. She walked a perfect little circle on those two front paws before tumbling forward onto her back. She put all six paws in the air and looked up at Ales expectantly. Ales took a piece of dried meat out of her pouch, and tossed it towards Lia. Lia snatched it out of the air in her jaws and rolled back to her paws. She sat down at Ales' side again, like a perfect obedient pet.

The guard smiled and waved them through the gate.

Ales walked through, giving Lia a long wink as they passed the guard. Lia pealed her lips back from her teeth in a terrifying feline grin.

"Careful, your ability to scare children is drastically increased with that kind of smile," Ales joked as they made their way down the main street of the Center.

{Alright, so just precisely how in the howling trench are we going to get close enough to Kiltik to get the information you want?} Lia asked.

"The same way you did," Ales said seriously.

Lia looked up at her, twisting her head sharply.

{Why would you think...}

"You knew it was the least damaged of the Minds, so obviously you have gotten to all of them in one way or another to assess the damage. Why didn't you just tell me?"

Lia swallowed uncomfortably.

{Not something we can repeat. In those last moments before it all went to the abyss, I was in direct contact with The Core, trying to find out exactly what was going on. When it happened, I was the last one in contact with the complete information grid.} Lia explained.

Ales stopped in the street.

"You actually felt it, didn't you. You felt them all die. Lia, that was not what was meant to happen when we built the grid. It makes your desire to end your own life much easier to understand. How could you cope with that?" Ales was amazed.

{Like I told you, with a lot of help from a stubborn god who was not willing to let me go so easily.}

Liassa stopped and lifted her nose to the air, taking a deep breath.

"What is it?" Ales asked.

{The Three are nearby.}

"They truly do not learn, do they?"

{I told you they were determined.}

"Will they try to attack us in the open like this?"

Ales looked around. There were dozens of people around them on the street. Some were looking at her oddly, obviously because she had been speaking out loud to Liassa. She didn't really care about that.

{They are the law here. They can do whatever they want. If you kill them, there will simply be a new set of Three to hunt us. It is as I said.}

"Well, if that is the case we will just have to discourage them." Ales grinned.

{And how do you propose we do that?}

"Oh the question is not how, little sister. It is who," Ales said with a smile that was absolutely villainous.

4

{So let me make sure I have this right. Not only are we going to break into the Royal Citadel so you can have a poke around to try to find Kiltik, but while you are there, we're going to just stroll into the throne room and have a chat with the King?} Lia groused. Her mindvoice held scores of disbelief.

"Lia, I realize that you have been alone on your own for upwards of thirty intervals, but you are not alone anymore, and we are Arcangineers. If we are to use our Vision to make this world safe again, we cannot fear petty fools and half-baked dictators. We have a job to do, and I will not let this stand in my way… though you should know all of this. You had thousands of cycles of experience while I slept," Ales said.

{You know what all that experience has taught me? It's taught me that nothing ever goes quite the way that we hope it will. I didn't spend those cycles toppling governments or trying to save the world. I spent them trying to reconstruct the inner workings of my mind. Do you know precisely how many of the Tier we lost that day?}

"No. I never really kept count."

Ales looked around the Center. The streets were paved with smooth stone that had been clearly assembled by Bondstructs. It had to have been maintained with them as well, considering the distinct lack of cracks in the paving stones. The buildings on the street were precise, square designs with bell-shaped roofs, bondstructed of glass and steel. The wall-to-wall windows were tinted to allow only some sunlight through.

{Well I know. Twenty-six million one hundred thirty-one thousand six hundred seventeen, counting myself and the six survivors. The psychic backlash from being connected to The Core at the time of their death did things to my mind. Bad things. I told you some of them.} Lia shook her head as if she were trying to shake the memories out of it.

{In truth, I am still not whole in my mind. I am sound enough, but I do not have access to all of my memories. My Structures are constantly in the process of rebuilding them. I don't know if they will ever come back,} Liassa replied somberly.

Ales noticed that they were drawing a lot of looks as they moved down the walkway. She then noticed other people walking with their pets. Each one had some sort of tether attached to their pet somehow.

"We need to get one of those." Ales made a motion toward one of the people walking a small four legged creature with long floppy ears that she did not recognize.

{A leash?} Liassa's mindvoice sounded puzzled.

"Everyone with a pet has one. If we want to maintain the ruse that you are my pet, we can use one. We can make it entirely cosmetic, so that it will break away if pulled too hard. It will actually be an advantage,"

{Ales, how are we going to maintain such a ruse? It is one thing with a single guard, but another to try to make everyone believe it.}

"I don't expect it to be iron clad. I think it will draw attention to us, but it is better than you slinking around the city wondering when you are going to be attacked," Ales explained.

Liassa sighed in defeat. *{Well, let's find a place to stay first. I can stay in while you get what we need.}*

Liassa took a right into an alleyway between two buildings.

"I don't think that will be necessary. Where are you going?" Ales asked, turning to follow.

{I've been here before. I don't know where to find a good place to stay, but I know someone who does.}

"You can't talk. How do you know anyone?"

{You know as well as I do that there is more than one way to communicate.}

"But I thought that you said…"

{I said that the Three were after me because a shop owner wanted me killed for paying him for the goods that I took. I may have entered his shop without his knowledge, but I paid him amply for the goods taken. I didn't say that I hadn't made friends.}

The glass and steel buildings gave way to more mundane structures of brick and stone as they moved into another section of the Center. The streets here were narrower than the ones in the main section, but still nicely made. Ales opened her Vision and examined the buildings. While they were somewhat plain, the mortar was also bondstructed. She had a guess that the city here had sprung up very quickly when it had been built. There was no doubt that it had been designed by the Tieran Mind. The layout was perfect, but it was the placement of the city that truly stood out. It was hard up against the mountainside that surrounded what had been the Nasmath Forest.

The royal family had obviously used the Tieran Mind to build the whole of the Center. Considering how amazing that it would have looked, founding a kingdom would have been an easy task. Their continued work with Kiltik would have simply made them look like gods in a world without the Tier to police what they were doing -- in a world where the population didn't believe in Avaara and Zezzhz. Their gods were simply imposters. Every twenty marks along the walk was a bluevein tree. The azure teardrop shaped leaves fluttered in the wind, and their movement reminded her of pelting rain.

Ales and Liassa made their way down the quiet street. Only a few men and women passed them. Their clothing was strange to Ales. It was tight fitting, and in the case of the women, the dresses seemed to restrict movement so that they swayed rhythmically with each step. Ales noticed they were looking at her again. The dress she had on was obviously not anywhere near the same neighborhood of fashion. She did not like the idea of wearing one of those tight fitting dresses. Wearing such a dress would make moving quickly impossible. Fighting in those clothes would be even more so. The male clothing would work better for her, but she didn't know the taboos here. She would have to learn quickly.

"I don't like the clothing here," Ales mumbled.

{Sadly, their society is patriarchal. Females have very defined roles in society. You noticed your dress is making you stand out?}

"Yes. We should get off the street."

{Yes, and we will in just a few minutes. If I had to guess, we are going to the blue house at the end of the street.}

Liassa picked up her pace. She trotted down the street and Ales kept pace with her. The brick buildings were oddly dyed in different colors. Apparently, these people were concerned with architectural aesthetics.

At the end of the street, the bricks of the house were dyed almost the same baby blue as Liassa's fur. A young girl's face appeared in the window next to the door. The door swung open, and it turned out that the young girl was not a young girl at all, but a woman grown. She wore a tight fitting dress made of the same pliable fabric that Ales had seen on the other women. It clung to every part of her body, with frilled fabric at the wrists and around the ankles. The dress tapered inward, encasing her legs all the way to the ankles. Her steps were restricted by the tight fabric to maybe a mark, but she moved more quickly than Ales thought possible. She clearly didn't seem to mind her dress very much. She carefully knelt in front of Liassa and put her arms around Lia's neck.

"Thank the gods that you are still alive. I was certain the Three had tracked you down by now. And who is this?" She had a beautiful, high voice, and she smiled at Ales.

"I am Alessandra. I am Liassa's sister. Can we go inside?" Ales looked around suspiciously.

"Of course, of course. Come inside, please." the young woman said as she led the way into the house. She carefully closed the door behind them.

"Can I ask how she is your sister? You are two different species," the woman said with a small smile.

"That is a very, very long story. May I first ask your name?"

"I am Igran," she said.

Her house was atrocious, but not because of disorder. There was wood everywhere. Ales shuddered as she looked at all of the dead wood. The floors were made of it, as were the stairs. Her Vision told her there were planks inside of the walls as well.

"Mother's End!" Ales cursed. She looked around horrified. "How could you?" Her voice got quieter as she went on. "So much death."

{Ales, please try to understand. They do not know because they cannot see,} Lia said, her mindvoice filled with panic.

She had been among these people for too long. Liassa had become accustomed to the idea of building things with dead wood. To Ales, however, the idea of killing wood instead of using Bondstructs to build was abhorrent. Killing trees like this was a sin.

{How can Avaara bear this in silence? Tree killers, Liassa? This is who you bring me to?} Ales asked.

{Ales, they do not know the old ways. They do not have anyone with the Vision to show them why this is wrong! Please, Ales, I felt the same way when I first came to this place. But it was Avaara who taught me to forgive them for what they have done. This one is not among them,} Liassa explained hurriedly through mind speech.

{But...} A single tear rolled down Ales' cheek before she was able to pull her emotions into check. She took a long look around and then closed her eyes tightly.

"I am sorry. My family are descendants of the Highlanders who lived on the opposite side of the Ahlyn Divide. We knew very well of the Tier, though not many of us survived the Cataclysm. As the world turned, though, we could no longer hold onto the old ways. More and more it became clear that those who came into possession of your science did not want the Tier to return. They liked having control of the power you used to wield. I am sorry about the trees. I did not build this house. I only live in it." The woman's voice was solemn.

"We left behind so many. I remember the Highlands. I remember your people. You were friends to the Tier." Ales sighed.

"Yes, we were. We still are, though there are only a few of us in the city. I can help you get clothing, and I know of several places where you can get accommodations. Until you find somewhere to stay, you can stay here with me," Igran said.

{She is quite nice, and the only one of the Highlanders that I have found. She has recently relocated. When I was last here, she was not living in this house. It took me a little while to catch her scent in the other places that I had seen her,} said Lia.

"So you didn't think that you should tell me about her?" Ales asked as they followed Igran into the kitchen.

It was well-appointed. The kitchen was square with an island in the middle, and there was smooth-polished black tile covering the floor. The counters were bondsteel, and the cupboards were open entirely, lacking doors. Ales opened her Vision and looked around. There was an elementary energy grid running through the house that powered the lights and many of the devices in the kitchen. A section of the countertop was marked with a black border, and it was there that Igran put down a kettle. As she did so, a circle of red glowed around the kettle. Ales eyed it suspiciously. It was some sort of induction heating plate. She shrugged and closed her Vision.

{I didn't know if she was still here, especially when we walked through her neighborhood and I didn't catch her scent. No point in getting your hopes up when I wasn't sure if we had help.} Liassa explained.

"Fair enough," Ales said.

"Hmm?" Igran hummed inquisitively.

"I apologize, Igran. Lia cannot speak, but we are in mental communication," Ales explained.

"Oh, I see. I'm making myself some lisan tea, would you like some?" Igran asked.

"No, thank you, but if you could put some in a dish for Lia, she would enjoy it," Ales responded.

{*You remembered,*} Lia said.

"Of course I remembered. You couldn't stomach anything but lisan root for a span after the change," Ales replied.

"It must be amazing to be able to speak like that," Igran pondered aloud. "May I ask why you are here?" The kettle started to whistle.

"Because we have been gone for three thousand cycles and our technology has not done good things in our absence. We have been asked by The Mother herself to bring peace back to the world. Tell me, Igran, what happens to people who go against the Royal Family here in Vilhena?"

Igran got a faraway look in her eyes. "There hasn't been anyone like that in a long time."

"That is the kind of thing our technology was not meant to do. We will do our best to stop it. Somehow, I get the feeling you don't like dressing like a hobbled maevea."

"I don't mind the dresses. My husband enjoys the way they make me look, and so do I," Igran said with a rather beautiful smile.

Ales sighed. "What is your husband going to say about us staying here?"

"My husband is one of those people who would like to speak out against the royals, but really enjoys breathing. So I dress how I am supposed to, and we do what is required of us for now. And we hope. My husband was very happy when Liassa found us. She gave both of us hope, and we would like to give some back. He will be home soon."

"We really only need things that will help us blend in. We have money, and we do not want to put you into any danger. Believe me when I tell you what we are planning will be very dangerous. You are not ready for that. We just need a place to stay, and clothing. Actually, with cloth like that, I can make my own dresses. But before anything else, there is a problem we have to take care of. We need a leash for Liassa if we are to keep up the ruse that she is an exotic pet," Ales explained.

"A... pet?" Igran burst into giggling laughter. "Did you actually... get the gate guards to buy that?" she asked haltingly between fits of giggles.

Ales grinned. "I can be very persuasive when I try to be. It also helps that my Vision allows me to see people's emotional state. It's easier to nudge them when I am using it," Ales explained.

Igran looked a little taken aback at that. She looked at Liassa.

"No, she can't do it the same way I can, and you can always, *always* tell when one of us is using our Vision. All you have to do is look at our eyes. If we are using our Vision, they will glow, like this."

Ales opened her Vision. Cool light bled through her eyes and filled the irises completely. They appeared as if someone were shining a bright light through a pane of colored glass. Igran drew a sharp breath and covered her mouth with her hand.

"It's beautiful!" she gasped.

"How come I have never seen you do this?" Igran looked down to Lia.

{Tell her it is because I have never used my Vision in front of her,} Lia said. Ales passed along the message, and then Lia looked up opening her Vision. Her eyes brightened to a luminescent glow, one orange and one gold.

"There is more to it than that. We can open and close our Vision extremely quickly. You can always see us do it if you are really paying attention, but most don't because it happens so fast that they are left wondering what they actually saw. It is even truer now that no one has seen the Tier in thousands of cycles," Ales explained.

"Everyone in my family was told stories about the Tier when we were little. All of the Highlanders were. The stories were not enough."

Igran almost fumbled the kettle as she poured the hot water into a teapot. She picked up the pot by the handle and spun it slowly in the air to stir the lisan grounds. She then filled a cup for herself and a dish for Lia which she placed on the floor. Lia made a little bowing motion with her head as a gesture of thanks. Ales was always amazed at how Lia could make simple motions and gestures into words. It was an ability that she had gained after she became one of the Wild. It was little things like that which made Ales sure that Lia was meant to be one of the Wild.

"Can you get the cloth today, Igran? I don't know what sort of hours that crafters keep in this time. Solid colors or maybe something in a flower print?" Ales asked.

"Like this?" Igran gestured to the dress she was wearing already. "I will see what can be done. Until then, you can use the back entrance when you return. Will Liassa be staying until you get back?" Igran asked, and Lia looked up from her drink. Ales shook her head.

"No. I think a little while longer will be safe. We can explain more when we return."

5

{*So what are you planning? You don't want to be a normal person here, so why the clothing?*} Lia asked.

"We are going to be here a while, Lia, before we can even start looking for The Core. We need to find the other remaining Minds. One isn't going to be enough. It is just going to be a start," Ales explained. They walked down the street, back towards the parts of the Center that held shops and businesses. It was still mid-day, and Ales did not want to run into the Three just yet, but she had to discourage them from following her somehow.

{*You don't know how we are going to get the Three off our back, do you?*} Lia said.

"Actually, I do. The Bondstructs they got into your fur. We're going to use them to send them on a wild gantha chase to start, but I have other ulterior motives for all of this. I need to create a separate persona for myself, someone who is part of this society, if I am to get close to the king. For that, I will need you to stay out of sight. But for the purpose of getting the resident police off our collective backs and onto mine, they need to believe that you are in fact my pet. You need to be seen with me. It won't exactly keep you safe, but scant protection is better than none. I hope that it will keep them from attacking you for fear that I will come down on them. This way we can always face them together. There is something else we'll need eventually – Verdant. Did it make it out of the blast?"

{*The last contact I had with it, it was hurtling towards the Weilen Abyss. Considering I have had no contact with anyone who has Cellstructs in over a millennium, I can assume that no one has found it. It was not badly damaged as the facility where it was kept was on the outer edge of the blast radius, but I have never been able to find it.*}

"I assume Hylina was destroyed in the blast. Its facility was the least shielded," Ales said.

There had been ten Tieran Minds in all. They were the most advanced technology of the Tier. Some of them were Structure designers, others were used for facilitating communications, and still others had other functions. Hylina was the Mind that controlled the daily functioning of the city of Ahal.

{It was one of three that were taken in the Cataclysm. Hylina, Los, and Juria were destroyed in the blast,} Lia explained.

"Mother's End. Giri is still out there somewhere? Have you had any evidence?" Ales asked, trailing off when Lia shook her head.

{There hasn't been any evidence of it. I don't think anyone could access its abilities without our Structures, anyway. I hope they cannot.} Lia didn't want to talk about the nightmares that just thinking of someone using Giri for selfish reasons had given her. It would be disastrous.

"Well, let us hope that Verdant didn't fall into the Abyss. I would rather not have to get past the Defenders to retrieve it. Do they still exist?" Ales asked.

{I have accounted for Kiltik, Noas, Jingi, and Moer. That leaves Giri, Fahmor, and Verdant. And yes, the Defenders still hold the abyss. Nobody goes there.}

"Fair enough. We can safely make the assumption that Fahmor has not been damaged, or was destroyed entirely. If it were malfunctioning, I think that Zezzhz would have sought you out about it by now."

Ales finally found what she was looking for – a small shop with floor to ceiling glass windows that displayed long coats made of hide. It was near the edge of town, in one of the less savory sections that had grown up around the city proper. The hidebinder's shop. The inside of the shop was filled with racks of practical hide garments. The shopkeeper was a balding little man with a fringe of red hair around his head and a ready smile that instantly disappeared when he saw Liassa.

"Wot is tha' doin in her'?" he choked out, his accent odd to Ales' ears. Liassa sat down by the door and tried to look as unthreatening as three hundred and fifty spheres of katali could look.

"She appears to be sitting calmly at the door. She will not hurt you. She's my pet."

"Pet?! Wot ya gonna use for ah leash on tha monsta? Best get yerself an anchor chain!" the balding little man exclaimed.

"She is quite well trained, sir. I was hoping to find a leash for her here, as well as a long coat. I would like it tailored to fit, of gantha hide if you have it."

"Fer a monsta like tha, I'd have ta make somethin'. Th' coat is ner a problem. I have two er three in ta back tat might fit ya. Will have ta take in ta waist a bit, 'tis ner a garment tha many ladies ask fer around here. An' I dun know what gantha is, but I would mak't of good strong baran hide."

{Baran is just another word for gantha,} Liassa filled in for her.

"That would be fine, and the leash. As I said, she is very well trained, and my voice is a better leash than any piece of hide that I might attach to her collar. So if you could make something that would conveniently break away if she tugs on it?"

"Tha is somethin' I can do. When do ya need it by?"

"Now would be good. I also need the services of a tailor that can make me serviceable clothing."

Ales danced a number of gold pieces across the back of her fingers. It was a skill that always caught the eye. They tumbled off of her fingers onto the countertop in front of the shopkeeper. His hands darted greedily toward the coins, but Ales slapped her hand down over them.

"There is more in it for you if you tell me who can make me those clothes and then pretend you never saw us."

The man nodded eagerly, and she took her hand off the coins. He snatched them up and quickly pocketed them, telling her there was a tailor two shops down that would make the clothing she wanted. He took some measurements, and said the coat would be ready in a few hours.

{I'm not going to like the whole of this plan you are coming up with, am I?} Liassa asked as they stepped onto the street again.

"You have it all. I'm going to use the money we have to get close to the king by becoming a part of the high society crowd around here. That should afford me a way to get in contact with Kiltik without starting a huge fight. Smashing my way out of the place without hurting anyone is a lot more likely than going both ways, especially when I will need some time to commune with Kiltik. At the same time, we are going to use our abilities to give a little real justice to this place."

Liassa eyed her suspiciously.

{You're lying.} Liassa's mindvoice was full of the suspicion on her face.

"I am, but I haven't worked it all out for myself yet, Liassa. I promise you that I will consult you on every part of my plan as I work it out."

They made their way into the tailor shop. A few requests for clothing and subsequent measurements later, she paid the hulking man, whose profession was entirely disparate to his size, before heading back into the city.

"I hate wearing this dress," she groused.

{I said I was sorry, but I was never sure why you hated dresses so much. You look rather cute in one.}

Ales scowled at her. "That, is the precise reason I hate them. I am not supposed to appear cute."

Liassa tilted her head in puzzlement. *{Why not?}*

They turned a corner into an alleyway that ran between the buildings in the Low Center to head into the High Center. In the alleyway, there were three men waiting for them. They were not armored, but they were dressed roughly.

"This is why I don't like to look cute. Because disgusting men with no conscience target you because they think you are vulnerable."

Ales reached through the pocket in the front of her dress, which she had modified it so that she could reach within. She pulled out two bands of black metal. She slipped one over each hand so that the ovular bands covered her knuckles with a strip of metal. She touched them together, and there was a buzzing sound of energetic discharge from them. Ales grinned.

{You know I can just sit here. They only want to rape and kill you.} Liassa's mindvoice had a sing-song quality to it. She gave a feline grin to Ales.

"What?!" Ales exclaimed. "Me?! I am so frightened!" She feigned a high, frightened voice.

Then she darted forward in a blur. The men had certainly not expected that. The first man tried to grab her in a bear hug. She slammed her fist into his stomach. The Spark in her hand delivered an elementary energy charge into the man. He went into violent spasms and collapsed to the ground. The other men gaped at her in shock. They did not get the chance to recover. She slammed her fist into the left shoulder of the second man. She was careful about where she struck because if she wasn't, the discharge from one of her Sparks could stop a heart. For the last man, she went to one knee and punched him in the groin. He twitched once and fell to the ground.

"They're lucky I don't rob them for the trouble."

{This one's boots look like they are small enough to fit you,} Liassa noted absently as she stepped over their unconscious bodies.

"As much as a good pair of boots might be nice, those are not a good pair of boots." Her eyes glowed briefly. "They're infested with biting nisce. Little monsters are eating them alive."

Ales stepped over their bodies as well. She slipped the Sparks back into the pouch strapped to her leg beneath her dress.

{Gross.} Lia squeezed past them, making sure not to let her fur touch them lest the tiny biting insects infest her coat. Nisce were a disaster to someone with fur. In three thousand long cycles, she had only ever gotten them once. It was not an experience she cared to repeat.

{So, what are we going to do now?} Lia asked as they walked between the tall buildings between High Center and Low Center.

"First, I need your help. I need some of your Cellstructs."

The microscopic machines that inhabited Liassa's body were slightly different than hers. Everyone who became one of the Wild experienced a physical transformation, and their Cellstructs remembered it. They could be used to make small changes in other people.

{Certainly. What are you hoping to change?} Liassa asked, interested now.

"Just my hair and a few cosmetic things. I will need to make more drastic changes in the future, which is why we need Verdant, but for now, a few of yours will suffice."

{You're not thinking of...} Liassa began.

"No, I do not want to become one of the Wild. It was, at first, a tempting thought to me. It would have been an escape from three thousand empty cycles, but no. Still, I fear we have a long way to go before this is done, and it is very possible that we will be recognized."

{I am not changing my fur,} Lia groused.

"Does anyone have advanced tracking methods in this time? Body structure recognition? Anything like that?"

{Not that I'm aware of. Perhaps in one of the Stoneward centers where Jingi came down. Not here, though. They have only thought of direct applications for Bondstructs here. Without the Vision, there is only so much Kiltik can teach them.}

"Thank Zezzhz for little blessings. So only those three knights actually know you by sight?"

{It's possible they have recorded images from their armor, but they have only gotten glancing looks at me before the other day.}

"So much we don't know. I want to Cut my way into their armor to find out more. Can you catch their scent?"

{No, too many nasty smells around here. I can't pick them out, but they haven't been following us since we got back into the High Center.}

"We'll have to wait for them to make a move. So until they do, it's time to start setting up my new fake life here. Maybe if I am quick enough, I can get them out of the way before they even become a problem."

6

"My Lord, when we caught up to the creature, it had somehow gained a protector. A woman with weapons unlike any I have ever seen. Our armor was not proof against it. She destroyed our lancers, and I am certain she could have just as easily destroyed us. We were unable to retrieve her," Urin, the first of the Three, explained. Lord Faln scowled.

"Incompetence! I should strip you of that armor and give it to someone more worthy. That creature could be the key! As it has so amply demonstrated to you, it is not simply a katali," Lord Faln growled.

Wind blew through the open windows of the well-appointed study. Polished burgundy panels covered the walls and floor to ceiling windows sparkled in gilded frames. The three knights knelt in front of those windows. Faln considered kicking Urin out of the window. It wasn't likely to kill him, considering the armor he wore. He needed that creature.

"My lord, her protector seemed considerably more powerful. Should we not consider capturing her first?" Traed asked.

"It is obvious that she's beyond your abilities. Only the King has armors powerful enough to deal with a threat like the one you describe."

Faln walked back to his massive ebony desk.

"But, my lord, if the woman is protecting her, we will need to focus on her anyway," Luma argued. She was the only female knight he had ever seen. She was a hard woman with solid grey eyes.

"The weapon she used somehow moved and shaped air. She was strong, m'lord. My armor registered levels of strength far beyond anything I have ever seen."

She was a knight for a reason. She was observant and intuitive about the armor in ways that the other knights were not.

"You are unfortunately correct, Luma. If you were not so young and inexperienced, I would put you in charge of this entire operation. Know this, all of our lives depend on this. If the royal family learns what we are trying to do, it will be the end of us. Go now. Do not return without that creature." Lord Faln commanded.

The three knights saluted by putting their fists to their hearts. The door opened and they left. Something moved in a darkened corner of the room. It was as if the darkness detached itself from the wall. Faln did not turn when it happened.

"This is a dangerous game you play, Faln. If King Roa finds out what you are doing, they will not find enough of you to know it is you," the figure in black said.

The voice was raspy, as if the person behind the black cloak and mask had a damaged throat. Faln knew better. All the agents of the Darkness sounded like that.

"That is what I am paying you for, Darkness. You have made a contract with me. You will honor it."

The figure in black blurred across the room. Small as the figure was, it wrapped its hand around his throat and lifted him from the ground.

"You will not sully our honor with your filthy tongue."

Faln made a choking sound as he dangled in the grip of the figure.

"Insult the Order again at your own peril, Faln. I will honor my contract, as ever those of the Order do. You know the penalty for crossing the Order."

The figure dropped him and he hit the floor hard. He gasped for air, and when he looked up, the figure in black was gone. One of his guards came into the office a moment later. His eyes went wide when he saw Faln gasping on the ground.

"M'lord, what happened?" His head swiveled around frantically, searching the room for any threats.

"Nothing, Kin, nothing happened. Leave me."

The guard nodded once and closed the door behind him. Faln folded his hands behind his back and stared at the Citadel. The king's time would come, and Faln would be there to take what was his.

7

Avaara stepped through the doorway, a doorway that she had bent into reality. Though her power had waned in the cycles since the fall of her Tier, she was still the goddess to this reality, and always would be. But without the Tier to help guide them, her children had run wild. They had stopped believing in her and taken what the Tier had given to the world. They had bent it to their own desire for power. So much had gone wrong due to the actions of her child Alizar. Even to her, an immortal, three thousand cycles was too long to wait. And so the doorway, a bridge through space and time, had taken some effort for her to create.

She looked around, not recognizing where the doorway had brought her. She had created the portal into Zezzhz's home in the same place that she always had, but everything was different than it had been the last time she was here. It seemed that Zezzhz had, at some point, gained a desire for something beautiful. The hallway she was standing in was made entirely of perfect crystal where once only simple stone had been. It was shot through with flora. The plants followed paths through the crystal that had obviously been cut precisely for them. She had never seen anything like it, but it was clearly Zezzhz's work. The carved paths had perfect symmetry to them. He always did like his math. She wondered if he had noticed her opening the doorway, and then suddenly he was standing there, not ten marks away from her.

"I see you still like your straight lines," Avaara said.

Zezzhz was made up of straight lines. His body, though humanoid in shape, seemed to be made entirely of gemstones – massive slabs of sapphire carved into a human shape. He had softly burning emeralds for eyes. His squarely carved chin was home to a squarely carved beard of pure white opal. He hovered bare ticks above the floor, so as to avoid the effect his power would have on the world if he contacted the ground.

"As if my essential nature would change due simply to the passage of meaningless time? I exist in all times and all places. You choose to let time exist for you," he said in a slow, measured voice that was deep and cultured. It was a mirror opposite in tone to Avaara's own.

"Are you aware that the child has awakened?"

"What manner of foolish query is this? Am I not the Architect of this world? The Father of all that you create."

"Zezzhz, you have been sequestered in this place for three thousand cycles, unwilling to see anyone, even me. Do you recall your last remarks to me?"

"If my memory serves me, as it always has, I told you that there was no point in you darkening my door henceforth until such time when our wayward children were ready to return to our guidance."

Zezzhz recited the words perfectly, despite the fact that he had said them hundreds of cycles earlier. He said them with the same exact tone and inflection he had when they had last spoken.

"That time has not yet come," Zezzhz growled.

"And you let them call you Father. Do you not even care at all for what you helped me create?"

Zezzhz's face darkened. His whole body darkened physically. His body drew down to almost black, except for his burning green eyes. The eyes of an angry god.

"You accuse me of not caring for all that we have created? Where did you place yourself when the Cataclysm came for our sons and daughters? I was there! I had to oversee the sacrifice of the lives of our beloved Children for the salvation of our world. The Child was safe where she was, but you did not have the strength of will to watch as the rest of our Children were destroyed!" he roared.

The walls shook and the crystalline hall shattered as he loomed over her. She straightened and stared defiance at his anger.

"And what would have happened if you had failed?!"

"You were always so sure of yourself. So positive that your solutions were perfect. I couldn't take that chance! I forwent one last moment with our Children, the only moment I would ever have with them again to ensure that one survived! Even if we manage to revive their selves from The Core, they will not be the same. Their lines will have been broken. Do not dare accuse me of trying to avoid that pain! I felt it more keenly than you could possibly imagine!"

She seethed with rage at what he had accused her of. Her love for her Children was boundless. Without The Core, neither of them would ever see any of them ever again. Only two remained that had not gone to The Core.

Zezzhz's gemstone body brightened back to its normal shades. All of the anger drained out of him as quickly as it had come. He floated to the crystalline wall and touched it. The shards of crystal that had fallen from the walls reassembled themselves. They floated up from the floor and fit themselves back together into their beautiful pattern.

"I offer profound apologies, Avaara. I must refine my ability to interact with those around me. The millennia have not improved my disposition, it seems."

"Nor mine. You know as well as I, though, that while we will survive this catastrophic chain of events, our world will not."

"Perhaps if we were willing to make the same sacrifice our Children did it would not come to that. We could trade our power..." He trailed off when she shook her head.

"That, my love, is not a solution. That is your fear speaking. What joy is there in baseless servitude?"

"None, but they would be alive, and protected even from themselves."

"You are, however, right. We must gamble. You know how good I am at gambling."

Zezzhz, by his very nature, could not gamble in the traditional sense.

"Then I will bear the burden of gambling for both of us. We will bet on our Children. I believe they can do what we cannot, if we are willing to help them. Together?"

It had been a long time since they had done anything together.

"They will go through things that will be hard for us to watch, but our Children are strong. They will endure." He nodded. "We will do this together."

He frowned then.

"I have not eaten a decent meal in several intervals. Perhaps you could help me to improve my manners?" Zezzhz asked.

"I'd be delighted."

- END OF PART 1 -

"I <u>saw</u> her, Da! With my own two little eyes, right here in my own little head. It was one of the Tier! She beat three men half to death faster than I can tell you about it!" She squealed with delight.

"The Tier are just an old legend, Ilsa. They never actually existed," her father replied. "Keep your mind on your work."

She scowled at him through the lavender locks falling across her face.

"They are real! And tonight, I saw one of them. She had on a strange dress, and when she hit those men, there were bright flashes of light around her fists. She was amazing! And she had a katali for a pet too! And she wasn't wearing any shoes."

The square jawed man looked up from what he was tinkering with at his workbench as her jabbering trailed off.

"Ilsa, where do you come up with this nonsense? You can't make a katali a pet. Have you been reading dusty old books in the King's library again? What were you doing in the Low Center, don't you realize it is dangerous there?" He peppered her with questions, and she stammered, trying to answer them all at once.

"I just went to pick up the packs like you told me to!" she protested.

It didn't matter in her mind that she had taken the longest possible route, the one that went through the Low Center, to get to the hidebinder's shop.

"Ilsa," Lerand said angrily.

"Come on, Da! I'm safe when I'm there. I stay on the main streets when I go out, mostly, and I always keep the guards in sight. But I'm not lying, she really was one of the Tier. She had two different colored eyes, and they glowed," she said seriously.

He turned from his bench, wiping grease from his hands with a towel. The pieces of a lancer that he had been repairing for one of the King's guard sat on the bench. He looked at her and frowned.

She wore a tight-fitting white dress with a red and orange sunburst on the chest. She had just come of age, and she was so very proud of wearing a lady's dress. Lerand didn't care for it much, but she was eleven, and that meant it was time for her to start wearing a lady's dress. He just wished that putting on that dress would make her as mature as she should be. She wanted to be just like her mother, who commanded the palace servants as if she were the Queen herself. They wouldn't get much done without Ellena to keep it all in order. Somehow, Ellena could walk into the seediest part of town, buy whatever she wanted, show as much coin as she liked, and come out again unscathed. Lerand thought that woman could jump into a lake and come out dry. It was amazing, the power she wielded in a world where men were supposed to be in control. He shook his head.

"Alright, alright..." he said, pulling the stool away from his workbench so he could sit down across from her. "So where did you see this woman that you are so sure is one of the legendary Tier?"

"I was on the rooftops down by shop row. And there was this woman coming out of Rorak's shop. She had a katali with her, a blue one with white spots. It had a collar on it, like it was her pet. And three men stopped them in the High Center alley. I thought it was weird that she didn't sic her katali on them. She just grinned at them and she took something out of her dress. She put it on like a pair of gloves, and then she ran towards the men. They were rough men, Da! They had lancers, but they thought they could just take her. She was so small. She hit them, only once each, and when she did, there was a flash of white light. They collapsed as if they had taken a day of beatings, Da! After she left, I checked on them. They weren't dead, but they weren't getting up anytime soon. I think she saw me before she left. I don't know how, but she looked right at me for just a second. Her eyes glowed, Da, like they had a fire behind them. Blue and purple. I could see them all the way from the rooftops," Ilsa finished, her eyes bright with a grin on her face.

"The rooftops, Ilsa? You know they have another name for that. And how did you even get up onto the rooftops in your dress?" he said with a frown.

"The thievesway," Ilsa said unhappily. "Da~!" She drew out the word. "You aren't listening to me!"

"Neither are you, Ilsa," he growled.

"Alright! I won't go into the Low Center again if you promise to listen!" Ilsa whined.

"At least stay off the rooftops. You can't move quickly in your new dresses. I don't want you to fall. I know I can't keep you out of the Low Center, but the thievesway is too dangerous. And I *am* listening. I know you've always been fascinated with the legends in the palace library, but one of the Tier? Even the tomes say that they were gone for centuries before they were even written. How could one of the Tier be here now?"

"Daddy, if I knew, I would go looking for her on my own. But don't some of the ones in the palace libraries say they are right from the Tier? Maybe they could tell us more about her."

"Ilsa, those books are in closed sections. Only the Royal family are allowed to see them."

Ilsa's face froze over with determination.

"Oh Mother and Father, I've seen that look before. Ilsa, why is this suddenly so important to you?"

"I'm eleven, Daddy. I'm old enough to know I'm not going to be like Mama. And no one is ever going to let me be a Fixer like you. I would like to do what Ma does, but..." She shrugged as if that was the only way to explain.

"I think I want to be a Searcher for the King's Library. If I could prove the Tier were not gone, that they were still alive, it would make it easy for me."

"So you did not set out to find the Tier, this is just a happy coincidence?" Lerand rubbed the bridge of his nose. "What am I saying? This is crazy."

"What if it isn't, Da?"

"Taker"

9

Cole sat in the back of the pub. He sipped his drink, but it was a lot more likely the potted tree behind his bench would get drunk than he would. The two guards at the bar, on the other hand, were definitely inebriated. He hated being in the Center, even the Low Center, but that woman had utterly vanished since they let her and her katali pet through the gates. They hadn't known just how much gold she had been carrying. He hadn't, either, but she had been interesting enough to follow, considering that she had claimed to be with a menagerie that didn't exist and had a katali as a pet for proof. Then she had started spending the gold and Cole got really interested. The two guards had been his only lead to finding her again, but they hadn't seen her since, either. The booth creaked as someone filled the bench across from him. He looked up and started when he found the woman from the gate sitting across from him.

"Did you think that I hadn't noticed you following me? Watching me spend enough gold to buy half the shops in the Low Center?" Ales said.

"Don't know what you're talking about," Cole said, and then made the mistake of looking into her eyes. They were two different colors. One blue, one purple. They glowed softly with a ghostly inner light as she studied him.

"You're a thief, Cole. One of the best in the Center, from what I've seen, but I am not a mark. If you want to get to the gold in my pockets, you will need to do it the old-fashioned way."

Cole was about to say something.

"And before you attempt to act like you're drunk and I shouldn't take you seriously, don't."

It was exactly what he had been about to say. He stared at her as the glow faded from her eyes.

"I want to pay you, Cole, to be my back up plan. I want you to steal something that is quite likely to get you killed, even if you can do it without getting caught. But if you do, I will pay you whatever price you ask. Enough gold to buy a kingdom, though I suggest you use it to make yourself scarce until I can use what you will steal for me."

"Who are you, lady?"

"I am Alessandra. I am one of the Tier."

"And, Alessandra of the Tier, what is it that you could possibly want me to steal that could be worth this sort of price?"

"Information, Cole. You're not just any thief, you're the kind of thief who knows what's going on. No one who stays free as long as you have in your profession is insensitive to the state of the world. Not only that, you broker information. You have seen the state of this world. You pray to the Mother and the Father. You're one of the few I have seen. I am here to restore that state back to peace and freedom for all."

Ales pointed at the glint of gold inside the collar of his jacket. He touched the collar, then turned it out. Inside there was a gold pin, a circle with a hexagon border carved into it. Inside of the border was a trefoil leaf, wrought in clear blue chips of stone. It was an old symbol by the standards of this time, and one that Ales knew very well. She bowed her head. The symbol of the God and Goddess.

"You've seen one of them, haven't you?" Ales said knowingly.

"Why should I tell you anything about myself? To you, I'm just some tool to be used and discarded when you are done with it. Pick another thief and do it to them," he said, and immediately he knew he shouldn't have.

Her brows drew together, and her eyes narrowed at him as if he had accused her of doing harm to a child or kicking a hiluk pup. It was righteous indignation the likes of which he had never seen before. Suddenly, he wasn't sure he was going to make it out of the pub alive.

"I am of the Tier. It has been three thousand cycles since we protected this world, and now we return to do so again. Our reason for being is the protection of all life, even one such as yourself. But if you ever again dare to accuse me of so carelessly discarding a life, I will show you how much care I use when taking one."

There was something about the way she said it. It was final. Not a matter of if she could do it. It was only a matter of when.

"I'm sorry," Cole said, and found that he was. It was the only thing he could say, though the words felt strange to him. He hadn't apologized to anyone for anything in cycles.

"What, exactly, is it that you are paying me to steal?"

"So, can you fix it?" the grey bearded gentleman asked as Warran turned over the old clock.

Warran propped his chin up on the palm of his hand and stared at the ancient mess of gears and small bluevein wood panels the man had called a clock.

"Of course I can fix it. The question isn't if I can fix it, it's how much it will cost to fix it. What did you do to it, anyway? It looks like you ran it through a compactor unit. Half of these gears are just about as useful as a one-legged man in an ass kicking contest at this point," Warran grumbled. He put the pieces of the clock into a bin on the shop counter.

"It's a family heirloom, sir. If you can repair it, I will pay the cost."

Warran looked at the old clock, and blew out a breath.

"It'll take a few days, and I will need eight pieces of silver to do it."

The gentleman eyed him for a long moment. Eight pieces of silver would barely cover the cost of getting the necessary parts to fix the clock. By the look he gave Warran, the gentleman knew that as well. Warran knew this man. He did not have much money to spend.

"Thank you, Warran. I'll check back in a few days."

The man left the shop, but as Warran picked up the box holding the clock, he got the sense that he was not alone.

"Hello, Cole. Come right in. Lock the door, if you would," Warran said unhappily as he put the box down behind the counter.

"Hello, Warran, ready to put those magic fingers of yours to work for me?"

"I told you I'm not doing that kind of work anymore. You want to break into someone's vault, you'll have to find some other Fixer to help you. I have a real job now, a real life, Cole."

"Oh, and all those times what I did put food on your table wasn't good enough?" Cole said angrily.

Warran just grunted. "Cole, can we not do this again?"

Warran made his way into the back of the shop. Cole slipped in behind him and leaned against the wall next to the door.

"Fine, Warran, I just need a climbing rig. Something that I can set up easy that I can climb quickly with, but more importantly, something that will control my descent if I jump off a building."

Warran sighed. "Does it need to self-attach?"

He started taking the parts of the clock out of the bin and laying them out on his work bench.

"I would like it to, if it is possible."

"Won't be cheap. I need Bondstructs to build the..." Warran started to mumble to himself.

"Whatever you need, I can cover it with the advance."

Warran looked up from his mental planning on the device. "You'll have to get the materials. If I am going to build this for you, it can't be traced back to me. I will always help you, Cole, but I have a family to protect now. It is more important."

Cole's face finally changed from the determined scowl it was usually fixed in. He got a small smile.

"Where is the little carpet shark, anyway? Isn't she usually hanging around here staring raptly at whatever you happen to be building?"

"Napping upstairs. So, what do you need this for? What is it you're trying to steal now that is going to require you to jump off a building to get away?"

Warran sat down at his work bench and began to disassemble what was left of the clock. His hands worked without his attention. Taking things apart was easy for him.

"The Archive Tower," Cole said.

Warran's hands froze, and he dropped the gear he had been pulling out of the clock. It bounced off of the edge of his workbench and rolled to a stop, hitting the toe of Cole's boot.

"Are you out of your Father Cursed mind?!" Warran growled. "The Royal palace, Cole? You want to take something I build and use it to break into the royal palace?"

Warran made a chopping gesture with the flat of his hand.

"No. Find another Fixer, Cole. You've been my friend for a long time, but I will not help you kill yourself and put my daughter in danger at the same time."

Cole started to speak, but Warran spoke over him.

"Get out of my shop, Cole."

"I'm doing this with or without your gizmo, but it'll be a lot easier to not get dead with it."

"Out, Cole. Don't come back."

"Please, Warran. I can do this, and it will pay more money than either of us could ever spend. You could leave the Center. Take your daughter somewhere safe. It would never trace back to you."

Warran sat back down at his bench. He rubbed the heels of his hands against his eyes.

"I swear, Cole, by Wood and Word, this is the last time. And if this does harm to my little girl, no place will be safe for you from me."

He pulled a sheet of scrap paper from one of the bins on his bench, and began to scribble the list of materials he would need.

"It's perfect, right in the middle. Far enough into the High Center to make sure it could belong to someone of the High Class, but close enough to the Low Center to make it easy to get out of the city if you want to," Igran said.

Ales fidgeted in annoyance at the tightness of her dress. The fabric that they called streic had elastic properties. The dress hugged her tightly from neck to ankles, allowing her to take only tiny steps of a mark or less. She found it demeaning, but she certainly looked the part of a High Class lady. The dress showed her figure and left little to the imagination. It had a pattern of vines embroidered into it that started at the hem enfolding her ankles and wound around her body. It circled her hips and shot up between her breasts to end in a beautifully embroidered flower on her left shoulder. The blue color of the dress set off her mismatched blue and violet eyes, or so Liassa had said. It had cost her a not inconsiderable fortune to put herself in a position of one of the High Class from outside of the Center. She hated having to play the part.

"Are you sure this will work? I mean, these linage documents are fakes, right? What if they check them? You do not have a companion," Igran warned.

"Only parts of the documents are fake. And I did, in fact, purchase a small Courtship outside of the Center. A Courtship with a recently deceased Lord that would have been absorbed by a very unfriendly neighboring Courtship without money and a new patron. Therefore, they were more than willing to remember me as a distant cousin to their Lord and allow me to take over his holdings. My place is quite secure. I don't have to choose a companion right away. It will give me less of a speaking voice with the king so it is not perfect, but it is secure. The best lies hold truth." Ales recited the words from her training. She fidgeted with her tight dress again and Igran eyed her.

"You really must stop that. One of the High Class would not be so uncomfortable with her dress."

"Wearing dresses like that one is a sign that you are of sufficient wealth that you do not need to do things for yourself. You can have others do them."

Igran smoothed her own dress down. Hers was not as snugly fitting as the one that Ales wore, as she was only of the lowest ranks of the High Class. Still, Ales couldn't imagine how she wore it so comfortably. The way it restricted her movements was irritating even to watch. Having to wear one herself was beyond mere irritation. It made Ales unreasonably angry for the women of this time.

"You're right, I know. But four hundred cycles of life, and I have never been forced to wear something so humiliating. Even my dress for the performance of the Grand Epic each cycle offered freedom of movement." Ales groused.

Mentally, she checked the Bondstructs that held the right-hand side of the dress together. If she needed to move quickly, she could give them a mental command to release the fabric and the dress would split up the side to her hip. She stopped herself from doing it right then. Igran was right, she needed to learn to move about comfortably in these clothes. This was her home for now, and these were her clothes.

"You should be wearing more. Someone of your status should be wearing a shape. You should have some servants with you. It will be frowned upon by the other ladies of the Class."

Ales had flatly refused the shape. Igran had pointed out some of the High Ladies on the street wearing them. They were repulsive to Ales. It was a garment made of polished hide that was tightened around the waist to make it smaller, to shape the body of the person wearing it to some bent ideal of what was appealing. Liassa had tried to assuage her about the idea, but something about the thing just seemed entirely barbaric.

"No. I will not be squeezed into one of those things. As for servants, I will hire some, but I will not be followed wherever I go. I do not want to risk someone seeing me using my Vision before we are ready. I don't want to have to kill or maim half the royal family to get in contact with the Tieran Mind."

{Then I believe we both suggest that you get over your aversion to wearing the things a Lady would wear. This is your plan, after all,} Liassa chimed in from her hiding place outside.

Ales sighed, but she knew her sister was right.

"Igran, you know someone who can make shapes for a High Lady?"

"There is a hidebinder in the High Center that can make them. I will make you an appointment for later today. He works for the Royal family, and he can usually deliver within a few hours, though who knows how. It will take gold," Igran replied.

Ales reached into the small handbag she had hanging over her shoulder, taking out a small hide pouch that chinked heavily with coins. She handed it over.

"We need to find a way for Liassa to come in here without being seen," Ales said as she looked around the well-appointed rooms she had purchased.

A heavy thump rang out from the balcony outside of the sitting room. Igran startled and spun to face the balcony. Liassa slipped in through the curtains.

{I can easily make the jump from the adjacent building without anyone seeing me. I doubt that anyone else could make it besides you, Ales,} Liassa said.

Igran held her hand to her chest. "You scared the life out of me!"

Liassa bowed her head towards Igran.

"Her apologies," Ales transferred the message.

"Don't you go crazy relaying messages for her?" Igran asked.

"It's a new development. In our time, our people could hear her thoughts, so she had a lot more people to talk to."

Ales fidgeted with the tight skirt of her dress for a moment, pulling it to the right and then the left before she mastered herself.

"How does that work?" Igran asked.

"All of the Tier have microscopic symbiotic machines living in their bodies. The machines interact with us through a synaptic interface."

Igran held up a hand. "I don't know what that means."

Ales nodded. In some ways, this world had technology now that the Tier could not have matched, but in many others, the death of the Tier had plunged the world back into a literal dark age.

"In simple terms, it means that the machines can talk to us in our heads and to each other. And in that way, we can talk to each other mentally."

Ales looked around. Their new home was an entire floor of a glass and steel building just at the edge of the High Center. It had a commanding view of the interior of the Center. It was ten gorgeous rooms of glittering white norstone floors, wall to wall glass windows, and polished steel surfaces. Ales looked into one of those polished surfaces and grimaced. The artful blonde tresses that framed her face were just not meant to be on her head. She wished she could disguise her mismatched eyes, since they were no longer a common sight, but she knew better.

"I look a proper fool," she said.

Igran stared at her incredulously. "You look like a fool? You're beautiful in ways that almost none of us can imagine being. I'm jealous."

Ales couldn't help but blush. Igran seemed surprised.

"The Highlander stories make you out like you are gods, but you really aren't, are you? You are definitely special, but you are people."

"In more ways than you know," Ales replied. "Igran, I appreciate all of your help thus far, but this game is going to become very dangerous from here on out. I am forever grateful, and should you have need of us, we will come. But this should be your last part in this. You've showed me around the Center and taken me places I needed to go. I can ask no more of you."

Igran shook her head.

"My family, all of the Highlander families, have been telling those stories for hundreds of cycles. To actually be the one to see the return of the Tier, it's my pleasure to help. I wish I could do more than just show you the sights, and help you find a place to live."

"Maybe someday, Igran, when the Tier are strong again, you can. I think you would have done well among us."

"What do you mean?"

"You do not know? I thought the Highlanders stories would have told the most important part."

Igran raised a delicate eyebrow.

"Those who actually become the Tier were not born the Tier. We were chosen, each and every one of us, for our willingness to serve and our ability to learn. If we still had the means, I would sponsor your test myself."

Liassa nodded her agreement.

"Anyone could be like you?"

"Not anyone," Ales hedged, "but those of us born with the Vision are extremely rare. Almost all of the Tier, even those born among us, were chosen. The Vision is not what makes you Tier. Being one of the Tier is a choice that those with the right qualities are offered. Sometimes we are given signs that someone should join our ranks, but sometimes more complex tests are needed before we can make the offer. That is how some non human members of the Tier joined our ranks."

Igran seemed in awe of them now, more than ever she had before. Igran looked towards Lissa, an earlier question popping into her mind.

"So she isn't really your sister?" Igran asked.

"Oh no, make no mistake, Liassa and I were born of the same mother."

"You were human once?" Igran asked Liassa, who nodded in response.

"But why?"

"Because sometimes, when faced with the need to do violence to others of our own kind, the mental strain on one of the Tier is too strong to simply manage. Instead of languishing in sorrow and pain that cannot be soothed, they remove themselves from the pain by becoming another species. It makes it easier to maintain sanity in the face of the idea that you have taken the life of another just like you. It affords them some separation from what they have had to do."

Ales looked worriedly at Liassa. She did not want to tell the story with Liassa right there. What she had done was right, but it had hurt her in ways that Ales did not properly understand. Liassa looked up to Ales and then chucked her chin towards Igran.

{It's alright, Ales. It has been a very long time, and the Change did its job well. I am alright. Tell her how it happened. She is curious, and we owe her that much for her help.} Liassa's mindvoice was somber, but sure.

Ales mentally checked the time with her Structures.

"If I am going to get shapes made before my little appearance at the King's Lordhale, we will need to get moving, but we have time for a story that none but one of us knows."

Liassa climbed carefully onto the hide couch. It was always adorable to watch her trying as hard as she could to keep her claws from destroying something she was walking on. She sat down sphinx-like on the couch next to Ales.

"Liassa used to look a lot like I do. A little shorter than me, and her eyes were orange and gold instead of blue and violet like mine. But she had the same blue braids, the same blue freckles splashed across her face, and as she was so proud of her big sister becoming one of the Tier and an Arcangineer that she wanted nothing more than to do the same thing.

What I knew, though, is that Lia was a kinder soul, a gentler person. I tried to warn her away, because the Tier are protectors above all other things. An Arcangineer, more than all, was given the job of defending those who cannot defend themselves. Eventually, you will have to hurt someone. Eventually, when you live a life as long as ours, you are forced to kill someone who will not be reasoned with.

She was working what she thought was a diplomatic mission to another Kingdom. She was a guest of a Queen who thought she could hide something terrible from an Arcangineer. For cycles, she had been housing a slave trade. Buying and selling people, children especially. They were not kept in good conditions. Outraged, Lia confronted Queen Ysrin. Being in a situation where she was to be dethroned, Ysrin decided it would be better to kill Lia and take her chances with the next Arcangineer that the Tier sent.

Lia was forced to kill four men to defend herself and the children she recovered from Queen Ysrin's dungeon. She kept her head and brought the children back to Ahal, safe and sound. That didn't change the fact that killing those men nearly destroyed her sanity. Because for the Tier, killing is not like it is for anyone else. We suffer not only the mental effects of doing harm. When we kill, we see the soul leave the body. We experience a piece of the pain of their death. It is a check to our power. We kill only when we have no other choice because it hurts us to do so.

Sometimes, it hurts too much. But the Mother and the Father did not wish to see us destroyed by our grief. So when it became clear that one of us was unable to manage the guilt of killing another human, we were given the choice to become an animal. It creates a mental buffer between you and the grief. It still hurts to kill, but for those of us who cannot get past the grief of making that necessary decision, the pain is a little less when we no longer share a species with those we need to hurt to protect others. Just enough less that we can cope with what we need to do."

Igran looked at both of them with a sort of respect that was usually reserved for gods and legends.

"I don't think I could do anything like that. That..." She looked humbled. "How can you do something like that?"

"Because it was what we were made to do. We were made to protect this world from those who covet power. We are the check to people like Queen Ysrin who would destroy the lives of others for their own gain. The Tier and the Arcangineers who come from within the Tier. We were charged by Avaara and Zezzhz to keep this world safe. In many ways," Ales gestured around to the Center, "we failed. This is our second chance as a people to do what we were made to do. What we swore oaths to do."

"What is the difference between an Arcangineer and one of the Tier?"

"There isn't a wide difference. All of the Tier have two things in common. One, we all have the Vision, which you know of, and two, all of us were chosen. The difference is that you cannot become an Arcangineer unless your Vision goes deep enough to see things for what they really are. The Vision always allows us to understand the things we can see, but some of us can see much more. You need to be able to see much more, because we go out into the world and protect people. We need to be able understand things right away, even if we are not familiar with the situation. The more succinct version is that an Arcangineer was a warrior among the Tier. All Tier were protectors, but Arcangineers specialized in fighting."

Ales mentally checked the time again.

"I promise we'll tell you more, Igran, all that you want to know about us. But for now, if you could be so kind as to make that appointment for me while I lay a few things into motion?"

Igran bowed her head and got gracefully to her feet despite the tight confines of her dress.

"Of course. How long will you need?"

"Tell him to be ready for me at the highbell."

Igran left, and Ales scowled at Lia.

"You and your big mouth. This dress is bad enough, but you just had to take her side about the shape, didn't you?"

{Oh, you are whining like a kicked hiluk. Get over it! Besides, I think you look good in that dress.}

"Oh, you would. The game is ready to begin. Come on, we have work to do, you lazy fuzzball."

Ales' blonde hair began to change, darkening down until it was a light blue with hints of purple. Her natural color. She twisted it into two long braids. She folded her arms up behind her back to unzip the dress. She had to change for where they were going.

{You know braiding your hair like that makes you look like a five cycle old girl, right?} Lia's mindvoice held loads of sarcasm.

"You know those spots make you look like you're walking around with a pair of testicles between your legs, right?" Ales said with a sardonic grin.

Lia made a choking sound, and Ales began to laugh.

12

Ales sat on the side of the road. It had taken them a while to find what Lia had told her existed in this day and age. It was not terribly amazing, just so different. It wasn't that there weren't traveling performers in their time, but that was a time when the Tier protected the roads. Not that bad things didn't happen on the road, but they happened a lot less when highwaymen had to worry about Tieran protectors showing up to put an end to their thieving.

"Does it happen a lot more in this time?" Ales asked Lia.

{Does what happen?} Lia asked.

"Robbery on the road?"

Lia's face twisted in a grimace.

{I do what I can when I see it happening, but yes, it's distressing just how much it happens. Traveling performers band together and then pool their resources to hire guards.}

"Guards." Ales said it with some disdain.

{We haven't been here to protect this world, Ales. Did you think they wouldn't find a way to help themselves?}

Ales swallowed hard. "I hoped that they would learn from our example."

{When did they ever do that?}

Ales shook her head. Lia's ears twitched to one side.

{They are coming.}

Lia sat up and tried to look non-threatening with marginal success.

"Lots of places, they never listened, but some, they did. I was hoping that those would have been the places to lead in our absence."

{It's unfortunate, but only a few of those places exist anymore. I'll take you to some of them when we're done here. If you want to see them.}

A pair of red skinned maevea appeared over the horizon, pulling a large. A man and a woman sat on the seat. They were not elderly, nor were they young. The man had frizzy hair that looked like it never quite paid attention to anything he tried to do with it. He wore traveling clothes – grey pants and a shirt that used to be white, though it wasn't dirty. The clothes fit him well, though, which meant they had some success as performers. People of that ilk did not do things like waste clothing simply because it was stained. His companion wore a green dress with vines in a darker green embroidered on the arms and bodice. She had long brown hair that was twisted into a complex braid.

They noticed Ales and Lia right away. She snapped the reins once, and the maevea came to an obedient stop right in front of Ales, and Lia.

"Good day to..." The woman trailed off when Ales and Lia looked up showing their eyes. Her reaction was not what Ales had expected. The woman's mouth fell open and she stared openly.

"Mother and Father hold my soul," the woman said in a devout whisper. "This can't be a coincidence."

The reins fell out of her hand and she climbed down from the seat. She showed no fear of Lia when she reached out to touch her face. She ran her fingers through Lia's fur. She stopped holding her face on either side of her eyes.

"No wild katali ever had eyes like these."

"Amazing that you recognize us so readily. Lia tells me that legends of the Tier are not very common in this day and age."

"Lia is right."

"So how do you know what we are?"

The woman smiled at Lia and released her face. "When I was a little girl, my mother was a priestess in the Temple of Life at the foot of the Black Spire."

{The Black Spire is what they call the Kalic Basin Volcano in this time. It went dormant about fourteen hundred cycles ago. The volcanic soil is very rich and the farm land is highly sought after. They are devout worshipers of the Mother and the Father, though they are more dedicated to the Mother for somewhat obvious reasons. They are also known for fiercely protecting their supposedly massive libraries.} Lia supplied. She eyed the woman with some interest. *{They are not known for striking out into the world, though it does happen. This is quite the coincidence.}* Lia's mindvoice was smugly amused.

{Coincidence,} Ales said, making her mindvoice playfully scornful.

Ales smiled politely at the woman.

"She told me all about the Tier. A thousand stories about your people and how you all protected the helpless and the defenseless. How you all disappeared suddenly. Sadly, many people have abandoned their beliefs in the Mother and Father. And their belief in you."

The woman's mate finally joined her.

"So, my dear, do we have two fine additions to our little group?" the man asked jovially.

"Aran," she hissed.

"Show some respect," she whispered.

He looked at her, and then back to Ales and Lia, his hair waving about insanely in a stray breeze.

"Can't show something I don't have, woman," he said jokingly.

Ales chuckled.

"Please forgive my mate. He is quite literally a fool."

"And I am the best fool you have ever seen. What has you in such a bunch, Halli?" he said in consternation.

Ales and Lia watched with some amusement as they prodded at each other with affection.

"Gods, Aran, if you used your eyes for anything but ogling other women, someone might mistake you for having a brain in your head. They are Tier," she growled.

Another man began to approach them.

"If we could discuss this somewhere more private, please?" Ales interrupted, looking meaningfully at the man approaching.

"Yes, of course," the woman said.

"Though I think that your companion may wish to wait outside for his comfort," Halli said.

"Her comfort," Ales emphasized the her.

The woman looked at Lia with interest, but said no more.

"And yes, I think she will wait outside."

{I'll be able to hear everything,} Lia said.

Aran waved off the burly looking man, who had been walking up from the rest of the wagons.

"Go on inside. I will let everyone know what is happening," Aran said.

Ales eyed the wagon's wheels with interest. "Where did you get this wagon?"

The wagon was like a tiny house on wheels, but those wheels were set on the axles with a very specific type of bearing, one that had been originally invented by one of the Tier. It would never wear out, and would always glide perfectly smoothly. It was made with a gel that removed absolutely all friction. They were notoriously hard to put together because the gel had to be injected into the bearing once it had already been assembled.

"It was built by a number of craftsman in the village near the temple of life," Halli said.

"These are Tieran designs. I'm surprised that any of this survived the Cataclysm."

"We don't believe that they did in the traditional sense. The only reason we have these things is that our craftsman were taught how to make them by the Tier. No one has figured out the secrets of them yet, and so we sell them to others."

Ales made an annoyed noise. "Our technology was not meant to be kept secret unless it was dangerous."

Halli gave her a rueful smile, but it was Lia who explained.

{It's a different time, Ales. These people do not have the support that we did to simply give away our safe discoveries.}

Ales gave her a mental nod.

Halli began to try to explain, and Ales shook her head.

"I'm sorry. This is a new world. I should not try to judge you by my old standards."

"I imagine that you have quite a story to tell, but it seems you have some business with us?" The woman's raised voice on the last word made it a question.

Ales followed her into the wagon. There was a table and chairs nailed to the floor, like they might be on a ship. Bookshelves lined the walls, and there was a bed near the front of the wagon. It was neatly kept, clean, and decorated beautifully with red draperies that had gold edging and tassels. Halli invited her to sit at the small table with a gesture, and Aran joined them a moment later.

"Leave the door open if you please, so that Lia may hear us?" Ales asked.

Aran nodded, joining them at the table. "Of course."

"My name is Alessandra, and as you have guessed, my katali sister and I are Tier. I know we have just met and you owe me nothing, but I have need of your help. I will see you well paid for your services. I don't think it will be dangerous for you, but it won't be completely safe, either. You may not be able to return to the kingdom of Vilhena at all. This is a lot to ask, but I need you to act as a cover for my sister and myself. The only suspicious thing you will need to do is stay near the city for as long as we need you, and tell anyone who asks that Lia is one of your performing animals. She'll spend some days in one of your cages so that people see her there, and she will even give some performances, if you would have her do so."

They exchanged a look.

"The legends say that there were animals that were members of the Tier. She's one of them?" Halli asked hesitantly.

"It's more complicated than that, but yes, she is one of the Tier. Please don't think of us as gods. We have special powers, but it is not beneath us to do what we must. Besides, Lia enjoys playing for others. Right now, what we really need is to lay temporary false trails that will keep anyone from finding the truth about us too quickly. We want you to be one of our false trails."

"And what about our people? Can we tell them about this?" Aran asked.

"I think it would be better if you didn't. When Lia is here, you should treat her just like any of your other trained animals, though I do suggest that you inform your animal keepers that she is well trained and understands spoken word as well as you or I do. A locked cage door is no barrier to her, so they need not leave it to chance that someone will notice something amiss."

"I think that we would like to help."

"I don't wish to sound materialistic, but you mentioned compensation for our services?" Aran asked.

His mate gave him such a look that Ales had to laugh.

"No, it's alright, Halli, your mate is quite right. I have enough with me to cover all of the expenses for everyone for at least five rotations. Once I have more time, I will send a letter of rights with Lia to allow you to draw a fair amount for your services from my accounts at any Countary on the continent."

Ales took four heavy hide purses from beneath her jacket.

"There are five hundred pieces gold in each of these. Please take your wagons along the stoneward road around the city. Lia will go with you and show you where you can take up residence. No one will bother you there."

"That would be an unusual delight. Many people think that because we are always traveling that we are thieves," Aran said.

"Well, I am the owner of the land where you will be placed. So no one will bother you. It is along the moonward road."

{If I am to sleep in a cage, please have them move it away from the other animals. I would rather not smell them all night,} Lia said, her mindvoice amused.

"Lia requests that you keep her cage a fair distance from the other animals. She has a very sensitive nose," Ales relayed.

"I'm sure that'll not be a problem," Aran said with a chuckle.

"Can you show us?" Halli asked hopefully.

Ales tilted her head.

{She wants to see our Vision, Ales. Everyone who recognizes me for what I am asks me for this.}

Lia put her front paws up onto the back of the wagon and poked her head inside the wagon door.

{At least, people who want to believe.}

And then she opened her Vision, and her eyes glowed, one gold, one orange.

"Ahh, of course," Ales said.

She opened her Vision, and immediately knew they had chosen right with these two. They were not afraid. Ales closed her Vision and Lia did likewise, dropping back down to the ground.

"My mother would have loved to meet you," Halli said.

"Perhaps when we are done here we can visit your home."

"You would find a warm welcome among us."

Ales stood up and hopped out of the back of the wagon. She stopped as Halli came out.

"One more thing, Halli. Do you know what bondarmor looks like?"

"We have been to Vilhena a time or two. We have seen The Three before, and some of their soldiers in bondarmor."

"If anyone in bondarmor comes and asks about Lia, you tell them that she escaped the night before. She will see them before you and make herself scarce. If that happens, Halli, once they have left, you pack your things and leave. Don't ever come back to Vilhena unless we visit you and tell you that it is safe."

13

There was one other thing to be done this night. This was the most dangerous part of her many plans, the part that she wouldn't tell her sister about. She had always known that her connection with The Core was something special. Even though she couldn't locate The Core as she made her way back into the city, she could definitely feel its presence. It seemed like it was immeasurably far away. She scaled the Center wall with little difficulty, and then, pushing open the first level of her Constraints, she jumped across the gap between the wall and the nearest roof in the low center. She knelt there and sighed.

"Mother of all things, giver of life, source of nature, hear my call. I would have a discussion with you."

Ales opened her eyes and, to her surprise, Avaara was there. Her appearance had changed. She was not nearly as thin as she had been, and it appeared that she was making the transition to her springtime affectation. She was plump and looked far more motherly than she had a few spans earlier.

"Hello, Avaara. I would like you to answer a question for me if you can. I know you cannot divine for me directly where The Core is. That being said, my theory is that it has been displaced into a pocket dimension created by the elementary force discharge from the device that Alizar left behind. Am I right?"

Avaara hesitated for a long moment before she spoke. She gave no indication if Ales was right.

"I cannot answer that question, my Child. You must discover that on your own. However, I sense that there is a question that you want to ask me that I *can* answer."

"I'm about to make it perfectly clear that the Tier have returned to the world. Am I correct in thinking that this will awaken the Core?"

"Yes. Even Zezzhz and I are not sure how Newlings happen. What we can tell you is that Newlings each have a special connection with the Core. You were chosen to be a Newling for a reason."

Avaara looked at her curiously for a moment. Ales was about to ask her last question when Avaara spoke again.

"Alessandra, you should trust your sister more."

"I trust Lia with my very life. It isn't trust that's the problem, Mother. I never know what I am going into, and until I do, I always have to keep everyone safe."

"My daughter, your sister has passed all of the same tests you ever did, and with less resources. Do you think she is unprepared to face what is ahead?"

Ales rubbed the bridge of her nose.

"Mother, I don't know what to do with all of this anger. It's making my protective instincts go into overdrive. I do not think my mind is fully sound. I don't know if it is ever going to be."

Avaara watched her for a long moment before her face finally pulled a frown.

"And you will try to use this to bleed off some of that anger?"

"I want to do some good in the Center, and yes, if I can use taking down thugs, rapists, and murders to calm this anger within me, I will. But I don't need to tell you this, Mother. You already know my plans."

"Yes, I do, and they are good plans. You are trying to keep innocents out of harm's way. How could I not condone such plans when it would be so much simpler for you to simply attack? Do you have any more questions, Daughter?"

"If the Core awakens, we'll see new Tier right away, won't we?"

"It has been three thousand cycles. The Core has been disconnected completely from this world all that time. With this act, you will bring all of the world to know that the Tier are alive and well. That knowledge, spread to so many souls, will provide the conduit to the world that the Core needs to begin releasing the long-lost power of the Tier. I would not be surprised if you saw two or three Newlings emerge almost instantaneously. But be certain, you will find new Tier right away, as you surmise."

Ales wanted to ask if what she was about to do was right. It wasn't a question she could make herself ask. She already knew that what she was about to do was right.

"Child, do you truly think that you would have been allowed to walk this path you have chosen if you were to misuse the power you have been given? Protect those who cannot protect themselves. Defend those who are without defense. Free those who've had freedom taken from them."

It was a truncated form of the oaths. Avaara smiled. That smile made Ales feel like all was right in the world.

"Will the new ones choose to be our brothers and sisters?"

Avaara watched her quietly, and suddenly Ales felt like she was a child again.

"The ones you need will," Avara said.

"Thank you, Mother."

"Of course, Daughter."

And then she vanished.

Ales sighed. And then she rose, her face set with determination. She knew where she was going because she had been there before. Two dozen times in the past few spans, she had watched them from the warehouse across the river. They thought that their spot at the end of the piers made it impossible for anyone to observe them without being seen. They were wrong. All of the buildings surrounding their warehouse belonged to one person.

High Lord Lineus was the only monster among the nobles who was possibly more despicable than Nivus. She would deal with *that one* after she had inserted herself into the nobility. Lineus used the river here as a shipping stop for a slave operation. Slaving was definitely illegal in the Kingdom of Vilhena. Across the Iborian Sea, it was perfectly legal, something that would eventually change if she had anything to say about it.

Ales jumped from the roof of the building and landed silently, flexing her knees to absorb the impact. She slipped across the bridge like a shadow. She opened her Vision and focused on the Circle of Taking. No guards stood watch outside, but that was normal. The windows of the slaver's warehouse gave them an uninterrupted view of the entire perimeter of the building. The long rectangular building had thick brick walls and a bondstructed steel roof that appeared to a single piece with four large skylights in it.

Ales decided it was no time to be subtle. She closed down the Circle of Taking and then mentally forced open the doors on the first four levels of her Constraints. She shook out her limbs, feeling the increased strength and speed pour through them. She looked up at the roof, opened two Circles, and squinted. Distance and Observance were not her two strongest circles, but she had worked diligently to master them.

Her Cellstructs complained about the sudden increase in neural load, but settled down after a moment, spreading the load to the rest of the Structures in her brain. The roof was precisely twenty five marks from the ground. She crouched, and then jumped, clearing the roof absolutely perfectly. Her jump was arrested by gravity exactly one width above the roof. Her feet came down upon the roof in perfect silence. She took her Windblade from inside of her coat and held it ready, took a deep breath, and raised it.

"Mother, forgive me for what I must do to restore balance, and protect me from corruption."

She snapped the blade from left to right, a high-pitched screech ringing out in its wake. The skylight nearest to her exploded into myriad shards of shattered glass. Metal screamed as the frame was sheered away from the roof and twisted into a mangled heap of broken steel. Shouts of surprise came from inside the warehouse.

Ales darted across the roof and jumped down through the hole. She landed on top of a large wooden crate. Glass crunched beneath her feet, but the Cellstructs gathered in her soles to protect them from cuts. The lights in the warehouse had been doused. Ales opened the Circle of Light, and the body heat of everyone in the warehouse lit up before her. She swept her sight left and right. Her Cellstructs marked in her mind where each of the warm bodies were. There was a large group somewhere beneath the ground level. Those were the slaves. The group above ground all carried weapons, which meant that everyone in here was fair game.

The warehouse filled with angry shouts. Ales hopped from one row of crates to the next, landing behind the first of the men she found. He was roughly dressed in a homespun black shirt and pants beneath soft hide armor. He turned, trying to aim a lancer at her. She smashed her left fist into his wrist and it broke with an audible snap. The lancer spun away, clattering to the ground. The man screamed, clutching his wrist. She tangled her fist in his shirt and slammed him up against one of the heavy wooden crates.

"Do not think it is luck that smiles on you this night, filth. It is for no person to enslave another, and I will see to it that you pay for that crime with your life, but I will let you keep your life for a while longer. You will be one of my messengers. You will tell all who will listen what you see here this night. Tell them that the Night Lady did this. Make them believe in me. Make them believe that no place is safe from me."

She spun him around with her left hand and slammed him into the outside wall of the warehouse. She raised the Windblade in her right hand and swung it in a blur towards the interior of the warehouse. A howling like the winds of a tornado erupted. Crates exploded apart, flung away from them in an arc that crossed the entire floor of the warehouse. The wind smashed everything into a pile on the opposite wall.

The carnage was as horrific as Ales had meant it to be. The broken and bloody limbs of cadavers protruded from the wreckage of the crates. There was only one justice for men like these. Only death could erase the sins of a life like this. She used her rage to shield herself from the pain of the deaths of twenty three souls, but she would feel it later. She would ache from those deaths. She had to hurry. She could only delay that pain for so long.

She swung her blade again in a sharp motion. The sound was a barely audible shriek. The bay doors to the warehouse sheered in two and blew off their hinges like they had been hit with a battering ram. She shoved the grubby man towards the door and he took off at a run faster than any normal man she'd seen before.

She looked around with her Vision open and found the doors in the floor that lead into the basement. She slid her Windblade back into her coat. The heavy steel lock looked shiny and new despite the fact that the doors were dry, heavy planks at least a hundred cycles old. She knelt down and took the lock in the palm of her hand. She closed her fingers around it and squeezed. The steel housing crumpled in her hand and the lock popped open. She pulled the doors open.

What she saw did not surprise her, but it did stoke the fires of her rage. The basement floor of the warehouse was smooth, bondstructed stone that stretched about three quarters the size of the warehouse floor. People were everywhere, and the smell was awful. The people were chained hand and foot, each tethered to an eye bolt set into the floor or wall. It was clear that they were to be taken across the sea as each was branded on the shoulder with a slave mark. They cowered when she came down the stone stairs.

"Do not be afraid. I know that you have been mistreated, but I am here now to see you set free. The men who did this to you have paid for their crimes with their lives."

A young girl with bright red hair and amber eyes stood up.

"They do not all speak your language."

Ales moved to her, and the young girl shrank back from her.

"Do not worry. I will not harm you, child. I meant what I said, but I need to make sure everyone understands so that no one runs when they are freed."

The girl came forward. She was filthy and underfed, but thankfully not emaciated. Her hair was ragged and frizzy. Her clothing was little more than sack cloth. The only thing that looked new on her were the chains that bound her hands and feet. She couldn't have been more than eight cycles old at most.

Ales closed down the two Circles she had open and then opened Breaking. She tried not to look at the people because she knew what she would see. A living body should have very few of the kinds of weak spots that Breaking revealed to her, but these people would have hundreds. Weak bones, injuries, and so many other things that would make her wish that she had not killed those men so quickly.

"What is your name?" Ales asked.

"Aetta," she said, watching Ales warily for any sign of turning on her.

"And do you speak their language, Aetta?"

Ales examined the shackles around her wrists. She touched the first, and cracks suddenly crazed the surface of the shackle. Ales tapped it with her knuckle and it simply shattered. She repeated the process with others around her other extremities.

"Yes, we were all taken from the same village. My parents owned the wayhouse and taught me other tongues."

Tears filled the girl's eyes, but she did not cry. Ales had seen it before. She had cried herself out.

"Can you speak a little of your language for me?"

Ales didn't mention her parents because she knew that her parents were dead. She would not pick at that wound any more than the girl already had. The girl called out in a loud voice, and everyone looked to her. A long moment later, Ales' Cellstructs began a running translation of the words.

"... is here to free us. She says she will help us."

Ales smiled at her. "Thank you, Aetta," she said in the girl's language.

The little girl looked up at her, startled.

"You can speak our tongue?"

"I can now." Ales raised her voice so everyone would hear her. "I will free each and every one of you. The men who hurt you have paid for that crime with their lives. They will never harm you or anyone else again."

Ales set about fulfilling her promise. She broke shackles and continued speaking.

"I will take you to a safe place. I'll supply you with money and care until you are strong enough to return to your home, or I will make a new place for you to call home." Her words came slowly and calmly.

"I would ask if there are any souls among you brave enough to say here in this place for a time and help me with my work. I will see you protected and well taken care of."

She finished breaking the shackles off the last man. He was the biggest of the lot. He towered over Ales and watched her with intelligent eyes.

"None of you have to stay, and even if you do, you won't have to stay long. I simply need a few to spread the story of what has happened here."

"We owe you our lives. I will stay and help you," the big man said.

"And I," said another. A number of others who stepped from the crowd and volunteered their help.

"Thank you, all. Let's get you someplace safe and fed."

14

Ales pulled the blue dress up over her legs and slipped her arms into place. The dress clung to her body, and she made a frustrated noise at the tightness of the garment. It wasn't uncomfortable per se, but it made her *feel* uncomfortable. She examined her yellow gold curls in the mirror.

"Did you have to set them to make me blonde? I mean you could have gone with black, or a nicer blue," Ales groused.

{Because having hair ten shades closer to your real color is a great idea for infiltrating this place,} Liassa said.

Ales picked at a loose thread in the glittering gold embroidery on the dress.

{Stop that, you're like a child when it comes to those dresses,} Liassa growled both mentally and audibly.

The maid on the other side of the room startled and dropped the leather garment she was measuring out laces for. Nisa was a middle-aged woman with long golden-brown hair and kindly grey eyes. Ales had hired her on with two other servants to take care of the needs of her alias, the High Lady Brightwater.

"It's alright, Nisa. Liassa will not ever harm you."

"Yes, M'lady." Nisa replied as she picked up the shape.

The hide garment was beautifully made, even if it was barbaric in Ales' eyes. There were a dozen garments like it hanging inside of the spacious wardrobe in her bedroom, each in colors to match her new dresses. They were made to go around the waist, shaping her body to make her look more aesthetically appealing when laced closed. At least, more appealing by the standards of this time. It squeezed her body into a shape very similar to an hourglass.

"Come help me into that."

Ales lifted her arms and Nisa pulled the garment around her waist like a belt. Ales waited as Nisa laced the garment, tightening it about her waist. It took her a few minutes to get it fully secured. By the time she was done, Ales was not gasping for breath, but it certainly left her short of it. Still, the garment was not actually physically uncomfortable. It was a tight fit, but she wasn't going to pass out from the restriction by any stretch of the imagination. The shape was blue, with white flowers embroidered throughout the hide. The springy metal rods in the garment were perfectly conformed to her body. She looked at herself in the mirror. It certainly emphasized her feminine curves. Mentally, she made a nervous check of the bondstruts she had placed in the shape. Like her dresses, if she needed the thing off, a simple mental command would split it up one side so it would fall away.

"You look beautiful, M'lady," Nisa said.

"Thank you, Nisa. You can retire for the ending. Please tell Reynard to prepare something suitable for Liassa to eat. She will pick out what she'd like him to cook. Once he's done, he may retire as well. I will not require help undressing when I return."

"Yes, M'lady. Enjoy the Lordhale."

Nisa left the room silently. Ales slid her feet into the blue velvet slippers she had had made.

{Not hating this quite as much as you thought you would, I see.} Liassa's mindvoice held genuine happiness. She liked seeing her sister enjoying herself. It wasn't a common sight. Usually, she was far too professional.

"Nonsense, it's just a job."

Liassa could see the blush in her cheeks.

{You know I can tell when you're lying?} Liassa's mindvoice held a smug, sing-song quality that made Ales blush even brighter, but her voice was not embarrassed.

"Lia, you know I've always enjoyed being pretty and dressing pretty when there is time for it. But me wearing this dress is not the same as the men in this time using confinement like this to oppress women. Are all the kingdoms like this?"

{Not all. Only about half have become Patriarchal societies. There are even a number of Matriarchal kingdoms in the lands stoneward. Probably half treat males and females equally like we did. Vilhena just happened to be the best place to start, and it is ruled by men. I'm sorry, I just remember the times when I came back for special occasions. I remembered how happy you looked dressing for the Grand Epic. We have a sacred duty, Ales, but we are also alive. I spent a hundred cycles running myself nearly to death because I was so focused on trying to forget that I was not simply a machine. Avaara noticed and put a stop to it. Lesson learned, Ales. Have some fun tonight.}

"Alright, Lia. I hear you. I'll try to enjoy myself. If I'm going to be hiding in plain sight, I suppose I need to at least pretend to have fun. If you go out tonight, be careful. The

Three have been looking for me. I hope they'll stay away from you, but no guarantees. I know you don't like it, but if they force the issue, don't let them follow you back here. Kill them if you must. I know you've been purposely avoiding violence. You wanted me to believe their armor was too tough for you to penetrate, but that is not true. I can tell when you are lying too, Spook."

Lia bowed her head.

{*I'm sorry, Ales. I just...*} Ales cut her off.

"It's alright, Lia. I understand fully why you became one of the Wild. I know violence hurts. But there are only two of us left, and I can't be this or do these things without you. Defend yourself, Lia. They won't hesitate to kill you. Do not let them."

Ales picked up the small handbag that held only those things of greatest need.

{*Before you leave, let the chef retire as well. I will hunt tonight.*}

Ales nodded. "I'll tell him on my way out."

She drew in a long breath, as deep as the shape would allow, and let it out.

"I'll be back in a few hours, Lia."

Ales made her way down to the carriage she had called for. It was pulled by four sleek, black maevea. They were one of the creatures of Ahlysim that Ales knew for sure were created directly by Avaara. They were unlike any other. Maevea had long, featureless faces, and by all appearances, no method of breathing, seeing, or eating. Yet, their sides rose and fell as if they were breathing. They absorbed oxygen through pores on their glistening black skin. Though they came in many colors, black maevea were the most common. Sprouting from their heads were antennae that looked much like the ears of other animals, but on closer inspection, it was clear that they looked more like a fern than an ear. They were amazingly sensitive to sound, movement, and even light. They had thick, long legs that allowed them to run amazingly fast.

Their hooves made a clacking sound as they stamped them impatiently on the cobblestones. They drank in water through their hooves just like a tree through its roots. These hooves still glistened with wetness. It meant that driver, a young man with blue eyes and a tight-fitting black jumpsuit, cared for them well.

"M'lady. Shall we be on our way?"

"Certainly."

15

Liassa prowled across the top of the High Center gate. No one could see her so high up, and the gate was only a marker, anyway. Sure, there were two token guards but they only stopped people who looked suspicious. They wouldn't notice her. No one ever looked up. She slunk off the side of the gate, digging her claws into the wall to control her descent, and silently made her way down to the Low Center. She had to get out of the city and attend to her body's needs, but there was someone she had to find first.

She leapt from the side of the High Center gate to an adjacent rooftop in the Low Center. It creaked under hear weight but held easily enough. She stood on the rooftop for a long moment, breathing deeply until she caught his scent. The Taker that Ales had hired was nearby. Lia turned sunward and followed the scent. She hurdled from one dilapidated roof to the next, until she found him standing in a dark alleyway. Ales had said he was an honest man for a Taker. He didn't look so honest to Lia, standing there in a shrouding cloak. It didn't matter to her, though, as long as he did what they asked him to do.

Lia leapt over the side of the building, landing beside him in absolute silence. It was a trick that she could pull off only because she was a katali. It had become apparent to her when Ales had spent nearly a cycle trying to duplicate the feat. The human body just wasn't designed to arrest motion in the same way as one of the katali. She eyed Cole for a long moment. The hood had prevented him from seeing her. She did not want to roar at him. As gratifying as scaring the life out of him would be, attracting the guards' attention wouldn't be the best of ideas. She moved as close to him as she could without actually touching him and then growled. There wasn't much of a middle ground in the sounds she was able to make. Her voice box just didn't give her a way to be quiet, so the sound she made was something akin to a running airplane engine falling down a mine shaft just beside his ear.

Cole let out a startled yell and nearly jumped directly out of his skin. He sent his cloak flying open, drawing both of his lancers from holsters under his arms. Lia simply sat where she was, watching him with a look that called him an idiot.

"Oh, ha-ha, very funny, you disturbing pile of fur and fangs. Fine, you scared the shit out of me. Happy now? Hey, I thought only male katali had markings like that." Cole said sarcastically, pointing at her face.

She growled at him more seriously this time and thrust out her chest to hold up the hide bag hanging around her neck. The movement said she dared him to take it. He put his lancers away and approached warily. Lia held her pose, standing still as a statue in a way only predators could manage. Cole's fingers trembled as he took the bag. Lia snorted, and Cole jumped back, clutching the bag. Lia pulled her lips back from her teeth in a terrifying grin and lifted her wide paw, extending a single claw.

Cole watched wide-eyed as she scratched words into the paving stones. It said, "not an animal". She looked up at him and her eyes glowed with a ghostly inner light to emphasize the point. It worked.

"Alright, I understand. You aren't really a katali."

Lia shook her head. She looked back down at words in the cobble, then scratched the words "I am Tier" into the stones. She looked up at him and then crouched down before leaping easily onto the first landing of the fire escape above them. Cole watched her go for a long moment, and then shook his head.

"What in the Abyss have I gotten myself into?" he wondered aloud before slinging the bag over his shoulder.

Lia watched him go from above. When she turned to leave herself, she nearly ran face first into the floating form of Zezzhz. She startled back and then bowed her head in respect.

"Hello, my Child. You seem to be enjoying yourself," he said in his slow solid tones.

{I... am sorry, Father.}

"Do not apologize, my Child. In any case, that young man deserves a bit of a fright," Zezzhz replied, his gleaming diamond teeth sparkling in the sinking sun.

{Father, it has been a very long time.}

"Too long, my Child. I have been away from our world for far too long. You needed me, and in my despair, I hid myself from you. Some god I have proven myself to be. I am not here for self-recrimination, however."

Zezzhz shook his bejeweled head. His shining hair tinkled like bells.

{It's happening, isn't it? Now that she is awake.}

"People have seen you. Truly seen you, and some even recognize what you are. Even now as we stand here in this place, the word spreads that the Tier are once again in the world. Avaara is correct in her assumption. The retrieval of The Core is tantamount to the return of your people. For the two of you, to accomplish this task will tax all of your abilities as Arcangineers. Avaara has given us the gift of returning Ales to us. For you, I have a gift as well. Come, I must be very careful not to touch you. Lean your head back. I must get to your collar."

Lia didn't say anything, she just leaned her head back. There was no arguing with those gemstone eyes. He was her god. She prayed and cursed in his name. If there was anyone she could fully trust, it was him. She felt a light, brief touch on her collar. It became warm to the touch for a long moment, and then he stood up, floating back away from her.

"This is something I will do for you and you alone. When such a time comes as The Core is recovered and the Tier are whole again, this device will return to me. Alternatively, if a time comes when you feel you are finished with it, I will accept it back. I have made a modification to your collar that will allow you human speech. It is important that you be able to communicate in this time. However, the Change, the commitment of becoming one of the Wild, is to be something other than human. As such, you are not meant for human speech. You have been of the Wild long enough that I do not think this will interfere with your separation from humanity. Do you agree?"

{I agree, Father. I will not abuse this ability.}

"I would hear you say something, my Child."

Lia nodded. She wasn't sure how it would work. She had not formed human words other than inside her mind for literally thousands of cycles.

"Do not hesitate, my Child. With the collar, I have restored your familiarity with human speech."

"Thank you, Father." Lia's human voice was replicated exactly. Zezzhz remembered everything.

"It is strange to speak with a human voice again," Lia said. *{I think I prefer the mental method.}*

"I thought that you might, but I noticed your conundrum with the young man. I believed that you would find it a gift to be able to make quieter noises and to form human speech once again. May I ask where your Sister is this night?"

{As is usually the case with my sister, she has three plans to make contact with the Mind, Kiltik. You remember, it was the least damaged of the Minds, and we are hoping that it will give us a better idea of what actually happened at the onset of the Cataclysm. It may lead us to the Core.}

"Ah, so it is a hunt for the Minds, then? As good a tactic as any."

{Father, I know it is not my place to question you,} Lia began.

"And yet, you have questions. Above all others, however, much like your sister, you wonder if Avaara and I could do more to assist. If somehow we could have even stopped the Cataclysm from happening."

{Yes,} Lia replied, feeling ashamed at the accusation in her question.

"There is no need to feel ashamed, Lia, and it is a fair question. The answer is complicated. Our abilities are several orders of magnitude beyond that of even your sister Alessandra. It would seem then that we could easily solve the concerns that you are now facing. We should be able to answer all of your questions without straining our cerebral capacity. However, Avaara and I cannot be thoughtless with the information we dole out to our Children, as it is our wish that you make your own decisions and follow your own paths. If we were to simply tell you what we see for you, it could damage your ability to live your lives. For instance, if I had informed you of the possibility of the Cataclysm when you had just completed your schooling as a member of the Corps of Arcangineers?" He tilted his head making it a question.

{You knew?} Lia asked, startled.

"No, my Daughter we did not know with any certainty that the Cataclysm would come to pass. Nor did we know in advance the details of the mechanism that The Traitor would use to attempt to destroy us."

{But if you had, and you had told me... Wood and Word, it would have destroyed me.}

Zezzhz nodded, hearing her thoughts.

"Yes, Lia, I am left with the terrible decision. Do I, knowing what may happen, attempt to change it by putting the burden on one of you my dear Children, or do I allow things to play out as they may and trust that my Children are strong enough to shape their own future? I almost always choose the second, but there are times I do not wait." Zezzhz took a deep breath and sighed.

"The Traitor designed the device to resist my attempts to decipher it. Your abilities as Tier are small pieces of my own ability to understand the universe on an intrinsic level. I should have become suspicious of Alizar's studies on the nature of the Arcangineers' powers and stopped him. The past is the past, and we can do nothing but move forward. Go, my Child. You will find the best hunt in the forest moonward. Return swiftly and safely, my Daughter."

And then he was gone.

{Thank you, Father,} Lia said, knowing that he could still hear her. She turned moonward.

16

Ales made her way through the massive norstone entry hall. Everything was made of the glimmering white stone. Massive columns supporting the roof lined the hall on either side, each wound around with bands of silver that looked like ribbons, but were, in truth, metal set into the stone. It was not the equal of the Tieran Embassy in Ahal, but it was certainly a gorgeous achievement of bondstructing. She didn't dare open her Vision to look at it all. Someone would certainly see the glow. However, there was a telltale lack of seams and joints in the stone that told her it had been bondstructed.

She took small, careful steps, keeping her composure as she moved towards the ballroom. The guards lining either side of the entry hall were dressed more colorfully than they normally would be, decked out in the greens and blues of the royal family. A crier stood at the entrance to the teeming ballroom. Dozens mingled, enjoying their drinks and talking about the happenings of the day. Ales took a deep breath and entered the hallway.

"The High Lady Brightwater!" the crier announced.

Heads turned to look at her. She did her best to move into the ballroom with grace. She wasn't sure she pulled it off until a server offered her a glass. His eyes were slightly wide, and he could hardly stop himself from staring at her. She finally let a smile creep onto her face as she took a glass from his tray. She sipped the dark blue liquid inside. It was a delicious spiced alcohol blend that she couldn't quite identify. It took her Structures a few minutes while she was mingling to identify the components of the drink - phirefruit and rindspice. She realized that someone was talking to her.

"Lady Brightwater?"

The man standing before her was whipcord thin and wearing the most ridiculous feathered hat that she had ever seen. A narrow brim surrounded a domed top, with feathers arranged around the dome in a rainbow pattern. Despite the hat's ridiculousness, she did not laugh. This man certainly hated her. This was High Lord Nivus, her only direct rival at the Lordhale, at least that she knew of. He had been the one attempting to absorb the Brightwater estate when she took it from him.

"Ah, Lord Nivus, how does the Lordhale find you?" she asked.

"Intrigued as always, my dear. Your arrival was such a surprise. I was unaware that Lord Brightwater had any relatives left."

He smiled thinly at her. She did not scowl, though she did think about killing this man. She didn't have time for these idiotic political maneuverings. Still, if it was a dance he wanted, she could dance.

"I believe if you check the central registry, you will easily find me there. It should not be too difficult for you to spot a niece on his family tree," Ales said sweetly.

The man's expression soured into a scowl.

"You are not a relative. I knew each and every person on that line. I do not know who you are, or how your records were placed in the central registry, but I will find out. And then, Lady Brightwater, those lands will be mine to claim." His whisper was threatening, and just loud enough for her to hear.

She leaned forward, putting her face almost right against his. She opened her Vision for just a second, just long enough for her eyes to flash with light and power. He almost startled back, but she tangled her fist in his cravat, holding him stock still.

"I suggest that you apologize for your false accusations, Nivus. I know that the death of Lord Brightwater's daughter was your doing. I know that you've hidden her body in the catacombs beneath your bloomward estates, and I can prove the deed was done by the hand of your personal assassin, Lonblont. I can prove *my* accusations, but you have no way to prove that I am not Lady Helena Brightwater, for that is who I am."

His eyes went wide. "How could you possibly..." he started, but she cut him off.

"It's not important how I know. It's only important that you know that if you try to pursue me, I will destroy you for your crimes against the Courtship of Brightwater. Do we understand each other, Lord Nivus?" Ales growled.

Nivus nodded sharply and she released him. He skittered away from her, disappearing into the crowd. She nodded with satisfaction and sipped her drink. A deep chuckle sounded from behind her. She turned to find High King Terrin Roa standing behind her.

"Lady Brightwater," he said.

She put her cup down on the tray of a passing server and bent gracefully at the knees, holding her hands elegantly out to either side of her. She bowed her head.

"My King," she said in the high, clear voice she had adopted as Lady Brightwater.

On his arm was a beautiful woman, dressed similarly to Ales, but her dress shone with bits of gemstone sewn into the fabric in a sinuous pattern that encircled her body, running around the hem and neckline. Ales made a similar bow to her.

"My Queen. I hope that the Brightwater donation to the Lordhale banquet was adequate?"

"Adequate? Lady Brightwater, it is exquisite. It will be the centerpiece of the banquet. Might I ask who it is created such an eloquent work?"

Ales blushed, but it was a hard-earned skill more than any feeling of praise. She did not know these people yet. She knew only how she needed to act around them.

"You flatter me, My Queen. It was a creation of my own hand. Please, I insist that you accept it as a gift to the crown."

"Truly? You must be the best kept secret of Lord Brightwater, Mother hold his soul."

"Oh no, My Queen. My art is far from the hand of a true master. I am finding that I should have spent my time studying the business of our family instead."

The Queen waved her hand. "Please, enough of my title. I tire of being the Queen already this ending. Call me Aisha, and you are far too modest. The sculpture is the most beautiful piece I have seen in all my cycles."

Ales found that she could actually like this woman. There was not a bit of deceit in her, unlike what she had heard of her mate the King. Perhaps she would not have to break in to get close to Kiltik, after all. It was possible she could befriend the Queen and use that friendship to get her close enough to connect with the Mind without doing any harm, mental or physical.

"As you wish, Aisha. My King, I trust that you found it equally enjoyable?"

The King affected boredom, but it was an act. No one could lie to an Arcangineer. For some reason, he was very interested in her, though it could just be that he suspected she was an imposter just as Lord Nivus did. By all accounts, the king was an intelligent, and shrewd player in the game of politics.

"I had not seen your contribution yet this ending. My lady wife always keeps the Lordhale banquet something of a secret from me until I see it with my own eyes. It is always a delightful surprise."

His smile was genuine, so he truly did enjoy the company of his Queen. Ales was not sure what to make of this man yet. She would have to observe him more. A pleasant bell chime sounded throughout the room. The banquet was ready. Everyone started to move towards the banquet hall.

"Lady Brightwater, would you be so kind as to join us at the high table?" the Queen asked.

"Only if you would be so kind as to call me Helena."

The Queen nodded. Ales made a gesture for them to precede her, and smiled.

17

Liassa looked up from her kill. The sound that had drawn her attention away from the elderly gantha she'd brought down came again. The buck was far past its prime, and she had chosen him carefully. One of the important parts that she learned as one of the Wild was that if you wanted to eat, you had to follow the patterns of nature to maintain balance. Otherwise, you'd draw the attention of Avaara very quickly. Many thought it was the easy way out, and in some ways, they were right. However, they rarely thought about the fact that in nature there were no taverns, no wayhouses, and no ready sources of food. If you didn't hunt, you didn't eat. None of the Wild ever became an herbivore. It was dangerous enough being so isolated, but being anything other than a predator was ill-advised.

The noise came again, like the sound of boots crunching on gravel. She looked up again. This time, she opened her Vision and scanned the forest around her. Those with the Vision had many ocular powers, but she had been gifted with the Circle of Light. She was able to shift the sensitivity of her Vision to see in different spectra. She concentrated, and her Vision began to cycle through them. When she shifted through the infrared spectrum, she spotted it. There were men moving towards her in the forest. Between the dark spots that were trees and the cooler air of the nighttime forest, they showed up as a glow of red and orange.

She got her feet beneath her and rose to a crouch. She noted three separate bodies moving slowly through the forest, in a loose skirmish line. Professional soldiers or hunters, then. It was likely the Three. She decided it would be a good time to use her new power to speak. She might be able to resolve this without bloodshed, despite what Ales had told her. They obviously had some way of detecting her in the forest, though it wasn't the same tracking Structures they had used on her before. Ales had taken care of all of those, but as soon as she started to move, they all froze in place as if listening for her.

She concentrated on her Vision and shifted her sight back to normal, albeit with one major difference. She increased her sensitivity to light to account for the darkness of the forest. She placed her paws just so, finely tuned animal instincts allowing her steps to stay absolutely silent. She moved, seeing her chance, quickly circling to her right, flanking the three knights. She kept careful track of them, but they didn't seem to notice where she had gone. Perhaps they were using some sort of auditory adaptation provided by their armor to track her. They started prowling forward again, just as she pushed her head through a bush to get a better look. They didn't look like hunters. They looked like children. She watched them for a moment, but then pulled back silently. She hurried back to her kill and carefully began to drag it deeper into the woods. She didn't want them to stumble over the half-eaten gantha, and start looking for what killed it. Besides, she was still hungry.

"... saw it leave Jai. It jumped over the wall right from the ground. No katali can jump that high. It's thirty marks." The voice was female, but Lia did not recognize it.

"If it's that strong, should we really be out here looking for it?" a male voice said in the darkness.

"Jai is right, Ilsa. Your Father is going to kill you! Your mother is going to have a fit about you going out wearing that," another male voice said.

"If you two cowards want to run back to the Center, you can go. I'm going to find that katali. It won't hurt us," Ilsa said.

Lia let out a low groan of annoyance. Determination filled the girl's voice. Lia decided that if she wanted to finish her meal in peace, she had to get rid of them.

She stood up, shoving the first level of her Constraints open. Her body tightened, her muscle tension ratcheting up to twice her normal strength. She crouched down, bending all six legs before leaping straight into the air. She landed silently on a branch halfway up the nearest needlebark. The thorns broke off against her paws, the pads kept safe by a thick layer of Structures. She looked down towards the children, who had found the trail that she had made dragging the gantha. She let out a little sigh of annoyance. She didn't want to terrify these children, but she knew exactly what Ales would say in this situation. Better to give them a scare than let them find out a truth that might get them killed.

She knew this type, this girl. If she found out what Lia was, she would never leave it alone. It could put her in the crossfire. If she befriended this child like her first instinct urged, it could turn her into a target for the people who wanted to hurt Ales and Lia. She braced herself as they neared her kill. Then she sprang. She landed with a heavy thud between the children and the kill and then drew herself up, roaring with enough volume that thorns showered down from the limbs of the needlebark, blanketing the children. The boy on the left actually pissed himself. The one to the girl's right tried to scream, a sound strangled off as he began to run. The girl simply fell backwards, unconscious.

Lia's roar cut off abruptly when the girl collapsed. She groaned loudly. The first boy stared at her with absolute incredulity when her roar cut off. She eyed him, and then she bared her teeth, opening her Vision wider, causing the gleam in her eyes to flare to incandescent brilliance. She growled, and the boy had clearly had enough. He turned and ran, back towards the Center with everything he had.

{Great,} Lia thought. {Now I have an unconscious girl to deal with and no one to carry her back.}

Lia pushed her muzzle underneath the girl's stomach and nosed her over onto her back. She inspected the girl with her Vision. She was in no immediate danger, but Lia couldn't leave her out here. Another predator might find her. Lia shook her head and padded back to the gantha. She ate her fill, and then settled down in the bushes to watch the girl. Ales was going to have a mental break down when Lia was neither in the apartment nor in range of her thoughts.

Thankfully, it wasn't long before the girl started to stir. Lia sighed in relief. The girl sat up and put a hand to her head. She looked around in the dark and then reached into her pocket, fishing out a small glass globe. She shook it violently and it started to glow. With her night vision on, it nearly blinded Lia. She closed off her Vision and watched as light filled the little patch of ground around the girl. Lia queried her Structures for the girl's name just in case she needed it. The boys had called her Ilsa.

"Are you still here?" the girl asked. When no response came, she scowled and started to curse. "Wood and Word, this is just what I need. I find one of the Wild and one of the Tier, and I can't even talk to either of them. How in the howling trench am I going to find them again?!"

Lia watched intently from the shadows. The girl got to her feet and held the globe of light up over her head. She eyed the child for a long moment. She sensed that Ilsa was not scared. Lia had shocked her but not actually frightened her. This girl was something different, something that Lia just barely recognized. Did Zezzhz know that this would happen when he came to give her back her voice? She rose to a crouch and pushed through the bushes. Ilsa startled when Lia came into view.

"Do not be frightened, I will not hurt you," Lia said, her voice still sounding strange to her own ears.

"You can talk?!" Ilsa exclaimed.

"It is a temporary necessity. It's not something I can always do, but I somehow suspect that a higher power knew that I would need to be able to speak to you. Ilsa, if my instincts are right, then you are what we call a Newling. I know I look large and intimidating, but you were drawn to me. Can I come closer?"

Ilsa hesitated, and her eyes went a little wide when she realized how large Lia truly was. Ilsa swallowed hard and looked back over her shoulder. Then she turned back, her face filled with resolve. That was good. There was a difference between a Newling and someone who simply wanted to become one of the Tier. A Newling was born to the Vision. They were so rare that only two had ever been recorded. One of them was Alizar, the Traitor, and the other was Ales. Lia stayed entirely motionless while Ilsa considered.

"I think I came out here looking for you. It's not like I could run fast enough to get away if you wanted to hurt me."

She was smart, that was for sure. "I am not a monster, Ilsa. I am, as you suspect, one of the Wild, though I am surprised that you have any idea of what I am."

"My parents live and work in the royal palace. I was educated there, and the libraries have old books passed down through the royal line for hundreds of cycles that tell about the Tier, and they have some things about the Wild in there. I don't know much, only that you were Tier that somehow became animals."

Lia nodded. "Well, I don't know anything about you, but I have instincts that tell me you may need to know more about the Wild than you suspect."

Lia padded closer and Ilsa took an involuntary step backward.

"I promise I will not hurt you, but to be sure, I need to look into your eyes."

Ilsa mastered herself quickly and stood stock still.

"I need to look down to be able to see what I need to see. On one knee please?" Lia said.

Ilsa sank down to one knee, looking up into Lia's eyes.

"Understand, Ilsa, if I am right, your eyes are going to go blurry on you. They will take a few minutes to clear but it is nothing to be afraid of."

Lia had never done this before, but she knew the how of it. She opened her Vision as deep as it would go and looked directly down into Ilsa's eyes. In a normal person, she would see the muscles, along with the rest of the parts of the person's body. In one of the Tier, the response was much different. Ilsa's eyes flared brightly and Lia stepped back as in her Vision, Ilsa's entire body was glowing with living energy. She had been right. Ilsa had been born with the Vision. So rare was she that it was like finding one specific snowflake on a mountainside covered in fresh powder. Isla, for her part, waved her hands out to either side, trying to regain her balance.

"Sit down, Ilsa, it will help. The feeling will pass in a few moments. When it does, I will tell you everything you want to know about the Tier. You'll need to know because you are one of us."

Ilsa plopped down onto her backside and stared blankly at Lia. Lia joined her. They both had to do something now. They were two different things, but they were both going to be almost impossible.

18

"How are we going to get past them?" Ilsa whispered. She was standing right next to Liassa at the edge of the forest.

"We won't. You're going to climb up on my back, and I'm going to jump the wall. How did you get by them on the way out?"

"With a hat, and wearing boy's clothes." She gestured at her distinct lack of a dress.

"I don't know if you've noticed, but the gate guards are about as useful as a shirt with a back pocket." Ilsa said.

Lia made chuffing noises that after a moment Ilsa recognized as laughter.

"That doesn't sound like the language of someone who lives in the palace. Come on, climb up on my back. If you run your hands through the fur around my neck, you'll find my collar. You can hold onto that. Hold on tight." Lia laid down in the grass, and Ilsa threw her leg over Lia's back. "It's going to be jarring when I land. It might hurt. Try to be quiet."

Ilsa slipped her fingers beneath Lia's collar and took a tight grip.

"I'm not going to choke you?" Ilsa asked.

"Just hold on as tight as you can."

Feeling Ilsa adjust her grip, Lia pushed open her first and then her second level of Constraints. Lia bolted as fast as she could towards the wall. Ilsa gasped, but did not shout. Lia leapt, and it was then that Ilsa did let out a shout, but it strangled off quickly as Lia cleared the wall. She bent her legs and did her best to mitigate the impact when she landed on the nearest roof.

Ilsa let out a small grunt of pain when they hit. Lia skidded to a stop, lashing her tail once to help her balance. She waited for Ilsa to slide down off her back, but a quick look over her shoulder showed her Ilsa clutching to her collar with her eyes closed. The poor girl hadn't realized that they'd stopped moving.

"You're fine, Ilsa. You can get down now." Liassa said gently.

Ilsa opened one eye, and peered around. "I'm not dead?"

"You are, in fact, not dead."

Ilsa slid down off Lia's back.

"Ilsa, we have to talk before we go any further. You unfortunately have no choice about whether or not you develop the Vision. It will come to you in the next cycle, and if we don't teach you how to control it, it will be problematic. It will be very disorientating until you learn to control it, which can take cycles without anyone to guide you. So we can teach you, but that does not mean you have to be part of what we are doing here. It will be dangerous in ways that someone as young as you cannot understand. I know it's unfair to ask you to make a choice right now, and I will not do that. But eventually, you'll have to choose whether to stay with us or not. You need only stay as long as it takes for you to learn to control your Vision, but to teach you everything will take two dozen cycles or more."

Ilsa looked down at the flat tiled roof.

"Why me?"

"Oh, child, you do not know how many times my sister asked that question when they found out she was a Newling. Nobody has the answer to that, though, not even the Mother and Father, for we have spoken to them. Newlings are as rare as summer snow, and no one truly knows how you get your powers."

"Not even the gods who made us?"

"Not even them, but you can ask them yourself. All of the Tier meet our Mother and Father. You will too."

Ilsa's eyes went kind of wide. "You..."

"Yes, I mean that they do truly walk in our world, and they will find us when the time is right. They tell each of us something to help guide us on our way."

"What did they tell you?" Ilsa blurted out.

Lia's face screwed up in an expression Ilsa could not place. It took a moment to tell that Liassa was embarrassed.

"Ilsa, that is not a polite question. What they tell you is extremely personal. It's not something you share with others." Liassa's voice showed her embarrassment.

"Oh, Mother's End, I am so sorry. I didn't mean..." Ilsa covered her mouth. "I didn't..."

"Do not worry, child. They do not take offense to curses. Avaara is quite creative when it comes to cursing."

Lia padded towards the opposite side of the roof.

"You can't possibly be serious," Ilsa said.

"Child, I spent twenty-two hundred cycles in the company of the Mother. I assure you, the idea of besmirching her name with a curse is outlandish. Come on, you can climb down here."

"May I ask where we are going?"

"Into the High Center. My sister will be able to help you more than I can."

"Your sister?" Ilsa asked as she swung her leg over the wall and onto the ladder leading down to the first level of the building's fire stairs.

"Alessandra is a newling like you, but she has been fully taught how to use her Vision just like I have. She is special, different. No one had ever seen anyone quite like Ales."

Lia jumped down to the first landing, and then over the side, landing silently in the alleyway below. It took a long minute for Ilsa to make her way down the stairs to the alleyway.

"Aren't you worried about being seen?" Ilsa asked as they made their way across the street and into the High Center alleyway.

Lia slowed as she entered the alleyway, looking down at the ground. "They won't see us as long as you keep walking."

"How?"

"Just a trick of my Vision. I can tell when people won't look at me. You'll be able to do it eventually. It's about watching how everyone is moving and understanding the pattern," Lia said as she stopped in the alleyway. "Well, that isn't entirely true. You won't be able to do it as well as I can, but you will be able to come close enough."

"Why do you look so sad?"

Lia took a deep breath and then started walking again.

"Ilsa, you are young, and I am not sure you will understand, but The Tier are one family. Not all related by our blood, but we are..." She paused.

"We were one," Lia said.

"What happened to the Tier, Lia? The books all say that something happened, but no one knows what it was. Just one day you were here and the next you were gone."

"There was a skirmish on the boarders of Ahal. A small band of nomads, just people looking for food who didn't understand our language or who we were. There were no

Arcangineers on the border, so it took the Tier on the border time to decipher their language. By the time they did, they had frightened away the nomads by defending themselves. A child got left behind, and we took him in as scouts were sent out to find the nomads. We wanted to return the child. The scouts found the nomads, but they had been butchered on the road. We tracked down the mercenaries who had done it and brought them back to Ahal, where we imprisoned them.

So, there it was, a child with no family and no one we could return him to. One of the houses of Ahal took him in and quickly discovered that like you, he was a newling. We taught him to use his Vision, and eventually he became one of the most powerful Arcangineers among us. He fought beside us, Ilsa. He was our brother. What we did not know about him was that he never recovered from the trauma of the deaths of his people.

I will not go further into this as it will be much easier to show you everything once you are further along. All that really matters is the result. Alizar built a device, shielded from our abilities to decipher its purpose. It exploded and disrupted the tectonic activity below Ahal, causing a massive volcanic blast. Our family died that day. Millions of Tier were killed in an effort to stop an explosion that, if allowed to continue unabated, could quite possibly have consumed our entire world. I am sad, Ilsa because you may choose to be our sister, but you may also choose not to. We will not feel ill will if you choose not to, but we will be sad because Ales and I are alone in this world as it is now. We desperately need family."

19

Ales sat at the high table and attempted to affect polite interest in whatever it was Lord Whizen was joking over. She'd been attempting to ignore him all ending while focusing on processing everything that happened. Whizen came to the punchline of his joke. Ales covered her mouth politely, and laughed at his joke. It had not been funny. It was time to take control of the conversation.

"So, my King, the word from the border is that traffic stoneward is no longer safe. Are there any leads as to where the missing caravans have gone?" Ales asked.

"I'm surprised that word has made it to your estate so close to the capital. Yes, we've been experiencing problems with bandits stoneward. Currently, one of the Three is being dispatched to investigate the situation."

Ales suppressed the grin that wanted to spread across her face. She always marveled at how easy it was to steer a conversation with just a little information.

"I have heard so much about the Three Knights. Is it true that their armor somehow makes them faster and stronger than a normal person?" Ales asked blithely.

"Yes, that is true. Their armor is a marvel that was discovered by our Searchers. It was all made right here in the castle. Even now, they are working to find ways to make more suits of armor like those that will allow us to better defend our borders."

"Truly amazing, your majesty. How is it that they go about making such armor?"

Ales wasn't sure he would answer. It seemed that all of the Bondstructs that they used were carefully guarded secrets. They were all operated by Fixers who were employed by the royal family directly. That was what she had guessed, at least. She did know that Kiltik had to be in the castle somewhere, however. The Bondstructs were crude, but they were still Tieran made. After examining the ones that had been clinging to Lia's fur, it became quite clear that they had been enlarged to allow those without the proper equipment to manipulate them more easily. They were by no means gigantic, but compared to the Bondstructs that Kiltik produced in their time, they were practically archaic.

The King's eyes narrowed as he looked at her suspiciously, but it lasted only a moment before his affable expression returned. "That is a question I fear that I cannot help you with. Our Searchers are the only ones who understand the process in creating the armor."

He turned to one of the other Lords, and the conversation turned to unimportant politics of moving grain into the bloomward provinces from the Izari nation. Ales cursed inwardly as she followed the conversation absently.

The Queen leaned a little closer from her right.

"If you have interest in search studies, Helena, there are many books available in the royal library on the subject. I could show you around, if you will be in the Center for a time?"

Ales smiled. "I think I would like that, my Queen."

The Queen scowled at her.

"I'm sorry, Aisha. When?"

"It will be a few days, as I'm sure you realize these overstuffed fops will monopolize my time for days after the Hale," she replied with a smile.

"Perhaps I could accompany you and attempt to save you from some of their attempts to impose upon you?" Ales offered.

The Queen grinned positively delighted with the idea. "I would not subject you to such punishment, though. You shouldn't have to endure their silly squabbles over the latest fashions or the state of the whole Hale of Nobles. It's such a bore," she said with a little laugh.

"It can't be any more boring than the stacks of financial books that are waiting for me at the estate. I would be delighted to have a few more days away before I have to dive back into that horrifying mathematical morass."

"So if it is not too presumptuous of me, Aisha, I would be thrilled to help you fend off your discourteous courtiers."

20

Ales climbed down from the carriage with little difficulty. Over the course of the night, she had become more and more comfortable moving in the dress and shape. Now she barely noticed them. That didn't mean she wouldn't love to have them off, however. As soon as she closed the door to her apartments behind her, she used her mental connection with the Bondstructs. She caught the shape as the seam split up the side. The dress split at the side up to her hip moments after, and she strode across the norstone floor towards her bedroom.

{Ales, please do not be startled. I have brought a friend.} Lia's mindvoice was nervous.

"Lia, who have you brought? Did you drop off the package with Cole?"

{I did. I also had a short visit from the Father. He gave me a gift. Well temporarily. I can speak again.} Lia's mindvoice was still slightly nervous.

"Why do you sound so nervous?" Ales asked as she turned the corner into her bedroom.

There sitting on the edge of the bed was a beautiful young woman. She had long navy-colored hair bound into a practical ponytail. She wore rough clothing, a brown linen shirt with a heavy tunic and trews. Her boots were made for hard wear. But her eyes were what drew Ales' attention. They were sapphire blue, alive with intelligence in ways that Ales was all too familiar with. She strode across the room and stopped directly in front of Ilsa.

{I've already Confirmed her, Ales. She is a newling. If I had my guess, she'll be three quarters your strength, perhaps a little more. Much stronger than me. I can tell you she has the Circle of Finding, but none of the other patterns I saw were familiar, so she doesn't have the Circle of Taking.}

Ales looked Ilsa over. The source of Lia's nervousness was apparent. If the girl chose to fight, and was not left the option of the Wild, she could quite possibly go mad.

"She is very young, Lia."

"I didn't find her, she found me. Besides, does it really matter? She is a newling. The Vision will come out in her eventually. I have looked for newlings, Ales. For three thousand cycles, I have been on the alert for them. Why now?"

Ales blinked and looked at Lia. She had heard what she had said about Zezzhz gifting her with human speech but it was jarring.

"Because of me. I have a connection with The Core unlike any other except for the Traitor. When I woke up, it was obvious that I woke The Core as well. With The Core awake, there will be new Tier in the world. All souls come from The Core, and now that I have awakened it, so too will the powers of our dormant brothers and sisters. I can only hope it will be slow at first. It should only be people near to us."

Liassa nodded slowly. *{I think that was the Father's thought as well. If I had a guess, the return of my voice was meant to allow me to teach if necessary.}*

She put heavy emphasis on the word necessary. Lia did not like to teach. She became too attached in the process. She felt responsible for everything one of her students did or did not do with their Vision.

{Until we can retrieve Verdant, there is no way to make it so others can hear my thoughts.}

Liassa's mindvoice was almost sad. She didn't like speaking out loud. It was a stark reminder of the pain she left behind when she became one of the Wild.

{How certain are you she will be one of the Wild?} Ales asked.

{I can't be completely certain, but you know that all of the Wild feel a certain kinship, and I feel it with her. It's not a sure thing, but we talked. I don't know if her mind could handle the stress of having to hurt someone, much less kill someone. Perhaps she will choose the path of the Finder instead of becoming an Arcangineer.}

"I'm sorry, I don't want to be rude, but I feel as if there is a conversation happening that only you two can hear," Ilsa finally said.

"Quite right. I apologize, we were simply discussing your options for the future," Ales replied.

"Am I part of that decision?"

Ales smiled reassuringly. "Of course you are, child. I meant only that we were deciding what options we could offer you. That is not to say that you must take them."

"And what are those options?"

Ales looked down into her eyes and opened her Vision. Ilsa lost herself for a moment. She shivered when Ales finally looked away.

"Mother's End, that feels strange," Ilsa groaned after a moment of balancing herself.

"I apologize for the necessity. I had to get a better feeling for your abilities. You have a number of paths before you. You are in possession of three of the seven ocular circles."

"Circles?"

"Circles are how we refer to areas of study within the Vision. The Vision itself allows you to see and understand more about the world around you than any normal person can. However, almost all of the Tier have specialized powers that stem from their Vision. Usually, mastering an area of ocular ability takes anywhere from two to five cycles. The reason Lia could only understand one of your Circles is because you can only understand a Circle if you possess it yourself."

"So you have the same ones that I do?"

"I possess all seven ocular Circles."

Ilsa's mouth made a little 'O' of surprise. "Which ones do I have?"

"Finding, Repair, and Breaking. Ilsa, before I tell you anything else, it is getting very late. You have parents, people who will miss you?"

"My parents. We live in the palace. My Father repairs weapons for the palace guard and my mother is the Head Mistress of the palace servants."

"That makes some sense. Your Father is talented?" Lia asked

"Yeah, very talented. So was my grandpapa. He built the first lancers. My Da says that he made the armor that the King uses when he fights."

"It explains the Circle of Repair and the Circle of Finding," Ales said.

"You mean, I got them from my father? Does that mean they are Tier too?"

Ales shrugged in response. "The Vision is a power that we all have the potential for at birth. Usually, though, we have to be taught how to access it, and so almost all of the Tier choose to be with us. You have the same choice with one exception.

Regardless of whether or not we teach you, your Vision will come out, but that does not mean you have to be one of the Tier. What it does mean is that you are in a very dangerous situation, because you need a Tieran teacher."

Ilsa nodded her head. "What's going to happen to me if you don't teach me?"

Ales sighed. "You're too young. It would only frighten you to know," Ales said.

"But we are going to tell you anyway," Lia added.

"If you go untaught, within a few rotations, your Vision will be triggered by something. You will see something that will rouse your abilities. The problem is, you won't know how to turn them off. It takes spans of mental training to learn simply how to close your Vision, and if you don't have a teacher, you have rotations of seeing the world overwhelmed by everything the Vision shows you before you can learn to close off your sight and return to normal," Lia explained.

"I don't understand what you mean," Ilsa said.

"I will help you understand," Alessandra said.

She looked down into Ilsa's eyes again. There was no feeling of disorientation this time, but suddenly, Ilsa was blinded by blazing lights. It was too much. She closed her eyes, but it didn't help. She could see countless tiny motes floating across her line of sight. They moved and danced in unrecognizable patterns.

"I can't see anything!" she said with a frightened tremor in her voice.

"No, that's not it. The problem is that you see absolutely everything. At this level, you are seeing every tiny particle that everything around you is made up of. Now imagine having to see this all the time, for spans on end. You wouldn't be able to sleep because closing your eyes simply shows you the particles that make up your eyelids. No one would be able to tell why you were unable to see or function, or why your eyes were glowing all the time."

Suddenly Ilsa's eyes went back to normal. She nearly pitched forward as everything snapped back into clear focus.

"I can't..." Ilsa started then stopped. She realized she had no idea how to express her distress.

"We will teach you how to control your abilities, but it will take cycles. More importantly, it will take trust."

"I think I can trust you," Ilsa said.

"You misunderstand, child. We must trust you," Ales said.

Ales and Liassa watched as Ilsa made her way into the servant's entrance of the palace. The sky was starting to lighten sunward.

"We need to get outside of the city and talk to the Mother or the Father. I'm not happy about this, Lia. I don't feel right pulling a child of her age into our affairs. This is not Ahal. There is no one here to defend her until she is ready," Ales said.

{We are here, and she is hardly a child, Ales. She is a woman full grown.} Lia's mindvoice was firm.

"And what of her parents? What are we are to tell them?"

{The truth. That their daughter is very special and is going to need to learn how to control her abilities or she will hurt herself or others.}

Lia replied as she turned and padded back towards the Low Center. Ales made an unhappy noise.

"Why did she have to have Breaking? Why couldn't it have been some nice quiet Circles?" Ales asked.

"You remember your first experience with Breaking?"

Liassa nodded solemnly. *{But not having the power myself, I remember yours better. I remember the look on your face. Fear and confusion as to what was happening. Arcangineers darting everywhere, pulling people out of the Hall of Listening as the eastern wing collapsed.}*

Her own had been much less devastating. Watching Haw repair a person's broken body was far less impressionistic than seeing a building destroyed with a touch. It was how Ales found out she was a Newling. She had been six, and all she had done was put her hand against the wall of the Hall of Listening. When she did, the wall had simply crumbled away from her hand. Breaking was by far the most dangerous Circle to be out of control of. It showed you all of the weaknesses of physical things. Seeing things through the Circle of Breaking made it possible to heal even the direst of wounds by immediately knowing what was weakest. It could also let you start a chain reaction with a touch that could destroy entire buildings. The Hall of Listening had been one of largest buildings in the Learning quarter of Ahal. No one had been killed, thankfully, as the Learning quarter was also where the

Arcangineer's Corps had been located. They had reacted quickly and pulled everyone out of the building. Ales had been fairly traumatized by the event, though, and as a result, she rarely used the Circle of Breaking unless the need was dire. When she did, the results tended to be terrifying.

"You weren't even born to remember that."

{I wasn't, but The Core never forgets, and you, of all people, should know how easy it is to see the memories of a blood family member when communing with The Core.}

Ales frowned and changed subjects. "We are deluding ourselves Lia. You know what this means. She has Breaking. She will not simply choose another path."

{It is not a sure thing,} Lia said, but her mindvoice held no true confidence.

"There were many Arcangineers such as yourself who did not have Breaking. How many of our folk do you remember who had Breaking that did not eventually seek out the Arcangineers Corps?" Lia looked down.

{None, but that doesn't mean she won't find some creative use for it. Lots of people used it for things other than fighting. Haw never broke anything with it in his life.}

Ales just shook her head as they made their way around the palace.

"Haw was an exceptionally gifted healer that I think would have wept for an entire rotation if he had accidentally killed even a tiny nightwing. Even he sought out the Corps. He may have had different reasons, but in the end, he joined us. This girl has a fire in her, Lia. I can see it. I don't know how she will react in a fight, or to having to do harm. You may be right, she may end up as one of the Wild, but she will be a fighter, Lia."

{Not everyone has to follow you, Ales.}

Ales looked hurt. "You regret your decision to follow me to the Corps."

It wasn't a question, but Lia shook her head immediately.

{No, not for a second. Not in three thousand cycles has that ever been a regret of mine. No, I regret what it did to you. Other people can believe whatever they want, but I know how you would feel about what Alizar did.}

Ales straightened up a little. She didn't want to talk about it, but three thousand cycles is a long time for a wound to fester. Lia wasn't going to let it go now that she was on to the topic. Ales grunted unhappily as they squeezed past a pile of refuse heaped against one of the clean stone walls of the alleyway. Lia sneezed at the smell and hurried past it. It smelled of ammonia and rotting fruit. She squeezed past Ales to try to get away from it. When she looked back, Ales was staring very hard at the disorganized mound of trash.

"This is the first time I have seen garbage anywhere in the city."

She eyed it suspiciously. Lia made a grunting noise, and Ales spun, deepening her Vision. Her sister had collapsed onto her side, a dart sticking out of her hindquarters. By her mental command, her Cellstructs analyzed the dart and calculated possible angles of entry. It took only a moment for them to tell her that the dart had come from the roof of the small building behind the wayhouse across the street.

Everything around it faded as she picked out the attacker. They were dressed in black and counting on it to hide them where they laid on the roof. They had not moved, but in her Vision, the shape of the person was outlined in bright blue. She stopped next to Lia and pushed off her Constraints. The mental blocks opened, and she felt her body tighten with speed and strength.

"Are you alright?"

{Neurotoxin with a tranquilizer. My Cellstructs are filtering it now. Go.} Lia groaned inside of Ales' head.

Ales nodded and then bolted across the street. An overwhelming show of force was what was needed here. No one should know who they were, but already someone was trying to kill them. That was unacceptable. Ales had leapt the short fence around the stables and landed right next to one of the three stable buildings by the time the assassin knew what was happening. The assassin had picked the empty building probably thinking that the maevea would not notice him.

Ales triggered the Circle of Breaking. She grimaced as lurid red lights appeared, covering everything she was looking at like polka dots for a long second. She focused, and all of them faded except for one on the side of the stable building. The assassin jumped up, but it was far too late. Ales slammed her fist into the bright red dot on the side of the stable. The wall simply disintegrated beneath her hand, stress fractures shattering the wood. The whole small building began to collapse in on itself with a groan of buckling beams. The assassin fell into the middle of the tumult, disappearing among the wreckage.

When the sound finally quieted, there were shouts coming from within the wayhouse. Ales ignored them and stalked through the wreckage. With her increased strength, it was easy to shove aside broken walls and fallen beams. She found the assassin trapped beneath a thick beam. The woman eyed her dazedly and Ales took in the damage. She had a broken collarbone and her leg was crushed beneath the building's center beam. Ales hunkered down beside her and paused over her in a crouch.

"Who sent you?" Ales asked softly.

The woman smiled at her with bloodied teeth. She said something in a language that Ales did not understand. It took her Vision, aided by her Cellstructs, the space of three deep breaths to translate it. It was a much closer derivative of Tieran than Vilhenan.

"You couldn't possibly understand me, witch, and my purpose in killing the beast I will never speak." came the translation.

The woman spat blood onto Ales' coat. Ales tossed the heavy crossbeam off of the woman without any visible effort. She moved her face closer to the woman's, their noses almost touching.

"Oh, but I *can* understand you," Ales whispered. She tangled her fist in the woman's jacket, her eyes flaring with spectral light. "And you will tell me everything I want to know," Ales grated.

The woman's eyes widened in naked terror.

- END OF PART 2 -

Cole eyed the palace walls and shook his head. He'd beaten the defenses of a dozen strong holds in his time, but the Vilhenan Royal Palace had been the one place he'd always been told was entirely impenetrable. He unrolled the scroll he had taken from that insane woman's pet katali. The scroll was unlike anything he had ever seen. Not just what was drawn upon it, but the paper itself. It was easily the finest quality writing material he had ever seen. The layout of the palace and route he would take to reach his destination was laid out with such precision that it almost seemed to leap off the page and into his mind.

Still, it wasn't everything he needed. There were parts of the plan that she had left entirely up to him. The scroll clearly pointed out that to clear the route, he would have to bribe, cajole, or blackmail at least one guard. Not only that, there was nothing to show where he was going once he reached the cellars below the palace. If there were any defenses below there, he would have to be ready for them. Once he reached the royal palace, he would not be able to retrace his route, either. He'd have to find a way down from the top levels of the Citadel without passing through it. That meant he was going to need more specialized tools.

"There's no way I can do this on my own, Warran" Cole said.

"I said I needed a look at the Archive Tower, not that I would go in with you."

"I hear a but..."

Warran grunted. It was a form of communication with him. It meant that he had an idea. "But there are people who have been wronged by the King that would be willing to help you," Warran's gleaming green eyes locked onto the Archive Tower and he began to rubberneck around, looking at all the buildings surrounding the palace.

"I'm not sure my client would like that. I will have to enquire," Cole said.

"The grapple can be shot from one of your lancers to that rooftop over there. Then you can use it to descend from the

Archive Tower. You still use those old Harn Sidekicks?" Warran asked.

"They're reliable," Cole hissed defensively.

"They are."

"They're also slow and would have a hard time penetrating the armor of the royal guard. I have a pair of Stoe Model Eights that I have retooled with self-repairing Bondstructs. They'll fire every time."

Cole eyed Warran for a long moment. "How did you get a pair of Stoes?"

"Built them myself, just used the Stoe designs."

"You built them? How did you get the designs?"

Ronald Stoe was a legendary designer and maker of lancers. Besides Harn, none were more widely recognized for making a reliable iron.

"A gentleman came in a few rotations ago. He'd taken a tumble and cracked the grip on his Stoe. He couldn't load the weapon and needed it repaired. I took it apart and memorized the design," Warran explained.

Cole stared at him gape jawed. "Memorized the design? A lancer design?"

Warran just shrugged in response. "It's just something I do."

"I ever mention how much you freak me out with that brain of yours?"

Cole watched the guards moving around the perimeter of the palace. He would have to time it just right to get down from the Archive tower over the wall without being spotted.

"Once or twice. Who is that?" Warran said, shrinking back into the alleyway pulling Cole with him.

A sally port door opened in the palace gates and a man came through it with a guard on either side of him. He was wearing a full suit of bondarmor that appeared to be painted with red and gold. It wasn't. The structures it was made out of were just those colors.

"That, my dear Fixer, is High Lord Faln, Commander of the Royal Guard, and if luck favors me, the man I will bribe to gain entrance to the lower reaches of the palace."

Warran let out a little spluttering sound. "Are you mad? You can't bribe the Guard Commander!" Warran backed down the alleyway a little further.

"Relax, I am not meeting him here. I'm meeting him over there. Truth be told, it's more blackmail than a bribe, but I was trying to be circumspect."

Cole pointed to a building across the wide main road. The Blue Mare was one of the highest class establishments in the city. It boasted wine cellars that were said to rival the Royal Palace itself, and contained over a hundred suites that Cole would have robbed blind in a heartbeat given half a chance. There was no chance. The Blue Mare also boasted some of the best security measures shockingly large piles of gold could buy. The rumor was that everything in the entire wayhouse had been tagged with bondstructed tracking devices. If anything went missing at all, the owners would know where to find the thief. Cole was fairly certain the last was a rumor. That many Bondstructs would bankrupt even the Royal coffers. They did, however, have security alarms and autonomous motion sensors that were bondstructed. Cole eyed the place with suspicion.

"I have to go, Cole. I can't be seen with you."

"I know. It's alright, go ahead. If I don't walk out of this, I have arranged it so that the advance that insane woman gave me comes to you."

Warran shook his head. His friend was making no sense whatsoever. What could he possibly have to blackmail a High Lord with? Warran just shook his head again and turned back down the alleyway.

Cole put on his usual swagger, adjusted his long coat, and strode across the main street. He checked his lancers with a quick touch of his fingers and walked right past the doorman, who gave him an ugly stare but didn't raise any objections. Perhaps Faln had paid him to let Cole pass.

The common room of the Blue Mare was opulent. Cole almost stopped and stared. Almost. It was nothing like the outside, which fit into the halfway modern halfway archaic skyline of Vilhena perfectly. Every surface within was polished and modern. White norstone floors gleamed with flecks of shimmering silver. The walls were covered in gleaming silver metal, brushed rather than polished. The walls curved like a bowl towards the back of the massive common room. On the left-hand side in the back, a massive black sorstone staircase disappeared to the upper floors of the building. On the right, a pair of unmarked bluevein doors loomed, fitted with gold that looked like they were worth enough to buy half the kingdom.

Everyone was better dressed than he was, and for a moment, he felt out of place, but he knew better. He was not part of this shining lie. They might call him a thief, but he was a rank amateur compared to the demons in this room. He might steal gold and jewels, but these creatures stole people's very lives. He swaggered to the bar, a gleaming steel surface with a black sorstone base that curved to match the front wall of the room. The stock on the shelves behind the bar was the most extensive collection of liquor he had ever seen.

His eyes were immediately drawn to a bottle of Aluvian starn that was older than he was. The warm emerald liquid in that bottle was worth enough money to feed him for a cycle. He eyed it greedily, but only for a moment before he mastered his desire to steal it. He turned back to the room and scanned the crowd for Lord Faln. It took him only a moment to spot the scaled red and gold pauldrons that would extend into a full suit of armor, should the man need to defend himself. That was good. If he got in trouble he could draw fast and put a bolt into the Lord before his armor could transform. Once that was done, he could go out through the window. He made his way across the room and brushed by one of bodyguards Faln had brought. He reached into the man's coat and nicked his coin purse as he slid onto the posh gantha hide bench across from Lord Faln.

"So, the boy arrives. Much younger than your reputation makes you out to be," Faln said.

"I am told I am exceedingly talented, m'Lord. I do not believe it, but all of these things keep appearing in my pockets that speak to the contrary of my belief." He dropped the coin purse he had pickpocketed from the guard onto the table. The guard's eyes went wide and he scrambled to pick up the pouch of coins. Lord Faln barked out a laugh.

"It seems your reputation is hard earned, boy. So, tell me why I shouldn't dump you in the royal dungeon and let you rot?" Faln's smile had disappeared.

Cole grinned back at his stern expression. "Why, Lord Faln, I thought you would never ask. Tell your babysitters to take a walk."

The two guard's faces fell into cold scowls.

"Careful, boys, you keep looking like that and the ladies won't have to guess how ugly you are. Walk."

Faln waved them away. Cole reached into his jacket and Faln stiffened visibly.

"Relax, if I wanted you dead I wouldn't do it from three marks away."

Cole pulled a thick envelope from one of the many pockets inside of his coat and placed the crisp, white package squarely before Faln. Faln opened its flap and took out a sheaf of papers. His eyes widened when they fell on the seal at the bottom of the page. These were exact duplicates of the contract with the Darkness from his private study. He looked up at Cole suspiciously.

"You will find, m'Lord, that the originals are in my possession. More accurately, they are in the possession of someone that will ensure that they make their way to the King if anything should happen to me. This person is not connected to me in any way, and attempting to track down those close to me will only result in the documents immediately making their way to the King. This is your one and only chance to contain this. As I am sure you well know, breaking your contract with the Darkness will only result in your immediate death. Is all this really worth one little tour of the Citadel?" Cole employed his most reasonable tone.

"Allowing a thief into the lower reaches will result in my death just as quickly as breaking contract with the Darkness," Faln said cooly. His eyes were like frozen knives boring into Cole.

Cole, for his part, affected nonchalance. "You are a clever man, Faln. I'm sure you will think of a way to clear my path to the lower reaches in the next two spans. Find a way. I'll be in touch." He pushed himself to his feet, swaggered to the bar, and pointed to the bottle he had been eyeing earlier. "I'll take the bottle of Aluvian back there. Compliments of High Lord Faln."

The barkeep scowled and eyed Faln. The High Lord simply nodded and waved his hand in response. Cole eyed the bottle appreciatively as he headed for the door. Just as he made it, there was an enormous sharp, snapping sound and an immense racket coming from somewhere behind the wayhouse. Cole had no delusions of being a hero. He ran.

Ilsa heard her Father's boots in the hallway. She groaned and pulled herself out of bed. She had gotten a whole two hours of sleep.

"Ilsa, are you awake?" Her father's soft voice came through the door.

"Sure, Da. Just let me get dressed."

"It's alright. Can I come in?" Lerand asked.

"Yeah, but I'm warning you, I look awful."

The door cracked open and Lerand slipped through, closing it behind him. As Ilsa slid out of bed, her nightshirt fell around her ankles. She took a brush off of her dresser and pulled it through her hair a few times before beginning to braid.

"You were late last night," he said carefully.

She paused in twisting her first braid for a long moment before her fingers began their work again. "I tried to be quiet when I came in."

"I talk to every guard in the City twice a span, Ilsa. Did you expect I wouldn't find out where you were last night?"

She didn't know how to answer him so she just continued to braid her hair. She walked over to her open wardrobe, where she pulled a bit of blue ribbon out of the door and tied off the first of her braids.

"You weren't very careful last night. If anyone who mattered had seen you wearing those clothes, your mother would've had a serious breakdown." He was avoiding the topic because he didn't know what to say either.

Ilsa took a long deep breath as she tied off her second braid. "I was right." She started on her third braid.

"About what?"

She took down a blue dress with a floral pattern in it. She stepped behind her dressing screen. "The Tier, Da. I was right about the Tier."

She pulled the dress up over her legs and then put her arms though it. She turned her back on her dressing mirror and took a lace puller down from a hook. Using it, she pulled the laces up the back of her dress closed and then reached behind her back with practiced ease, tying the laces into a bow at the small of her back. She squirmed, trying to settle the tight-fitting fabric before starting to braid the other side of her hair. When she came out from behind the dressing screen, her father was staring at her with a skeptical expression.

"Are you sure, kitten? That sounds..." His speech cut off as she looked at him full in the face and her eyes flared with brilliant luminosity. They were two different colors. One was her normal deep blue, but the other was bright and amber colored. When the light faded, both of her eyes were blue again.

"I'm sure, Da, and they told me it won't be long before my eyes stay two different colors permanently. They said maybe a few days, at the longest, a few spans."

Lerand just stared at her. "They did this to you?"

Ilsa shook her head. "Nah, Da. I was born this way. They just knew it, that's all."

"But it's just a legend," he said, seemingly beyond belief.

"Da, you know how I've been feeling lately. You told me when I was little that I would know what I was meant to do when I was older. This is what I'm meant to do. I'm supposed to be one of the Tier."

Lerand tilted his head and that quiet smile crept onto his face. "You know, when you started wearing those dresses, you looked awkward, like you didn't even know how your body was supposed to work yet. And that awkwardness hadn't left since. But now." He made a wordless gesture that took in how she was standing. Even as feminine as her dress made her look, no one who walked into that room would look anywhere but at her. Not just because she was beautiful and feminine, but because she commanded the room. Just like her mother.

"Does that mean that you aren't going to try to stop me?" she said skeptically as she tied off the last of her braids.

He burst out in a hearty laugh. "Stop you?" He seemed genuinely perplexed and amused by the idea. "Dear child, how would I ever accomplish such a thing?" he asked, his quiet smile back in place. "Your mother may have something to say about you gallivanting around doing whatever it is that you will be doing."

He stood up and held out his arms in a wordless request that no child would fail to recognize. She made her careful way across the room and hugged him.

"She told me that part. The Tier protect people who can't protect themselves. But I promise I'll be careful, Daddy."

"Remember what I told you about careful, kitten."

"I shouldn't be too careful with my life or I will miss it all together."

"That's my girl, " he said as he released her. "When do you have to leave?"

"I think it will be soon. She said that I probably should wait to tell you and Ma until we could all sit down and talk, but you knew something was different. I think that they are doing something the King would not like, but I believe in them, Da. Whatever they're doing, it is important."

He didn't seem surprised by this. His lack of surprise surprised her, though.

"I've done good work for the King, kitten, but I have never deluded myself with the idea that he was a great man, or even a very good one. He keeps the kingdom stable, but only because it is to his advantage. Kings are rarely as good as their image makes them out to be. Often, they're forced to do things they would rather not. I can't claim to know the mind of our King, but that doesn't matter. You have my blessing, kitten. Chase those dreams. Be sure to visit when you can."

She took tiny steps back from him and sighed. "I don't know if it will be safe for you and Ma if I come back. It might be better if you were to disown me."

He eyed her for a long moment. He could tell it hurt her to say it, but she had done it anyway. It was an amazing transformation from one day to the next. Could it really be that she had been coming into this for much longer than he had thought? He pondered it, but what she said demanded an answer.

"No, your mother and I will leave the palace and find a new life before that." He saw that wasn't going to be enough for her. "Ilsa, you are my only child. Your mother and I trust you with our lives. Neither your mother nor I are going to be separated from our child just because someone else might not like you for doing what you believe in. Your mother may grouse, but she would never stand in the way of you doing what you want with your life. She just worries, just like you are worrying for us. No, we are your family, and that is that." He made a chopping motion with his hand, ending the discussion.

Her face softened, and she smiled at him like she had when she was little.

"Thank you, Da."

"FIXER"

24

Warran watched from the shadows as Cole disappeared into the Blue Mare, and then turned to start back towards his shop. He had to help Cole, but he would have to be very careful not to leave any mark of his on what he built to help his friend. He took the twists and turns of the back alleys of the center exactly as he had memorized them. He mumbled to himself, going over what he would need to put together, not only the grappling device, but also a few other surprises that would keep Cole safe. He wasn't really seeing anything around him as he went, his mind entirely focused on what he needed to do. That all stopped when a soft but distinct thud came from the alleyway ahead of him. He looked around, but when he saw only the lengthening shadows, he shrugged away his sudden rush of apprehension. Then she appeared, sliding out of the shadows as if she had been part of them. The katali prowled forward, watching him keenly. It took him a long moment to pull his mind from the depths of what he had been doing. Then he backed away from the enormous feline.

"How did you get into the center?" he said mostly for lack of anything else to say.

"Mostly, I just walked," the katali replied.

Warran leapt back. "Father's Stones!"

"Lia? Why are you terrorizing that man?" Ales came around the corner, sliding her Windblade back into her jacket.

{Did you finish breaking down the poison?} Ales added, purely mentally.

{It was not terribly difficult. What did you do with the assassin?}
{Stashed her in a room in a wayhouse a few streets away.}

Lia answered her question about Warran out loud, "Because he looks like fun, and besides, you know what he is."

"Only if he chooses to be," Ales observed.

"What are you?" He looked between them.

"He got the first question without even trying, and right on the tail end of the shock. Promising," Ales said.

Warran started to speak, but Ales held up her hand to stall him.

"Let us answer first, then you can ask and we will see how far this goes. We are the last of the Tier. The only remnant of our people. We are here to bring this world back into balance." She gestured to him.

"It's out of balance?" He had never really thought about it.

Lia made a wordless gesture to him with her forepaw as if saying she had told Ales so.

"Yes, to the average eye, I am sure things seem quite normal, but what Tieran technology is being used for is not what it is meant for. We are here now to correct this," Lia responded.

"You're talking about what the King and people like him use their Bondstructs for. But they've always used them for things like that, haven't they?"

"Not always. When we made these things, they were not for war. They have stained our efforts with the blood of the innocent. Our technology was not meant to hold power over others. It was meant to protect and guide," Ales said.

"I've never believed in the Tier or the Gods, but if what you're saying is true and the Gods did set you on this path, then..."

They waited patiently while he worked his way through it all.

"That means something terrible is going to happen, something that is going to affect everyone, everywhere, doesn't it?" Warran said. He looked to Ales' solemn face, and she nodded.

"That is what we think. We don't know for sure, but that is the most likely scenario." Ales and Lia exchanged a glance.

"Then I only have one more question," Warran said, thoughts of his daughter in danger flashing through his mind.

Ales nodded encouragingly.

"How can I help?" Warran asked.

"That, dear boy, is the right question."

PART 3

25

{*You think it is a coincidence?*} Liassa asked as they returned from Warran's shop.

"Coincidence?" Ales raised a brow skeptically as they turned into the alleyway behind the building they were calling home. In truth, it was the apartments of High Lady Brightwater. That was the name Ales had taken to infiltrate the collection of nobles. She had already befriended the queen and was hoping that she could get access to Kiltik without the need to hurt anyone. There were other ways they could go about it, but Lia trusted her sister. They had argued at the beginning. Liassa thought they should have just broken into the palace and taken Kiltik. The Mind was Tieran, and it belonged with them. Ales had argued that Kiltik did not belong to them. It was a life of its own, if an artificial one. It had to choose. If they were to represent all that the Tier stood for, then they could not force Kiltik to their will any more than they could any other living being. It was not the way.

{*I know, once is a happenstance, twice is coincidence, three times is undoubtedly a pattern. I am the Finder, if you remember. Still, you think the Theif is one of us? He uses his abilities to take for himself. He thinks of no one else,*} Liassa said.

"I'm not so sure about that, Lia." She made the jump up to the steel stairway on the outside of the adjacent building. Lia landed next to her a moment later, and they made their way up in companionable silence.

{*Well, tell me why I am wrong then?*} Lia asked.

Ales jumped across to the balcony and Lia made the jump a moment later, as soon as there was room.

"Every fifth day, if you go into the low center in the early breaking, you will find a single gold piece on the back stoop of every honest shop keeper that is struggling. No one could tell me where the coin comes from, and yet it comes every fifth day. Who better to know who is honest and who isn't than a thief?" Ales said as they parted the curtains, and went inside.

{*Hmm, I suppose you could be right. Change of subject. I've been listening at windows like you asked. I think you are right about High Lady Wryn. She is not nearly as important as everyone thinks she is. There is someone in her house standing behind her calling the*} *shots. She takes private meetings three times a day, but no one can seem to find out who she is talking to.}*

"If she is just a pawn, then it is the one who is moving her that is concerning."

{Have you discovered how many of the High Lords are scheming against the king?}

"Out of the twenty or so High Lords and Ladies, there are four I can say for certain are attempting to overthrow him actively. Faln is the closest to him, and the closest to accomplishing the task. He is the only one who is attempting to take control of Kiltik, as he is the only one who knows the real source of the king's power. Nivus is attempting to collect all of the holdings that ensure that the kingdom survives in a financial sense. I have momentarily stalled his efforts, though that can become a more permanent solution if I have to make it one. Illad is the one the King is focusing on. As Commander of the Stoneward Wall, he has control of the stoneward army. He's been having secret dealings with the Halla tribes in the stoneward flats. The nomads have been attempting to retake the flatlands stoneward since Vilhena forced them out three centuries ago. Apparently, Illad is promising them control of the flatlands if they will provide an army to take the kingdom. They could do it, too. If I am right, the Halla are descended from the Craigmen. You remember how many times we had to go to the Craig to settle disputes?"

{Three times a cycle, never less. Though it wasn't always us. They were savage fighters, but not actually savages.}

It wasn't uncommon for the Craigmen to start wars over their territory. They were reasonable enough about most things, but they believed that the land they occupied was theirs by birthright. They would defend it fiercely.

"The High Lady Wryn's activities are probably the most dangerous, since we aren't really sure where she is going with what she's doing. Perhaps she is undermining the king, but the subtle way that she is influencing the armies, buying officers commissions so randomly like that. No one else is likely to notice the pattern. She's playing a long game, and has been for cycles, but I'm not sure what game it is that she is playing. What other state enemies does Vilhena have? Perhaps Lady Wryn is a plant for one of them?" Ales guessed.

{It's possible. I'll see what I can dig up on my own. What are we going to do with that woman who attempted to murder me?}

"I'm going to find out exactly who sent her. I have an idea, but no evidence. I think that Faln has been trying to capture you because he knows what you are. He thinks he can use you somehow. When I spoke with him at the Lordhale, he became agitated when I mentioned his hunt for you. But he wasn't angry, he was frustrated. He wants you for something other than any perceived thievery. That frustration was born of purpose beyond the simple pursuit of a criminal."

Liassa interrupted, *{That's not sound. He's charged with the protection of the realm. I'm not only a thief, but a killer in his eyes. It's someone he would pursue with intensity.}*

"It became apparent when I tried to delve into why he was so focused on you, Lia. There are a dozen other criminals he is in pursuit of that have committed more heinous crimes than you have. He would readily speak about them. He was calm and collected about them. However, when I tried to steer the conversation to you, he was extremely evasive. He didn't want to discuss anything about you. When I pressed the conversation in that direction, he became overtly frustrated and hostile. This, coupled with what we know about Faln's desire to be King, gives us even more leverage Lia. Especially since he doesn't know it was us who stole his contract with the Darkness and his maps of the upper palace."

{We don't need all of this, Ales,} Lia said.

"Again Lia? I thought we had agreed?" Ales asked tiredly.

{Because you aren't telling me everything. Why, Ales?}

Ales sighed. "Besides you, Lia, I am drifting. You know we are not fanatics. It isn't enough, Lia, just to have the word from Avaara. I need to feel... something."

Tears began to slide down Ales' cheeks. Lia stared for a long moment. She had not seen Ales vulnerable in a very long time. She'd always thought of her sister as invincible. She had only seen her this fragile when they were children.

{Ales, I'm sorry. I've just been waiting for three millennia for you. I remember the you before all this happened,} Lia responded carefully.

"I had healthy relationships back then, Lia. I had our family, I had Bann. It's likely that I will have to really fight soon. I know you were not exaggerating when you said there were people with devices made from our technology that could be truly dangerous to us. I can't do that without seeing the good things that come from what we are doing. I can't just let the world burn because I know that when the fire dies down, it will be a better place. I'm not ready to go that far." Ales put her head down and her unbound hair fell around her face.

{I didn't think I would ever see you turn into such a blubbering sissy again.} Lia's mindvoice held gentle humor.

"You ruin everything," Ales mumbled, but Lia could tell she was smiling. Ales wiped the tears off of her cheeks.

{You have to open up to me. For now, all we have is you and me. If you feel that this is the best way that you can stay stable and we can still do what we are meant to do, then I will follow your plan. We will help these people and accomplish our mission. Just tell me that what you are planning is going to work?}

"It will work, one way or another. That's why I'm using Cole as our backup plan. Just because I do not want to destabilize this kingdom to do what we must doesn't mean I won't do it. But I think there is a better way. Get to know them, get to Kiltik without anyone feeling betrayed, and it will help us in the long run."

{You mean to dethrone the king anyway, don't you?}

"That depends on how much of a monster he is."

"All monarchs are monsters." Lia said it out loud, which was a small indicator of how deep her feelings ran on the subject.

Ales gave her a concerned look. "Yes, but some become so by necessity. Others were born monsters," she chided.

Lia sighed. *{You know how I feel about people lording over other people. It isn't necessary.}*

"No, not the way you mean it. But what do we do, Lia? Do we not shelter the people around us to keep them safe?"

Lia glared at her. *{That is nothing like what kings and queens do out in the world.}*

"It can be exactly what they do. Sometimes, it is. I hear you, Lia. We both suspect that Terran Roa is not a good person. But a smash and grab will get people killed, innocent people. I will only do so as a last resort. I will not entertain any discussion beyond that. It is the way it must be."

{That is why you hired the Theif, isn't it?} Lia said, realization dawning. *{You mean to control the situation. You do the smashing without really hurting anyone, and he does the grabbing. That's why you gave him such a specific time table, the night of the Skyfire festival.}*

Ales grumbled, "Would it kill you to just trust me, Spook?" but she was smiling again.

{It might,} Lia said.

"I rather mean for it to go the other way around. I mean for him to be a distraction. To plant a number of controlled explosives in the Citadel as a ploy to trap the palace guards and keep everyone away from the lower levels while I work. I also want him to ferret out a secret for us. We need to know if the Royal family takes off their armor when they sleep. It's not concrete, but I have guesses that their armor may be more than we think it is."

{It'll be safer for him because he can just keep moving. A good thought. So what role am I meant to play in this little fiasco of yours?}

Ales nodded. "None. There are more important things for you to be doing. You need to be our Teacher. Ilsa and Warran will need to know about their abilities and you have to be the one to teach them. Cole, too, if we can entice him to our cause."

Lia sat up sharply and shook her head emphatically. *{Oh, no, I am no Teacher,}* Lia said, waving both of her front paws at Ales.

"Lia, there is no one else. Over the next three rotations, I will be spending most of my time building my place as High Lady Brightwater. That leaves you, unless you think you can tempt the Mother to teach them?" Ales asked. Lia looked almost as if she might try. Ales grinned with amusement.

"And what of this Night Lady persona you are cultivating? What is your plan for that?" Lia tried to change the subject.

"Three thousand cycles, and you are still terrified of trying to teach," Ales said with a little laugh.

Lia looked away shamefully. *{She scarred me,}* Lia said, her mindvoice petulant.

"It is of little consequence. Silis is not here to torment you, and only you can teach. I do not have the time, so it is you."

Lia grumbled something under her breath. *{Fine. I'll start tomorrow, but only if you can get the Three off my back. I will not spend my teaching time worrying about them attacking us.}* Lia hopped down off the couch and curled up in the far corner of the room.

"I think that will not be a problem," Ales said.

"The Night Lady?" Lia pressed.

"That's just me trying to create some confusion, just like the menagerie. It is clear that there are already rumors of the Tier. I told them to spread rumors of the Night Lady to just give the King one more rumor to investigate. You know that we will just be racing time until people know exactly who we are. The Tier, by our nature, cannot remain hidden for long once we become involved in events," Ales said as she got up from the divan. She did not change into her night clothes and instead went back to the balcony doors.

Lia lifted her head from her paws. *{Where are you going?}* Lia's mindvoice was concerned.

"Nowhere I will be in any danger, Lia. Sleep, you are going to need the rest," Ales said, and disappeared out of the room.

26

Ales closed the door to the room. The wayhouse she had chosen in the Low Center was clean but not prestigious. She wanted something where she wouldn't have to smell sour sweat and bad noug. The foul brew that men drank when they were looking for something cheap to get them drunk made her skin crawl. She needed something that would not be high profile enough to draw attention when she paid the owner to close it down for over a rotation. She had restrained the assassin quite harshly, but she wanted to leave no chance that the woman would escape. Ales unbuckled the strap that lashed the woman's elbows together behind her back and then removed the one holding the wad of spongy material in her mouth to serve as a gag. She removed it and clamped her hand over the woman's mouth when she tried to scream. This woman was an enigma to Ales. She somehow knew what Ales and Liassa were, but she still had attacked with poison. It was foolish. There was no chance that poison would work on one of the Tier, much less an Arcangineer.

"There is no point in screaming. The walls are thick stone, and I have paid the housekeep enough to keep this wayhouse empty for spans. No one will hear you."

The woman's eyes were wild and darted everywhere in an insane pattern. They were deep amber, almost brown, but still showing hints of gold. Her eyes focused on Ales' face and she calmed considerably. She started to jibber in her native language and Ales' structures began to translate.

"You are the one the voice spoke of. The one too strong to take. It hates you and your sister." Then the woman spoke, as if she had memorized it, in perfect Tieran. The voice was not her own.

"Alessandra and Liassa of the Ahal House. Immortal, chosen protectors of the gods and of this world, strongest of the Tier. Your brother, Alizar, failed to stop us and so too shall you fail."

Then, as if something inside of her had burst blood poured out of the woman. Her nose, her mouth, her eyes, every orifice evacuated until the bed she had kept the woman on was covered in deep navy liquid. Ales stared dazedly at her for a long moment, and then opened her Vision. The woman's heart had literally burst in her chest. She focused her Vision, trying to get an idea of what could have caused such massive damage. Her sight drew down until she was seeing microscopic particles. That was when she found them. Cellstructs. Lia had said she had not seen anyone with Cellstructs since the cataclysm. They were so crude that they were doing more harm than good. They were unable to bind to the woman's cells as was proper, so her own immune system had been attacking them. What had happened was a foregone conclusion, but it had happened sooner than it should have. What could cause a person's Cellstructs to turn against them like this? Shaken, she got up from her scrutiny of the chilling body and tried to decide what she could do about this new puzzle.

27

The voice roared into Terran's mind with a haunting shriek of anger that reverberated from the walls of his skull. He groaned as he woke a mere two hours after passing into the freedom of sleep.

"Up, Filth. There is work to be done."

The seething buzz of the voice would not be denied, and Terran's body sat bolt upright in bed of its own accord. The king felt as if he might vomit. He had long since stopped sleeping in bed next to his queen so that she would not be roused by the creature's invasions upon his body.

"What is your bidding?" he responded, lest he rouse the creature's anger and become the focus of its rage.

"I knew they would return, that They had hidden them away somewhere, and one day they would plague us again," the voice babbled inside of his mind. Clearly, it was not talking to him, but with whom it might be talking, he had no idea.

Images were forced into his head, one of a woman with long light blue hair and eyes of two colors that glowed with unnatural light - one blue, one violet. She was well-muscled and those glowing eyes seemed to bore into him, like she was peering into the deepest corners of his soul. The second image was of a katali, a massive blue-furred specimen of the breed. It had white spots on its face and down its back. Around its neck was a collar. It was hard to see since the leather was the exact color of the katali's fur. The distressed brass-colored nameplate affixed to the collar was in a language that was not familiar to him.

"These are what remains of the Tier. The animal Liassa must die and the woman Alessandra must be captured!" the voice snarled.

Terran started to reply that he would put bondarmored soldiers on the task immediately when the voice howled over him again.

"The filth Wryn has finished her task. Be done with her!" The presence of the voice fled from his mind without another word.

The pauldron clamped onto his shoulder creaked when he stood, and he groaned. It appeared as a thin coating of metal on his shoulder, but would expand into armor if required. He examined the ports in his arms and legs - metal disks implanted in his flesh that opened his body, allowing his armor access to his "elementary energy pathways" as the creature had described them. He gave the mental command to encase his body in the armor and it extended from the pauldron to protect him. He leapt from the balcony and enjoyed the feel of the armor enhancing his strength as best he could. The five stories of the palace tower flashed by, and he landed with a thunderous impact at the bottom. He disappeared into the night, making his way through the jungle of buildings towards House Wryn.

High Lady Wryn turned the key in the door to her personal quarters. She left the key hanging around her neck. She sat down on the divan, and waited. She watched the window nervously, smoothing down her tight-fitting gown over and over again. She tensed when a black-clawed hand curled over the windowsill. A long-armored body slid into view past the sill, covered from head to toe in black plates of what looked like polished steel.

"Good ending, My King," High Lady Wryn said.

The muscular man drew himself over the sill and his black armor receded from his body, leaving him clothed in a golden suit with the royal seal emblazoned upon the chest. That black armor remained in the form of a single pauldron on his right shoulder.

"Good ending, Lady Wryn." The king's deep voice filled the room. He was a presence. He made his way to the deeply cushioned hide chair across from Lady Wryn. "How does the plan progress?"

"Very well, my King. I have bought commissions for every open position in the four armies, and each of them has been outfitted with proper Bondarmor per your instruction. I have kept my part of the bargain. In return, I ask that you now uphold your end."

"As you wish, your family will be set above all the others. They shall be the richest family in all of Vilhena, second only to the royal line. I shall leave them sovereign for ten generations as agreed," he said as his armor spread to cover his entire body again. It slid over his hands, turning them into clawed talons.

"They? What about me, my King?" Lady Wryn said.

"You have outlived your usefulness."

The King's clawed hand darted out blindingly fast to wrap around her throat. He used his Bondarmor's enhanced strength to snap her neck in one fast motion. She never made a sound.

"That was unnecessary," the king said, seemingly to himself, but his voice had changed. It had lost the dark baritone register that it had when he had been speaking with Lady Wryn.

"It was entirely necessary. She knew too much." The baritone register was back. Two entirely different voices from the same throat. The king examined Lady Wryn's limp body hanging from his fist. He slung her body over his shoulder and then looked out the window. It was clear, so he leapt out, disappearing into the night.

28

Lia waited in the alleyway across from the servant's entrance to the Citadel. She had Warran with her, and while she didn't relish the thought, she would collect Cole next. She didn't have long to wait. Ilsa came out of the door after a long few minutes. She had anticipated the dress Ilsa was wearing and brought more suitable clothing for traveling outside of the Center. She wasn't a maevea to carry a person on her back, but if Ilsa insisted on keeping her dress, she would have to carry the girl. She made a low growling noise that made Warran stare at her. Ilsa whipped around and stared into the alleyway.

"Liassa?" Ilsa said in a near whisper.

"Yes. It is time for you to start learning to be one of the Tier. I will be your teacher. Have you spoken to your parents?" Lia asked.

"One of them. My father said I should do what I thought was right," Ilsa said.

"Your father is a wise man," Lia replied.

"He is. He will convince my mother as long as I promise to visit when I can." Ilsa made her way into the alley.

"Would you mind changing out of your dress into something that lets you move a little more freely?" Lia asked as Ilsa stopped. She had seen Warran tinkering with something behind Lia's large form.

"Is that a Stoe Model Eight?" Ilsa asked.

Warran almost dropped the pieces of the lancer that he was deftly assembling. "How did you know?"

"My father repairs them pretty often. The nobles don't care for them properly. They take them out in the weather and then do not properly clean them."

"That is the truth if I have ever heard it," Warran said. He finished reassembling the receiver for the magazine without even looking at it.

Lia cleared her throat, which sounded half like a monster of some sort was roaring behind them.

"Ilsa, this is Warran," Lia introduced them.

"He will be a Fixer. You have the same circle but repair is his natural talent, so he will probably be a little better at it than all of us. I think yours will be Finding, though it is obvious you have an affinity for Repair as well."

"Pleased to meet you," Warran said. He made a polite little bow, which Ilsa returned.

"And I, you," Ilsa said remembering her manners at the last second.

"You should change. There is one more person we need to get before we can start." Lia nosed open one of the bags hanging from an arrangement of straps that fit over her shoulders like a back pack. It left the bags hanging on either side of her body, between her middle and hind legs. Inside, there was a change of clothing for Ilsa – a loose skirt, and a blouse both in blue.

"Right here?" Ilsa said, looking dubiously at Warran.

"He will turn his back and I will stay at the mouth of the alley to make sure no one sees you. Don't be such a prude. Get changed," Lia said.

Ilsa huffed in annoyance, and began pulling the garments out of her bag. "Well, at least I am less likely to draw attention in a skirt."

"Please close the bag for me?" Lia asked.

Ilsa pulled the flap back down, and it snapped closed as soon as the flap got close the side of the bag. "How does that work?" Ilsa asked, looking at the bag with interest.

"Two small pieces of metal with opposing elementary force charges. They are sort of like the rails inside of a lancer. They are much less powerful, though. No energetic power source," Lia explained.

Lia trotted to the end of the alleyway and sat on her haunches. She was nearly as tall as Ilsa. Warran turned his back without comment, still fiddling with the Stoe lancer. She could see there was another of the weapons in a holster, hanging off the belt behind his back. It was a quick draw holster.

"I need some help with my laces," Ilsa said.

Warran turned back. "Um..." he stammered.

"Oh, just help her undo her laces, you fool." Lia said exasperatedly.

Ilsa turned her back to him and he dropped the pieces of lancer into a pouch at his side. His deft fingers undid the laces in just a moment, and he turned his back again, fishing in his pouch for the parts of the lancer.

"How do you get dressed without help?" he asked without turning back around.

"I have a little set of hooks that I can use to pull the laces in the mirror." Ilsa stripped out of her dress quickly and pulled the skirt up a moment later. She tightened the laces on the skirt and spun it around. She pulled the blouse over her head, tightening the laces in the front, tying them off in a tight bow.

"Makes sense." Warran was the perfect gentleman. He finished assembling the second Stoe. He slid a magazine into the receiver, and pulled back the slide chambering the first bolt. It was the third time he had assembled the gun, so he was certain of the operation of the energetic driver. It wouldn't overheat, and would fire true every time. He held it out to Ilsa.

"Liassa says we should be armed until we learn how to control our talents. I assume you know how a lancer works?" Warran said.

Ilsa stared at the lancer.

"I have adjusted the energetic discharge so that there is quite a bit less recoil from the discharge on this model. It should be a little softer on your wrists. Keep in mind that it is slightly less powerful this way, too, though it isn't much different. It will still go through even Bondarmor at close range like it is paper, so don't pull the trigger unless you mean to kill someone, understand?" Warran admonished her.

Ilsa took the lancer gingerly, and Warran held out a belt and holster that matched it.

"I understand," Ilsa said.

"The belt has gantha fur on the inside so you can wear it right next to your skin without it chaffing."

Ilsa looked it over with a businesslike efficiency.

"Never seen a woman Fixer before," Warran said.

Ilsa narrowed her eyes. He held up his hands in a placating gesture.

"Didn't say you wouldn't be good at it," Warran said defensively. "I was just hoping my little girl would be the first," he said with a smile of fatherly pride.

"If you have the Circle of Repair, it is likely your daughter will have it as well," Lia said.

"Changed," Ilsa said as she finished buckling the belt around her hips. It was just high enough on her waist that her blouse hid it.

"Do you know how to use that thing?" Lia asked.

"I've been shooting since I was old enough to hold the lancer steady. Nothing as fine as this Stoe. I wish I had some way to pay you for it," Ilsa said.

"It cost me much less to build than you think," Warran said with a grin.

Ilsa folded her dress neatly. "Do you mind?" She asked Lia, gesturing towards the saddle bags Liassa was wearing.

"Not at all. We need to fetch Cole," Liassa said.

"Cole?" Warran said suspiciously.

"I believe his full name is Aloysius Cole, though he hates his first name so he uses his sur," Lia said.

"Shards!" Warran cursed. "Cole is a thief!"

"Cole is a Taker. He uses his abilities to steal, yes, but if you really know him, you will understand that he doesn't just steal for himself. And without training, a Taker will turn to thievery in a heartbeat. They don't know what drives them. They just know they can take whatever they want, and it is almost impossible for anyone to stop them,"

Lia remembered very well how her Taker's instincts made her feel until she had them fully under control. The Arcangineer's Corps had made thievery into a game to keep all of the Takers on a more harmless path until they learned how to direct those instincts properly. She would have to be more creative as she did not have the Corps resources.

"You really think you can make Cole avoid stealing? He breathes theft," Warran said as Lia walked past him back into the alleyway.

"I think Cole has spent his life without any other options. And once he discovered he was so good at it, he didn't think that he should be doing anything else." Lia said.

Ales had convinced her that Cole was one of them. She reminded Lia how she had been the only Taker in her group to never be caught stealing anything.

"You haven't even spoken to him yet, have you?" Warran asked.

Lia narrowed her eyes at him. He was far too perceptive for her liking. Ales had said he had only the Circles of Repair and Distance, but he displayed intuition like a Seer. But no seer had ever been able to read minds, just actions.

"It is his decision, Warran, just like it was yours. It doesn't matter if I have spoken to him or not. He has to choose to be one of the Tier."

They followed a path of back alleyways towards the Low Center. They crossed main roads only when it was necessary and kept out of sight otherwise. Lia did not want anyone to see them. It took them about an hour to reach Hunter's Rest, just on the edge of the Low Center. It was Cole's choice of wayhouse when he was staying in the city. Lia led them into the alleyway between the back of the wayhouse and the High Center wall. There was a door There, but it was locked tight.

"I assume that you can bypass the lock, Warran?" Lia said.

Warran reached into a pouch beneath his Stoe, from where he extracted a small cloth package. Opening the neatly tied package revealed a number of long, thin pieces of metal in various shapes. He took two of them and inserted them into the lock. It took only a few tense moments before the lock clicked open. Warran pulled the door open and motioned Ilsa inside.

"He is usually in the last door closest to this stairwell," Warran said.

"I don't want to scare everyone going in there and Warran can't be seen with Cole right now, so you will have to fetch him, Ilsa. Try not to shoot anyone," Lia said.

Ilsa looked at the door. "This is not a good place. My father warned me to stay out of here," Ilsa said hesitantly.

"Hence my admonishment to attempt not to shoot anyone. I don't want to be seen, but if anyone accosts you, simply shout, and I will come in to help," Lia said.

"Alright," Ilsa said. She went inside her hand on the grip of the Stoe behind her back. She stopped before she got all the way through the door.

"What does he look like?" she asked over her shoulder.

"Little shorter than me, stocky looking, light blue hair cropped short, and amber colored eyes," Warran said without pausing.

Ilsa nodded without turning around. She went up the back stairs to the rooms above. She knocked on the last door closest to the stairs. There was a noise inside of the room. Some cursing followed, and then the door was yanked open.

"Shards, Noven, I paid you for a full..." He stammered to a stop when he saw Ilsa standing there. He didn't have a shirt on, and while he would appear stocky with a shirt on, there was nothing of that in his actual body. His rippling stomach muscles were taut, and there was not an ounce of fat to be seen anywhere else on him.

"Well, who might you be?" he said, a smile growing on his face.

"Don't get any ideas, you lecher, or I will have a mutual friend come up here and take a bite out of you. Let's go, she wants to talk to you," Ilsa said.

His eyes narrowed. "How can I have a conversation with that creature? I don't speak katali."

"Then it is fortunate for you that she speaks common," Ilsa said.

Cole made a growling noise. He turned from the door, and when she saw his back, she gasped. His back was crisscrossed with scars. Dozens of lash marks where he had been whipped at some point in his past.

"What's the matter, half pint, never seen someone who has been whipped for thieving before?" he said over his shoulder.

"So many, how are you still alive?"

"I didn't get them all at once, but becoming a master thief is not an overnight process, girl. It is very much trial and error."

He pulled a shirt from a pile of clothing and pulled it over his head, hiding his scars. Then he took a long coat from the same pile. He laid that across the narrow bed and took his lancers from the bedside table. They were in a shoulder rig, which he shrugged into. This put the grip of each lancer underneath his arm. They were much bigger than the Stoe that she carried. He slid his coat on over them, hiding them almost completely. When she didn't move out of the doorway, he prompted her.

"Come on, princess. Let's get a move on," he said.

She narrowed her eyes at him and frowned. "I am not Highborn," she growled.

"Whatever you say," he said, holding his hands up in a placating gesture. He turned and locked his door. He didn't put much faith in locks, but then again, he didn't have anything of real value stashed in the room. He followed her out of the wayhouse, and into the back alleyway.

"Finally! What took you so long?" Liassa hissed.

Cole jumped back, waving his arms as if to ward off an attack. "Sweet Mother's Tits, it can talk?!" Cole shouted.

Lia flattened her ears at the curse. "Gods, you have a foul mouth," she grumbled, and Warran looked positively red from hearing the curse, though it was hard to tell in the dim light of the alleyway.

"And if you call me <u>it</u> again, I promise I will snack on some unimportant part of you when you are sleeping. Perhaps an earlobe." She snapped her teeth at him, and he jumped just a little. Then she made a chuffing sound of laughter.

"You are creepy in ways I do not have words to describe," Cole said.

Liassa rolled her eyes. "Cole, you know Warran already, and this is Ilsa. Against my better judgment, I am going to make you the same offer we have made them. My sister believes you have it in you to be one of the Tier. I am skeptical, but you have shown that you are more than a mere thief. You have good in you."

"Whoa, whoa..." Cole said, holding up his hand in a stopping gesture. Then he pinched the bridge of his nose with his free hand. "Hold on, let me get this straight. You want me to do what now?" C

"Cole, you can learn to use the Vision. I can teach you to be something more. I can teach you how to help people, and I want to teach you, but it has to be your decision. I can't force you, and I'll tell you the same thing I told them. Being one of the Tier is dangerous, and you can easily get dead doing our job, but you will know that you help people. You will know that you make the world better."

Cole opened one eye, and looked at them. "Are you so sure I am good?" Cole said, still pinching the bridge of his nose. "Are you really that sure?"

"You want the truth?" Lia asked.

"I have to lie so much. How much do you think I value the truth?" Cole said.

"No, I am not sure. My sister is more sure, but we have to do everything using the old ways. We feel a certain kinship with those ordinary people who have the potential to be Tier.

But besides Ilsa, I will have to teach you and Warran for a number of rotations before I can be sure of who you are. At least come with us today. See what I can do. See, what you can do."

"What is so different about her?" Cole chucked his chin at Ilsa.

"Ilsa was born with her Vision already open. Truly, it is only the lack of the Tier in this time that has kept her Vision from coming out sooner. Everyone has the potential to learn how to use the Vision, but Ilsa has no choice. We can either teach her or risk that she goes entirely mad when her Vision finally comes out. I promise you, you do not want to see someone lost in their own Vision, especially someone like Ilsa who has Breaking at her disposal."

29

Ales made her careful way through the Citadel. The two guards escorting her were more for her protection than anything, but she did not trust them. They ushered her down a long corridor of polished grey stone that she could not identify without her Vision. The columns were gorgeously carved sorstone. It was breathtaking, and perfectly made. There was no question that a Tieran Mind had created this precision. It was a wonder that in some ways rivaled the beauty of Ahal itself, or at least a small part of it. It didn't quite have the human element to it that Ahal had. It was clear that when they used Kiltik to build this place, he was the only one involved in the design. It was entirely mathematical, but math could be beautiful when used properly. The door at the end of the hall was emblazoned with the royal crest. Just below was the Queen's seal.

"Thank you, gentlemen. If you please?" Ales said, matching her voice to Lady Brightwater's precise accent. She knocked politely on the massive door. A moment later, the door swung silently open to reveal Queen Roa.

"Lady Brightwater, so good to see you again!"

"Please, my Queen, Helena."

Ales took three careful steps to get inside the door, and then two tiny ones to the side so the Queen could push it closed.

"Very well, Helena. What is the purpose of your visit today? Your missive seemed quite urgent."

"Oh dear, no, I didn't mean for it to seem that way," Ales lied. The note she had written to the Queen had been very carefully worded to imply that urgency should be felt, but never actually said outright. She could almost like the Queen if she wasn't careful. She kept reminding herself that Aisha would not be pleased with what she was planning.

"However, after spending time helping you fend off your courtiers, I thought it might be nice for us to simply have some time to talk amongst ourselves," Ales said.

Aisha smiled, and seemed genuinely delighted.

"Well, this is a fortunate distraction in an otherwise boring and tedious day of discussions with the merchant houses," Aisha said.

Ales nodded and Aisha led the way into a well-appointed sitting area. She turned right, passing that room and moved through a sorstone hallway with glowlamps lighting the path. The next room was similar in size and dimensions, but the furnishings here were far less formal. They also looked far more comfortable. The queen lowered herself into a plush chair and invited Ales to take the chair across from her with a wave of her hand. Ales had been right about the comfort of the furniture. It was old, well worn, and very comfortable indeed.

"I would have thought that intermediaries would take care of things like that for you," Ales said. A kingdom as large as Vilhena was bound to have at least two dozen merchant houses. Having one person conduct all of the kingdom's business with them was somewhat ludicrous.

"Oh, we have a whole staff for such things, of course, but once every rotation, I have a discussion with each of the heads of house to ensure that things are running as smoothly as our clerks tell us they are."

"A wise measure, My Queen."

"Thank you, Helena, but if you call me My Queen once more, I think I may have to scream. Please?"

"Usually when I meet a Queen, they are quite a bit more concerned about their title than you are."

"There is a time for that, but not when we are in my private rooms, and especially not when I'm trying to make someone feel welcome in my home."

Ales laughed. "Fair enough. So, what was the fallout from our little discourse among the nobles?"

The queen laughed high and clear.

"Oh, not very much. I am the queen, after all. I can treat those fops any way I wish. If they weren't such a gaggle of idiots, I might treat them with more respect, but they're all so concerned with their own well-being that they think nothing of the kingdom we rule over. There are a bare handful of lords and ladies that are actually worth respecting," the queen said matter-of-factly.

"Is that how the king designates who gets Bondarmor? Those who are actually worth respect?"

"What a strange question. If that were the case, we wouldn't be scrambling to make more suits of Bondarmor as fast as we can. No, we do not do it that way, but we do regulate their relative strengths. All of the armors are designed for maximum protection, but we are careful about how much stronger they make others. There are only a few suits of Bondarmor that are more powerful than the rest. The King's, our Children, The Knights Three, and the Guard Captain. The rest are all identical."

"I must confess a fascination with the armor. I've always wondered how it was made?" Ales tilted her head, making it a question.

"I, too, wonder how the Searchers make their marvels, but they say it is a delicate process. No one is allowed to contaminate the environment. They keep it sealed off. My husband has promised me that one day he will take me in to see them work."

"Perhaps he can be persuaded to grant two passes?" Ales said with a small silly smile.

"Perhaps! But enough about the boy's toys, what of your estates? I had heard that Brightwater was in dire straits since the death of his Lordship."

Ales nodded in response. "That they were. However, I've made a fair fortune in my travels in the world. I was able to use that money to pay down the debts of the Courtship. We are now free and clear. The fields have been put under new management and we expect a new crop in less than three rotations. I may see some problems getting crops into the city. I believe High Lord Nivus wished to possess all of the food production in the city. However, I am prepared for anything he can do to stop me."

"It sounds as if you have everything well in hand. I do not like Nivus, but he hasn't done anything illegal in the past. At least not in view of anyone. The man crawls lower than any other while attempting to look like he is a gift to all mankind," the Queen snarled.

Ales' eyebrows rose slowly. The queen truly hated Nivus for some reason. It had to be personal for the kind of hatred Ales saw on her face.

"Perhaps this is presumptuous of me Aisha, but what did Nivus do to you? You obviously bear a great hatred from him."

"It is presumptuous, Helena. How could you possibly know that?"

"Reading faces is something of a talent of mine. It helps when I attempt to sell my sculptures. It is just a trick, My Queen. I apologize for asking. I will take my leave if you wish, My Queen." Ales said, feeling a fool for having asked the question. She had to remember she was High Lady Brightwater here. She was not one of the Tier who stood outside of the laws of other nations and worked always for the good of everyone. She was not that person, not yet. She got up from her seat. She bowed, holding her hands out to either side of her hips gracefully.

"No, Helena. No, it is alright, I was simply startled. Please sit. I didn't think it showed as badly as it does. Before I became Queen, my Father was High Lord Ranus. He was partners with Nivus in a mining venture. My older brother was overseer at the mine. There was never anything to link it back to Nivus, but he hired a second crew to dig into deposits from a different part of the mountain. Then they detonated explosives in the mine. My brother was in the mine at the time and was killed. We knew that Nivus was behind it, but there was no proof. He is very good at making sure things do not connect back to him. We suspect he hires the Darkness to cover up his business."

Ales sat back down in the comfortable chair. She wanted to ask what Aisha meant about the Darkness but her brush with disaster made her wary.

"Somehow, I find myself unsurprised. I think that man may be the lowest form of life I have ever encountered," Ales said meaning every word. She had met some real scum in the past, but that man made her skin crawl. There were some very few times that she wished she could simply kill someone and have done with it. This was one of those times.

"You've had some run in with him?" Aisha asked

For a long moment, Ales considered handing over all of Nivus' dirty little secrets and letting Aisha bury him. She might have actually been able to trade it to get close enough to Kiltik to communicate. She sensed that there was something larger at play here, but it was just out of her reach. There were a lot of things that didn't add square. She believed Aisha's story about her brother, but she held her tongue anyway. The fall of Lord Nivus could be an important bargaining chip later in the game.

"Much like you, I have no concrete evidence for what he's done, but we've always suspected he was responsible for the disappearance of my cousin, Lady Leona Brightwater. My uncle never recovered from her disappearance."

"It's nice to know that not everyone is fooled by his exterior. It drives me to find what he is hiding so that he can be dealt with."

"Perhaps it's something we can both work for."

"Would you permit me a question?"

"Of course."

"Your eyes are so strange. I've never seen anyone with eyes of two different colors. Who were your parents?"

"Oh, that is a story, but I think I can shorten it to something reasonable. Three generations ago, a fourth son to the House of Brightwater decided to strike out on his own. He began by asking for a few innocuous pieces of art, nothing that the then Lord Brightwater thought would be valuable. He made his way moonward and took a ship across the Grey Tide. When he arrived on the other side of the ocean, he sold the art, rare on that side of the sea, for a very large sum. He became very successful in trading works of art all around the world. While he was on a trip across the ocean, he met a Liqualy woman with eyes of two colors. She had a daughter, and so on and so forth until I appeared,"

Aisha smiled. "I've never heard of a people by that name,"

"The Linqual are a large tribe of nomads who follow and protect the herds of maevea that roam across the endless sea of grass on the other side of the Grey Tide. They have since time immemorial," Ales replied. "They are, by their nature, hard to find. Their customs are strange, but they have a great love of beautiful things crafted by the hands of men. It was only natural that they would seek out a great trader in the arts."

Aisha looked at the clock above the mantle, and frowned. "I apologize, Helena, I must get to my meetings with the Merchant Houses, but our talk has been a delight. Will you come again?" the Queen asked as they both rose.

"Of course. Would it be too much to ask to petition access to the royal library? I would very much like to study my family line and learn more about how the Bondarmor is created."

"I believe that can be arranged. I will let the librarians know that you are to have complete access as soon as I am free to tell them. It should be arranged by tomorrow."

Aisha made a graceful bow, and Ales returned the gesture.

Lia led them into the Low Center. Cole had finally opted to follow them, for the entertainment value, he claimed. He had already pickpocketed three nobles, Lia noted. before Warran picked up on it and scowled at him.

"What?" Cole said.

"You're stealing from people, and if I get caught with you, who will take care of my daughter?" Warran hissed.

"He won't get caught," Lia mumbled.

"Now stop bickering. We're drawing enough attention between alleyways as it is," Lia said. Ilsa was holding the leash clipped to her collar.

"Are you sure this is alright?" Ilsa asked as they were passing between two buildings.

"It's fine, Ilsa. It's better that they think of me as a very scary pet, but a pet none-the-less."

"I feel like a fool," Ilsa groused.

"How do you think I feel?" Lia said.

"I don't think you feel as much a fool as I do," Ilsa said.

Lia looked back over her shoulder and grinned in a way no animal had any right to do. "You will find, Child, if you live as long as I have, that you will rarely have more fun than the times you feel a fool."

They got through the Low Center, passing the perfectly laid out grid of streets mostly unnoticed. Lia stopped at the mouth of the alleyway across the square to the gate. It was nearing dusk.

"I can't talk from here on out until we are well past the gate. My sister and I have made a habit of coming through here once a span, though, so the guards shouldn't give you any trouble. They'll think you're taking me out to hunt. Warran, keep your hood up no matter what you do. They won't know who you are. Cole, I assume you can pass the guards?" Lia asked.

"It shouldn't be a problem with you drawing all of their attention."

"Let's go," Lia said. She tugged the leash, fearing that Ilsa would be too afraid to follow her. To her surprise, the leash was slack and Ilsa was right next to her. Ales had been right. This girl had fire in her. She would be a legend someday.

"So, taking the beast out to hunt again, huh?" one of the
two guards said as they neared the gate.

"She gets restless if we don't take her out now and then,"
Ilsa said. Her voice wavered slightly, but the guard didn't
seem to notice.

"Back before sundown as usual. Gates will be closed after
that," the guard reminded.

"See you then," Warran said.

They made their way past the gate without trouble and
headed down the road.

"Well done, both of you," Lia said, padding down the path.
Ilsa unclipped the leash from Lia's collar as soon as they were
out of sight of the guards. She stuffed it into Lia's bags.

"Do we need to be back by the time the gates close?"
Warran asked nervously.

"No. There have been a few times we've stayed out for two
days or more. I think they figure that Ales has to chase me
down after letting me loose."

"I can't believe they think you're a pet," Ilsa said.

"Believe it or not, in the high places stoneward, katali are
domesticated and used as mounts in places too cold for
maevea. They're also kept as hunting companions to the
Linqual across the Grey Tide," Lia explained.

"But they're so dangerous!" Ilsa objected.

"It isn't common because, like you, most people think
they're wild and untrustworthy. In reality, it depends on how
they are raised. Sure, we are dangerous, but so are many full
grown hiluk breeds. Yet you see folk with hiluk as pets all the
time. Katali are extremely intelligent, and quite loyal if they're
socialized with humans from the time they are cubs. Truly,
they are only dangerous if you do not treat them with the
respect they deserve," Lia illuminated.

"Does it bother you?" Ilsa asked.

"What, that other katali are treated as pets?" Lia asked with
amusement.

"Well, doesn't it seem insulting?"

Lia barked out a sound meant to be a laugh. "Gods, Ilsa, I
am Tier and all creatures have a purpose. Those katali are
treated with love and reverence in places where they are kept
as pets."

"Come out, Cole," Warran said suddenly.

Cole wandered out onto the road a few moments later. He slipped between the trees without a sound.

"How do you always know?" Cole asked.

Warran just shrugged.

"He's unconsciously tapping into his abilities with the Vision to a minor extent. Everyone does it, even ordinary people. The Vision is not so much a magical power as it is a massive enhancement to what you are already seeing all the time. It does grant a few abilities that are truly mystical, but they are more in support to your Vision than anything else. Once you awaken it properly, you can never go blind, and if your eyes are damaged, they will always heal. Controlling the Circles, on the other hand, is truly superhuman. If you think that Warran is great at fixing things now, wait until you see how fast he can do it with the Circle of Repair at his call," Lia explained.

"Can I ask a question?" Warran asked.

"As long as you are a student of mine, I will accept all questions, but if you ask me personal things, I may ask you some in return," Lia said.

"Were there more like you? People who decided to become animals?"

Lia paused. "Yes, there were many of us once." Sadness was weaved into her words.

"Did any of them have kids?" he asked.

"There were only two in my memory that had children, but their children were grown. Both children were Tier before they made the change," Lia explained.

"What about anyone who was a fixer? I mean how can you be a fixer with paws?" Warran asked.

"There were some. They used their abilities in different ways once they made the change, but you needn't worry, Warran. I do not believe you will find it difficult to deal with the pain of having to hurt someone. You can look at your little girl any time and know exactly what you are fighting for. For others of us, it is different."

Lia didn't like the way this was going. The story of how she had become one of the Wild was not one that she liked remembering. She didn't regret who she was now, especially once she understood how proud her family was of her.

Becoming one of the Wild was never an easy decision for any Tier, even when it eased their pain.

"How is it different?" Ilsa asked the question that Lia had known was coming.

"Well…" Lia hesitated for a long moment.

"What is it?" Ilsa asked.

"I do not want to frighten you away too soon. Being one of the Tier will be one of the most rewarding experiences you can possibly have, but it's also going to be one of the most difficult things you can possibly do."

"Did you think that we all came here thinking it would be easy?" Cole finally spoke up.

Lia nodded as she walked deeper into the woods. The others had to pick their way around trees and other detritus that Lia slunk through uninhibited despite her massive size.

"Right now, you feel a certain empathy with other people. Everyone does, unless you're mentally damaged. It's because in the end, we are all the same people. We all come from the same place. In small ways, we are all related because all living things came from the Mother, so we can all feel that small piece of ourselves inside of others. For us, the Tier, it's much different.

When I open my Vision, I can quite literally see that piece of me in others. The connection becomes something physical. For one of the Tier, even if it is self-defense when you hurt someone else, you are hurting yourself. You will be able to see every ill you cause to another living thing. It will hurt, and the only armor you will have against that pain is knowing that you are put here to help others. To defend those that cannot defend themselves." Lia stopped as they came into a large circular clearing.

"If you don't have people very close to you to make that connection with, to know what you are defending, that armor gets awfully thin. Sometimes, it isn't enough," Lia said as she sat down on the edge of the clearing.

"How does changing help?" Warran asked.

"It makes your connection different. There are no others like one of the Wild. We are still a part of all living things, but each of us is an entirely unique form of life. It thins our sympathetic connection to other living things. You can still see that connection. It will still hurt, but it's not the same kind of hurt. It doesn't go so deep. If you want a better explanation of why it works, you would have to ask the Mother herself."

"You never wondered?" Ilsa asked.

Lia shrugged. "It was never so important to me to know. But when you know enough, she will come to speak to you. If you ask, she will do her best to explain in a way you can understand. Can you all find your way back here on your own, or help each other?"

"Why?" Warran asked.

"Because I am not always going to be here instructing you, but this is where you should come to learn. You all can't see it yet, but this place in the forest is special. Anyone who comes here and tries to do the Tier harm will quickly find themselves in the kind of trouble that no one ever wishes to see," Lia explained.

"So is that what we are now? Tier?"

Lia padded towards the center of the clearing. When she got there, she faced them and sat down.

"Not until you say the words. As a people, the Tier each choose to be a part of what we do. It has to be a choice, but we find it comforting to believe that everyone who has the potential to be one of us will be until they choose not to be."

"So, we have to decide now?" Cole asked.

Lia tilted her head at him. "Do you really have to decide?"

"I don't," Warran said.

"Me either. I want to help people," Ilsa said.

Cole looked at them both, his brows going up. "Oh, you think that I'll be duped into putting my hide on the line because they will?"

Lia's lips peeled back from her teeth in a feline grin. Cole wasn't sure if that meant she was happy or that she was going to bite him.

"Not at all, Cole, and having the powers of the Vision should not sway your decision either. No matter how well you learn to use your powers, you may one day come to your end because you will be compelled to stand in the way of people who wish to harm the helpless. You must decide on your own to put yourself into that position. I am simply showing you this so that you all know that if you do this, you will not do so unaided." Lia said, and then she turned, disappearing into the trees. Her voice drifted out , a ghostly sound in the burgeoning dusk.

"See me, if you can." Lia opened her Vision and looked at them. They had spread out into a loose group. In her sight, there was a glowing blue line on the ground that wound between all of them. It shifted its path back and forth as they all looked in different directions. It was a path that she could walk on where none of them would actually see her. It wasn't the only power that Taking gave her, but it was the main one.

She followed the line precisely, her paws falling right on top of it with each step. She moved as it shifted. She stopped standing between all three of them and sat down. Ilsa saw her first.

"Howling Abyss!" she cursed when she finally turned around enough to see Lia sitting between them. "How did you get there?"

"My Vision shows me where to walk, shows me when you are going to be looking at a place, and if necessary, deters you from actually seeing me. Want to see it again?" Lia said with a small smile in her voice.

"There is no way you can do that again," Cole said.

"Care to make a wager on it?" Lia asked.

"What are we betting?"

"I'll bet you a full rotation of paying the shopkeepers in the Low Center that you couldn't catch me if I stole the gold right out of your pockets." Lia wiggled the toes of her forepaw at him.

"And what am I paying if I lose?"

"You spend a rotation at least watching us learn. You don't have to join if you don't want to, but you'll be here every day watching," Lia said. It was a safe bet. He had absolutely no idea how talented she was.

"Oh, you are on. There is no way you can get anything off of me with those paws."

"Oh, but I already have."

Lia turned herself so she could push her muzzle into the bag hanging off her side. She pulled out one of his lancers. She had taken it out of his coat when he was busy goggling the scenery. He'd never even seen her, despite the fact that she had been right in front of him. Warran immediately began to cackle. Lia carefully placed the lancer on her upturned forepaw.

"And that, my dear Cole, is our bet. So, take a lean up against a tree over there and get an eyeful." She held out his lancer.

He narrowed his eyes at her and snatched it off her paw in a blur. He shoved it into its holster as hard as he could without breaking anything or shooting himself.

"You cheated!" he grumbled.

"Did I?" Lia showed him her teeth and stalked closer to him. If she had one regret about becoming one of the Wild, it was that she had to look up at almost everyone. Despite her size, when she was on all six paws, she was only just as tall as the shortest of adults.

"Are you saying that I welshed on a bet? Did I not take your lancer from you without you knowing?" Lia snarled.

"No, you took it without me knowing," he said quietly.

Lia lashed her tail once. "That's what I thought." Lia stalked away.

"Now, I will try to teach you something that no one has learned in over three thousand cycles. Learn well."

31

Ales walked the Citadel hallways by invitation of the queen. She thought about how she was lying to Aisha. She didn't like lying to anyone, and now she was truly becoming friends with Aisha. It made her even more uncomfortable with the situation. She made her slow way down the hallway, cursing herself inwardly for the necessity. She resolved that she would tell Aisha the truth once this was done. Maybe even before that. It didn't matter that it might cost her a friend. You couldn't base a friendship on lies.

She turned right down a hallway, towards the Royal Libraries. It took her a relatively long time to make it to the doors at the end. The doors to the royal library were enormous, but they were wide open and invited her in. An elderly woman sat behind a desk, thumbing through what looked like a large ledger.

"Good miday to you, Lady. Might I be able to help you find something?"

Ales took a folded piece of paper from the handbag she carried. It was signed and had the queen's impression on it. She handed it to the woman.

"If you would be so kind as to direct me to the old histories?" Ales asked. "And if there is anything in the restricted sections about the making of Bondstructs, it would be of great interest to me."

The woman scanned the paper and nodded. "High Lady Brightwater, of course. I can show you the histories, of course, but none of the texts on Bondstructs are kept here."

Ales frowned.

"Apologies, High Lady. You must petition the king to gain access to those texts."

Ales shook her head. "No apologies necessary, Keeper. Please, the histories would be delightful. How far back do they go?"

The woman made her way out from behind the polished stone desk. She suppressed an annoyed sound when she saw the woman was wearing a loose skirt that allowed her freedom of movement. She must have kept in shape because despite her obvious age, her back was straight and she walked like a much younger woman. Still, Ales offered her arm and the woman smiled at her.

"A little old-fashioned, aren't you?" The woman put her hand on Ales' arm.

"More than you know, Keeper." A

The woman looked her full in the face and drew in a breath. "The histories go back to the origin of the empire, about three hundred cycles ago, but I have traveled to other libraries with histories that go back much, much further. I recall a text from the Stonelands that spoke of the Tier. It was old, and there was not much that had survived, but I remember that it said that the Tier had eyes of two different colors."

Ales did not betray anything with her face. "Is that so, Keeper? I got them from my mother, and I know very little of mythology, though I am always interested in learning."

The woman smiled at her knowingly. "It is possible you are descended from the Tier. Some claim that they are, though I have only met one family who had the eyes. Before you, that is." The elderly librarian led her up a winding sorstone staircase.

"Where my mother's family came from, they kept only oral histories. She only knew of her family for three generations back. I suppose it is possible, but from what meager legends I know, I thought that their abilities were what changed their eye color." Alessandra said. It was the kind of comment that an average person who had only ever heard the stories of the Tier would say. It didn't matter that it was true.

"It is certainly possible, so your mother came from sunward?"

Ales nodded. She was born in a remote village near the edge of the Whitelands. My father had just returned with a caravan from the Sahnia."

The Librarian hummed in response. "Have you ever been?"

"To Sahnia?"

The woman nodded.

"Twice," Ales said. She had not actually been there, but Lia had. She had seen her sister's memories of the place.

"And is it true what they say about the palace?" she asked as she directed Ales up a spiral norstone staircase.

"That it is a shining tower made entirely of polished metal? Yes, it is true. It sparkles during the day like a thousand stars. They say that the Tier built it for them thousands of cycles ago."

Ales knew the truth. The Tier had built the tower as a tribute to Zezzhz. It had amazed her to learn Zezzhz had seen the monument as great enough a gift that he had spent considerable power to transport it to a place where he could view it in all its splendor without interference. Within a few generations, a Center had grown up around it despite the inhospitable land on which it sat.

"My, but that might be a sight worth seeing," the woman said. She went around the end of a number of bookshelves and turned back towards the center of the library, to a set of carved wooden doors.

"Here we are. Now, to access the histories, we will need a bit of your blood. Morbid as it may sound, the door will not let you pass without a drop of your blood." The woman gestured to a small pedestal next to the door. It had a round plate of metal with a handprint embossed into it.

Ales nodded. She put her hand on the plate. Her Cellstructs rushed to the palm of her hand, and when the needle pierced it, not a drop of blood was released. She released her Cellstructs into the device and instantly made a connection with the Bondstructs within. It was a fairly simply device. It read her helixical code to verify who she was. Her Cellstructs bypassed the door's locks as if it had recognized her blood. She rubbed her hand, but her Cellstructs had already knitted the skin closed. The doors clicked and swung open to reveal rows of shining black shelves.

"I think you are the only one here today, Lady. It should be quiet for you," the elderly woman said. She released Ales' arm.

"How is it organized, Keeper?" Ales asked. She could just find out for herself, but she felt terrible for lying to the woman.

"From the left, it is organized by cycle front to back. Please be careful with the oldest books, Lady. They are fragile."

"I will, Keeper. Thank you."

Ales moved towards the oldest books and walked down the first isle. She reached out and trailed her fingers along the book shelves. Millions of Cellstructs poured out of her fingertips and onto them. Her Cellstructs couldn't last more than a few hours outside of her body, but she didn't expect to need more than a couple. They couldn't go very fast, small as the tiny machines were, but with so many of them crawling through the books, she could cover everything in the library in a single day. She hoped she would find something useful here.

Something in the back of her mind was telling her there was something terribly wrong. Something just beyond the reach of her memory. She and Liassa had spoken a half dozen times about the subject. Lia said that her fears were unfounded. It was a feeling that she had felt before. As she sat down in a comfortable chair waiting for her Cellstructs to assimilate the knowledge from the books, it struck her that she knew the feeling. She had absolutely no memories of her fight with Alizar, but the feeling she had been getting since she had first seen the King was the same feeling she had gotten when she realized that Alizar was the Traitor. Her instincts had not been wrong then, and she would not ignore them now.

32

Lia watched Ilsa critically as she worked through the mental drill that would allow her consciously control her Vision. She had quickly learned how to bring herself to the verge of opening her Vision, which caused her eyes to glow brightly. She could even get over the verge and open her Vision, but when she did, it would simply dive to the deepest level, allowing her to see every particle of the world around her in glowing detail. Then she was stuck there and Lia would have to help her return to normal. The drill was simple, yet very difficult to actually accomplish. After a full span, she was still no closer to getting it right. Ilsa groaned as her Vision snapped open once more. Lia put her paw against Ilsa's forehead and through that contact, she was able to feel the magic coursing through her eyes. She carefully guided her Vision closed. Ilsa stumbled back and then scowled.

"This is impossible!" she growled.

"No, it is simply difficult. You're attempting to teach your mind to do something that it cannot possibly understand how to accomplish until it is done. Once you do it once, it will become instinct. It will work eventually if you have patience," Lia said calmly.

"No I won't! Didn't you hear about the impossible part?!" Ilsa stalked off towards the tree line.

Lia held up a paw, but said nothing as Ilsa disappeared into the trees.

"I hate to say it, but I think she is right. Are you sure about all of this?" Warran asked. Lia growled at him, and he held up his hands in a placating gesture.

"You, Fixer, are very close to losing something unimportant to your continued survival but that you hold very dear." Lia gave him a very predatory grin as she slunk closer to him. "Perhaps a finger, or a toe?" She asked sweetly. Then she snapped her teeth at him, sending him scrambling backwards, falling onto his ass in an attempt to get away from her. She made a chuffing sound that he quickly realized was laughter.

"I hate you. This gives us migraines, you know." Warran said.

She gave him a sour look. It was amazing how expressive her face could be for someone who wasn't human.

"I know. The mental acrobatics necessary for working comfortably with your Vision are difficult. It's just like any other muscle, the more you use it, the stronger it gets. I warned all of you that this would be difficult. I learned it the same way I am teaching it to you. Close your eyes and make yourself believe that you're opening them for the first time. If you can't make yourself believe absolutely, you cannot open your Vision, nor can you close it. This is just the first step. If you can't do it, you can never advance to higher control of your powers."

"I've never believed in anything in my life but what I could touch and what I could fix," Warran said. He flexed his hands, which were long-fingered and, if not precisely delicate, they were clever, to say the least. It wasn't very often, but occasionally Lia missed having hands. Her hands had been like his. Clever ones that could do amazing things. She didn't usually dwell on being human because she also remembered the pain.

"If you wish to be one of the Tier, then you must learn to believe in more, Warran. Not everything is simply what you can see, and touch. The world around you is alive with wonders that your eyes can never behold without the Vision to aid you."

Lia felt like an idiot using the words that Avaara had once said to her. Not because of the words themselves. They were the right words. It was something that, if you spent more than even a few minutes with Avaara, you knew she was a goddess if for no other reason than that she always used the right words. It was a subtle distinction that you could only really understand if you had met her before. Not everyone got to meet their creator.

"Oh, now that was a good line," Cole said sarcastically.

She didn't growl at him. She stared him down with cool feline eyes until he finally looked away.

"You don't know anything about real life, with your magic and your Vision. You live in a fantasy world," Cole groused.

"If you think that my powers make my life easier, you are more a fool than I thought you to be, no matter what my sister thinks of you," Lia said dispassionately.

He opened his mouth to say something, but she went on.

"How many times, Cole, have you had to heal from a broken spine? How many times have you had to watch as your entire race was destroyed before your eyes? How many times have you had to feel a piece of your own life ebb away because of something you had to do? How many times have you had to know that it wasn't going to stop? That you would do it again and again?" She said bitterly. Then she did growl at him.

"You think that it's just so easy for me? I know about you Cole, all about you. You were a noble once, when you were young. When you were six, your family was killed, and you think that because of that tragedy, you are justified in the things you do. That anyone else who has something you don't have is to be preyed upon, and that anyone who has less is someone who should accept whatever you give them." She looked him up and down, then shook her head.

"Go, Cole. Do my sister's bidding and get on with your life with your riches. I would not teach you now if you begged me. You do not have it," she said, and turned away from him back to Warran.

"What is it that you think I don't have that makes you so special? You aren't even human." He knew it was a mistake the second the words left his mouth.

She rounded on him, her lips pulled back from gleaming fangs. Her eyes glowed with sullen light. His first instinct was to run, because he knew that she was going to hurt him. He knew he deserved it, and he knew without a doubt that she would catch him. Knew that it would be worse. So he stood frozen, staring into those burning eyes. One like molten gold and one like blinding orange fire.

"You, little man, seem to be mistaking my kindness for weakness. You think that just because I don't walk on two legs that you are somehow more than me?"

She reared up onto her two pairs of hind legs. She drew her front paws back, wicked claws appearing on each toe, and roared at him. The overwhelming sound brought some primal part of his brain to the fore and he scrambled backwards, trying to get away from her as fast as he could. Her roar cut off abruptly and she fell back to all six paws. The glow faded from her eyes and she watched him for a moment.

"You will never understand. You are only human." She turned and stalked away. "Don't come back, Cole. I don't want to see you here again," she said coldly.

Cole didn't run from the clearing, but it was a close thing. He had not felt fear of anything since he lost his family. Whatever she had done, though, had made him fear her.

Lia sighed as soon as he left the clearing. Warran was staring at her in awe and a little fear. She folded her ears back shamefully.

"That seemed unnecessary," Warran said soberly.

She growled at him but there was no real feeling in it.

"I know it was. I'm not stupid, Warran, as you well know."

"Well, what you did there seemed pretty stupid," he said, and there was bite to his words.

"Warran, there are things you do not say to one of the Wild. We do not regret our choices, but we do remember what it was to be human. With that memory comes pain, the pain of losing who we were and the pain that we felt that made it impossible to keep that person. So to remind us we are no longer human hurts more than most people can imagine." Lia sat down on her haunches, arranging her two front pairs of legs for comfort.

"And that is an excuse for terrifying him?" Warran asked.

"No, it isn't, but I am not so foolish as to think that I am perfect, Warran. And I do not want him here if all he is going to do is destroy your concentration and belief in yourself. The Vision is in everyone and our gods are real. This is not some fantasy, Warran. This is reality, and our gods think that if we do not act, something terrible is going to happen to it. I don't know what, but Ales feels that there is something that we don't understand happening in our world. I was her partner for over two hundred cycles, Warran, and I have never seen my sister's instincts be wrong. Never."

"Your sister is very scary."

"She would not appreciate that like the compliment that you meant it to be, Warran."

"I know, good people don't enjoy the idea that they terrify people. And despite how frightening she is, I know with all certainty that she is better than I, better than all of us, except maybe you."

She nodded. "You'll have to get used to that eventually. It's something that many people who are not the Tier feel for the Tier. We do things that other people think are impossible. It is who we are. Even those of us who were not Arcangineers made sacrifices. It's part of being Tier. We are not better, but people think of us that way."

"What about my daughter? Will she have to do this too because I am?" Warran asked.

"No, she doesn't have to be one of the Tier, but I have hope that she will want to be one day," Lia said.

Warran sighed with relief.

Lia grinned a feline grin. "You know that she'll grow into a woman one day, and if you hold her too tight, you will lose her."

"I know, but until that day, I must protect her so that she can grow into that woman."

"Wise words, but I've let you change the subject. I'll talk to Ales about Cole. I don't think she is wrong about him, Warran, but I was never a very good teacher and he upsets me in a way I thought was beyond me."

Lia's ears perked forward, and Ilsa came out of the trees.

"I just saw Cole storming off towards the Center. He looked like he was running but he wished he could run faster," she said. "What did you do to him?"

"He said some things that opened an old wound of mine. Something he should not have said, but he didn't know that. I reacted badly and frightened him. I will rectify the situation as best I can. Have you found some of your patience, Ilsa? Would you like to try again?"

Ilsa sighed. "I'm not sure patience is what I need. I think that I have to be doing something wrong. I know I can do this. I know it. I believe, Lia. I've seen my Vision work but I can't control it."

"Believing you have the Vision and that you can use it is not quite the same as the mental trick of convincing your abilities that you're calling on them, Ilsa. Words fail to convey the difference, I know, but mentally, the difference is there. Be patient, you will not get it on the first try, or even the fifth, or the tenth, and probably not even the first hundred or so times you do it. It took Ales a full rotation to figure it out, and I've never seen anyone learn about the Vision faster than her. Try again," Liassa encouraged them both.

33

Liassa made her slow way through the alleys of Vilhena. She had made sure that Ilsa and Warran had made it home safely. She had made it almost halfway back to the apartment when she spotted her tail. She grinned at the expression, thinking about how many times her sister yelled at her to keep her tail down. She considered how to deal with the person following her. It could be someone harmless who was just interested in what a katali was doing wandering in the city. She didn't want to open her Vision and give herself away. It was dark, and the glow of her eyes would be like a floodlight to anyone who was watching her.

She concentrated and forced open the first level of her Constraints. Then she pulled a trick out of her bag that she had learned over the long centuries. Her claws were very sharp but not sharp enough to penetrate brick or steel. She pushed some of the Cellstructs out of the tips of her toes around her claws. The tiny machines encased and reinforced her claws. It was a slow process, but that was alright. Her tail was still far enough back that she wouldn't worry too much about it. Finally, she took a path towards a dead-end alleyway. She turned the corner on the alleyway and then darted down the last hundred marks in a blur of speed even Ales would have trouble matching. When she reached the wall of the building that dead-ended the alleyway, she leapt onto the wall. Her claws bit deeply into the brick and she scrambled up the side of the building without slowing down. By the time the person following her entered the end of the alleyway, Lia was watching them from far above.

It was a man of average height and build. He was swathed in a black cloak that seemed to move on its own. Lia opened her Vision then, focusing fully on the man. Her vision swooped in until she was looking at his cloak, which covered his entire face with a deep black hood. Her gaze sharpened and her face twisted with anger. She shoved open the second level of her Constraints and flew off the roof in a fury. She slammed into the ground in front of the man, throwing off dust and chips of cobblestones. He stumbled back from her with a startled yelp. She knew her eyes were glowing as she bore down on him.

"What in the abyss are you?!" His voice sounded like slabs of stone grating together.

Her lips pealed back from her teeth and she growled.

His cloak was made of Antistructs. They had been designed by the Tier to leave no lasting impact on the environment. They could break down any material on a basic level. They were extremely dangerous in the wrong hands and they should never be in this person's control. She lifted her right forepaw. The gesture wasn't really necessary, it simply helped her to focus. Her Cellstructs made a connection to the Antistructs that made up the man's cloak. She felt the mental chime that indicated her Structures made the handshake with the Antistructs, and then her Structures identified themselves as belonging to one of the Tier. They responded to her request just as they should.

The Antistructs flowed away from him to the ground like water that had been poured over his head from a bucket. They slithered across the ground in a black stream that looked like mercury rolling across the ground. Then they gathered into a ball at her feet, roughly half the size of a man's head. She lowered her paw to the ground and stared daggers at the man. He was wearing black leather armor with dark clothing beneath. He seemed completely at a loss for words, staring hungrily at the ball of Antistructs at her feet, face hidden by his mask.

"You do not know the power you toy with. Where did you get these and how are you controlling them? It can be only a tenuous hold at best," Lia demanded.

The man startled when she spoke, obviously not expecting her to do so, though he knew there was something different about her. It must only be an instinct on his part, and his first question made her pause, but only for a moment.

The initiation of any Tier was their first instinct, and there was a subtle difference to the minds of those who would be Tier which influenced the way they asked that first question. He had said what, not who, just like Warran had. There were other ways to tell, but this was the simplest one if the circumstances worked out to reveal it. But she had ruined it by asking him a question. It broke the cycle. She couldn't muster the desire to care. What this man was doing with Antistructs was beyond her, but he had no idea the danger he was creating by walking around with them unbound by Tieran control. A ball this size could eventually multiply and destroy until there was not a single thing of human creation left. She fervently sent a mental prayer to the Mother and Father, giving thanks that she had found this person before he could unleash such desolation.

"My patience grows thin. Answer my questions, and if you lie, I will know," Lia said.

The man's eyes widened. He stepped forward further into the alleyway, obviously not wanting to be seen.

"Gods…" he whispered. "You are her. The last of the Tier." His voice was awestruck, even reverent. "The tomes say six survived, but only one was still walking Ahlysim."

It was Lia's turn to be startled, though she didn't show it. How did he know? The Tier were legends, but shapeless legends. That he knew what she was, that was not a shock. It was the one enduring truth about the Tier that she encountered everywhere she went, that their eyes glowed when they were using their Vision. It wasn't the first time someone had recognized it, but it wasn't common that she let anyone see her do it. But for him to know that she had been the only survivor until Ales had woken was not even a secret. It was a fact lost to the ravages of time.

Only eight beings in all the world had known she had survived the destruction of Ahal. That meant there were only two possible explanations for his tomes. One was that one of the five remaining Tier had been able to do what they had separated to do thousands of cycles ago. The other was that Avaara or Zezzhz had passed down knowledge of the Tier to these people. The second option was so unlikely that she could not even calculate the odds of it. Lia wasn't sure what to say next. She had questions to which she almost certainly already knew the answers. She couldn't ask them here, though. She was exposed. She turned back down the alleyway and the ball of Antistructs fell into a puddle behind her.

"If you wish to keep these, I need answers about what you do with them and how you control them. Come with me."

She leapt up to a steel fire stairway and pushed the ladder down to him. As he passed, he stepped into the puddle. When his bare feet touched it, the puddle swirled up from the ground. It climbed up his body like a snake wrapping around a tree branch. It swirled around his neck, and then flowed out into a deep black cloak. It made it clear that he had some sort of connection with them. Perhaps something synaptic. It was possible that they were connecting into his central nervous system somehow. She noted that only his hands and feet were unclothed besides the holes in his mask that allowed him to see. He climbed the ladder, and once she was sure he would follow, she stalked away across the rooftop.

- END OF PART 3 -

"FINDER"

34

Ilsa closed the door on the small apartment in the High Center that Ales had established for her. She couldn't think of it as home. Not yet. She slid down to the floor with her back against the door. She couldn't move a muscle. At least she didn't want to. She felt like her brain was going to ooze out of her ears at any second. She looked around the apartment. Five rooms all to herself. She realized that she was sitting on her hair, and levered herself up off of it. She made her way into her bedroom, and flopped on the bed. She rolled over onto her back, and stared at the ceiling. She tried to ignore the pounding in her head but it was a real effort. Lia had been working with them nonstop for more than a few span. Eleven more days of torture and she was still no closer to controlling the opening and closing of her Vision. At least it didn't feel like she was. She was supposed to have been born with these powers, but she had no idea how to control them. She had experienced her powers dozens of times now, but each time the overwhelming amount she could see had made it impossible to concentrate.

A small tapping noise came from her window. She didn't want to move. A moment's thought made her realize that the tapping noise was either very good, or very bad. Her apartment was on the fifth floor. She tilted her head backwards until she was seeing the window upside down. There was a dark figure crouching there outlined by the light of the moon.

"Window's open. If you are here to hurt me, just make sure I don't wake up." She said. The list of people that could balance on that tiny ledge outside of her window was short. The window opened with a small squeak.

"Hello Ilsa, I am sorry it has taken me so long to come to you. Lia tells me that you are becoming frustrated with attempting to control your Vision. She thinks that perhaps I can help you." Ales said as she closed the window.

"Did your head hurt this much when you were trying to learn to control your Vision?"

"Only the first few hundred times." Ales said dryly.

"I can help with the headache." Ales offered.

"Please? Right now everything hurts. I will happily take one less pain." Ilsa said. The bed shifted as Ales sat down on the other side. Her hands were gentle as she lifted Ilsa's shoulders. Ilsa realized after a moment that Ales had folded her legs into a crossed position, and laid Ilsa's head in her lap. It felt odd having someone so powerful as Ales be so gentle. Ales began massaging Ilsa's temples, and then spreading her fingers carefully she massaged her whole scalp. Within a few minutes the headache receeded. That was when Ales spoke.

"Lia is teaching you the proper method for opening and closing your Vision. We call it hard belief. It is not just a matter of knowing something is, but a matter of teaching your mind to see the world as you will it to be. Teaching your mind to perceive the world in a completely different way than you have all your life. It is a nearly impossible task to accomplish to deny the truth of what you see, and replace it with a truth that you know is just beyond your sight. Part of the problem is that Lia is not used to dealing with Vision as powerful as your Vision is. When learning how to do this none of the others will have the same difficulties because their Vision will manifest pulled back to the lowest level. Which means that they have to work to see anything new at all. Your Vision, on the other hand, will be opened to a level where the incoming information is nearly impossible to process," Ales explained.

"How do I do it then?" Ilsa said.

"Honestly I can't tell you. It is a little different for each of the Tier, and moreso for a Newling. But I can advise you on what worked for me. Perhaps you can adapt it to yourself. When I was first learning, I had to focus on all my other senses when I opened my Vision. I had to distract myself from what my Vision would show me or I would be overwhelmed. It took me a solid rotation to figure out how to distract myself from that crushing barrage of information. For me it was sound. I learned to pick out a single sound, and focus on it completely. Everything in my mind was that one sound. The wind, the twitter of a bird, or the sound of people talking. They all worked for me." Ilsa felt amazingly better from the short massage, and she looked up at Ales. She noticed the glow of the Vision fading from Ales' eyes.

"Magical fingers?" Ilsa said with a grin.

"A small application of Breaking makes it easy to massage out the problems. Muscle cramps are not something the Tier ever have to worry about." Ales said. Then Ilsa asked her something she hadn't expected from someone so young.

"So not only do I have to learn what Lia is trying to teach me, but I also have to learn to ignore being blinded by being able to see the whole Mother Cursed universe all at once?" Ilsa grumbled.

"Power like you are seeking has a cost Ilsa, but it has just as many rewards. I want you to keep in mind the way I originally used might not work for you. Every Tier feels a special relationship with one of the Circles. And it alters how you interpret your Vision. My bond is with Breaking. It means that I tend to look at things in terms of strengths and weaknesses. Which means that focusing down to one thing is easy. I can instantly pick out the loudest strongest sound. Lia and I have guesses that you will be a Finder. That means you'll see the patterns of things all around you. Hence you might need to adapt. The key is focusing on something other than what you will see when your Vision is open." Ales finished.

"Lia told me about how you ended up here. Is it worth it Ales?" Ilsa asked.

Ales wanted to tell her yes unequivocally that it was worth it but that wouldn't be the whole truth. "To me it is. But when I became one of the Tier it was in a time when there were millions of other Tier. It was easier back then because with all of us having our Cellstructs we could feel the love, and support we all had for each other. Until we can find Verdant to manufacture your own Cellstructs we cannot pass this on to you all."

"Lia hasn't told us much about Cellstructs, what are they?" She asked.

"What do you know about Bondstructs?" Ales asked. She didn't move, and Ilsa seemed content to leave her head right where it was.

"They are tiny machines that can be used to build things." She said.

"That is an accurate, if simplistic assessment. There are several varieties of Tieran Structures. Each type is a microscopic machine that can manipulate matter on one level or another. Bondstructs are used to create bonds between materials. They can be made out of a base of almost any building material, though stone, steel, and glass work best. Cellstructs live inside of our bodies. They are designed to integrate with our bodies on every level to strengthen us in every way.

After our early ancestors were taught how to use their Vision by the gods it became clear that we humans could not possibly utilize the full potential of our Vision on our own. So we began to experiment with increasing the strength of our bodies to allow us to better utilize our magic. After many efforts we arrived at the creation of Tieran Structures, and subsequently Tieran Minds to tend to the creation of new Structures as they were needed." Ales explained.

"Tieran Minds?" Ilsa asked.

"Tieran Minds were the greatest of our creations. They are hard to describe. They are intelligent thinking machines that help us understand our world. Sadly it seems that people in this time have focused on the machines part and not the intelligent part. At least that is what I have collected. Minds are alive as much as you and I are, and to use them simply like they are just another machine is cruel. They helped us of their own free will, and we provided for them experiences that they could not have themselves." Ales explained though she wasn't sure Ilsa would understand.

"I think I understand. They don't have bodies?" Ilsa asked.

"No, there were plans in place to give them their own bodies. That is all gone now. What is important is that Verdant was the Mind who helped us create, and search for new information about Cellstructs. Without Verdant we cannot give you the enhancements that Lia, and I enjoy. We wouldn't give them to you at first anyway, but until we can you are vulnerable in ways we are not. I will come to teach you as I can, as there are things Lia will not be able to teach you not having a human body." Ales explained. She carefully lifted Ilsa's shoulders and unfolded herself from the bed.

"Would it be rude of me to ask what else you are doing?" Ilsa asked as Ales neared the window.

"Not at all Ilsa. I have many tasks. I am ingratiating myself with the nobility here, and trying to find out exactly what happened to our people. We have magical senses Ilsa, and you will learn to listen to them eventually. Mine are telling me that there is so much more to our destruction than what we already know. I must find out what that is, and despite having absorbed the entirety of the royal archive I still find myself far from that goal." Ales explained.

"Can we help?" Ilsa asked.

"I suspect that you will at some point, but no not right now. Right now I must make use of the night while it lasts." Ales opened the window.

"Ales?" She asked.

"Hmm?" Ales hummed.

"Thank you." Ilsa said. Ales' smile was beautiful, and her glowing eyes simply enhanced that beauty.

"Any time Ilsa." Ales said. Then she leapt out of the window.

Cole sat at the bar of the Wandering Balath. Haleb behind the bar watched him with worried eyes. He had known Cole for a few cycles now, but not in any really personal way. But he had never seen Cole in such a mood. The serious way he was trying to drink the tap room dry showed just how dark his mood was. The tap room was full, but of greatest interest to Cole were the four men sitting in a booth near the back of the bar to his right. They were all members of the guild of merchants, but more importantly, they were mercenaries hired by the guild to protect their shipments. They were always the best source of gossip when you wanted real information.

"Rumor is that she killed twenty men by herself. They say she is a creature from the Howling Abyss," one of the men said. The one across from him with sandy colored hair and the best gear of the lot laughed.

"She killed twenty-three men in that warehouse, but why would one of the wraiths care about slavers? No. She is not one of the wraiths. She is just someone who is very good at killing. Slavers are not known for their martial skill," he said.

"No woman could kill twenty-three men on her own. I saw the inside of that warehouse. She didn't just kill them. I've seen battlefields cleaner than the inside of that warehouse. It looked like someone lined up ten catapults and threw bolders into it. That's not the only thing I hear about her. There isn't a slaver left for a hundred lengths, and they are saying that anyone who has taken a contract with the Blackhands has gone missing along with all of the Blackhands themselves. The assassin's guild hall has been empty for spans," the third man added. He was a red-eyed man that Cole had seen before on his trips. He had paid the man on a number of occasions for information about which merchants were most deserving of being robbed.

"I'll drink to that. Filthy throat-slitters. Would be a service to the realm if the Night Lady killed 'em all," the fourth man toastedand raised his tankard. That was when Cole noticed Haleb eyeing him. He held up his glass for a refill, and Haleb shook his head.

"I think that is enough for tonight Cole. Your room is empty. Go on up and sleep it off." Haleb said. Cole eyed him with annoyance. He was odd when he was deep in his cups Haleb remembered. Odd in the sense that he never seemed to take on the drunken stupor that other people did. He was able to think and reason with near all of his cognitive powers even when he had drank enough spirits to kill nearly any other man.

"If you won't give me what I need Haleb I will take my business elsewhere." Cole growled, and made to get up from his stool. Haleb waved him to sit down.

"You came in here tonight because something has rattled you. I've never seen you rattled Cole, but you are now. What is it?" Haleb asked. The tap room was starting to empty. Cole grunted, and then sat back down.

"You ever said something that you knew right away you should have kept your big stupid mouth shut?" Cole asked.

"A few times. Felt like a right idiot after I did." Haleb said.

"Well I did it only much much worse. I said something I can't ever take back. I can't believe I did something so stupid. I could have been killed. I think that would have been a blessing." Cole said. He couldn't figure out why he was so angry with himself. He had not felt any sort of attachment to anyone besides Warran since he had been a child. Why now did he feel like he had done something irrevocable when he had shouted at Liassa. He worked for them not anything else. He looked up at Haleb.

"I don't know why I think that. I work for her. She is paying me to do my job. Why isn't she like any other client that I can just work for and forget?" He asked. Haleb shrugged.

"Can't tell you that lad. But I know the feeling for certain." He held out his hand for the glass Cole was clutching in his right hand.

"And I also know for certain that you've had enough for tonight. Go on up to bed, on the house."

Cole handed him the glass, and pulled himself off the stool. Haleb held out a key, and Cole took it. He made his unsteady way towards the stairs at the back of the room. He headed up them slowly as the buzz of the drink made him slightly dizzy. He looked at the key in his hand, and thought slowly started to trickle in. Haleb had never given him a key before. Even drowned in drink there was no lock that Cole couldn't pick. Likely faster than he could use a key.

His paranoia ratcheted up to super human levels. His eyes darted about the hallway looking for anything that might be out of place. His immediate instinct was to flee. He could go down the back stair and be gone in under ten seconds. Once he got to the thieves way they would never be able to catch him. The key might be Haleb's way of warning him. He had made sure Haleb received portions of his thieving on numerous occasions. Perhaps he had not been careful enough in spending what he had been given, and someone had gotten to him. Cole watched the last door on the right by the servants' stairwell. It had become his habit to stay in that room in wayhouses all over Vilhena. A habit that he would now break.

He shook his head. He was drunk, and not ready for any sort of fight that might be hiding behind the door to that room. He didn't think going back down stairs was an option either. He turned to the door nearest to him, and slid his lock picks out of a pouch on his belt. He was through the door in less than ten seconds. He pulled up his hood hiding his face. When he entered the room there was a startled intake of breath from the bed, and he turned to see a woman sprawled naked on top of a man in the bed.

"Do carry on. I am simply passing through." Cole said with a grin.

He pushed the door closed behind him, and went to the window. Before the woman could scream he swung open the window, and pulled himself up onto the sill. He caught the lip of the roof above. No mean feat considering it stuck out two marks from the wall. He had to lean backwards, and count on his long cycles of practice to make sure he didn't fall and break his fool neck. But he kicked the window shut, and scrambled onto the rooftop in one smooth swinging motion. The woman inside never did actually scream. Cole startled when a woman's voice came from the peak of the roof above him.

"Took you long enough." The voice said. He stood up, and peered up the incline of the roof. Someone was sitting up there.

"Thought you might drink yourself to death and save me the trouble." The voice said, and he finally recognized Ales' strange Ahalyn accent.

"What are you doing here?" He asked.

"I am here for two reasons. The most important of the two is that you need to know you are part of my plans. The second is at the behest of my sister." Ales explained. Cole shrank a little at hearing that she was here because of Lia.

"It was that bad was it?" Ales asked. Cole shook himself, and then stood up straighter in a failed attempt at male bravado. He did not fool her. He seemed to notice it right away, and he deflated. He slumped into a desultory posture. Before he could say anything she went on.

"Do you understand why she was so angry with what you said?" Ales asked.

"I think so." He replied. Ales lifted her eyebrows letting him know he should go on.

"I think I do. She was human once, and I made her remember. It hurt her." Cole said.

"I'm a little surprised that you see it. People who take the Wild do it because hurting other people damages their minds. It does not make them less Cole. It simply means that they are different, and must take a different path. It isn't just pain, but that is the easiest way to describe it. It's a pain that for them does not dull with time, and can't be justified in any way. Most cannot imagine what it is like to not be able to accept something you have done with your own two hands. When you make them feel less because they are different it is deeply upsetting. Each of the Wild always harbors small fears that they should have been better somehow." Ales explained. Cole looked down at his hands, and grimaced.

"I didn't see it when I said that too her. But I know exactly what that feels like." Cole said. His mind wandered back to the memory of hiding as his family was butchered. It didn't matter to him that he had only been a child. He should have been able to do something.

"You look like you do." Ales said. Cole just shook his head.

"I have no excuses for what I said. I'm not like you Ales. Not like Lia. I'm not meant to do what you do." He shrugged.

"I will fulfill my contract with you. I won't have any trouble creating the kind of mayhem that will draw the whole attention of the palace." Cole said. He walked past her across the roof towards the High Center. A fire stair was even with the level of the roof where he stopped. Ales watched him go with sad eyes. He was meant for something more than just being a thief, but she knew forcing him was not an option. He turned at the edge of the roof.

"Hey do you know who was waiting for me in my room down there?" He chucked his chin towards his room in the wayhouse. She shook her head, then turned to look at the roof below her. She opened her Vision, and a moment later the glow faded from her eyes. She turned back to him.

"A couple of thick fisted thugs. I suspect someone meant for you to take a beating. Who did you steal from now?" Ales asked an easy smile sliding onto her face. The braids in her azure hair made her look cycles younger than Cole even though he knew she was so much older. Cole just shrugged affecting nonchalance.

"Everyone." He said. He turned, and jumped to the fire stair landing with almost no sound. Then he was gone.

"FIXER"

Warran twisted the screws into the handle of the grapple that he had painstakingly constructed over the last few days. He had to work on it between more lucrative projects, but it was finally done. He picked up his triggering tools. The small set of picks, hooks, and awls were charged with elementary forces enabling them to program Bondstructs. He took a tiny scoop of black sand from the white dish on his work bench. He shook a few grains into the recession where the screw had gone in. He pushed the tiny tip of the pick tool into the minuscule pile of grains. The grains spread out away from the pick, and he dragged it into circular motion. The grains seemed to melt into a liquid, and then he pulled out the pick. They solidified into a single piece sealing the screw into the handle. A small white dot appeared where he pulled the pick out of the handle. The indicator would be necessary if he ever had to maintain the equipment. The Bondstructs he had used in the construction of the grapple were self-repairing so the likelihood of manual repairs becoming necessary was small. Considering Cole though anything was possible.

"Daddy?" A small voice came from the workshop door.

"Kayna, what are you doing out of bed?" He asked without looking up.

"My fault I'm afraid." He recognized the voice.

"She is very bright your little one." Ales said.

"Oh?" Warran asked.

"She saw my shadow outside of her room when I came in through the attic, and bravely came right out to make sure I wasn't a thief. She told me that her uncle Cole is a thief, and he comes in that way sometimes. She said he didn't steal from you though. He only steals from bad people." Ales said, and ruffled the little girl's bright red hair. Kayna smiled, and nodded her little head.

"All true. But I think it is past her bedtime. Back to your dreams little one." Warran said. Kayna turned to Ales, and gave a curtsey.

"Nice to meet you Miss Ales." She said.

"Nice to meet you too Kayna." Ales said. She ran back up the stairs outside of the workshop door.

"I apologize for sneaking in here like an assassin Warran. I was hoping not to wake anyone. Your little girl seems to be a bit of a night owl." Ales said.

"Takes after her father." Warran said as he held up what looked sort of like an oversized barrel for a lancer. She resisted the urge to open her Vision and examine it more closely. She was here for something far more important.

"I came here to talk to you about Cole. About what happened between him and Lia." Ales explained. Warran set aside what he had been working on. He carefully put his triggering picks away before he looked up at her.

"I do not think I have ever seen anyone, man or beast, so angry as she was when Cole said that to her. I thought for a moment that she was going to kill him. All I could think was that I couldn't get there fast enough to stop her." Warran said.

"No matter how angry she may get Warran she will never hurt any of you. Lia is utterly incapable of harming anyone she cares about. Teaching people things makes her testy at best. What he said to her though it was." She shook her head unable to describe how much it would wound one of the Wild to hear that. What she had said to Cole seemed so inadequate.

"It was ill advised." She said simply. Warran nodded. She still cringed on the inside when she walked onto the hardwood floors.

"She explained it to us. She regretted it afterwards." Warran said.

"I tried to get him to come back. He is one of the Tier. He is meant to be with us meant to know the Vision." Ales said.

"Why are you so bent on getting him to do this?" Warran asked. Ales shrugged.

"I guess I am just amazed that he might not want to be one of us. In my time to be one of the Tier was a great honor. I still see it as such. I guess in this time others might not." Finally Warran pushed the grapple away and sighed.

"Look, Cole has good in him, but he also has a lot of bitterness. I've known him a long time, and he never quite got past the idea of what he lost when his family was killed. He is a devout believer in the Mother, and the Father but I can only imagine it to be so because he claims to have met the goddess.

I don't know that he will ever fully trust anyone but himself.
You are asking him to give up his life for people he doesn't
even know." Warran said.

"Not without reward. I do not simply want to take from
him." Ales mumbled. It annoyed her that she was seeking
help from someone hundreds of cycles her junior. Yet the
more she thought about it the more she realized the truth of it.
She had never really noticed that age had much to do with
how wise a person was. Bann had been a hundred cycles her
junior, and he had known things that she was certain she
would never understand. She had never been very good at
reading people despite her impressive abilities with the Vision.

"I'm not questioning your motives Ales. I joined you
without question when you explained it all to me didn't I?"
He asked. She sighed. He went on before she could speak.

"I believe in what you say, and maybe one day when I meet
them I will believe in the God and Goddess as well. Cole
though, he doesn't believe in much of anything but himself.
Cole is my brother if I ever had one. He saved my life when I
was younger, but that doesn't mean I am blind to who he is.
He is a thief. I am not even sure I could call him good. He
never steals from anyone who will truly miss it, and many
deserve it. But thieling is still not good. I would not lie to
myself about that, and you shouldn't either." Warran said.
Ales nodded.

"I'm not going to just forget about him Warran. He's one of
us." Ales said stubbornly. Warran blew out a breath.

"You obviously don't need my help to find him. What are
you really here for?" Warran asked.

"I guess what I am really asking is that you talk to him if
you see him again. We need him Warran. We need all of you.
Two of us will not be enough to set this right." Ales said.

"Do you even know what <u>this</u> is yet?" Warran asked.

"I'm getting a better idea. The histories I got from the
palace are helping, but it is a lot of information. Without
access to the Core it is taking a while for my Structures to
process it all especially since I am working with limited
space." Ales explained.

"I have no idea what you are talking about." Warran said.
Ales rubbed her temples.

"I'm sorry this is going to be difficult to explain. No one in this time thinks of the abstract uses of Structures. They can be used as storage devices for information. Mine, and Lia's especially are designed to aid our minds in storing and understanding information. My Cellstructs have absorbed all of the information in the Royal Library. But right now I don't understand the written language of this time. Lia did not exactly spend a lot of time reading, not being human and all. So my Cellstructs are having to decipher the language before I can attempt to apply my abilities as a Finder to it to see if there are any patterns to the last three thousand cycles that I have missed. However my reconstructed mind was already heavily saturated with information." Ales explained.

"Wait there is a limit on how much a person's brain can hold?" Warran asked. Ales nodded.

"Yes there is a limit, and I am nearing mine. Without access to the Core to offload my memories I am going to start losing things if I do not find some sort of secondary storage soon. But for this I have enough." Ales explained.

"Isn't that dangerous? Could you forget things you need to know?" Warran asked. Ales shook her head.

"No, my structures would give priorities to memories that are accessed more frequently than others. I would have options as to what is removed and what is not to free space." Ales said. Warran raised a brow.

"I have so many questions at this point I don't even know where to start." Warran said.

"Welcome to being one of the Tier." Ales said.

Lia watched the man warily as he lowered himself slowly onto the couch across from the love seat that she had perched on. It was just large enough to hold her. His posture said that he wasn't going to tell her anything. She suspected he had told himself that he was only following her to give himself time to find a way to escape with his Antistructs.

"Do not fool yourself. You are a child by comparison, and I can supersede your control of those Structures whenever I wish too." Lia said.

"How did you spot me?" The man asked.

"Your Structures are a beacon to anyone who can properly sense them. I knew you were there when you came within a length of me." Lia said, and he just stared at her. He seemed unable to respond. Just as he was about to open his mouth there was a soft noise on the balcony. Ales came through the glass doors, and eyed Lia.

"Is this going to become a habit?" Ales asked tartly. Lia lifted her lips it a terrifying approximation of a smile.

"Perhaps if I keep finding strange and interesting people to bring here." Lia replied, and Ales grinned. It was an easy exchange. Something they had done thousands upon thousands of times. The man recognized it for what it was.

"You two are sisters? How is that even possible?" He asked incredulously. Lia's imitation of a smile disappeared and she glared at him.

"How is that any business of yours?" Lia growled.

"Lia manners?" Ales asked, and Lia folded her ears back shamefully.

"Young man you are an oddity in an odd world. I think that she has many questions, and she is not boiling over with them only because she has been waiting for me so she doesn't have to repeat everything. Go on Lia."

Ales made a gesture, and sat down on one of the comfortable looking chairs. She leaned back into the heavy padding. Her posture said that she knew the chair would slow her getting up, but also that he would still be to slow to come anywhere near her.

"It is also because I'm not sure where to start asking questions. I think the first is that it is obvious that somewhere you came in contact with the Tieran Mind called Giri, but how did you manage to access it?" Lia said. He did not answer but stared at Ales for a long moment.

"Prove you are of the Tier." His gravel voice was strong. Ales narrowed her eyes at him.

"You seem to misunderstand the situation. We two have far too many questions, and far too few answers. I will have answers for how you came to possess your cloak of Antistructs." Her voice was iron, and brooked absolutely no argument.

For the first time in cycles since he finished his training he was afraid. She hadn't even shown her Tieran powers, and he was certain she could kill him more easily than he was drawing breath.

"The Tieran Mind Giri lives in a monastery in the Kurian Mountains of the Nysan Empire across the ocean sunward. And my name is Niemand Kiener." The man said, his voice scratchy.

"Well that is a good sign." Ales said.

"How did you gain contact with the Mind?" Lia asked. At the same exact time Ales asked the same question. Niemand Kiener looked back and forth between them unsure who to talk too. He decided to answer the question first.

"A long time ago we were simply monks searching for the best place to find peace." He began. Ales stopped him immediately.

"How long ago?" She asked. Niemand shrugged.

"We don't know for sure. Over two thousand cycles we know that much. Can't say for sure at all. In the end we found the Mind embedded in a boulder in the Black Wilds. They built the monastery around that rock, for the Mind glowed with the magic of the Mother, and the Father. We hoped that if we stayed, if we kept it safe that one day they would come to us. They did not however. One of the Tier visited us. He was very old." Niemand explained.

"What did he look like?" Lia asked. She knew the Tier that had survived the Cataclysm. They had gone their separate ways each of them looking for one of the Minds. Lia had only run into three of them again before they had died. None of them wanted to live forever with the rest of the Tier gone. She had known they had died, as Avaara had told her with each death that they were gone back to The Core.

"He was like you. His name was Hallai. He made the monks understand that if they touched the surface of the mind he could communicate with them." He explained.

"Figures that the Ghost of the Highlands would have survived." Ales said. He had not been very old when he had gotten that name.

"He hated that name." Lia said.

"That doesn't change the fact that he earned it." Ales said.

"What did you mean when you said that was a good sign?" Niemand asked. Two pairs of dual colored eyes turned to him as if he were a particularly intelligent dog.

"That you see the Mind as a living thing, and not just a piece of machinery like everyone else seems to think." Ales said, and then they both ignored him again. He could tell that they were exchanging some sort of conversation that he did not understand. He started to get up, but subsided when Ales' eyes turned to him. There was a faint lambent glow in those eyes, and suddenly he knew she had only been focusing part of her attention on him before. He felt as if she had torn away all his clothing, and then that not being enough for her had stripped him right down to his bones.

"What did he look like?" Lia asked.

"He was a rowunalf. Generally he shaped himself like a hiluk. He took various forms though."

"Well at least he isn't lying about that." Lia said.

"Can't you tell when I am lying?" He asked.

"There are ways to lie to us if you have the kind of mental control that you have. We are not perfect, gods, or invincible. We have some power that we work very hard to gain." Ales said.

"Niemand it is clear to me that you have excellent control over those Antistructs given you. Still I have questions about how you use them." Lia said.

"He taught us what the Antistructs could do unchecked. And so we use them as best we can. We use them to help people keep secrets. But we only take a contract after we know everything about those we are working for. We do not take work from those who would misuse our abilities as we were taught by Hallai." Lia, and Ales exchanged a glance.

"A contract you say. Would your contract be with Lord Faln?" Ales asked. Niemand nodded.

"Yes, my current contract is with Lord Faln." Niemand said.

"Then you know that he is simply vying for power over others?" Lia growled.

"Is he? Lord Faln is ambitious. I will not deny such. But no one knows what makes we of the Darkness take a contract, and we have watched him. His actions speak for themselves. He knows that there is something wrong with the King, and as we agree with his assessment so we have agreed to aid him in overthrowing this government."

{Could this be the source of information you have been searching for?} Lia's mental sending was hopeful.

{I think he just might be. If they are following tenants that Hallai set down for them then they will have recorded what history was available to them accurately.} Ales replied.

"So you also believe there is something wrong with the King?" Ales asked. She opened her Vision a little more, and the man hesitated. He guessed that with her Vision open so she would know for certain if he was lying despite what they had said.

"It is a pattern we have noticed as a group in the last few intervals. Two of the major kingdoms who had for centuries maintained their borders, and their stance that there was a need for peace became quietly aggressive. Vilhena especially." He explained. Lia looked at him with some suspicion. He shrank in his seat a little bit. It was subtle, but they both caught the movement.

{He's not lying. But he's trying to protect something about Faln. Something he thinks will anger us.} Lia said. Ales nodded.

"Why were you following my sister tonight?" She asked outloud.

"Faln has had the Three trying to tail you for spans, and then he was ordered to put the Three on another task by the Queen herself. He was frustrated and turned to me to attempt to acquire you. He has not quite made it to the idea that you could be one of the Tier but he is almost there. He knows that there is something very odd about you. I think that he has the impression he can study you to learn something." He said.

Ales' response was a grin that was positively deranged. Niemand looked as if he were trying to disappear into the cushions of the couch he was sitting on.

"Mother's End, it was you. You persuaded the Queen to use the Three to put down the bandits in the bloomward dutchies." Ales' face slid from insanity into an expression of complete innocence.

"I have no idea what you could possibly mean." Ales said in a too sweet voice.

"But how? I've never seen you with the Queen. Why would she listen to you?" Niemand asked. Ales shrugged.

"Those are our secrets." Ales said. The expression on his face changed to irritation. Ales could tell that he was a man who was used to everyone being afraid of him, or at least showing him a modicum of respect. He seemed completely unsure how to deal with his current situation. He stood up.

"I think that I have been more than forthcoming when I did not have to tell you anything. I'm leaving now." He said, and he strode towards the door his cloak swirled around him.

"Peace Niemand. We must be careful what information we share about what we are doing here. We are only two, and in this world there are many threats to the return of the Tier." Ales said.

"But knowing what we know now I believe we can share some of it." Lia said. He did not seem reassured. He seemed afraid.

"If the Tier return what will become of our Order?" Niemand asked, his voice seeming more gravely than it had been.

"We will not lightly take from you thousands of cycles of history Niemand. I think that it is possible that yours will not be the first group we will need to make ties with." Lia said. Ales nodded in agreement.

"My sister is right. I believe that you do good work with your Structures. I think we will need to share more information, but the situation is delicate right now. Be patient with us, and we will help you in kind?" Ales tilted her head making it a question.

{Are you any closer to figuring this out?} Lia asked.

"Somewhat. The royal histories show a distinct change in the ruling nobles of Vilhena about a hundred cycles ago. There are a number of events that normal historians would not place together as similar. But when I applied the Circle of Finding to them the pattern emerged rather quickly. You would almost certainly see it better than I would. You were always a better Finder than I." Ales explained.

{I don't have enough space left to take in everything you have.} Lia said.

"The things I wouldn't give to have access to the Core are few right at this moment." Ales said.

{Perhaps, we could call on the Father?} Lia suggested. Ales paused for a long moment. It was just the sort of help that the God would be able to provide.

"What was that call you used to say for him?" Ales asked.

{Oh Gods, no not that.} Lia looked mortified.

"I seem to remember..." Ales started. Lia waved her foremost paws.

{Don't, that was awful!} Lia begged her.

"But he came right away!" Ales teased her. Lia put her head down on the floor, and covered her head with her massive front paws.

{Augh, don't remind me! Do you know how many times I have heard that story from his side in the five hundred cycles I was with him?} Lia complained.

"Fine, fine. Perhaps something more traditional. How many people still call to them Lia?" Ales asked. Lia took her paws off her head, and looked up at the serious question.

{I would say about a third. Most folks don't believe in magic anymore, and so they don't believe in our gods. I think we will have to make them believe again.} Lia said. Ales sighed.

"Will you call with me? I know you are uncomfortable speaking human languages now, but it has been a long time." Ales asked her hopefully.

{Of course I will.} Lia said. Ales lowered herself to the floor, and folded her legs. She put her hands on her knees, and took a deep breath.

"Father of stone, we call to you by stone, in stone your will is written, in stone we know your hand, by stone we show our reverence, through stone we call your name." Lia intoned. She ceremoniously spread the toes of her right forepaw, and pressed it against the stone floor. Then Ales spoke.

"Father of wind, we call to you by wind, in wind your voice is revealed, in wind we feel your touch, in wind we speak our tribute, through wind we call you to us. We your children beg you, heed our call, see our need."

Ales closed her eyes, and held the spread fingers of her right hand towards the ceiling. There was a long moment when everything seemed to stop. Neither of them breathed. Then the moment passed. The Father did not appear, but it was likely with the formal call that he would as soon as he could. That moment made it obvious that they had drawn his attention. Lia seemed a little disheartened that he did not come immediately.

"Don't worry Sister. We belong to the Father, and Mother. We are theirs, and they will heed our call when they can. There is still a lot of work to do before Skyfire, and only two span to do it in. You have new ones to teach, and I have to go over the plan with Cole so he doesn't get himself killed." Ales said.

{Tell me about the bits you have pieced together?} Lia asked.

"A delegation visited Vilhena from the Relasal Empire far moonward. They brought gifts including two swords that are described in the history as peculiar. With black blades, and strange gemstones in the hilts one would think they would be well cared for. However, no one is sure what happened to them.

An uprising in the Greenlands past the borders of Vilhena killed one of the Royal Family who was traveling the road through that area. But later, that member of the family returned alive and well despite the fact that there were verified reports of their death. The most disturbing fact is that the uprising was sponsored by a faction of the Linqual in retaliation for an attack that Harrad Roa, one of the princes at the time, made on a convoy of Linqualy traders. But none of the information I have obtained has ever shown that to be in the character of the Linqual. Worse, by all reports, the assassins took the body of Stanta Roa with them. He just appeared at the gates of the palace all on his own.

Directly after his return, they began construction on an entirely new wing of the Searchers compound below the palace. And finally tying all of those things together is the disappearance of a ship bringing materials from across the Grey Tide. Materials used specifically in the creation of Bondstructs which was later found adrift with no sign of its crew. Yet not a single bit of the cargo had been touched, there was no damage to the ship. It just floated into the Vilhenan harbor at Nestral all on its own. This from the Kingdom of Tiaqua also moonward on the other side of the Sea of Grass."

Lia was certain that the facts that she laid out had not been put into such order in the history texts she had absorbed, but when put in this order...

{I would need to see more of the data to make a full decision. But what does Finding tell you?} Lia asked.

"One final piece of information. The materials that came off of that ship, were brought directly to the palace. Care to guess what they were used for?" Ales asked.

{Is there record of it?} Lia said with growing unease.

"No, but I know. Because I have seen it. They made five sets of bondarmor. Five sets that have been used in perpetuity by the Royal Family."

{You think...} Lia began.

"I'm not sure what I think Lia. My Vision tells me that something happened to that armor that changed the way the rulers of Vilhena treat with the nations around them. Until those events happened they ruled with quiet strength. They defended their borders, and their people, but they never sought to conquer neighboring lands."

{So you do think someone is using that armor, and those structures to control the royal family somehow?} Lia said. Her mindvoice held a mixture of horror, and disgust.

"That is the pattern my Vision shows me. It is further evidenced by what happened with the assassin who tried to kill you. She had rudimentary Cellstructs, and when I began to question her they turned against her. She died almost instantly." Ales explained.

{When were you going to tell me about that?} Lia said angrily.

"When I knew enough to make it meaningful. The Cellstructs destroyed not only her but themselves before I could find out more. In other words, now." Ales said. Lia narrowed her eyes, and bared her teeth at Ales.

"What a grump." Ales said. Lia folded her ears back.

{Am not.} She said, her expression returning to something much less threatening.

"Whatever Spook, not going to argue with you." Ales said.

{Am not.} She repeated, and Ales grinned.

{So what are we going to do about it?}

"For now, I think I am going to go and find someplace with a good drink." Ales said. Lia nodded.

{When you see Cole...} Her mindvoice sounded guilty.

"I will do what I can Lia, but you know I can't force him." Ales said.

{I know, just tell him I am sorry. Again.} Lia said. Ales nodded, and headed for the Balcony.

"Like as not I won't be here when you get back. I have a date with the Queen tomorrow breaking." Ales said.

{Please be careful. I'm still not sure that Niemand will keep your secrets from Lord Faln. I don't want you walking into an ambush in that silly dress with none of your weapons.} Lia said.

"I will, but I think that one knows how to keep secrets that are not his." Ales said. She ducked out onto the balcony, and disappeared into the night.

39

Niemand slipped through the window to Faln's study. The lord had called him through their normal channels. He wore a furious expression.

"Have you caught her?" Faln asked. His voice held barely contained rage.

"No I have not, nor shall I be in the near future. You seem to have stumbled upon something that you do not quite understand Faln. That katali is one of the Tier, and I could no more catch her than I could pull the sun from the sky." Faln's furious expression fell away into quickly hidden fear.

"Gods, I..." His voice trailed off as if he had lost all of his words.

"Gods indeed. And we both best hope that they do not take interest in that little activity of ours lest we both find out exactly how real they are. I was, surprised as well." He said, and suppressed his near laugh ruthlessly.

He would have sounded utterly mad had he laughed with that thought running through his mind. Those two had scared the wits right out of his head. Faln though seemed to be having some sort of crisis of faith right then. Niemand eyed him, then shrugged.

"I can see you need some time to process this my Lord. Perhaps I should return at a better time." He said. He slid closer to the window, but Faln shook himself like a hiluk would shake water from its pelt and straightened.

"Can you find her again Darkness?" He asked. Niemand turned back to him.

"I think that might be possible. But do not ask me to attempt to capture her. I cannot. She is beyond the limits even of our entire order." Niemand answered.

"No, no of course not. I would simply like to speak with her if that is somehow possible?" Faln asked. He seemed different somehow. Niemand thought that he was broken. Lia had only been a small part of a much larger plan, but somehow finding out that she was one of the Tier had destroyed it for him.

"I must warn you Faln, our contract is at an end. I am unable to complete my assigned duties. The funds held in escrow will be returned to you within the day. If you attempt violent action against her I will not stand on your behalf. Believe me when I tell you she has held back until now. She is not an enemy, and if you had not pursued her with such wanton abandon your man would not have died. She defended herself nothing more." Niemand said.

"I know. I am not a petty man Darkness. I try not to be, but I knew the second that I saw him after his coronation that Terran Roa was not the same man I grew up with. Perhaps it is selfish of me to topple a kingdom for my reasons, but the Terran Roa that I knew would not have done the things he has these past cycles. I want my friend back, and if that means I must put my trust into mythological people then that is what I will do." Faln said.

It was more sense than Niemand had been led to believe Faln had. Perhaps in the face of the Tier no one could keep hold on what drove them completely. He certainly hadn't.

"I will see if it can be arranged. They will want to meet somewhere netural, or likely inaccessible to others." Niemand said.

"I will go wherever they will meet me. I will come alone." Faln said. Niemand nodded. He stepped onto the window sill and disappeared into the night.

40

Ilsa closed her eyes. She concentrated on her belief. It irritated her that Warran was so quickly outpacing her with his Vision. He had learned to gain control two spans ago, and had been learning about the Circle of Repair. He was sitting cross-legged on the ground a few marks away. In front of him was a tarp covered in the parts of some complex machine. She wasn't sure what it was even though she had some of the same abilities as he did. She wasn't sure he knew what it was for. It was something that Ales had fabricated for them as a challenge for their Fixer abilities. He spoke up.

"This can't be what I think it is." He said.

"What does your Vision tell you? You have to learn to trust it Warran." Lia said. His fingers ran over the tiny pieces and parts.

"It tells me that this is a legend. One of the great works of the Tier." He said. Lia grinned in that terrifying feline way she had.

"I'm not sure I would call it a great work. Though it was the source of many a story." Lia said.

"But I thought that these were magical?" He said.

"They are magical, but not the way you were thinking. They require Fixer magic to assemble properly. You can't meld some of the pieces together otherwise. Windblades are amazingly useful tools, but they are more delicate than the stories would lead you to believe. They need constant maintenance, and repair. They also require greater than human strength to use at their full capacity. This was one of the tests of a newly minted Fixer. To properly construct a Windblade shows that you have made a strong bond with your magic." Lia explained.

Warran slid back away from the tarp. "I can't build this. I don't have the tools."

Lia scowled at him. It was a fearsome expression.

"You are Tier. The only tool you need to accomplish any task is your mind. Your mind Warran, builds, not the tools. Open your Vision. Believe." Lia encouraged him.

He swallowed then nodded. His eyes had not made the full change yet, but she could see ruby red bleeding into the green of his right eye. It was only a matter of time until his eyes showed the world what he was. Then it became fully red as the Vision lit his eyes. Hesitantly he picked up a piece, and then another. They fit together with a click a moment later. He would exhaust himself in a few minutes. He did not have enough practice yet using his Vision, and it exhausted him quickly. The mind like any other muscle in his body would need time to adjust to operating at such levels.

She turned back to Ilsa. She had taken that disk of metal out of the pack she carried, and was running her finger over it. Her eyes were glowing with her Vision. Lia padded silently closer to her, and sat down a few marks away in anticipation of helping her close down her Vision. Ilsa ran her thumb over the pattern carved into the steel disk. She did it over, and over again as if she were trying to memorize it by touch alone. Finally her face broke out into a smile. She closed her eyes, and when she opened them again they were bright. But not with her Vision only with excitement.

"I did it." Ilsa said.

"And you were right, I can feel it now. No wonder it is so hard to explain the difference between knowing, and truly believing." Ilsa said.

"I thought I did a fair job." Lia groused, but her eyes sparkled with contentment.

"What is that?" Lia pointed towards the metal disk in Ilsa's hand with her nose.

"Ales visited me, she explained something about being a newling." Ilsa said.

"She said she was going to try to help." Lia said.

"She explained that our Vision is slightly different when we first open it. That was why just opening it for a quick second, and closing it wasn't a problem. But once I focused on actually trying to see anything I got overwhelmed. Why didn't she just tell you all of this?" Ilsa asked. Lia shrugged.

"I simply trust my sister, and she extends me the same trust. Likely she wasn't sure what was wrong until she actually got a look at you."

"Well when I open my Vision I," She paused trying to think of how Ales had explained it.

"She said I was zoomed in down to as far as my Vision would let me see. So I couldn't really focus on any one thing, it was just too much to process." Lia was nodding.

"It makes sense. When I open my Vision nothing really changes until I start focusing on things. If you were seeing all of that it is no wonder you got overwhelmed. I'm sorry I didn't even think of it." Lia said.

"Your sister said you are not a newling so you were unlikely to know." Ilsa said. Lia shrugged again.

"She's right for the most part. Most Tier start out the same, but newlings are all a little unique in their Vision. I've never taught other Tier, and it's been three thousand cycles. I'm a little rusty." Lia explained. Ilsa smiled, her delight at finally having taken control of her Vision was obvious.

"Congratulations Ilsa Ulwren, my sister, you are one of the Tier." It was the same way she had congratulated Warran when he had finally gotten control of his Vision after almost ten span of fruitless struggling. Lia stood on her two hind sets of legs, and put her paws lightly on Ilsa's shoulders so she was face to face with the girl.

"Never forget Ilsa. Believe." Lia bent her head, and put her forehead against Ilsa's.

"Anything is possible, if you simply believe." Lia took a deep breath, and released her. She put all six paws back on the ground.

"I won't forget." Ilsa promised.

41

Ales met with Cole in the High Center Square just in front of the Royal Citadel. She led him back through the alleyways towards the apartment.

"You know we don't need to go over the plan again Ales. I have it down. I will keep moving they won't catch me. It is what I am good at." Cole said.

"I'm not terribly worried about that Cole I need something more. Lia will not approve of what I am going to ask you to do. This is the part that I spoke to you of about your life being in danger." She lead him to the fire stairs outside of the glass, and steel monolith that held her apartments. He didn't have any trouble scaling the stair right behind her. Once they were comfortably ensconced within she sighed.

"I want you to understand how serious this is Cole. If you are caught, you will almost certainly be killed. You are my back up plan. We explained something too you of Tieran minds. There is one in the Citadel. Your distraction will provide me with the opportunity to make contact with the mind. However in the event that the Mind does not have the information that I need to make a decision. I need you to check on five rooms in the Citadel. Five people who wear the bondarmor of the royal family."

"Please tell me you don't want me to steal anything from the Royal Family." Cole said. He sat on the edge of the love seat where Lia liked to sprawl.

"No, but I need to know if they take their armor off. I need to know if they shed their armor when they sleep. Can you do it?" Ales asked. Cole shook his head.

"Sneak into five rooms, and see if they wear their armor when they sleep. I think I can handle that." Cole said.

"Do not take this too lightly Cole. Lia believes that the armor in the possession of the Royal family is strong enough to rival our power in some ways. I have something for you."

Ales reached into the black bag sitting on the divan next to her. He hadn't noticed it before because it was exactly the same shade as her long coat. She took out a pair of lancers. They seemed almost simple in comparison to his reliable old irons.

"I have rebuilt these myself, and have made several improvements to Stoe's design. They won't ever jam, and they will fire a bolt at almost four times the velocity of your lancers. They will fire under water, and filled with sand. They fire every time. The solar cells are the same design as Stoe's so you can use solar cells of that design in these lancers, but they will offer you far less shots. I have made you eight extra cells for each weapon. They recharge in the presence of heat and sunlight at twice the rate meaning each cell can be recharged in about three hours."

Cole looked at them skeptically.

"Don't be a fool Cole, take these. Defend yourself. I will not be responsible for you if you are too stupid to take the help that others have offered you." Ales said. Cole frowned at her.

"You are not responsible for me Ales. I can take care of myself. I have always had to take care of myself. This is no different." Cole said.

"But I am. Paying you or not Cole, if I did not ask you to do this you would not go anywhere near the Citadel." Ales said. She proffered the bag again, and he reached out hesitantly and took it.

"Do you know what these are worth? I could live the rest of my life from selling these and never want for anything." Cole said.

"I suspect you could. Those are one of a kind, and I doubt you will ever see another set like them. The solar cells will never dull with time, so as long as you do not lose them you will never need to replace them. And for Avaara's Love do not let Warran anywhere near them. Maybe one day when his Vision is fully his, but for now do not even show them too him." Ales said.

"Be ready Cole. The Skyfire festival approaches, and we have little time to prepare for what is to come." Ales said.

"Do you have any idea what that actually is?" Cole asked.

"My suspicions are only suspicions Cole. I don't have any concrete proof of what I think will happen. What I do know is that whatever it is, Mother and Father have waited three thousand cycles for me to awaken to attempt to set it right. That tells me that whatever it is we are the only option left to them without direct interference. That would harm not only us, but them beyond all conceivable measure. So whatever threatens our world I will do whatever I must to stop it." Ales said.

He seemed to stare off into the distance for a moment finally getting a better grasp on what they were going to do.

"How do you do it?" Cole said.

"I've been in tight situations before, but this is so much. Yet there you sit talking about toppling a kingdom like I would pick a pocket." Cole said exasperated.

"Toppling a kindom?" Ales grinned.

"Is that what we are doing Cole? If we were only to topple a kingdom I promise you the Gods would not be involved. We would not need a directive from the Gods to topple a corrupt government. We would merely proceed." Ales said.

"I'm going to die." Cole groaned.

"Everyone does." Ales said cheerily.

42

Ales worked her way into the green dress with more skill than Lia would have thought her to have developed considering her self-proclaimed hatred for the outfit. Lia huffed out a breath of annoyance.

{Are you sure it is a good idea to do this before you make your move?} Lia asked.

"No I'm not sure. I'm not sure what I am going to do tonight until I do it. I want to find out how much the Queen knows, she is the only member of the royal family who doesn't wear any armor. The Lordhale tonight is to discuss the Skyfire celebration, and I have my own plans to set in motion. All the necessary distractions for the Lords so that Cole and I can move through the castle with as little resistance as possible will begin tonight." Ales sensed that Lia was going to challenge her plan again.

{I know you have explained before. But why are we doing all of this?} Lia asked. Ales sighed. *{Why do you always do this? Every time you try to take, and do everything? Do you think me incapable of taking care of myself? You have seen my memories. In three thousand cycles I have survived. You lie to me.}* Lia's mindvoice was sad.

"I don't lie." Ales mumbled.

{And what would you call it? Four hundred cycles Ales, and dozens of times you withheld your plans. You told me to defend myself. How can I do that without knowing everything you know?}

Lia wasn't going to stop pushing. She had always been a lot more sensitive about people than Ales was. Ales had given her perfectly good reasons. She didn't want to hurt anyone, and she did need to make herself feel like she were part of the world.

"Because I don't know how to stand up to the idea that I could lose anyone Lia. I never did, and now it is all gone. All of it. Bann, Father, Mother, and everyone else. I've lost it all, and it has not been without damage to me. I told you I am emotionally unstable, and I feel so much anger. So much rage that I am ready to boil over with it. Do you know what is going to happen if I lose control Lia?" Ales asked.

{Then let us step back Ales. I don't want to think about what would happen if you were to lose yourself in a fight.} Just like that

she knew the purpose of all of Ales' seemingly superfluous planning. Her unneeded desire to be part of this kingdom. Ales had never been simple in her motivations. She always had a half dozen reasons for doing anything.

{Gods Ales, why didn't you just say?} Lia asked.

"Do you even really need to ask that?" Ales asked. She took a deep breath and then continued to dress. She took one of the hide shapes off of the dressing dummy next to her wardrobe. She slipped it around her waist with quick practiced movements, and began to tighten the laces. She let out a breath, and pulled the laces fully closed. She tied the knot in the top of the laces, and then tucked the excess laces neatly into an elastic pouch sewn cleverly into the back meant to hide them.

The green of the hide matched her dress. There was a pattern embroidered on the dress in blue. It seemed to flow directly into the hide, and back out the other side. It was a pattern of trefoil leaves that started at her ankles, and wound around her body. It crossed the shape at her stomach, and turned sharply upward. It flowed between her breasts, and then down her arm to circle around her wrist. She looked at herself in the mirror. She untied her braids and teased her hair loose until it fell down around her face. Then it began to fade from her natural shade of light blue to bright yellow. It curled artfully in the process, and she looked at it for a long moment. The long mane of golden curls flowed down her back covering the laces of the shape.

{I'm sorry Ales. I didn't think that...} She trailed off. She started again. *{I always thought of you as...}* She stopped again.

"Invincible. Yes I know Lia. I know everyone thought that about me. But I am just as fragile as anyone. I always was. I tried to tell you, but..." Ales sighed.

{I misjudged. I am so sorry. I thought that what you said was just you trying to adjust. But this is deeper. Are you sure we should continue?} Lia asked.

Ales just shrugged. "What else can we do? I just can't hurt anyone who isn't due such judgment. I could break my mind for a long time if I go too far, and I have just recovered. Avaara believes I am strong enough. I must believe as well." Ales said. She fussed with the yellow curls framing her face.

"What do you think? I don't usually leave it down." Ales asked Lia.

{I like the curls. It makes you look less cute, and more distinguished.} Lia said.

Ales blushed for a moment. "Thank you Lia."

Ales focused on her reflection in the mirror again. The blue freckles that dusted her cheeks, and ran across Ales' nose faded into her skin as if they had never been there at all, and then her tan skin lightened to porcelain. The only thing that didn't change about her appearance was her eyes. There was no way to alter their eye color. It was something they had tried in the past, but their Tieran eye color asserted itself ruthlessly. The minor alterations that could be made by using structures that had gone through a Wild transformation didn't last forever either. They could only work if the structures came from a blood relation, and even then it took regular transfers of Structures as they did not survive more than a few spans outside of their host.

"We need to cycle your structures again Lia. I don't want any of these to die off."

Ales turned away from the mirror, and took a strand of her hair next to her face, and twisted it into a small braid threaded through with a thin strand of green ribbon that matched her dress. She tied it into a clever bow at the end of the braid. She held out her hand palm forward. Lia put her pads of her paw against Ales' palm. There was a familiar tingling feeling in her skin, as Lia's structures slid out through the pores of her skin. The tingling sensation faded for a long moment as the tiny machines made their way back into Lia's body. Then it came again as Liassa sent a new batch of Structures into Ales' body. Ales nodded.

"Thank you Sister." Ales said.

"I'll be careful I promise." Ales said.

Lia knew that it meant more than Ales keeping herself safe. What she was really worried about was that she would lose control. She would become the one thing that she could never be. A destroyer. Ales had never hurt anyone unnecessarily since the incident when she was a child, and if she ever did it would likely be the end of her.

{You do that, for all our sakes.} Lia said.

"So have you found anything about the disappearance of the High Lady Wryn?" Ales asked.

{The only evidence I have found that she was taken is a set of marks on the sill of her window. They appear to be claw marks, but

they are not consistent with any living creature that has claws. What is more is that there is a residue in the marks that I believe to be the husks of destroyed Bondstructs. You should have a look soon. They are beyond my Vision.} Lia explained.

"You think it was someone with Bondarmor?" Ales asked. Lia nodded.

{I think it was the King himself, but I can't tell you why I think that.} Lia paced back and forth as she tried to work it out.

{You should know to trust your instincts Lia.} Ales assured her.

{Do you think he knows about us?} Lia asked.

"Of course he does. He doesn't know us personally, but he knows there are Tier in the city. But only Faln, and the Three Knights actually knew what you look like. And the information I got from Faln's quarters told me he had no images of you to pass around. Not only that, but he didn't want anyone else to know about you. Have you been careful to keep the new ones disguised?" Ales asked.

{We have. Though I am starting to wish I could share my Cellstructs with them.}

"If only it were that simple. How far along are they Lia?" Ales asked worriedly.

{Not far enough. Ilsa at this stage needs you more than me. She needs to learn about Breaking. I worry for Warran as he has no real offensive Circles though it may be without cause. I've never seen anyone use Distance quite like he does. And I think anyone who truly threatened him would find themselves riddled with lancer bolts. I think he may be the most talented Fixer I have ever seen. He constructed the compression engine for his Windblade in under a span. I don't think you could do it faster.} Lia explained.

Ales shook her head.

"My first attempt took me eighteen days. I can do it from scratch in four now, but I was never great with Repair. I don't have the affinity for it like he does. What about the rest of the royal family?"

{Word is that they are out overseeing battle fronts. They only return periodically to report to the King, and leave just as quickly. Cole has paid a number of people around the city to watch for them.} Lia said.

"I didn't see any of them at the last Lordhale." Ales said suspiciously.

"They have to come back sometime." She grumbled.

{I will see what I can find out about them while I am prowling around tonight. I like that word, prowling.} Lia gave a grin.

"Do you actually go in anywhere, or am I going to hear about someone seeing you clinging to the side of a sheer stone wall?" Ales asked. She grinned when Lia scowled at her.

{I may be a Finder, but I also have Taking, do you really think anyone will see me short of you?}

Not waiting for an answer, she trotted towards the balcony.

{Have fun with your hoity-toity friends!} Lia said as she walked through the curtain.

"They aren't my friends!" Ales growled.

"Some of them are!" Lia's voice drifted in like a light breeze. Ales scoffed. Then she turned back to the mirror, but she was finished.

Everything was in place.

43

Lia sunk her claws into the stone of the Archive tower, and pulled herself up to a nook just below the lowest balcony on the side of the tower. Hanging there was not terribly comfortable, but springing her first level of Constraints made it much more bearable. She arranged her second pair of legs so she braced herself horizontally giving her a good look at the open courtyard below. She had beaten Ales to the palace by a fair margin. She wasn't worried about anyone seeing her at this distance, though the guards on the wall might spot her if they were truly lucky.

She watched the High Lords and Ladies mill about in the courtyard. She didn't dare invoke her Vision, as the glow would give her away instantly. Instead she called up her Cellstructs, and her vision swooped in closer until it was like she was walking among the well-dressed crowd below. Her structures were able to enhance the image, and then feed it back into her optic nerves giving her a zoomed in view. It was a trick that was especially effective with her natural katali night vision. She stayed where she was watching more pairs of courtiers enter through the gates.

Finally the carriage that Ales regularly hired to carry her to the palace appeared. She watched Ales take careful steps down the stairs, and move into the crowd with the grace of a dancer. Lia felt a slight pang, not being able to be down there with her. It passed quickly, and she watched Ales with interest. Even she couldn't hear what was being said at this distance, but she knew what Ales was doing.

Part of Ales' plan to keep the guards busy while she looked for Kiltik involved Cole. However the other part involved her arranging it so that certain people would be in the right place at the right time to cause disruptions to the response time of the guards. There was no doubt in Lia's mind that she would succeed. Ales had always been good at getting people to do what she wanted them too. Lia shook her head. They would never know what hit them. But that was not her concern tonight.

She turned herself, and walked along the side of the tower. She kept her center legs splayed out wide to stabilize her horizontally as she made her slow way up the tower towards the roof. Niemand waited for her at the summit, his cloak of Antistructs trembling in the breeze. It was an odd motion almost as if the cloak itself was cold. Standing next to him was the High Commander of the King's guard. Lia watched him warily for any signs of sudden movement.

"Well Niemand you asked for this meeting. Why did you bring him?" Lia chucked her chin towards High Commander Faln. Faln's face showed surprise when she spoke, but it passed quickly.

"You can talk. Why haven't you spoken to my people before?" Faln asked.

"It is a recent development fool. Not that it would have mattered. They watched me, with their own eyes, do things that no katali ever would. It was not enough. So what good would a few words have done?" She snarled.

"The purpose of this meeting please gentlemen? Or I can simply leave." She turned, and padded towards the edge of the roof.

"Please wait." Faln said. Lia looked back over her shoulder, and narrowed her eyes.

"Reasons?" Lia growled.

"I only wish to speak to you. I had no idea that you were one of the Tier. I thought that at best you were in league with whoever, or whatever has taken the mind of my King." Faln said.

Lia eyed the Bondarmor on his shoulder. "Say I believe a single one of your worthless words, what do you want?" Lia asked angrily.

A few simple words were not going to erase three cycles of being hunted relentlessly.. Even if they were true he was not her friend, and never would be. She opened her Vision before he started to speak, and he paused for a long moment staring at her glowing eyes.

"I want my friend back, or I want him dead. I knew Terran Roa every day of his life. And when he took his birthright he changed. No one else seemed to notice, but when I saw him on the battlefield." Faln shook his head.

"Terran had always gone to battle without fear, but he had never enjoyed killing. I saw a darkness in my friend that day. He killed with a smile on his face. Whatever inhabits my friend's body it is not Terran Roa. The Terran Roa I knew would rather be dead than do the things he has done these past cycles." Faln said.

Lia eyed him for a long moment. Then the glow faded from her eyes. She didn't want to believe him, but her Vision told her very clearly that he was telling the full truth.

"How unexpected to find an ally where I would expect an enemy. Know this Harran Faln I don't know what has taken Terran Roa, but we will do what we can to see him set right. If you want your friend back do what has been asked of you. Perhaps it will be enough." Lia said.

"What do you mean?" Faln asked.

"You were approached by a theif who blackmailed you to find a way to get him into the lower reaches of the palace. See to it that they are open when he asked for them to be." Lia said.

"Cole is working for you?" Faln sounded shocked.

"How much do you know about the Tier?" Lia asked.

"What can I know? You are legends. Legends generally do not have convenient books written about them." Faln said.

"Well Faln, the first thing you should know about the Tier is that each of the Tier were chosen, not born. Each of us can come from anywhere, and any background. We do not judge a person solely on their past exploits. Cole is not one of us, but he is skilled, and more importantly he is discrete. Considering the corruption of the nobles that he takes from we feel disinclined to look down upon him for what he does. You yourself have used the resources given to you by the people to your own ends." Lia said.

Faln started to speak, his face twisted with anger. But before he could get a word out he stopped himself. He stared hard at her, knowing she would hear even the slightest lie in anything he said. He knew she was right, and it did not sit well with him.

"Do better Faln. We were already aware of something wrong with the King. We are not sure what the trouble is yet, but we will discover the problem. We will do what we can to remedy it." Lia turned and padded towards the edge of the roof.

"I will make sure that when the Three return they will not hunt you any longer." Faln said.

"Do that. Niemand we will need to speak again before you go. Find me where we first met." Lia said, and then she leapt off the edge of the roof.

Faln held up a hand as she disappeared over the side, but Niemand stopped him.

"Don't. She is already gone." He said in his sandpaper tones.

"She was, not what I expected." Faln said.

"In what way?" Niemand said.

"She didn't attempt to kill me." Faln said.

"What made you think that she would?" Niemand seemed genuinely perplexed by the idea.

"The Tier were always made out to be like heralds of a vengeful god to those who did bad things. I guess I just thought she would be more..." Faln trailed off at a loss for the right words.

"Harran Faln, I do not think you or I ever want to see her when she is in the mood to exact justice upon those who do terrible things." Niemand said.

44

Ales moved through the crowd taking careful note of the people that she wanted to speak to the most. The guard commander Faln was nowhere in evidence, but he was only one part of the chain of command for the palace guards. Truly he wasn't necessary to her plan. The five Watch Commanders were all here by invitation of the King, and so would they be for the Skyfire feast. They would be the ones she would need to maneuver, or more importantly their guards were the ones to be maneuvered.

The palace guard had fifty members that worked the interior of the palace, and four of them were always on duty watching the entrance to the lower levels. She could deal with four fairly easily without hurting anyone. But if the whole guard showed up people were going to die. It didn't hurt that she had persuaded the Queen to allow her to take control of the planning of the festivities. Watch Commander Pheris was the first one on her list. If she was lucky she wouldn't have to speak with the others. She watched him speaking with the other commanders, and when they broke away from each other she stepped up next to him. Pheris was a blocky man, square jawed, and square built. His tight suit showed the muscle beneath emphasizing his strength.

"Commander Pheris, just the man I wanted to speak to."

His expression changed from the jovial unconcern he had had when speaking with the other commanders to one of wary annoyance. Pheris did not like her very much. Her eyes made him uncomfortable, and his attempts to find out more about her had made no headway. His concern was actually genuine, which made Ales hate herself for manipulating him. He wasn't sure why the Queen had taken a shine to her. Mother give me strength. She thought as he scowled at her.

"Lady Brightwater, a pleasure I am sure." He said in a frosty, but even tone. His bass rumble did not intimidate her like it did other people, and that was a second mark against her in his book.

She reached into her small handbag and removed a folded sheet of paper.

"These are the guard deployments for the festival night. I have two performing troupes coming in to entertain the guests, and I would rather not have the guards tripping all over them." She said briskly. He frowned.

"What does a Lady know of guard deployments?" He asked hotly. She stepped closer to him.

"Enough to know that they will be in the way if they are left as you have them now." She growled. He eyed her incredulously. It was as if to him she were some sort of odd new animal that he had never seen before. Something that he was thinking of eating, but he wasn't sure how it would taste.

"Unless you think the Queen needs to be involved in this matter?" She asked snappishly. That got his attention.

"No Milady. I can handle this. As long as it does not put the security of the palace in jeopardy I will see the guards are arrayed as you have outlined."

He took the piece of paper, and unfolded it. He examined it for a long moment, and then frowned. Ales grinned inwardly, but did not let her delight show on her face.

"I think that we can work with this just fine Milady. Might I ask where you got these?" He asked.

"You might. I drew them up myself using the palace designs. I think you will see that it will provide your men with more mobility while keeping them out of the way of the performers." She said.

Before he could say another word she spun on her heal, and slid away from him as quickly as her dress would allow. She didn't need to look back to see the dumbfounded look on the man's face. She couldn't be sure that he would use her plans, but her instincts told her there was a high probability that he would claim the plans to be his own. She had made certain that no one was looking at them when she handed over the paper. No one but she and the Watch Commander would know where the plans had come from.

She moved along to the next person on her list. Matron Silina was the mistress of the palace kitchens, and she was also going to be the one taking care of where the performers would be stationed in the palace. Ales stopped next to the banquet table. She didn't have to wait long for the Matron to come bustling out of the doors to the kitchens. She was a surprisingly thin woman for someone who spent her days in the kitchens. What she did have was that competent air of a woman who managed the kitchens as if they were a finely tuned machine. Her silver hair was done up in a neat bun, and she wore a pair of spectacles perched on her pert little nose. Her blue eyes focused on Ales who was currently standing between her, and the banquet table.

"Lady Brightwater?"

"Hello Silina. I wanted to give you the placements for the performers." Ales said, and she held out a crisp folded sheet for Silina.

"Oh, thank you Lady. I will see to it that this makes it to Ellena." Ales nodded her head graciously.

"I trust that the banquet arrangements I proposed are adequate?" Ales asked. At that the woman brightened with real joy.

"Oh yes Milady. I am so glad the Queen put you in charge Lady Brightwater."

The Matron scowled at a plump High Lady across the room. High Lady Gans had been in charge of the Skyfire celebration at the palace for the last five cycles. Matron Silina had bashed heads with the woman at every festival. It was a regular rant with the old Matron about how the woman organized the same tired old festival every cycle.

"Be kind Silina, she was the only one who would do the job." Ales said with a fond grin for the old Matron.

"Not much of a job." Silina grumbled. Ales could not contain a giggle. That got a wide smile out of the Matron.

"Everything is in order Lady Brightwater." Silina made a little bow of respect, and then bustled away making sure the tables were arranged properly for dinner.

Ales went on her way. She had one more person to talk to before she could enjoy herself for the ending. She made her way across the room to where High Lord Nivus stood. The commander of his house guard was with him, as he had been at every function since the first Lordhale she had attended. Both of them were dressed to the nines, and he was still wearing his stupid feathered hat. He saw her coming too late to move away. She was nearly standing on top of him before she drew his attention. His guard commander stepped up next to him. Ales eyed him. Her eyes roved over him once, and then she dismissed him. She returned her gaze back to Nivus.

"What's the matter little man? Afraid of a woman?" Her smile widened into something that was beyond all sanity. He opened his mouth to speak, but found that he had no response.

"Tell your bootlicker to scarper off. I would have words with you." Ales said. It was an effort to make the tone of her voice match that which she had chosen as the voice of Lady Brightwater. She despised this man, and wondered idly how people like this ever came from the First People.

The giant man growled at her.

"Now, Nivus, or I will teach him why he should fear me like you do." She said.

The gorilla clenched his hands into fists. She raised a brow at him.

"Do try it. Please." Ales said maliciously.

Nivus' bodyguard looked like he was about to do just that when Nivus held up his hand. He waved away his guard commander quickly.

"What do you want, imposter?" Nivus growled. It was an affectation. He was terrified of her.

"I want you to make yourself scarce. If you appear at the Skyfire festival you will not be seen again. No one will know what happened to you. Do not bring your guards, do not bring yourself. If I glimpse you anywhere in the city the span of the festival I promise you that no one else will ever again." Ales said. Nivus opened his mouth, and Ales hissed.

"I'm not done. While you are busy not being at the Skyfire festival you are going to be spending your time making sure that all of your servants, and all of your commoners are repaid for the last fifty cycles of financial rape and destruction your family has visited upon them. Convince me that you will be a High Lord that takes care of his people, or you will be a High Lord no more. Make no mistake Nivus there is no place you can hide from me. Now. Be, gone." Ales growled the last two words making him skitter back away from her.

Then he fled.

45

Niemand stood on top of the wall surrounding Vilhena. He couldn't stay for very long or the guards would see him. Fortunately he did not have to wait He saw her slip over the edge of a rooftop adjoining the wall right when she said she would. He got a short running start, and jumped from the wall. His cloak flailed out behind him, and gave him a short push across the gap. It stretched down below him at his mental command softening the impact as he landed on the roof. He went down to one knee in front of her, and bowed his head.

"Hello Niemand. Please stand. We are not the Gods. We are owed no worship." Liassa said. She sat down, arranging her six legs for comfort.

"You wished to speak to me Arcangineer?" He asked as he stood.

"Niemand, we never expected to encounter anyone using our technology like you do. But we are uncertain that you are safe. We ask that you return to your home, and inform your brothers and sisters that they should return to the monastery. Wait for us there. We will come as soon as we know more about the danger."

"I know more about the danger." A polite, cultured voice said.

Lia's eyes went wide, and she turned to the direction the voice had come from. She spread her two sets of front legs and bowed until she was almost prostrate.

{Goddess.}

Lia watched Niemand out of the corner of her eye. He was frozen, and she read such a mix of emotions on him that she wasn't sure his mind could cope with them all. Even the hardest man or woman could freeze up when meeting the Goddess for the first time. She had that effect on people.

"You should catch him dear one. He is about to collapse." Avaara said carefully.

Lia moved in a blur. She slipped around behind him, and he fell backwards against her side. She allowed him to slide to the ground, and stepped back at just the right time extending her second leg on the right to allow his head to slide to the ground without injury.

"Oh dear." Avaara said.

"That was not my intention." Avaara continued, but Lia gave her a look. Avaara sighed.

"All right there was a fair chance that he was going to pass out and I knew it." Avaara finished. She smiled. Lia almost couldn't bear to look at the beauty of it.

{Should I wake him up Mother?} Lia asked.

"I do not think his mind is ready to cope with encountering one of his deities Daughter. If you wake him there is a fair chance he will simply pass out again." Avaara said slowly. She adopted a sitting position floating a few ticks off the rooftop.

{A fair assessment. What can you tell us Mother?}

"I can tell you only that your sister is right. Something has infected our world through Tieran Structures, and you must discover what it is and stop it. I cannot say more than that. What I and Zezzhz can do is give you this." She reached into the wide sleeve of her dress and removed a small object.

"He heard our call?" Lia asked, a little astonished. She had gone so long without his attentions. She should not have doubted him.

"Of course he did my Child. We would never abandon you if we can help. We may not always be able to answer, but we will always be listening." Avaara said. She held the small cube of unidentifiable metal a tick off the rooftop, and let it fall the last little bit.

"This is a memory storage device?"

"Zezzhz says that this is a small piece of the magic, and technology that was used to create the Core. He asks that you please be careful with it. He does not think that anyone or thing could decipher what he has done, but it is better not to take the chance. Use it wisely my Daughter." Avaara said.

"I assume it is impervious to water?" Lia asked tentatively.

Avaara tilted her head questioningly. "Oh, you must carry it in your mouth. Apologies Daughter. Allow me."

Avaara held up her hands, and the moss of her dress began to grow around her wrists. It flowed away from her arms twisting around itself. Then it began to take a shape. It formed into a small satchel with a strap just long enough to fit over Lia's head. The moss detached itself from her arms, and the satchel floated between her long delicate fingers. Then the moss fell away dissolving to leave behind a small leather satchel of exquisite construction. It had threads of gold stitched through it. The pattern stitched into it she recognized right away. It was one of the only ways to identify one of the Wild from a normal animal. They were all marked with the symbol somewhere on their bodies. To those of the Tier they could use their Vision to see the symbol instantly. It showed up on the body of one of the Wild like a glowing beacon in the presence of the Vision.

Avaara picked up the small device, and placed it into the small satchel. It floated across the space between them, and slipped over Lia's head.

"Thank you Mother. Did you know about them?" Lia pointed towards the man lying on the rooftop with her chin.

"Lia I am sorry that this will be so difficult for you. I am sorry we cannot tell you everything we know. I am sorry that there are so many jarring things that you will have to discover for yourself." Avaara said.

Lia shook her head. Avaara's explanation had been more than sufficient to assure her that the God and Goddess would help in any way they could.

"I understand. We will do whatever we can to be your will in the world Mother." Lia promised.

"I know you will my Child. Be safe, and our blessing to you all." And she was gone.

Lia touched a paw to the satchel hanging around her neck. It felt warm to the touch, and oddly comforting. She wondered idly if that was Avaara's touch on it. She looked down at Niemand, and grunted when he did not stir. She made a connection to the structures making up his cloak, and mentally commanded the mask over his face to part for her. She sighed with resignation, and then bent her neck and licked his face.

It was not the first time she had had to wake someone this way. Of the options available to her it was the most gentle. However she had come to the conclusion long ago that people did not taste good. It wasn't so bad if they had salt on their skin from sweat but more often than not she could only taste the oils. Still she didn't have a handy bucket of water, and if she tried to slap him awake it was likely as not to leave him with gashes. Freakishly sharp claws were not always an advantage she noted absently. So she kept licking him until he spluttered and sat up.

He stared at her with a poleaxed expression. He made a Wordless squawk of disgust, and pointed at his face as if to ask what in the name of the gods she had been doing.

"You faint like a sissy girl, and it's not like you taste like a fine cut of meat let me tell you. Would it kill you to bathe every once in a while?" She said sarcastically.

He made a show of wiping off his face with his coat sleeve. "Beast." Was all he said, but it was said almost playfully despite his gravel voice.

"Be careful Darkness someone might be in danger of thinking you actually have a soul." She said sweetly. His face went blank as he realized that Avaara was gone.

"That was Her." He whispered. It wasn't a question, but Lia answered as if it was.

"It was. I think she would have liked to speak to you, but she assessed that you would not be able to stay conscious in her presence."

"I'm not sure what came over me." He said touching his hand to his forehead.

"It is a reaction to her power that some people have on being in her presence the first time. She does nothing without a reason, and if she did not mean to speak to you she would not have come while you were here. You will see her again soon." Lia said.

"Couldn't she have just woken me?" He asked.

"Can't she just do anything?" Lia shook her head.

"Not without consequences. Likely she would damage you if she had tried to keep you awake the first time. It's like being sick, and then getting better. For a while you will be fairly immune to sickness because of the antibodies your immune system generates. It's like that. Once you have been close to her once you won't have a reaction like that again." She said.

He eyed her skeptically. "I'm not sure I believe you." He said. She shrugged indifferent to whether he believed her or not.

"What I was saying before Niemand has become all the more clear. You need to pull your brothers, and sisters back to the monastery. You are in control of a power that I am not sure you fully grasp the damage it could do in the wrong hands." Liassa said.

"I think that we do. But you may be right. We have never fully deciphered everything that your Wild brother passed on to us." Niemand said.

"Come here," she said.

He stepped closer to her. She held up a paw, and a small collection of the structures that made up his cloak slid across the ground towards her. She turned her paw pads up, and the cluster crawled up one of her legs, across her back, and onto the pads of her paw. She mentally instructed them to obey only this one, and deny connections to anyone who was not one of the Tier. She waved her paw. The group of tiny machines fell to the ground, and slunk back to rejoin the rest. They would spread the instructions to the rest of the microscopic machines in his cloak, and subsequently to the rest of the Antistructs as they came in close enough contact with them.

"I have made an adjustment to your Antistructs so that they obey only you, and do not permit access to themselves for anyone except you or the Tier. It will spread these instructions to other Antistructures that get close enough to you. They will obey only their current masters. This is the best defense I can give you until we can come to all of you and do something better. Until then admit no one who cannot prove themselves to be one of the Tier." Liassa said.

Niemand nodded his head.

"By your command Arcangineer." He bowed formally.

"Good luck Niemand. I will see you again." Lia said. He turned, and his cloak propelled him up onto the wall again.

46

Liassa trotted across the rooftops of the buildings that followed the wall between the High Center, and the Low Center. She paused long enough to touch the bag hanging around her neck. It still felt warm even a long hour later. She took a few fast steps, and then made the jump to the next flat rooftop. As soon as her paws hit the rooftop her Structures blared alarms inside of her head. She fell flat to the ground tucking her tail between her legs.

Something zipped over the top of her head just missing the tips of her ears. She threw herself into a roll to the right, and opened her Vision to better process what her structures were trying to tell her. She threw open the doors on three of her five levels of Constraints, and then blurred forward across the rooftop. She jumped to the next rooftop without even a pause. Whoever was attacking her was fast, but not nearly fast enough. By the time the sound of boots hit the rooftop behind her she was already across the roof. She faced back the way she had come.

Standing across the rooftop was a figure clad in shimmering silver armor. He was just under five marks tall, but other than that she could tell nothing about him through the armor save for his scent. But his scent was all she really needed. Her Cellstructs told her that this man was one of the royal family. The youngest she thought, if the descriptions she had been given were anything to be believed. He was supposed to be an impressive swordsman.

"Well, it appears that you are rather interested in me." Lia said. He didn't stiffen when she spoke which was only mildly surprising. The Royals would hear all the rumors.

"Illya Roa." She said.

Then he did stiffen. It lasted only a moment before he drew his sword. It was a long curving saber slightly wider at the point than the hilt. It had a wide steel knuckle guard that protected his fingers

"So the rumors are true." His voice was oddly distorted as if it were coming down a long metal pipe.

Lia narrowed her eyes. Then opened her Vision wider invoking the Circle of Light. This was the moment she always feared no matter how many times it came. When she was forced to kill someone again. And there was no question in her mind that one of them would not walk away from this fight.

"Yes, the rumors are true."

Her eyes darted from side to side. There were at least a dozen men on surrounding rooftops in shadow black bondarmor. She could not out-run them all, but she could move the fight to somewhere where she might only be forced to kill the one man.

"What do you want?"

"You, dead by the order of the king." He said.

"You want my head boy, come and take it. If you can." Lia taunted. And she turned away from him.

The roof nearly shattered from the force of her paws as she pushed off. Then the city was a blur behind her. She had two more levels of Constraints to release, but she could not operate at a level higher than this without damaging herself. There were consequences to that kind of power. Chimneys and rooftop machinery went by like a picket fence as she ran for the forest. Then she was clearing the wall.

She landed outside, and sod flew from beneath her paws as she took off into the forest. She heard him hit the ground when she was a hundred marks from the wall. He was fast, and if he was well acquainted with his armor he would be able to keep up with her in a foot race. The armor was doing all the work for him. The run wouldn't last long. She needed just enough time. The lesser armors of the men he had brought with him would never be able to keep up with her. She needed just enough time to beat him. She ran for the clearing where they trained the young ones. She burst through the bushes at the edge of the clearing, and she felt it.

The presence of the Mother was strong in this place. It wasn't truly the Mother aiding her, but this place would favor her because of the Mother's presence here. She skidded to stop in the center of the clearing, and spun to face back towards the city. She lashed her tail once, and then stood perfectly still. The King's son appeared at the edge of the clearing. He stopped in a spray of dirt, and grass just before crossing out of the woods. Lia's luminescent eyes tracked his every movement. He didn't rush her though. He stood at the edge of the clearing just watching her. She knew he was waiting for his men. He was intelligent in battle that was for certain.

If he wouldn't come to her, she would just have to go to him. She pushed open the barrier on the fourth level of her Constraints. Every muscle in her body tightened to an obscene level. She felt taunt like a thread on the verge of snapping. Then she moved. A hundred marks across the clearing was gone in an instant. She leapt into the air, and hunched up her body lining her paws up with his body. She slammed her rear legs into his thighs. Her second set of legs hit his stomach driving the air out of him. The plates of his armor flexed almost to snapping as they fought to absorb the impact. The sound was like an explosion. Lia's structures flowed out onto the claws of her forepaws, and she dug them into his shoulders. They pierced his armor as if it were paper though they did not make it to his flesh. Overlapping plates beneath stopped her claws from penetrating completely, but she had accomplished what she needed to.

She pulled as hard as she could putting all of her weight into it. She overbalanced him and rolled onto her back pulling him on top of her. With her two rear sets of legs she pushed. She retracted her claws from his shoulders at the same time. The result was that he was thrown in a violent arc towards the center of the clearing. He was still in the air as Lia rolled to her feet. She bolted towards the center of the clearing. Halfway there as he was on the way down she jumped. It would have been easier if she had the Circle of Distance to help her, but she knew her body well. She flew into the air as high as she could manage, and came down on top of Roa. She bent her legs, and she landed on his back just as his body rebounded from hitting the ground. She pushed as hard as she could multiplying the force of her fall.

All six of her feet hit his body with tremendous force. There was a thunder clap of sound when his body hit the ground. The armor on the front of his body exploded away from him in a torrent of shattered metal that flew in all directions. Lia cringed inwardly as dozens of his bones shattered. He gasped once, and then was dead. She tried to brace herself, but there was nothing that she could do.

The pain of his death washed over her like liquid fire. She unashamedly let out a roar of pain that trailed off into a sob. It left an ache in her bones that made her wonder if she should have done something different as it always did. This had not been an animal she was going to eat, but his death had been just as necessary. It didn't help the ache that she felt as she steadied herself on her feet. She closed down the fourth level of her Constraints. Her structures rushed around inside of her body attempting to repair the half dozen badly torn muscles that had happened from operating at such a supernatural level.

"Mother protect your soul Illya Roa."

Lia stepped away from the cooling body. Then startled away as her structures shouted a warning into her mind. The Bondarmor that had protected Illya moved on its own. It flowed around him, and pooled in the grass next to him like mercury. A tendril had grown out from it, and was reaching towards Lia. Initial shock passed she examined the pool from a distance. The metal was definitely trying to get to her, and she tried to mentally connect to the Bondstructs in it so that it wouldn't attach to anyone else.

The sensations coming from her Cellstructs overwhelmed her immediately. Blaring alarms bounced off of the inside of her skull like a handful of ball bearings bouncing in a bucket. Lia groaned, and stumbled to one side trying to get control over them. She mentally assured them that she would not attempt to connect to the Bondstructs in the armor again. The cacophony in her head quieted. Voices shouted out from the forest around her, and she remembered the men Illya had brought with him. She did not want to leave his Bondarmor free, but there was no time to deal with it. When she mentally queried her structures about why they could not connect she found that the wireless handshake from the Bondstructs had been corrupted somehow. They were not controlled by Tieran intelligence any longer. There was something else there. She cursed herself inwardly for not being strong enough in the Vision to see what had happened to cause the corruption. Ales would have been able to do something, gain something from this.

The voices got louder, and she had an idea. She held up her forepaw, and added more Cellstructs to her claws. She did not want to lose any of her Cellstructs. Each one was tiny in the grand scheme of things but together they did so much for her. She darted forward, and swiped her claws through the pool of liquid metal. A tendril darted out towards her again but it was too slow. Her Cellstructs encased the tiny residual traces from the armor. She poured more and more of them out of her skin until there was a tiny pellet no bigger than the head of a pin in the center of her paw. This she dropped into the bag hanging around her neck. Then she stood, and waited for the men to make it to the clearing.

She checked her Cellstructs for the status on her damaged muscles. She found that they had done their job well, and that she was completely free of damage. They gathered at the edge of the clearing. Clothed in matte black armor from head to toe they made Lia shiver. They would all be under the control of whatever had infected Illya's Bondarmor. She waited until they began to move cautiously forward before she shouted.

"Let it be known to you whatever you are, the Tier did not begin this. The consequences of hunting us be on your head." She shouted.

Then she turned and bolted across the clearing. She fled into the woods. Many of the men chased her, but their Bondarmor was not up to the task of keeping up with her. It didn't matter. They would return to the city with news of her soon enough. Their ruse was over. She could not outrun that. She would have to be much more careful from now on.

– END OF PART 4 –

Ilsa picked herself up from the ground. It was not her imagination. She was getting better. Her bruises barely hurt anymore, and her body had hardened over the spans as she worked with Lia before Ales had started teaching her to fight.

"That was excellent Ilsa." Ales said.

"I still lost." She growled, and took the stance Ales had shown her. She centered herself using her Vision. She brought up her hands.

"Ilsa it is not about winning or losing. We are here to hone your skills. You will not learn everything I have to teach you in a handful of spans. Even then I have had hundreds of cycles to sharpen the skills I was taught. For now learn what I have to teach you. You are still leaving your left open. Ready?" Ales said.

Ilsa nodded to her. The exchange was quick. Ales threw a punch meant for Ilsa's stomach. Ilsa stepped aside using her left hand to push the blow away. Ales spun, and dropped down using her hands to balance herself she kicked a leg at Ilsa's ankles. Ilsa jumped over her leg. Ales saw the glow of Ilsa's Vision as she came back to her feet. She continued the spinning motion that was a hallmark of Tieran martial arts. Her leg lashed out as Ilsa was coming down from her jump. Ilsa saw it coming, and put both of her hands forward. The blow slammed into her palms tossing her into a backward flip. Ilsa controlled the motion though completing the flip.

She skidded to a stop a few marks away, and then dashed forward on the offensive. Ilsa spun, and threw a high kick at Ales's head. Ales caught her ankle, and planted her feet. She turned her hips, and dragged Ilsa off her feet. Ilsa tumbled to the ground in a tangle of limbs a few marks away. She flipped herself over, and laid there on her back gasping for air.

"I think that is enough for today. You are progressing extremely well in using your Vision Ilsa. I think that you should work with Lia on your Finder talents for the rest of the day." Ales said.

"What about Breaking?" Ilsa asked hopefully.

"Not yet. You are not ready for that, but I promise it will be soon Ilsa." Ales said.

Ilsa sighed dejectedly. "Fine. But I could help more with Breaking. My fighting would be better."

"Ilsa!" Ales snapped.

"Breaking is not like the other Circles. It is far more dangerous, and you are still too distracted. I will teach it too you when you are ready. Not before." Ales scolded her.

Ilsa looked down dejectedly.

"Ilsa, you are going to be one of the most powerful Tier ever to exist. You need to understand patience. With power like ours comes the need to be patient. To move only when you are sure of what you are doing. Before you use Breaking you must learn to use its power to see the consequences of what you do before you ever do anything." Ales spoke more softly to comfort her.

"I just feel like I am worthless to you right now." Ilsa said.

"You are not worthless to us. You truly do not understand how much you are helping us just by doing what you are doing. Besides your mind is and always will be far more valuable to us than your fighting ability." Ales explained.

She was worried that Ilsa was already unconsciously using Breaking when fighting. She had known warriors who had trained every day of their lives that would have been hard pressed to fight on an even keel with Ilsa. She would never be a match for Ales. She could never be that committed. But she would be more than a match for any man, or group of men once she got her Cellstructs.

{You sure you don't want to teach?} Lia's mindvoice was only slightly hopeful.

{Only if you want to put on a dress and be High Lady Brightwater for a while. Besides you are a better teacher than I am. You can school her in how to respond to unorthodox fighting. She is at the point right now where she simply needs to practice her technique. Especially against an opponent who is not of human shape.}

{I would be of better use if I were still...} She let the thought trail off. Not willing to say the words that would hurt her.

{Having a human shape would not make you more useful Lia. Need I list all the times your Wild nature has saved our lives? You know the time we didn't freeze to death in the Yuana Peaks because

you dug us a shelter out of the storm? How about...} Lia cut her off.

{All right! You can stop heaping praise on me.} Lia said sourly. Ales ruffled the fur between her ears playfully.

{I love you Spook no matter what skin you wear. That's never going to stop.} Ales said, and Lia leaned her head into the petting enjoying her sister's touch.

{It's about to get rough isn't it?} Lia asked as Ales scratched her behind the ears.

{Yes. You killed one of the Royal family. They will not take that lightly. It will make it harder to convince the Queen to help me once she knows I am one of the Tier.} Lia folded her ears back, and Ales rapped her on the head with a knuckle.

{I'm not correcting you. I wouldn't have done it different. He meant to end your life, and I told you not to let that happen so I can hardly scold you now. I doubt it will matter much to her that he was controlled by some unknown entity.} Ales explained.

"Can I get a piece of the conversation?" Ilsa asked as she folded her legs and sat down.

"I'm sorry Ales. I know you are right. I really have no idea how dangerous it is, and you have been using it for hundreds of cycles. I just want to do more." Ilsa said apologetically.

"That's good, because this will give you that chance."

Ales pulled the small cube of metal from a pouch at her side. Lia had discovered that the pouch that Avaara had given her had somehow become part of her collar. It was unlikely the collar was ever coming off. Every one of the Wild were given a collar like the one she was wearing by the God and Goddess upon their transformation. It had no clasp, and would magically adjust to size as needed. It was a wonderous thing. It also could not be taken off. It would not go past her ears if lifted even though it seemed like it would fit. The only way to get that collar off was to separate her head from her body.

Ales had made a pouch so she could carry the cube instead despite the fact that they were fairly certain that no one but Lia could access the one that Avaara had made. Lia felt more comfortable with Ales carrying it. When Ales had reached inside the one around her sister's neck was nothing in it. But when Lia touched the pouch anything she wanted out of it would roll out into her paw. When Ales had tried to examine it with her Vision she had been blind for three hours. It was a sure sign that it was a place that the Goddess had bent reality with her will. It was the same effect one got when attempting to examine the Core, and the small metal cube the god had given them.

"This is a memory storage device. It seems it is large enough to hold a half dozen long intervals of memories. More than we will need before we gain access to the Core again. Without structures of your own you will need to maintain contact with the cube to see the memories on it.

I want you to use your Finding to look for patterns in the memories on here. Something is infecting Tieran structures that are autonomous entities. Our personal Cellstructs seem immune to such infection, but Bondstructs seem susceptible. We are unsure if a Tieran Mind would be immune. However we are fairly certain that a Mind would be. We need ideas about what exactly is doing this. Any patterns you can find in all those memories will be of immense help to us." Ales explained.

Ilsa reached for the cube. Lia put her paw between Ilsa's hand and the cube.

"A small warning. Like your Vision the cube will attempt to show you everything it has stored. You have to force it to show you only what you want to see. Be mentally clear about what you want from the cube, and it will acquiesce to your will."

Lia drew her paw back and Ilsa reached out to tentatively touch the cube. Her eyes began to glow softly as she opened her Vision. Her fingers touched the cube, and she stiffened. Every muscle in her body went completely taut, and Lia looked as if she might try to pull the cube away from her. Ales held up a stalling hand.

{*Wait, I think that it is all right. Her mind is just trying to cope with everything the cube is forcing at her. Give her a chance. She's going to be strong Lia. She's never going to be able to match you in many ways, but in the sheer strength of her Vision she will be exceptional. I'm not sure she will quite make it to seeing into the subatomic levels, but the atomic level is a good possibility. She can do it.*} Ales said.

A long moment later Ilsa's body relaxed, and she let out a sigh. Then she started talking. It was impressive considering how new she was to trying to work with other people's memories. It meant that her Finder powers were not just strong but they were nearly on par with Lia's. That was incredible to say the least. Lia was one of the most impressive Finders anyone had ever seen. There were few puzzles she couldn't solve with the use of her Finder powers in a few minutes. But even her abilities had limits, and she had drawn every bit of meaning from Ales' scanning of the Archives that she could. She said that her instincts told her that she was missing a connection that was there.

"Stick with her Lia, and we can all compare notes tonight. We only have a few days left before the Skyfire. I'm going to go fetch Warran. We need to teach them how to properly call on the Mother, and Father tonight. They need to have somewhere to turn if something happens to us." Ales said. Lia nodded.

"I agree. I am trying to arrange a place for us to go. Which direction do we want to go from here?" Lia asked.

"Towards Verdant. These new ones need their own structures. Their Vision would not be enough to keep them safe." Ales said.

"Father's stones I hope it didn't fall into the Abyss." Lia groaned.

"TAKER"

48

Cole jogged across the rooftops towards the High Center wall. He jumped the short gap between the roof and landed on the wall in a crouch. He went to one knee, and pressed the grapple to the top of the wall. It clung to the stone seemingly impervious to being moved ever again. Cole jumped off the wall, trailing a thin wire from the grapple. It was a marvel that Warran had created. He squeezed the grip of the grapple and it began to slow his decent until he touched down on the ground on the other side without a sound. With this thing he could escape from anyone. Even someone in bondarmor couldn't keep up with what this little toy would let him do. He twisted the handle, and gave it a tug. It released the grapple from its setting. The wire zipped back into the handle of its own accord. He caught the grapple, and the wire slowed until it slowly drew the grapple back onto the handle. Warran claimed that even a hard swung sword would not cut the wire, and the handle would self-repair any damage taken in its use. He took out one of his new lancers. He slid the grapple over the end of the lancer, and it snapped into place as if it belonged there.

"He will make greater things than that in his time." A voice startled him from one of the side alleys.

He clutched his chest and gasped for air. "Could you not do that?!" Cole growled as Ales stepped into view.

"But it always so much fun." Ales said.

"I'm going to keel over dead of fright if you continue. That will show you." Cole said, and then grinned.

"He was always brilliant but this." Cole held up the lancer with the grapple attached to it.

"This is magic." Cole said.

"You noticed did you?" Ales said.

"It is a little too perfect. It fits any one of my lancers including the long barrel like it was made to fit there." Cole said.

"There is a bit of magic in there. The Tier can all do a little bending of reality. Not like the god, or goddess." She said quickly.

"It is all little things. We build something it works better.
We talk it sounds better. We want people not to look at us
they don't. It's part of the energy in our Vision. It sort of
pushes around energy in the world a little." Ales said.

"Why do you need me then?" Cole said.

"Mostly because it has limits, and because I can't be in two
places at once. The thing is Cole if I just try to blast my way in
there I'm going to kill people. Innocent people Cole. I know
how you feel about them, but they are just doing what they
think is right. And it hurts me Cole. Even when people are
evil it still hurts, but I can't kill innocent people no matter how
misguided unless there is no other choice. I have to make
plans so that I don't get into a position where I am forced to
hurt someone that doesn't deserve it. That is why I need you."
Ales said.

Cole sensed that she had revealed something to him that
she didn't tell just anyone.

"I'm sorry." He said. He seemed sincere.

"No it's all right. It's something you should know." Ales
said.

"You keep telling me these things like..."

"Like I still expect you to be one of us some day?" Ales
finished for him.

He scowled at her. "I will be so glad when this is over, and
I can get away from all of you insane people." He growled,
but Ales could see the lie for what it was. She just grinned at
him. But then her face hardened.

"There is something else Cole. Lia killed Illya Roa the day
before yesterday."

"What?!" He let out a strangled yelp.

"He left her no choice. He attempted to kill her, and
nothing short of lethal force was going to make him stop. His
armor would have protected him from anything less." Ales
said.

"Gods, they will never stop hunting us now." He said.

"Two days left Cole. Don't make me sorry I lugged all the
gold to town to pay you. If you get dead I will see you
resurrected just long enough for me to kick your ass. Be
careful." Ales said with such sincerity that he wasn't sure she
was kidding at all.

"I will be. I will make sure they never see me." Cole said.

Ales took two folded pieces of paper out of the black bag she carried slung over her chest. It looked like it should just fall open when she handed it to him but it remained tightly folded.

"I came to give you those. The first will not open until the day after tomorrow. It tells you what time you should start on Skyfire Eve. I will not see you again between now, and the festival. So follow those instructions exactly. The other will not open until the end of the span. It contains instructions on how to retrieve your payment should you make it out of this and I do not." Cole took it and slid it into a pocket.

"Do not try to open it early Cole. If you do it will simply disintegrate into dust. Only you can open it so don't give it to anyone else." Ales explained.

"All right I get the picture. If I skip out on the job I don't get paid." Cole grumbled.

"No, you still get paid you simply have to wait until after. I hope you don't suddenly turn into a coward. But mere gold is not enough for what I am asking you to do. It is your life Cole. I would not choose for you." Ales said.

"You mean that?" He said, incredulously.

She shrugged, and turned away. She walked down the alleyway towards the Palace Square. He stared after her for a long while after she had gone. Then he sighed.

He knew what she said was right. That was irrelevant though. He didn't deserve to be one of them, and he knew it. He hadn't earned it like she had. He pointed his lancer towards the roof of the building next to him. He pulled the trigger, and the grapple was launched high over the roof of the building. He grabbed the handle of the grapple removing it from his lancer. Then after he stowed his lancer back in its holster he gave it a short tug, and zipped off towards the rooftop his coat flowing behind him. He shook his head pushing away that vain stupid hope that he could do something better. There was only one thing he had to focus on. One last score, and he could be done with this place forever.

"FIXER"

49

Warran looked at the Terent sitting on his bench. The longbarrel on the bench had some sort of serious problem in the trigger mechanism. He eyed it with annoyance. He had rebuilt it twice already, but it still wasn't working right. He was going to have to get his measuring tools out, and that was going to cost. The things were so delicate that you couldn't use them without recalibrating them which took Bondstructs. He would have to get in touch with Haveran and find out if he wanted to spend the money to fix the old lancer.

He eyed it for a long moment. There was a better way to do this, and he didn't even need the measuring tools. He unscrewed the shielding plate, and pulled it away from the receiver. The connector plate for the trigger mechanism was the problem he knew it. It was just a few microns too wide. Which meant that it wouldn't provide the231onection to allow the flow of elementary energy to activate the force metals. But he couldn't shave it down properly without an exact measurement. He went out into the shop, and closed up for the night. It was a little early, but it wouldn't do to have anyone walking in while he was using his Vision.

"Daddy?" Kayna came down the stairs carrying one of the books he had given her to read.

"Hey Midget, done with that one?" She nodded, and handed it up to him. "Ready for another?" She shrugged, and didn't look pleased at the prospect.

Kayna had never been much for talking. Warran had never understood why she was so quiet, and for a time he thought she might have been mute. Then she had come into his workshop one day, and asked him what he was building. Right out of the blue like she had been talking all along. He had been so startled that he had dropped the current compass he had been working on. It had shattered all over the floor, and cost him a dozen gold pieces to repair. She had been so upset she hadn't spoken again for an entire span. Even now she didn't say much. But what she didn't say in words she made up for in brains. She was thoughtful, careful, and she never shied away from hard work which was why he had always let her set her own pace with what she wanted to learn. That mainly involved everything he knew.

"All right, how about you come watch your old dad do some magic?" Warran asked.

Her eyes lit up, and she nodded. "Daddy, what is wrong with your eyes?" She asked.

He cocked an eyebrow. "What do you mean?"

"One of them is red. It wasn't red before." She said, and eyed him skeptically. He got down on one knee so he was eye to eye with her.

"Remember when I told you I was doing something special baby girl? Something magical?"

She nodded.

"Well that is why my eyes are different." He winked at her with his new red eye.

"It's magic?" She said with a bit of awe in her voice.

"Sure is." He said, and he put his arms around her. He picked her up, and carried her into the workshop with him her braids swinging as she bobbed her head left and right. He put her down on the stool next to his. She looked at the parts of the old longbarrel.

"That's old." She said as she looked over the parts. Six cycles old, and she was as likely to be able to fix anything as he was. He looked at her with all the pride a father could have in his children.

"Yes, old and sick. What do you think is wrong with it?"

She looked at it. She picked up a few of the parts, and touched them together. She put them back down and shrugged.

"I dunno. Something small?" She said.

Warran nodded. "Something small is right baby girl. It's the strike plate on the trigger. It isn't fitting together right because it was machined a hair to big. Your old dad made a little mistake. Watch this."

He opened his Vision. She let out a little gasp when she saw his eyes glowing. He held up the strike plate, and the contact well. When he had them where he could see them both at the same time it became instantly clear exactly how much the strike plate needed to be shaved down. He pulled out a piece of fine grinding stone then put it down on the bench where he could reach it.

"Ready?" He asked. She nodded watching his glowing eyes. "Eyes on the prize, Midget."

He held up the square of metal. He tossed it up into the air, and then picked up the lower piece of the receiver. He snapped the contact plate back into place. Then as the strike plate began to fall he set the receiver down on the bench. He lifted the fine stone, and the strike plate scraped along it, and then fell into the receiver exactly as it should. It snapped into place with a quiet click. His Vision made it so easy to place everything exactly where it should go. He dropped the separation spring into the receiver barely even looking at it. It slid into the channel keeping the trigger strike plate separated from the contact well. He went about the process of reassembling the longbarrel barely even looking at it as he watched her eyes get wider and wider. He slid the bolt back into place finishing the lancer.

"Wow." Kayna whispered when he was finished. He had done it so quickly.

"Think it's fixed?" He asked. She nodded without taking her eyes off the lancer on the bench. "Let's find out."

He took the clip that fit the lancer, and filled it with little bondsteel bolts. He loaded it into the lancer, and walked across the workshop to the trap. The bondsteel box was specifically built to guide a lancer bolt into a fabric pad that was made of Bondstructs that would stop the bolt. He pointed it in the box, and pulled the trigger. The high pitched energy whine of the lancer discharge filled the shop directly followed by the bang of the bolt slamming into the trap. He popped the clip out of the lancer, and turned back to Kayna with a grin.

"What do you think Midget? Magic?" He said.

She just nodded wordlessly. A loud banging sound echoed from the front of the shop. The wonder was gone, replaced with fear.

"Daddy?" She said in a whisper.

"I don't know baby girl. Kayna you remember how to get to Ales?" He asked.

She nodded to him.

"Go out the back door. The way I showed you. I'll meet you there." He said.

"I'm scared Dad."

"I know baby. I know you are. But I can only get out of here if I know you're safe. Can you do that for me?" He said. He pulled his belt off the hook on the wall. He strapped it around his waist, which put two lancers on his waist. One was on his hip, and one was behind his back.

"Ok daddy. I'll go."

Suddenly there was a thunderous crash somewhere upstairs, and then something blurred down the stairs. He saw it only as a flash as it disappeared into the shop front.

"Go baby! Get to Ales!" he said, and then bolted through the door between the shop and the front room.

He brought his Vision up and drew the lancer from his hip in his left hand. The front room of his shop had become a tangle of wreckage. The front counter had been ripped from the floor, and been smashed halfway through the front wall. There were armored men lying in opposite corners. Their armor was in tatters, as if the metal were shredded cloth.

Outside in the street, though, was where the real fight was. There Liassa was surrounded by a half dozen men clad in black. They stood back in a loose ring around her, and another man in deep green armor. They were prodding at her with spears. So far she was dodging them with expert grace. The man in green though was much faster. He waited until she was in the air, and then darted in cutting at her with a thin bladed sword. Amazingly she twisted in midair barely avoiding the cut of the blade.

"Warran! Get out of here!"

He froze for a long moment. Two of the armored men turned to him. Then he shook himself. He couldn't possibly leave her there to fight them alone. He pulled his second lancer from the holster at the small of his back.

"Down!" He screamed in fury as he drew down with both of his Lancers.

"Don't!" Lia screamed but it was too late. She flattened herself to the ground in a split second.

His Vision allowed him to assess the distance to each man perfectly. Aiming was more a reflex than anything else. He squeezed the triggers, and the high pitched whine of the lancers echoed into the night. Men screamed, and pain slammed into him as they fell. He could feel them dying. It ripped through him, and there was nothing that had ever hurt so badly. He dropped the lancer in his right hand though he managed to keep a grip on the left through sheer determination. Tears streamed out of his eyes, and his Vision faded.

"No!" Lia roared. She hit the ground, and shot to one side. She slammed her shoulder into the man in green. It blasted him off his feet, and he slammed into the wall of a building twenty marks away. Warran heard bones snapping clearly even across the square. Lia turned to the rest of the men rage clear in her eyes, and the glow of her Vision blazed so brightly it pierced the night like two lanterns. That was the last thing he saw before he passed into unconsciousness.

PART 5

50

Ales wanted them to see her. It was clear that the King had pieced together the rumors, and now the royal family was hunting them. Sadly it had been a fruitless attempt to draw out the remaining members. She knew the King would not come himself until he had no other choice. She had strolled right through the High Center square wearing the long coat that had become the source of so many rumors about her. She lounged at the bar of the Blue Mare as if she owned the wayhouse, and everyone in it. She turned her stool back towards the bar.

The scream that echoed off the inside of her skull was wordless, and carried such overwhelming fear that it made her mind shut down for a moment. She stumbled off of the stool, and caught herself before she could fall down. She turned, and ran out the door of the inn. She slid to a halt when she nearly ran into a circle of guards in black. Standing behind them was a hulking man in blood red armor. She recognized him as Narran Roa. The second son of the royal family, and arguably the most dangerous behind the King.

"Normally I would love to entertain you. But just now I have no time to play with you. Move, or I will move you." Ales grated.

Ales opened her Vision, and forced open five of the seven levels of her Constraints. Her muscles twitched with barely leashed power. Cellstructs spread through her body in a wave, coating her bones, and infusing her muscles protecting her from destroying herself. The man in red spoke.

"You are under arrest by order of the King."

Ales did not bother speaking, she simply advanced. She jumped at the edge of the stairs leading down to the street. She cleared the men easily, and landed behind the man in red. He spun to face her but it was already too late. She threw her fist at his chest. He brought up his arms in a defensive X across his chest. Her fist slammed into his arms. It was as if he had been hit by a battering ram. His feet dug furrows in the ground as he was thrown back into his men. His armor absorbed most of the blow, but before he could recover Ales was already gone.

She ran as fast as she could. Buildings, and alleyways were nothing more than blurry impressions as she ran towards Warran's shop. The shout had been Lia, and she had been terribly afraid. Not for herself though. Something had happened to Warran. It had to be something beyond normal worries for Lia to reach out to her so strongly. To use her Cellstructs to broadcast a mental signal over that distance was risking brain damage.

Ales pushed as hard as she could. Cobbles shattered as she ran across them the force of her steps crushing them, and throwing tiny pieces of stone away in all directions. There were more than a few startled shouts, but they seemed very far away before they even started she had gone by them with such speed.

When she cleared the alleyway onto the street that held Warran's shop two men in black armor were carrying him towards the back of a wagon. Without slowing Ales threw herself into a flip. When she came over her feet slammed into the side of the wagon. An ear-piercing snap boomed off the buildings as the wagon nearly exploded. The tongues snapped off so violently that the black maevea pulling it were not even jostled. It slammed into Warran's shop like a wrecking ball. The front of the store crumpled in like wet paper. She landed not ten marks in front of the two men who had released Warran in shock. He had slumped to the ground bonelessly.

"You will not touch him again." Ales snarled and stalked towards them.

The two men stumbled back from her as if her pronouncement had been a physical thing. She was so angry that the only circle she seemed to be able to control was Breaking. It suited her as she was going to destroy one of these men. It was irrational, but she was not thinking rationally. She didn't care. These men had meant to kill Lia, and had done something to Warran that had caused Lia to risk her mental stability.

The men didn't seem to know if they should run or not. Ales rushed forward like a storm. She smashed her fist into the face of the soldier on the right. It hit with such ferocity that it crushed his helmet, and his head inside of it. Bright blue blood ran out of the face guard, and splattered his chest in gore. Ales spun, and lashed out with a foot. It caught the man in the shoulder. There was a resounding series of snapping sounds, and the soldier's body slammed into the cobbles with a crack of splitting stone. The pain of his death ripped through her, but she barely noticed she was so furious.

"You!"

She pointed a shaking finger at the remaining soldier. He tore his gaze away from the lifeless body of his compatriot. She just pointed down the street in a wordless dismissal. He ran. It seemed the lesser soldiers were beyond the control of whatever it was that controlled the Royal family.

She knelt down, and touched Warran's neck checking his pulse. He was breathing, and his pulse was strong. She looked at the scene, and tried to calm herself down. She slumped her knees folded until her rump touched the ground. She gritted her teeth against the pain of the soldier's death as it ate away at her. She needed access to her other circles to see what had happened here with any certainty. Her immediate guess was that Warran had killed someone entirely unprepared for what would happen when he used his Vision to end a life.

She picked up his lancers, and slid them back into their holsters. She snapped the straps over the handles of the lancers to keep them in place as she picked him up. Slowly the pain receeded, and she finally calmed down enough to access her other Circles. She opened herself to Finding, and the scene became a clear pattern. Blue light outlined the patterns of feet in the dirt, the paw prints from Lia as well. The intensity of the light around certain foot prints changed as her Vision discerned how the fight had gone. The patterns appeared quite quickly, and showed her that she was right. She looked at the two men with neat round holes in each of their chests.

"Gods help me." She said it fervently, and hoped beyond hope that it would be answered.

She hefted Warran's limp body, and put him over her shoulder. She went into the alleyway looking around carefully with her Vision wide open as she looked for something that would be very important to Warran when he finally woke. She had no trouble finding tiny footprints on the cobblestones.

She began to trot down the alleyway. Her need to find Kayna was singular, and she passed people with Warran over her shoulder not even realizing how much attention she was drawing. She hurried into another alleyway, and stopped. She had to make a decision.

Either she continued to draw attention in the interest of finding Kayna, or she took the time to take Warran someplace safe. She, and Lia had purchased several safe houses through proxies though they had never been followed home so the use of them had not been important. There was even one nearby. She shook her head. She couldn't wait, and chance someone picking up the little girl. She rushed forward following the tiny footprints outlined in blue. They were going towards the apartments, and if that was the case Ales had to catch her well before she got there. She picked up the pace, and had gone two blocks when Warran started to cough. She skidded to a stop, and put him down in the alleyway.

"Where..." He groaned, and clapped his hands to his head.

"I could feel them." He grated.

"I know. Just try to clear your head Warran. Just think of nothing." Ales explained. She prayed silently for a moment that Avaara would appear.

Amazingly, she did. She came in a bell tone of complete silence. It was as if the world had stopped. She came. Ales bent at the waist looking down.

"Mother. I am so sorry." Ales said.

Ales' worry was almost palpable. If Warran mentally attached the despair, and pain that he was feeling to the idea of what his daughter would think of him it could be disastrous.

"Be still child. The worry that you feel is not unfounded. I cannot do much, but I can keep him asleep until you have more time to deal with this. I cannot do more. Apologies Daughter." She bent quickly, and touched Warran's forehead briefly. He fell back into unconsciousness.

"Is the girl all right?" Ales asked.

Avaara looked at her for a long moment as if she were considering the question. "I cannot answer that. You must discover it on your own." Which was an answer in itself. Avaara had basically told her that if she didn't continue looking for the girl something would happen to her.

"Thank you Mother." Ales said.

Avaara nodded. "Be careful Daughter. The evil begins to reveal itself. It will become desperate soon." Avaara said. She vanished as quickly as she came.

Ales sighed. Picked up Warran once again, and started off down the alleyway to find Warran's daughter.

51

Lia was running. She lead them a marry chase through the city after she had drawn them away from Warran. She wasn't sure Ales had heard her mental sending, but she hoped. She had done all she could for Warran. She darted down alleyways, and weaved her way through the nighttime crowds. She had lost most of the soldiers after the first minute, but Morra Roa was very fast. Faster than her younger brother Illya had ever been. She managed to keep pace with Lia if just barely. Lia did not want to fight her. The shot she had gotten in was a fluke at best. Not only that. Hitting her had broken Lia's shoulder. Her structures were working double time to mend the bone as she wove her way through the alleyways of the Low Center.

Morra's armor was so much stronger than Illya's had been, and Lia wasn't sure she could beat her. The healing process finished, and Lia slid to a halt. With a mental command to her Cellstructs she boosted her speed, and strength. She staved in the rear door of the building to her left, and bolted inside. A quick look around, and she found the stairs going up. She carefully pulled down the door handle with her paw, and nosed it open. She slipped inside as silently as she could. She used her tail as a stop to let the door close as quietly as possible. As soon as it was closed she darted up the stairs. Her claws made tiny clicking noises as she ran but there was no way to stop that. She just had to hope that Morra would not hear.

She froze on the third floor when she heard the door to the stairs slam open. The sound of footsteps came from the floors below. Lia didn't move she had to wait until she was closer. She might decide to check each floor, which would give Lia time to escape. When the footsteps stopped on the first floor, she began to creep up to the next floor. The building was at least ten stories, and she needed to get to the roof. She hadn't chosen this building by mistake. It was the last one on the block meaning that there was nothing on the other side to assist in making the jump to the street. She could make it down to the street from the roof in one jump. It was the one and only way that she was certain Morra could not match her.

Her armor might be able to absorb such an impact, but her body would break.

She put her front paws up on the railing so she could look down the center of the stairwell. She called up the Circle of Light and her vision shifted into the infrared spectrum. Suddenly Morra Roa's body heat leapt out at her. She had been trying to sneak up the stairwell and was only one floor below Lia now. Lia snarled silently. She turned back to the stairwell, and she slid away up the stairs in dead silence. There was no way she was going to be beaten by someone barely into their thirtieth cycle. She had been sneaking into places that she wasn't supposed to be in for intervals before this child was ever even thought of.

She reached the top floor without a single sound. When she looked down she had to sort through a half dozen heat signatures of people close to the stairwell, but Morra was standing at the fourth floor. She had her head tilted as if she were trying to listen. Lia's lips pealed back in a feline grin. She would give her something to listen to. Lia drew in a deep breath, and roared a challenge down the stairwell. Then she turned, and streaked out the door to the roof.

She stood near the edge of the roof. She waited just long enough that she could hear Morra running up the stairs. Then she turned to the street side of the building and leapt off the side. She heard the door to the roof bang open just as she cleared the parapet. Morra ran for her at top speed. Suddenly Lia was afraid that Morra wouldn't realize the danger. There wasn't much she could do about it because even as fast as she was by the time Morra reached the edge of the roof Lia's structures were sending out frantic messages to her letting her know how to position her body so that she wouldn't damage herself.

She bent her legs, and let her body go almost limp. From the height she had jumped any tensing of her muscles might cause them to snap when she hit. All six of her paws hit the cobbles at the exact same time distributing the impact across her entire body. She bent her knees smoothly until her belly almost touched the ground. She straightened her legs, and then looked up. Morra Roa stared down at her through the slits of her helmet. Lia put her paw to her mouth, and then held it out to Morra as if she were blowing her a kiss.

"Catch me if you can!" Lia taunted her, and then turned and ran across the street towards the Low Center.

She sighed in relief now that there was no chance of Morra actually catching her. She needed to double back to help Warran. She needed to make sure that her family was all right. If anything had happened to them there would be a reckoning. She skidded to a stop when she heard something slam into the ground in the street. She wanted to turn back, but she knew it was not a good idea. A fight with Morra might not be one she could win. It would be better to wait until she had more backup. She turned, and disappeared into the alleyways. Her sharp ears brought her the sound of Morra cursing somewhere behind her. Considering the curses that were coming from Morra, the cracking sound that Lia had heard was not breaking cobbles, but breaking bones.

52

Ales' eyes darted back, and forth over the street. Her Vision told her that she was not being followed. Her Structures told her that it would be hundreds of times faster to find Warran's daughter if she wasn't lugging his unconscious body around with her. Not just because of the extra dead weight, but because she wouldn't be drawing so much attention. People were trying to stop her on the street. So she took to the back alleys and made her way to one of their safe houses.

This one was a small brick house in the moonward side of the High Center. The person who had owned it before Ales had paid them ten times what it was worth had had the bricks dyed a deep ugly purple. She opened her first level of Constraints, and jumped over the seven mark fence surrounding the small back yard of the house. It was the reason she had bought this place instead of one of the other one hundred and fifty-seven houses in this part of the city. The high fence, and its proximity to the alleyways was unlike any other house in the entire city. She opened the back door, and went inside. There were three bedrooms, and she put Warran down on the bed in the master. She wrote a quick note in case he woke up, but she didn't think he would. Avaara said he would sleep until she had time to deal with the problem. It was true magic.

"Which probably means he will sleep until I have time to deal with it whether I think I have time or not." She grumbled.

She left the note anyway and ran back out of the house leaving the first level of her Constraints open so she could run faster. She went back to the last place she saw Kayna's footprints. She opened several circles all at once. She didn't do this very often because so much information coming into her mind put a massive strain on her synaptic connections with her Cellstructs. But this was one of the times she couldn't afford to be subtle.

Circles of Light, Observance, Finding, and Distance. The world exploded with information. It assaulted her brain with knowledge, the distance between Kayna's footsteps indicated that she was walking not running. Finding showed the pattern that she was taking through the city indicated she was heading towards the Low Center. That meant one of two safe houses. When the spectral trail became more recent she focused more on Observance which allowed her to react more quickly. She began to run following the trail of Kayna's footprints towards the Low Center.

She burst out onto the high street, and ground to a halt. The footprints just disappeared as if she had vanished from the planet. The only explanation for that was that someone had picked her up. Ales concentrated, and her sight swooped in on the last footprint that Kayna had left. She focused on the molecular structure of what was in the footprint. It took her only a moment to separate the particles that made up Kayna's scent. She pulled her Vision back until she was seeing at the normal level again, and adjusted her Circles. Narrowing what she was seeing from the Circle of Light made her scent stand out to her like a green ghostly trail in the air. If she was hurt Ales' plans would go down the drain because she was going to kill everyone involved. Children were, for the most part, the most defenseless of people. They triggered the protective needs of the Tier more strongly than almost anyone or anything.

She ran through the streets keeping her speed down to something closer to normal human speed. She didn't want to draw to much attention. Having to deal with anyone when all of her mental capacity was absorbed into her Vision would not be a pleasant experience. She dodged between people some of whom shouted at her for almost knocking them aside. Her Vision told her before they even started shouting whether she had actually bumped into them or not. She didn't touch anyone she just got so close that they jumped back from her. She slid through the smallest of openings in the crowd.

Her mind raced uncontrollably. If something happened to her not only would she have failed a child, but it would destroy Warran beyond all repair. He would be so emotionally fragile after his first kill that he would simply break. Ales had seen it happen before she would not see it happen again. It was full dark now, and the trail was leading further out towards the edges of the Low Center. The most rundown part of the city. When she crossed the thoroughfare, and darted into an alleyway between two buildings Lia burst out of an alleyway behind the building on the right. She stopped dead when she saw Ales.

{Thank the Father that I found you!} She was panting hard which meant she had run a long way probably lengths across the city at top speed to catch up with Ales.

{They've taken Kayna, she was headed toward one of the safe houses when someone picked her up.} Ales said stopping next to her.

{Can you smell her?} Lia sniffed around the cobbles walking in a full circle.

{Yes, faintly. How did you track her?} She asked.

{A spectral light shift so that I can see the scent trail.} Ales answered.

{Which is quickly fading into the wash of molecules around us. Your nose is much better.} Ales replied.

{Well why are we standing here?} Lia said, and then trotted off down the alleyway in the direction Ales had been headed. She ran for about two hundred marks. Then she turned left and began to pick up speed.

{Her scent is getting stronger.} Lia said, and she reached a run. She galloped down the alleyway. Ales almost tripped over her when she pulled up short. The building had a basement stair. It was a business of some sort.

{She is in there Ales. She is bleeding. I can smell it.} Ales' knuckles creaked as she balled her fists.

{Lia you have to go in. I can't go in there. If I go in there I won't stop until everything is destroyed. I'm right on the edge of snapping. She's just a kid.} Ales said. Lia shook her head.

{Ales, I can't. I'm too big. The confines of that room are too small to let me move freely. I could hurt her.} Lia said helplessly. Ales growled. Lia was right.

{You are better with Light than I am. Can you see how many people are in there with her?} Ales asked.

{Easy for you to say there madam spectral light shift.} Lia said trying to lighten the mood.

{I was operating with four circles open Lia. You know what that is like it makes you do impossible things. It also gives you an impossible migraine.} Ales said.

{I have never managed a spectral light separation even with all three circles open Ales.} Lia shifted her vision to the infrared spectrum, and she could see the sources of heat on the other

side of the door. Only one warm body was present in the room.

{She's alone in the room right now. There are two people upstairs. Maybe we can do this quietly.} Lia said. Ales nodded. She looked at the door, and opened the Circle of Breaking. The oak door lit up with polkadots. They varied in shade from white, to bright red. Every shade in between.

{I need three hands for this. Lend me a paw?} Ales said.

{Sure, where?} Lia asked. Ales touched her finger to the door on one of the bright red dots. Lia touched her paw there. Ales put her hand over two more of them.

{On three apply pressure evenly. The door will just crumble.} Ales said.

{One, two, three.}

Ales pressed at the same time as Lia, and the door simply caved in on itself. Ales' hands blurred and she caught the two iron bands that fell away from the door. She set them silently aside. She slid into the room, and looked around. It was filthy. The floor was dirt, and the cobbles of the walls were striated with mold. There was a rickety set of stairs leading upwards to her left. Bound hand and foot to a chair directly in front of her was Kayna. She had a bloody nose that was still oozing, and she was unconscious.

{No one, come in please. There is something more wrong with her, and I can't focus.} Ales said. She wanted to go upstairs, and kill the people who had taken Kayna. Lia drew back at the door, and her face twisted into an expression of disgust

{She has a burn somewhere. They branded her.} Lia said.

{Only one reason you brand someone. Get her free Lia, take her out of here.} Ales said. Her mindvoice threatened to overwhelm Lia with the unadulterated rage that Ales was feeling.

{Ales I can't carry her.} It was foolish. Lia knew it was foolish trying to draw Ales' attention when she was so angry.

{Do not lie to me Lia. You can carry her just fine. Get her to the safe house.} Ales said.

{Ales…} Lia began. Ales cut her off.

{Slavers Lia! Slavers! You want me to just let them go? Get her out of here now!} Ales' mindvoice was a roar that made Lia whimper. Then she disappeared up the stairs.

Lia sliced away the ropes with her claws. She found the brand on the inside of Kayna's right wrist. Lia sighed, and carefully took Kayna's left wrist in her mouth. She was careful to keep the girl's wrist between her teeth so as to not pierce the skin. She turned her head, and the girl started to tip forward. Lia bumped the chair she was sitting in, and let go of her wrist. She bent her legs, and slid herself beneath Kayna's limp body. When the screams began Lia briefly looked upstairs. There wasn't anything she could do but leave. Lia trotted out the door to get Kayna back to her father.

53

The safe house was still quiet when Lia got to the back door. She eyed the door knob with annoyance. Turning door knobs was a disgusting operation for Lia. Her paws were too big to get a grip on the knob which was tiny in comparison so the only way to do it was with her mouth. No Wild would ever have this trouble in Ahal. The invention of the door knob, which had happened about eight hundred cycles after the fall of Ahal was one of the most disgusting things that had happened in her life. Hundreds of people touched a door knob in a day. There were thousands of germs on every single one. She had a nasty habit of looking at them with her Vision. It was not a fun practice because it made her want to vomit. She butted her head against the door in frustration. She couldn't help it.

She opened her Vision and looked at the black metal knob. It was suspiciously clean, and free of anything but the metal. Lia had never seen a clean door knob. Ales had known that Lia would have to open it with her mouth, and had cleaned it. It was the only explanation. Lia grinned inwardly. She carefully took the door knob in her mouth, and twisted her head. The door popped open, and she backed up until the door swung wide enough for her to slide her muzzle into the crack. It swung open. She slipped inside, and curled her tail around the door knob. It gave her just enough of a grip to pull it closed. She scowled at the stairs. All the rooms with beds were upstairs. The only way she could keep Kayna from sliding off her back was to go backwards up the stairs, and hunch her shoulders. She backed up the stairs slowly, negotiating the bend in them through sheer feline dexterity. When she finally made it upstairs the sound of movement made her stop.

"Thank the Gods. You found her." Warran's voice was haggard.

"I'm sorry Warran. She's not going to be completely whole. Slavers picked her up. She has a broken nose, and she had been branded with a slave mark. Nothing worse than that. We don't have what we need to remove the mark but we will soon." Lia said. Warran picked Kayna up off Lia's back. He looked at her sadly.

"She can wear something to cover it. But I can't ever cover up what I did." Warran said.

He carried her into the bedroom where Ales had left them. He laid her down on the bed. She saw the glow of his Vision, and he reached down. He straightened her nose out with a quiet popping sound. She started awake with a gasp, and put her hands up to her face.

"Ow, ow, ow." She looked up with tears streaming from her black, and blue rimmed eyes.

"Daddy?"

"I'm here baby girl. They can't hurt you anymore." Warran said.

"Daddy, I tried to get to Ales. Those dirty men kept me from getting there. They hurt me."

Lia looked her over quickly again. She was certain she had not seen anything but the broken nose and the brand. They had gotten to her in time. There was nothing more.

"I know Midget. Your nose will heal." He opened his Vision again, and looked her over. He let out a small sigh of relief when he saw the brand and the broken nose were her only injuries.

"Warran come here look into my eyes." Lia said.

"No. I need to stay with her." He was clutching her hand almost to the point of causing pain.

"Warran. Come over here right now, and look into my eyes." She sat on her haunches arranging her six paws carefully. He seemed to want to protest again.

"Warran she is fine now. Come over here. Sit down." Lia said.

He finally put Kayna's hand down. He walked over to Lia. His body posture told her everything. When he killed those men he had no idea what was going to happen to him, and there was only one way to solve this problem. He sat down in front of her. It made it so that he had to look up to see into her eyes. It was time for him to meet Avaara, and Zezzhz. He looked up into her eyes, and then his eyes widened.

"It's all right Warran. Open your Vision. See the path in my eyes." He opened his Vision. The glow in his eyes intensified until it was too bright for Lia to look into anymore. She closed her Vision, and stepped away from him. He would be there for a while. Her ears twitched when she heard footsteps on the stairs.

"Lia did you make it back?" Ales' voice came up the stairs.

{Of course I did.} Lia's mindvoice was somber almost sad. Ales came into the room, and eyed Warran sitting on the floor.

"Is he all right?" Ales said.

{He wasn't ready for fighting Ales. Not ready for killing. He was broken. I had to send him to the Mother and Father. Avaara will not be pleased with having to speak with him so soon. He was my responsibility.} Lia said. Ales switched to speaking mind to mind.

{Lia listen to me. They knew that this world is more dangerous to us now than it ever was in our time. They knew that we would have to make hard choices, do hard things, and anyone we taught would be in the same position. They will help him, and you if you would only ask.} Ales said.

{They have helped me enough already Ales. I accept that this is necessary. That doesn't mean I have to like it. Do you think your cover is blown?} She asked changing the subject. Ales ran her fingers through the fur on Lia's head gently, and then walked towards the bed.

{I think we are fine. They don't know I have any relation to Lady Brightwater.} Ales replied. Out loud she said.

"Kayna you were so brave. How are you feeling?" Ales asked.

"Better. M'nose hurts. Is Daddy all right?" She asked. Her eyes were fixed on her Father who sat motionless as a stone.

"He sure is." Ales said.

"He's just doing some magic. He will be done soon."

{Ales you have to go to that menagerie that you hired to be part of our cover. They are going to track me back there. I don't want any of them hurt.} Lia said.

Ales nodded. {Can you handle things here while I go to them?}

Lia nodded, and Ales opened the bedroom window, and slipped out into the night. Lia sighed when Ales was gone. It was clear that Ales was going to snap. Lia had no idea how many people were in that house, but she doubted Ales had left anyone alive. It was rare for Ales to get so angry that she couldn't control her Circles. Just then Warran gasped, and nearly fell forward. The glow of his Vision faded.

"It's all true, all connected." Warran gasped. Tears streamed from his eyes.

"They told me..." Lia almost cut him off, but he shook his head on his own.

"I believe." He finished.

Lia padded over to him as he groped blindly for something to get himself up with. She got close enough that his hand landed on her shoulder. He wrapped his arms around her surprising her.

"I'm sorry I didn't believe." He said.

"It is always hard to have faith in something you have never experienced for yourself Warran. They have been absent for three thousand cycles. They only occasionally show themselves to people in the best of times." Lia said.

"I'll never forget." He said

"They have that effect." Lia said. She put her paw around him, and held him for a few long minutes. He finally disentangled his arms from her.

"Lia they couldn't tell me much, but what they did tell me is important. We have a lot to do. We can't beat them by brute force. Even if we kill the ones here we need a new weapon to fight them effectively. I need to build it. I need Ales' Sparks."

54

Ales made it across the Center in record time. Luckily the land she had purchased to place the menagerie was just past the wall. Ales' scaled the Center wall without incident. She jogged to the clearing where they had put down their wagons. She was too late. Soldiers stood at the edge of the ring of wagons. Inside of the ring of wagons stood Morra Roa. She was with the master of the menagerie who appeared to be terrified. She had over thirty soldiers with her.

Ales invoked her Vision. She went cold with fear and helplessness when she saw what Morra had done. She had rammed a dagger under his ribs. He was dead where he stood if Ales didn't do something fast. Morra released the dagger, and he fell to the ground clutching the dagger. That was when someone let out a scream. Ales wasn't sure what to do. Lia had said that Illya was the weakest of the royal family, and she had said that she only beaten him so quickly because she had gone to her limits without holding anything back. Ales was considerably stronger than Lia but if she fought on that sort of level other people might get hurt. Ales came out of the brush, and stopped behind the soldiers.

"If you are looking for me you should leave them alone." Ales said it loudly.

Morra turned. She looked surprisingly hale considering what she had learned from Lia about their jump off the building. Maybe she had broken an arm, and her armor was supporting it.

"The Night Lady I presume. Or should I call you Alessandra?" Morra said.

Ales was not surprised her name was known. She had not been quiet about her name.

"I am she." Ales said.

"If you want me, you will leave them alone. Assuming you can take me." Ales taunted her.

That got all of them looking at her, which was exactly what she needed. She opened her Vision, and focused all of her concentration on the Circle of Taking. It was clear the moment it took hold. She had gotten inside of their heads. She was basically invisible to them. She had pushed into their minds so strongly that they wouldn't see anything for a few hours. They stood motionless as the mountains.

The ability of the Taker to make people not look at them was one of the most dangerous powers of the Tier. None of them had ever really been sure of what the ability did to the minds of the people it was used on. There had been several very solid theories in the past, but none had ever been confirmed. Ales grimaced at using it so strongly, because it had the reverse effect of making her feel very detached from reality. Some believed that it confused the mind of the individual somehow. Ales thought differently. Especially since she had seen Lia use the power so strongly that the target had stopped breathing. She believed that somehow that power of theirs created a sort of synaptic dissonance inside of the mind of the target. In the same way that bright rapidly flashing lights could cause the brain to malfunction. The more focused the use of Taking the greater the disruption.

Though not all of the Tier with that Circle could take it as far as Ales, and Lia could it was still dangerous. Ales shook herself from her thoughts about what she had done, and rushed around the group of soldiers. She knelt next to the dying man, and assessed the damage. The dagger had missed his heart, and with enough time Ales could repair the damage. It was time she didn't have. A woman knelt next to her.

"Can you fix him Antieri?" She asked.

Ales looked up at her startled. "How do you know that title?" Antieri was a title of respect given to the Tier who left Ahal to help people outside.

The woman began to speak again, and Ales shook her head sharply in negation. She remembered what the woman had told her on their first meeting.

"Not important, I can. I need a needle of bondsteel, thread, and a small knife. It must be razor sharp. And tell everyone to pack up, you must leave and never ever return to Vilhena. I will fix your mate Halli. We only have a couple of hours, and I will need half of that to save him. Go quickly." Ales said. She did not remove the dagger. It was keeping blood in. Instead, she looked down into Aran's eyes.

"Aran stay with me. I will take care of you. I will see you through this." Ales said.

The noise level increased around her as people began to shout, and things were packed into wagons. Halli returned with a small bright knife, the needle, and a spool of fine thread. Ales took the small knife first, and grimaced. She cut a slice across her palm, and commanded her Cellstructs to leave it open. She couldn't possibly push enough of her Cellstructs out through her pores for this in time. A steady trickle of her bright blue blood fell onto the dagger, and made its way into his wound. With it went thousands of her Cellstructs. They immediately went to work sealing the wounds. Once enough of her blood had fallen into the wound the cut on her hand closed up. She looked at Halli.

"Halli please hold his shoulders. He is going to make a lot of noise Halli but I promise he will be fine."

She could feel the tiny deaths of her Cellstructs as they gave themselves up to close Aran's wound. He would still have a lot of healing to do on his own but the muscles, and arteries around his heart would be fine. She couldn't put any more of her Cellstructs into him without triggering a massive response from his immune system. She took hold of the handle of the dagger. She nodded to Halli, and the woman pressed down hard on her husband's shoulders.

Ales drew the dagger out slowly giving her Cellstructs time to deal with the damage. He started to scream, as the dagger came out. Tears rolled down Ales' cheeks. This was a man she had failed to protect. He coughed up a gobbet of blood, and that was when Halli began to weep. Ales closed her eyes, and concentrated. Her tears shut off, and she focused on the job. The blade finally came free with a disgusting sucking sound. It was soft, but noticeable. The wound stopped bleeding almost immediately though due to her Cellstructs. She took the needle and thread. Aran was trying to whisper something, but Ales hushed him.

"Wait Aran, it will pass in a few minutes and you will be able to talk properly. Let me close this up. It's going to hurt." Aran nodded, and squeezed his eyes shut. Ales' quick fingers put fifty-four neat stitches into the wound. She tied it quickly, and eyed the wound critically.

"Thank you Antieri. Thank you." Halli wept freely.

"An hour or less Halli. I will carry him to your wagon. You have to be long gone by the time they snap out of it."

If they snap out of it at all. Ales thought. She could have just as easily destroyed their minds, which was not her intention. If they all died at once the shock would probably knock her out for half a day. She had managed to push through the deaths of the slavers on sheer rage, but she did not have any anger here to protect her mind from killing. She just felt sad. It was going to be compounded by the fact that using Taking so strongly was going to backfire on her in the next few hours. There was always a cost. She picked up Aran carefully, and took him to his wagon. Halli began cleaning up their camp, and was done in just a few minutes.

"Halli, take the caravan and go moonward. They will expect you to go stoneward to the nearest border. Take this." Ales pulled from her pocket a small black disc.

"Listen to me Halli very carefully." She waited until Halli was paying close attention. She held up the shining black coin.

"This coin is pure black sarsan gum. If you take this to a Searcher, or Fixer they will pay a king's ransom for it. But no one should have this much black sarsan. This coin is six pebs. If you try to sell it all in one place there will be questions. Don't sell more than one peb at a time. Keep it wrapped in a cloth at all times. Douse it in water before you cut it, and use a sharp knife. If there is any dust do not breathe it. If you inhale even one grain of this it will do permanent damage to your mind. Take no less than twenty thousand pieces of gold per peb. Do not sell it at all unless you are desperate for coin. Don't ever show the whole coin to anyone but Aran. I'm giving this to you as a last resort. It could cause you trouble to use it. I will find you again and collect what is left of it and pay you what it is worth as soon as I can. Do you understand Halli?"

The woman nodded, and reached for the coin. Ales held it away from her.

"Repeat it back to me." Ales said, and waited while the woman repeated back to her every word. Ales made her do it twice more before she was satisfied.

"Write it down as soon as you are on the road. Don't stop any more than necessary Halli." Ales stepped up on the back of the wagon so she could see Aran.

"I'm sorry for all of this Aran. I didn't think this would happen when I hired you to help us cover Lia's movements in the city."

But Aran shook his head. "It was our honor to help Antieri."

"Aran absolutely needs to rest for three days. If he gets up before then it could tear his stitches. Do you hear me?" She growled at him.

"I will make sure he rests." Halli said, and climbed up to the seat of the wagon. Somewhere in the confusion she had managed to hitch up two heavyset looking maevea. Beautiful white skinned creatures with delicate red antennae.

"Where did you get these?" Ales said walking to the front of the wagon. They were not just any maevea. Only a very few select breeds had different color antennae like these.

"A mating gift from my parents when Aran and I were joined." Halli said. She picked up the reins.

"They are gorgeous. You didn't have these when we met." Ales said. Halli smiled.

"We thought we had lost them to root rot, but they recovered in one of the wagons." Halli said.

"You should have told me I would have helped. They look strong enough now." Ales said patting one of them on the neck.

"And fast. Thank you Alessandra. Good luck." She said.

"No Halli, thank you. You have done more for my sister than you can ever know."

Halli snapped the reins and the maevea pulled away at a trot. Ales watched the wagon shrink down the road for a while until it was completely out of sight. She could feel the reaction headache from using her powers so strongly coming on but she had something else to do. She walked to where Morra Roa stood immobile. She walked around in front of her, and found that Morra was at least a couple ticks taller than her. It annoyed Ales to have to look up at the woman. Still, she should have been used to it by now, almost everyone was taller than her.

"I do not believe you to be in control of your own body, and because of that I will allow this to pass. But I urge you to converse with whatever power it is that animates this armor. If both of you value your existence you will save your ire for me. The next time you involve my friends in this you can expect me to overreact." Ales spun on her heel, and stormed away.

55

{Are you sure I can't help?} Lia asked.

"My cover is still safe. Everything is in place. I want you to take them outside of the city and wait for us. We will meet you in the clearing." Ales said. Lia just watched her with more worry. Ales sighed with exasperation.

"Lia I will be fine. I promise that if things become too chaotic I will use every power available to me to make it out. I will not leave you alone again. The best way you can help is to take our new family to safety." Ales said.

Ales pulled the blue dress up her body, and slid her arms into the sleeves. The elastic fabric stretched taunt over her body from ankles to neck. She straightened it carefully. Front and back there were whorls in the fabric that were sewn with hundreds of tiny cerulean gemstones. Her hair fell straight, and turned from blue to bright yellow. She started to braid it with ribbons that matched the color of the dress. She twisted ten individual braids into her hair, and then began to coil the braids onto the Back of her head making a tight bundle of coils. When they were all coiled they appeared to be swirling into one another. The pattern was not a mistake. It was beautiful, and it was their family mark.

{You look just like Mom.} Lia said.

{Mom would never have worn a dress like this.} Ales said.

{True enough. It isn't nearly frilly enough for her.} Lia said. Ales smiled. She took a choker made of fine golden chains dotted with sapphire stones off of a dressing bust. She fastened it around her throat.

"Thank you Lia. I promise it will be all right." She turned around, and carefully bent her knees. She tipped forward so she was kneeling on the carpet. She held out her arms.

{I'll get fur all over your dress.} Lia said worriedly.

"If you don't get over here, and give me a hug I will tie your tail in a knot Spook." Ales said. Lia padded over, and Ales put her arms around Lia's neck. Lia put her paw around Ales' shoulders and squeezed hard. Ales released her, and then rose by carefully rocking herself back onto her feet.

"Listen to me Lia. I understand now what your instincts have been telling you all this time. Something that anyone who wasn't one of the Wild wouldn't be able to sense. That the people inside of those armors are not in control of themselves. You thought they were stronger because you were subconsciously holding back. It is your imperative not to kill. You felt like you would be hurting innocents. I know because I felt it when I almost killed Morra Roa."

{You're certain of it?} Lia's mindvoice sounded stunned.

"I don't think it's every person wearing Bondarmor. I think only certain sets of it are controlled by whatever it is that the Gods have warned us about. Perhaps whatever is inhabiting the armor can only control so many people at once, or perhaps the armor requires a certain level of sophistication for it to happen. But I am certain that some of them are being controlled." Ales said.

Lia took a long slow breath trying to process that. She quickly reviewed her fight with Illya Roa. Her structures had recorded every emotion she had felt, for a moment it was like she was killing him again. She cringed at the mental vertigo that went with reviewing her memories like this. When she was done though there was no question that what Ales had said was right. Her instincts had been subtly telling her not to kill that man. She had killed an innocent man, and it hit her almost as hard as when she had done it. Her legs buckled, and it was by sheer force of will that she stayed on all six paws. Suddenly Ales was there inside of her mind, holding her up.

{Focus on me Lia. What you did was a release. You released him from the prison of his own mind. Don't ever think of it as anything else. You freed him from a life of being a puppet.} Ales said. There was a hint of hysteria in her mindvoice. It was tightly controlled but it was there.

{I'm all right I think. It was just overwhelming for a moment. I saw it and I didn't notice. He was in so much pain.} Lia said. She took long deep breaths. Her lungs worked like a bellows, and finally her legs steadied.

{You ended his pain Lia. You did a good thing.} Ales said.

{How can killing someone ever be a good thing?} Lia asked.

{When you put an end to something that cannot be endured. What would you be if you saw such suffering, and simply watched it continue? You helped him the only way that you could. Never be ashamed of that.} Ales said.

"Thank you Sister." Lia said softly.

"You were given your Vision for a reason Lia. Never forget." Ales said.

"I won't." She said, and then she slipped out of the balcony doors to collect the new Tier. Ales watched her go, and sighed. None of them were going to make it out of this unscarred.

56

Lia moved through the city like a ghost. She spared no use of her Vision, and no one even looked her way. She would not risk being caught tonight. She flowed over the fence and into the back yard of the safe house like water. Warran burst out of the back door to the safe house.

"Lia they took her!" Warran's face was a mask of fear and anger.

"Slow down, who took who?" Lia said.

"Ilsa. They grabbed her right outside of her apartments. How did they trace her back to us?" Warran asked.

"One of the guards must have recognized her. Who took her Warran?" Lia asked.

"I went to get her just like you asked. When I got there they were taking her away in chains. Morra Roa was there. The green armor just like you described it." Warran said.

"I couldn't fight them Lia. I just couldn't raise my irons." Warran said.

"I'm sorry. Why didn't we check on her?" He asked.

"It will take time for you to recover from the first time Warran. You're protective instincts will return soon. You will fight when it is time." Lia said. He nodded slowly in response seeming to regain some small margin of confidence.

"We weren't there because we thought it would be safer if we didn't visit. However they found her it wasn't because they followed us to her. Any one of us would have noticed someone following us. My suspicions tell me that they found her through her parents. But I will find out as soon as I get you and Kayna somewhere safe." Lia said.

"We will be safe in the clearing?" Warran asked.

"For a couple of days. She has marked you now, and that place is wild. A locus of her power. Anyone who attacks you there will not leave alive. If I hadn't killed Illya Roa before he could enter the clearing it would have been much worse for him. If we don't return to get you both in a couple of days..."

"I know where to go to get the gold. I know how to reach people at the Darkhold Monastery. I don't want to leave without any of you." Warran said.

"I know, but it is important that you do. You can come back once that task is done and find out what happened to us if you must, but that is too important to leave undone." Lia said. He nodded, and Lia changed the subject.

"Did you finish the Sparks?" He nodded, and reached into a bag he always carried with him. They were wrapped in black cloth.

"They're done. Whatever is controlling their Bondstructs is like an energetic infection of sorts if I had my guess. Along with their energetic discharge these Sparks will now also deliver a packet of patterned energy. Counter instructions that should release the Bondstructs from whatever it is that is controlling them." He said. He slipped them into the bag around her neck for her.

"I have something for you too if you will have them." He said. He brought out another cloth wrapped package.

"They won't impede your movement at all, and they will act like the Sparks. I made them with Bondstructs inside so they won't rub your fur off. Give me your paw?" he asked.

She lifted her right front paw. He unwrapped the package he had revealing two matte black bands of metal about as wide as a thick book. He picked one up, and snapped it around her leg above the paw. True to his word it fit perfectly, and didn't pinch or chafe when she turned her leg one way then the other. She lifted her other paw, and he fitted the second band around her leg.

"If you ever need to take them off for any reason, on the side is a small hole you can shove one of your claws into and the closure will open. The band's structures recognize when they are in contact with your own body so they won't discharge if you lie down on your paws." He said.

"Amazing. In our time things like this weren't needed." Lia said.

"Dangerous times now Lia. You need greater weapons than your claws. I have infused them with Bondstructs so that they are self-repairing. They shouldn't ever need maintenance as long as you provide the Bondstructs with materials to work with." He said.

Lia paused to consider what he said for a long moment.

"Warran, you need to start work on something else. But I can't show to you how to build it. Until you have Cellstructs of your own I can only explain and hope that your Vision can help you figure it out. We need something that creates an elementary force wave pulse. It would disrupt energetic devices within a certain range. Be careful Warran, done improperly this could disrupt our own Cellstructs momentarily. If you find yourself unable to be sure implore the Father, and he will assist you."

Warran looked uncomfortable. Lia put a reassuring expression on her feline face. This expression was much easier than when she was human.

"I know you are still getting a handle on your connection to the Gods Warran, but if you call for their help they will help if they can. Never forget that we are theirs. Given our power by their hand. Let them guide you." She said.

He petted her on the head, which she enjoyed for a long moment. It helped him too which was an interesting side effect of having fur that she had never quite understood. If she looked cute, and let someone pet her it made them feel better too. She didn't complain because a scratch between the ears always made her feel better.

"I will, and I'll think about the weapon. I think I understand what you mean, but I'm not sure what we could use for a power source. A normal thermal energy cell isn't going to be sufficient. It would need to be the size of a wagon to provide the power." He said.

"You need to learn about atomic merging. Gods I don't even know what you know in this time about energetic manipulation. You may have to call on Zezzhz directly to know more. Come on. Get Kayna we don't have any more time to waste. I have go after Ilsa." Lia said.

"We can go on our own." Warran said. But Lia shook her head immediately.

"No, I will not leave you vulnerable. They know too much, and we have been taking too many chances. I am too noticeable." She said, and walked toward the gate in the fence.

"It's not like you had a choice." Warran said.

"I'm ready Daddy." Kayna said from the steps.

"Ok Midget. Get Daddy's bag?" He said. She nodded eagerly. She put her bag down, and ran off into the house.

"No, it was just me and Ales. It doesn't mean I couldn't have been more careful not to associate you with us." Lia said.

"What did you teach me about self-recrimination?" He
said. Lia let out a little laugh.

"Aren't you a little young to be giving me advice?" Lia
asked skeptically. He held up a finger.

"I'm not. I'm just giving you back your own advice, and I
think you are more than old enough to advise yourself."
Warran said with a grin.

"Smartass." Lia quipped. Warran painted an
melodramatic expression of offense on his face.

"My Lady! My ass is of course incredibly intelligent!" He
said. She just shook her head. She looked over to see Kayna
standing at the door holding both her bag, and her father's.
She was listening quietly, and Lia padded over to her.

"Hey Midget, you want to ride?" Her eyes lit up, and she
nodded enthusiastically. Kayna handed her father his bag,
and slung hers across her back. Lia laid down at the bottom of
the stairs, and Kayna climbed up onto her back.

"Now lean forward, and hold onto my collar don't let go."

"Okay!" Kayna said.

She clutched Lia's collar, and Lia jumped over the top of
the gate. Kayna let out a little squeak of delight but nothing
more. Warran just shook his head, and pushed open the gate.
Even with so much danger all around she still managed to find
time to make his little girl feel good.

57

The carriage Ales normally rented had been replaced due to her generous donation with something much more upscale. The carriage that rolled to a stop in front of her was pulled by two absolutely gorgeous blue maevea. Their skin was dusted in white speckles. They were a rare breed. The driver was dressed in a tight fitting suit that he did not quite pull off. He was a little too thick around the middle for it to look completely right on him. Still he smiled and tipped his wide brimmed hat to her. The carriage was skinned in gold lacquer, with black norstone accents inlaid into the metal.

"High Lady. Do you need any assistance?" He asked. He was a polite man, and she had paid him a fortune to buy the maevea. The new carriage had been made especially for the Skyfire Festival. Though she had told him he could keep it after as her gift for being at her beck and call for the last few rotations. The skyfire would not begin for another hour.

"No thank you Rayno. I can manage."

She took hold of the side handle, and pulled herself up to the first step from the ground. From there her tiny steps made it difficult to get up the two stairs. Normally the driver would put down another set of stairs for a Lady but she never bothered with them. Her upper body strength made them quite unnecessary. She closed the door to the carriage a moment later, and Rayno moved them off at a slow trot.

"It's a beautiful Skyfire night eh M'Lady?" Rayno said from the driver's seat.

"I hope so Rayno." She replied.

"Do you know when the lights will begin?" He asked. It was a fair question. She suspected not many people knew what triggered the skyfire in this age.

"They will begin at full dark. You may feel free to take the carriage and watch them with your mate Rayno. They will last until first light. I would much rather see you spend the time with your family, and I will not be needing a ride back." Ales said.

"Are you certain M'Lady?" He asked skeptically.

"Not at all Rayno. I'm not certain of anything tonight except perhaps that you should spend it at home. I will take care of myself. Do not worry your payment will be for a full night." Ales said.

"M'Lady I am in possession of the finest transportation in the Center because of you. I would not take payment from you no matter what was offered me." Rayno said. He maneuvered them deftly through the streets toward the rising spire of the Archive Tower.

"I suppose that is fair. Thank you Rayno."

Finally the carriage rolled to a stop. The door opened a moment later, and Rayno held out his hand in an offer to help her down. She took his hand, and took tiny careful steps down the stairs. He had already put down the extra stairs, and she used them to make her way to the ground. The ramp up to the entrance of the Palace portion of the Citadel was a slow procession of High Lords, and High Ladies. There were hundreds of guests. Ales took a deep breath, and joined the queue. Rayno's voice called to her from the carriage.

"Good Luck M'Lady." He said.

She looked back towards him, but he just tipped his hat as he drove way. She wondered why he had said that. She watched him as he disappeared into the night. Only a few more carriages pulled up after hers, and she did not know any of the High Lords, or High Ladies who got out of them. It was just as well she didn't feel like conversing with any of them just then. They were not all bad people, and tonight she was going to manipulate them all. Sometimes she hated doing what was necessary.

"High Lady Brightwater?" An unfamiliar voice said Ales's name.

She looked around, and there was a young girl near the edge of the walkway. She wore a pretty blue dress that made Ales think of home. It was a wide skirt of blue cloth with white ruffles everywhere. The collar, the wrists, and the hem of the skirt were all puffs of ruffled cloth. Her waist was obviously drawn in by a shape, and Ales could see a huge cloth bow tied behind her back. The girl beckoned her forward. Ales made her slow way across the walkway to the girl.

"Lady Brightwater if you would follow me, her Highness the Queen has requested I bring you through to her table."

She spread her dress in a polite curtsey. The girl was one of the youngest of the palace servants that worked for Ilsa's mother. She wasn't yet old enough to wear a lady's dress. The girl was well trained in her role keeping her pace adjusted to the same speed that Ales was able to walk. Frilly or not Ales devoutly wished she could trade her dress for one like the girl was wearing. Many of the Lords, and Ladies glared at her as she walked past them and into the grand ballroom. She followed the girl to a table on one of three large daises at the front of the room. There were small stairs on the back side of the dais cut shallowly for woman wearing a proper dress. The girl curtsied again, and then left.

"High Lady Brightwater please join us." The Queen said pleasantly.

"I thought that perhaps you would like to be seated when the skyfire begins." She said.

"I apologize for my lateness My Queen, I had a minor emergency that I had to take care of." Ales said.

"Nothing to apologize for Helena." Aisha said.

There were only two other people at the table with Aisha. One was a very young High Lady Jusil who had just come of age. She was a robust young lady who's dress fit her tight and neatly. Her hair was a shade of seafoam green that was rare, and matched the color of her eyes. Her dress was the same exact color as her hair and eyes. The effect was quite pretty. Ales gave her a fond smile, and the young woman smiled back. They had shared a few fallings with the Queen. The other woman sitting at the table was Syle Roa. She was resplendent in bright white armor. Ales gave her the same pleasant smile. Syle Roa's helmet was pulled back. She had long white hair that was braided, and then coiled on top of her head.

Ales wanted so badly to open her vision and examine Syle Roa's armor. She knew though that it was somewhat pointless. She had tried to examine Morra Roa's armor briefly, but it had been like looking at energetic snow. There was something chaotic there, and a brief glimpse would not allow for her to figure it out. She needed hours. Maybe even days to tease out what was wrong with the Bondstructs. Lia's hope that they would be able to examine the Bondstructs from Illya Roa's armor had been dashed. She had opened the tiny pellet of her Cellstructs to find that the tiny dot of Bondstructs had self-destructed sometime after she had captured them.

"High Lady Brightwater, my mother has been telling me so much about you." Syle said. Her voice was incongruous. High, and pretty but somehow underdeveloped. She sounded like a little girl of four or five cycles.

"I have heard many stories of you as well Syle. It is so nice to finally meet you." Ales said.

She sat down in the last remaining chair at the Queen's table. Thankfully it was all the way across the table from Syle. Somehow Ales was certain that if she got too close to Syle she might be able to tell what Ales was.

"You two have something in common. You are both scholars in Tieran Lore." Aisha said. Ales didn't want to go down this road but she had very little choice.

"I have been searching the libraries of other kingdoms for many cycles. It has been fairly fruitless, though I have turned up a few gems." Ales began.

"Oh? I have found very little as well, though some of my own findings have been interesting." She said the last word with some emphasis.

"Well who goes first then?" Ales said with a grin.

"By all means." Syle said returning the smile.

"The Tier still have some descendants out in the world. And if you follow their family lines you can trace them back to the Highlands far bloomward. Even my family line came from that area. We can guess that the site of the Holy City was once located in the Bay of Anri." Ales said.

"That is a different theory. Most of the histories put Ahal far moonward. I thought that perhaps my mother was exaggerating when she said you were descended from the Tier. I can see she was not. Your eyes are beautiful." Syle said.

"Thank you. So? I shared mine." Ales folded her hands on the tabletop.

"Stoneward, there is a small group of towns that sit at the mouth of a rent in the ground that goes down for miles. Their legends say that thousands of cycles ago something fell from the sky, and made the hole. It was said to be a piece of the Tier that fell. Over the centuries the men and women of those towns have made themselves the fiercest of warriors. It is said they fight like the Tier themselves reborn to defend whatever is in that place. No one has been able to enter that place in all of recorded history." Syle said.

Ales had heard the rumor, but it was nice to have some confirmation. She believed that what had made that hole was Verdant, or what was left of the mind. It was a direction to go from here once she had Kiltik.

Servants arrived with the first course of the feast just in time for the skyfire to begin. The hangings were pulled back from massive windows that ran the length of the hall. Flowing curtains of light filled the night sky. Gasps and exclamations when up through the room as the lights undulated through all the colors of the rainbow. That was not normal behavior for the skyfire. It always cycled through all the shades of blue, but tonight every color imaginable showed through in the skyfire.

"What could that mean?" Aisha asked.

Ales knew. She wasn't sure how she knew, but she knew that it was a statement from the gods. She had no idea what that statement was, but only Avaara or Zezzhz could affect the skyfire like that. What does it mean? Ales wondered, but she pulled herself back to the conversation.

"I'm not sure. Perhaps the gods have once again become interested in what we do." Ales said.

"You believe in those old stories?" Syle asked.

"I have seen the goddess with my own two eyes. How could I not believe?" Ales regretted the words as soon as they passed her lips.

Syle's attention intensified to an uncomfortable degree.

"Have you now?" Syle asked.

"Yes, when I was a little girl I became lost for a time. She lead me back to where I should have been. Make no mistake they are very real." Ales said hoping it would be enough. She wasn't going to answer any more questions for this woman.

"If you were so young do you not think that perhaps you were mistaken?" Syle asked, and Ales narrowed her eyes at the woman.

"No, I do not. There is no forgetting a meeting with one's creator no matter how young one happens to be." Ales said evenly. She looked out at the shifting lights again. The rainbow colors were slowly fading back into the cool blue tones of the normal Skyfire. Ales knew then. The change in the skyfire had been a warning.

58

"Lia wait." Warran said as Lia reached the edge of the clearing.

"For what Warran? They have one of us, I have to go after her. With these I think I can get to her." Lia said. She lifted her front paw showing the band of metal around her leg that Warran had fastened there.

"Why didn't you let us come alone?" He asked. He had not closed his Vision since they left, but he had not seen any real dangers. It was hard to keep his head on a swivel all the time. Lia's eyes shifted to a dark corner of the clearing.

"Because of them." Lia whispered.

Warran followed her line of sight, and that was when he saw them. Two men in black armor. Their armor looked like they were members of the Three. But the Three had been gone for rotations. They were new, and Warran sensed the malice coming of them now that he had seen them.

"Will they attack us when you leave?" Warran asked. His hand crept toward the grip of his lancer, but then his fingers went rigid. His face twisted into pain, and self-hatred.

"I don't think they will, but if they do don't fight back. They won't make it thirty paces into the clearing. The Mother's magic here will only defend you if you do not defend yourself. It is too soon for you to fight again Warran. You need time to recover, to let what they told you sink in. You will be ready again one day, but not today." Lia explained.

"I thought that they couldn't help us." Warran said. Lia gave him a terrifying grin.

"They can't. It is known among the Tier that this effect is something that the Mother may not even be aware of. A sort of overflow of her connection with the natural world. She gives off power like body heat. No one has ever mentioned it to her. It is believed that if we were to draw her attention to it, the effect might cease." Lia said.

Warran let out a soft chuckle. "Omnipotent, and yet they don't know when they are causing parts of the world to go insane and protect us without their knowledge?" Warran said dubiously.

"Do you realize it when your body gives off heat? Do you realize you are breathing?" Lia asked. Warran shook his head.

"I wish I could help." Warran said.

"You are. Keep your little girl safe Warran. She's going to be one of us some day." Lia said. Then she turned, and trotted into the forest.

"Good Luck." Warran said.

Lia tried not to think about what she was going to do. Just as she got to the wall, the skyfire began. Undulating blue walls of light streaked across the sky. No matter where one was, the lights appeared to stream across the sky to the left and right. It was as if you were standing in the middle of a creek, and the water was flowing around you. As long as you could see the sky you could see the skyfire.

Lia pushed open the first two levels of her Constraints. She gave mental commands to her Cellstructs to keep those two levels open even if she were knocked unconscious. Lia crouched, and then sprang into the air. She reached the top of the wall easily. From there it was a short jump to one of the flat roofs of the shops in the Low Center. Traveling on the thievesway wasn't going to serve her well tonight. There were too many people looking up for her Taking to turn all eyes away from her.

She dropped silently into the next alleyway she came across, and began her arduous trip through the labyrinth of streets and alleyways that made up the Center. She paused when she noticed the lights coming off the buildings had changed. She looked up to the skyfire to see it rippling through with dozens of colors. Reds, blues, and greens flowed through the skyfire in a way that Lia had never seen before. She stopped, and stared.

The skyfire in her Vision had words swimming through it. They were in Tieran, and it was a short message. It wasn't really helpful though it just put her on edge. It read, "Take care Children. This night turns us towards a future. You must guide us into it with strength and mercy."

Lia closed her Vision, and while the colors remained the words vanished. She had to hurry. Ales wouldn't be able to open her Vision to read the message where she was. Lia had the sinking feeling that the message was about how Ales was going to react when she found out the King's men had taken Ilsa. When she did the results could be catastrophic.

59

Ales finished eating the second course of the feast. It had been a delicious baked skaln. If she had to guess from the flavor of the meat it had been fresh caught from the ocean within the last day. Whoever was preparing the food truly knew what they were about. Silina had found herself a master to cook this meal.

"If you will excuse me my Queen, I need to see to some of the arriving entertainers." Ales said, she rose and gave her bow to the queen.

"Of course Helena." The Queen said.

Ales made her way through the ballroom, and towards one of the service hallways used by the servants. She made a slow circuit of the labyrinth of hallways that surrounded the grand ballroom that would be the center of the night's festivities. At several intersections of hallways there was a medium sized room, and in each of these rooms a group of performers was setting up the things they needed to put on a show. Ales sighed, and folded her hands behind her back. She walked a slow path into another side hallway. Right on time Cole came around the corner at the opposite end of the hallway. He carried a small bag with him, and amazingly he didn't look out of place at all. Ales narrowed her eyes.

"Did you steal an officer's uniform?" She asked.

"That I did. Right off his back no less." Cole said with that stupid lopsided grin plastered on his face.

"Please tell me that he is still alive?" Ales asked. Cole nodded.

"He is sleeping it off in a store room. Considering how much brew I saw him pour into his face I highly doubt he will wake before breaking." Cole said.

Ales caught the shape when it split up the side, and fell away from her waist. Cole held out the bag, and she took it. Her dress split up the side as well springing away from her body, and freeing her from its confines. She changed into her normal clothing unabashedly as Cole eyed her body appreciatively.

"Pervert." She said. Cole put a hand against his chest in mock offense.

"Me M'lady? Perish the thought!" He said.

"Shame about the dress, you did look rather fetching in it." Cole said. Ales turned pulling on her jacket, and hiding her blush.

"Thank you Cole." Ales said.

"I've placed those little boxes where you wanted them. What do they do?" Cole asked.

"This."

Suddenly the palace shook under his feet. A deafening roar sounded down the hall as if he had stepped into a wind tunnel. He was blown off his feet, and Ales' jacket flew up fluttering in the wind like a cape.

"Father's Stones!" Cole groaned as he got to his feet.

"Do they take off their armor Cole?" Ales asked.

"Not for a minute. They retract it to a pauldron when they bathe, but nothing else. They even sleep with it on." Cole shivered.

"It's creepy."

"Get out of here Cole. Take your gold, and make sure they can never find you. Maybe one day I will see you again. Maybe by then, you'll change your mind about us."

Ales walked away toward the opposite end of the hall. Cole watched her for a long moment. In that moment he saw who Ales really was. She was never going to stop. She was never going to bend. She would do what was right even if it killed her. Someone like that had the power to do anything. He knew beyond any shadow of a doubt that he wanted to be that person. There was only one way to be that person. He pushed past his fear of what he might do with that kind of power.

"Ales wait." She paused at the end of the hallway, but she didn't turn back.

"I want it, Ales. The money who cares about the money? Real good isn't done with money. But I'm afraid I will do bad things with what you would teach me." Ales turned back to him, and she smiled.

"That dear boy is how you know that you won't. Go on Cole, get to the Clearing. You and the others will be safe there." Ales said.

"What if you don't come out of this?" He asked hesitantly.

"Lia will take good care of you. Don't be afraid of her Cole. Despite the fact that her sense of humor is sometimes frightening she will never hurt you. And despite her protests about being a teacher she will teach you things you could never learn anywhere else, not even from me." Ales said.

"Are you sure I cannot help?" Cole said.

She turned and came back to him. She put a hand on his shoulder. "No matter what, don't come back here on your own. You are not prepared for what will transpire here this night." Ales said.

Cole nodded he turned away so he could find his way out of the palace. Ales turned and began to jog. She had used up her pad with that conversation. She had no time to waste.

"I'm not even sure that I am prepared." Ales said as she followed the only remaining path that could lead her down to the Searchers quarters.

60

Lia stretched out into her run. Her Cellstructs told her that Ales would have already started. She pushed herself to go faster. She crossed the center in a blur. People were blown off their feet as she dodged between them. When she got to the High Center Citadel square Ilsa's scent hit her nose, and her reflexes made the disastrous choice to stop her right then and there. She dug her claws in, and it almost caused her to roll into a tumble that would have broken bones. But in that moment her Cellstructs took control of her body, and corrected her limbs so that she ground safely to a halt.

Letting her Cellstructs take control of her body was a trick she had been trying to pass on to Ales, but Ales hadn't been able to quite understand it yet. It was amazing to her that in many subtle ways she had surpassed her sister. Ales had always seemed so much more, and she was, but there were things even she could not do. She focused on Ilsa's scent, but there was really no point. She guessed that Ilsa had been taken to the Citadel jail, and it likely meant that she was going to have to step over corpses to get her back. She would.

She stopped just long enough to make a decision. The Citadel dungeon only had two access points that she knew of. If she went through the front door she would have to kill a lot of soldiers to get to Ilsa. She did not relish the idea of coming in from below. It would be a slog through the piss and shit of every criminal in the dungeon. But it was better than having to kill anyone. Besides it still looked calm inside of the Citadel. That meant Ales' plan hadn't quite started yet.

She groaned, and turned towards the opposite end of the Citadel square. She vowed that Ilsa would wash every square tick of her fur when this was done. She dashed across the square, and then followed the Citadel wall away moonward. When she passed the guard house atop the wall that was directly adjacent to the Archive Tower she began to count her steps. When she got to two hundred and seventeen she turned directly moonward. She pushed on her third level of Constraints, and it popped open. Strength surged into her body. Her run sped up to speeds that she knew were dangerous. If she tumbled at this speed there was no chance of all of her bones staying intact. She let her mind slip into the mild trance where her Cellstructs could aid her in correcting any small errors that would cause her to fall. She ran for five full lengths. Then she slowly tapered off to a trot, before coming to a full stop.

She had gotten into the Dark Wood at some point. The trance she had put herself into made her somewhat oblivious to the world around her. Her Cellstructs guided her until she came to a solid stone well. It was a single seamless bondstructed piece of stone. There was a solid metal cap on it. No one worried about anyone getting in this way because who would want to trek through five Lengths of shit, and piss to get into the Citadel? It was more than that. The cap had been bonded with the stone well. Getting it open would require supreme effort. The gas build up was dangerous in and of itself as well.

She studied it for a long moment. As part of their reconnaissance they learned of the sewer systems that kept the city clean. Despite their function, they were a marvel of engineering, running dozens of lengths moonward where they emptied into the great eastern sea. She put her front paws on top of the cap. She dug her claws deeply into the metal of the cap. Then she braced her rear two pairs of legs against the side of the well. She twisted her body, and the cap made a screeching sound of buckling stone. She snapped her body back straight, and the cap exploded free of the top of the well. It sprayed bits of stone in every direction as it broke loose from its moorings. She flung it to one side yanking her claws free of the metal. It slammed into a boulder, and slid to the ground.

She whimpered at the stench coming from the sewer. She took a deep breath, and then she was down the hole. She ran as fast as she could but she realized at the one length mark that she desperately wished she had simply gone in the front door. She could barely keep her stomach as she past the half way point. Then she started to think about the fact that what she was smelling was getting on her paws, on her fur, and on her everything. She skidded to a halt, and heaved up the contents of her stomach. Thankfully she hadn't eaten much in the past day. She panted for a long minute, and tried to mentally block out the vile stench engulfing her. Finally she started to trot towards her destination again picking up speed until she was running near as fast as she could again.

When she reached the Citadel she passed dozens of large iron pipes. Water and filth flowed from them and into the main drainage pipe. At the end of the tunnel was a massive bondsteel door that the Searchers, and city builders would use to access the tunnels in the event that they needed maintenance. Her Cellstructs judged how much power would be needed to blast the door off the hinges, and Lia picked up speed. Not for the first time she wished she had access to the Circle of Breaking. She would have been much less likely to hurt herself doing this if she could see the weak points of the door. Her Cellstructs warned her that striking at an incorrect angle could damage her, and she allowed them partial control over her limbs to help her correct her body. This was going to hurt.

She jumped. All six of her paws hit the massive bondsteel door at the same time. The metal buckled, and the frame was blasted from the stone on either side. The door flew away into the room shattering a heavy wood table. It slammed into the opposite wall, and then fell to the floor with a hollow boom. Lia landed where the table had been. She made a seething noise, and started to dance from once set of paws to the other.

"Oh gods that stings!" she hissed.

She realized a few moments later that there were two men in the room. They were still sitting in their chairs utensils poised as if they had just been about to dig into a meal. They stared at her absolutely astonished. She slowly lowered three of her paws to the floor, and only moved her eyes to each man.

"I don't suppose you would believe you were both dreaming this would you?" Lia asked.

The two men looked up at each other.

"You believe a talking katali just kicked down a bondsteel door, and tried to tell us we were dreaming this?" The man on the right said.

"Nope." The man on the left said. Then they calmly got out of their chairs and left the room.

Lia sagged with relief. She looked around the room but there didn't seem to be anything of value there. It was a simple guard post. She shook herself violently as only an animal can spraying the walls and floor with vile detritus. She was still filthy, but she didn't have time to think about it. She consulted her Cellstructs for a map of the Citadel. She was actually very close to where she guessed they would be holding Ilsa. She hoped she wasn't too late.

She ran up the stairs, and took a left. The hallway went about a hundred marks and then there was a t-junction. If she went left it would take her outside to a sally port in the city wall. To the right it went deeper into the dungeon. Lia started to have a bad feeling as she went down the hallway. When she came to the cells her unease increased to a healthy nagging paranoia. The cells were completely empty. Her nose told her that the cells had not been empty for more than a few hours.

Her ears pricked forward as she heard a soft whimper. Lia stopped and listened to the soft voice echoing down the hallway, but even her ears could not pick out the direction more than that it was somewhere ahead of her. The corridor she was going down was following the curve of the outer wall of the Citadel. Her mental map informed her that this corridor emptied out into a courtyard that they used to punish criminals who attacked the guards, or tried to escape. Lia's unease increased as she approached the courtyard door. She knew that this was going to be bad. When she got to the door it was closed. She eyed the door handle dubiously. She berated herself for worrying about germs when Ilsa's life was in danger.

She took the knob in her mouth and turned her head. The door thankfully was not locked. It popped open silently, and she released the knob. She pushed her head through it, and saw a disturbing tableau. Ilsa had been bound with her hands over her head to a stone frame. Her back was crisscrossed with at least a dozen slashes. Morra Roa stood coiling a whip in her fist.

"I will say this. I am impressed with your resolve child, but you will break eventually. You should just tell me where to find your friends."

Lia slipped through the door on silent paws. She opened her Vision, and invoked all of her Circles. The throb between her eyes told her that she could not hold so much power for very long. She had seen the aftermath of Ales working with all seven Circles open at once, and even her three were too much power for any mortal being to wield. She did not know how Ales could possibly manage seven.

She froze when she saw him. He was supposed to be at the celebration, he was supposed to be busy trying to get through the rubble of a half demolished Citadel. She had felt the vibrations in her paws when the charges had gone off. Yet there in the shadows across the courtyard sat King Roa calmly watching the interrogation. He did not see Lia because he could not. He could have stared right at her and his eyes would have slid away because the Circle of Taking made her all but invisible. This was a fight she knew she couldn't win. She would have to go with her second option to take Ilsa and run.

Lia slunk around the outside of the courtyard until she was in a straight line with Morra, and the King. She would use Morra like a cue ball. Slamming into her, and throwing her body into the King to momentarily disable them both. Lia gathered herself. Before she could leap another door into the courtyard burst open, and a young man with sandy colored hair came bustling through. He wore the black and gold of the king's servants, and looked flustered.

"My King!" The young man came to where the king sat, and went down to one knee.

"Go ahead boy." The king said. He waved his hand up for the young man to stand.

"I have made a circuit of the hallways My King. It seems that most of the Citadel Guard are trapped in the sunward wing. Only a few escaped the blasts. The Night Lady has been seen in the hallways." The sandy haired youth finished in a rush. Lia waited, as the king raised a perfect golden eyebrow.

"Has she now?"

The King got to his feet, and peered around the room suspiciously. His entire body language changed from one moment to the next. He went from relaxed and arrogant to an almost hunted body posture. He stood on the balls of his feet as he inspected the room his arms tensed at his sides as if he were ready to leap for the door. It was like he was two entirely different people stuffed into one body. Lia watched her whole body tense because it appeared he might attack the boy. But then he sat back down, relaxed once again. Self-sure he waved the boy away.

"Tell me when they have subdued her. Go on."

The boy bowed, and ran out of the room. Lia tensed her muscles, and struck. From her corner of the courtyard she took two massive leaps, and slammed her shoulder into Morra's side. The woman's whole body buckled, and she was driven away across the room towards the King. Lia's paws hit the ground, and she never stopped moving. The crashing sound of Morra slamming into the King, and driving both of them into the stone wall of the courtyard barely had time to register.

Lia reared up onto her hind paws, and cut the ropes holding Ilsa's wrists with one quick swipe of her claws. She was beneath the girl before she could fall, and Ilsa fell across Lia's back. Lia thought for a moment about putting Ilsa down, and giving them a real fight. She had the new Sparks that Warran had gifted her, but the motions she would have to make with them around her ankles would take practice. She decided that getting Ilsa away was far more important.

She turned for the courtyard door, and froze. The King, untouched in resplendent black scale armor stood between her and the door. She must have missed, but she had no idea how he had gotten across the room so fast. He kept his hands folded behind his back as if he were not concerned with her close proximity. Her Cellstructs were warning her to move, but their advice was not as helpful with Ilsa lying across her back. She stood stock still, trying to process the best way to handle the situation. But she couldn't ignore the warning from her Vision that Morra was coming up behind her. Lia dipped to her right to overbalance Ilsa so that when she moved Ilsa didn't slide of her back. A sword passed through the spot where she had been a moment earlier. The King had not followed her when she dodged out of the way, but Morra was advancing on her with a sword.

"I'm afraid we cannot allow you to leave. The girl and her parents are traitors to the crown." The King said.

Lia backed herself up into the corner of the courtyard. Carefully she tilted her body until Ilsa slid to the ground behind her.

"I'm glad that you think you can stop me. By your arrogance will you be undone."

It wasn't a hollow statement. They might stop her, but Ales would be their undoing. There were so many ways she had surpassed her sister. But in sheer fighting ability Ales was peerless. Lia had seen her fight with The Traitor through the memories of The Core. She didn't want to see her sister like that again, but they were fighting for their survival. She couldn't afford to be delicate. Lia pushed open all five levels of her Constraints. Not for the first time she wished she had the ability to bond more deeply with her Cellstructs. An extra level of Constraints might have made the difference here. She thought furiously trying to see a way out of this without fighting them, but she could not. She attempted to contact Ales telepathically. Either she was too far away, or she had entered the shielded areas below where Kiltik was kept. Having run out of options there was nothing left but to begin.

Lia drew in a breath, and roared as loudly as she could. She very often started a fight that way. Even if her opponents were prepared for her to do it the volume she could generate usually caused hearing damage. Morra screamed, and dropped her sword. She clutched her ears, and fell to her knees. Lia slammed into her claws first a moment later. She pushed off with her rear legs. This made most of her body fly past Morra. With her claws dug into the chest of her armor this wrenched Morra around violently at the waist.

The sound of Morra's spine snapping was gruesome. As if someone had fed a glass rod into a meat grinder. Her Cellstructs sounded a blaring warning inside of her head. It was too late though, she felt the blade slam into her back. She lost all feeling in her rear legs. Her Cellstructs immediately went to work on repairing the damage, but the blade was poisoned as well. It was going to take some time to break down the poison and close the wound. The poison was fast acting, and it was already making her light headed. It was blackhorn venom. She had not encountered it for at least fifty cycles. It was very rare. What made it worse was it was a paralytic. It would take her Cellstructs at least an hour to restore motion to her body. She gritted her teeth together when he twisted the blade. She refused to make a sound as he pulled the blade free.

"Now that I have calmed you a little we will have a long conversation about how you survived the Cataclysm, and where your dear sister has gone. A shame about Morra."

The King's voice had changed so drastically that Lia was certain that she was not talking to the same person. Whatever was running that body, it was not the King. It was working him like a puppet. He looked at his daughter's corpse, and his expression seemed as if he were looking at a pile of trash. His eyes though were distraught.

"I'll tell you a secret of the Tier, we cannot be broken. So if you are delaying killing me because you think that you will get information from me. I'll save you the time." Lia spat blood onto his boots. The paralytic venom finally spread, and her jaw muscles froze.

"I think you will find that you will not have a choice in the matter."

Lia could not close her eyes as he reached down to grab ahold of her collar.

61

Ales moved through the hallways soundless and unseen. She got past the remaining guards, and none of the Searchers had seen her so far. As soon as she had passed the outer doors she had gotten a psionic sending from Kiltik acknowledging that she was getting close but something was blocking them from accepting the mental handshake that would allow them to speak. The main hallway lead to a Y junction that indicated to her that this place was built to be as confusing as possible. The two halways off the junction looked identical, and appeared to have the same exact ninety degree turn about twenty marks down the hallway. One went to the right and one to the left.

Ales paused for a long moment. She gave her Cellstructs time to analyze what she was seeing. A moment later they communicated to her that there had to be some sort of indicator or people would constantly be getting lost down here. Not everyone would have the type of memory that would let them navigate a place like this. She realized that she had seen several Searchers, and not a one of them was without spectacles. At first she thought they wore them simply for protection, but it made more sense that they needed them to navigate the hallways. She opened the Circle of Light, and started to cycle through spectra of light besides those that were normally visible. When she reached ultra violet signs appeared painted on the walls. Ales found it somewhat amazing the strange way things had both advanced, and degraded in terms of technological achievement in thirty-one hundred cycles. The sign indicated that a restricted containment area was down the right hand path. That had to be where they were keeping Kiltik.

She went down the right hand corridor. She followed the polished white walls for hundred marks. There it ended in a blank wall with a door on either side of the hall. The glowing ultraviolet letters indicated that the left hand door lead to some sort of manufactory. The right hand door had the same restricted containment area label she had seen before. The door was locked and had some sort of bondstructed key.

She put her hand against the lock, and her Cellstructs poured out of her hand. They slipped into the lock allowing her to make an energetic connection to the lock. It only took a few short moments to Cut through the lock's defenses. The door popped open, and she slipped silently through the opening. She pulled the door closed, and the lock engaged behind her. She followed the signs on the switchback stairs down five flights to what she assumed was the lowest floor of the Searchers facilities. The door had a similar lock, but this one was much more difficult. This one required the blood of one of the Searchers to get through along with a key. She eyed the lock with annoyance. She could bypass it the same way she had bypassed the earlier lock, but it would take more time to Cut her way through the defenses.

She took a closer look at the door. It was bondsteel, and the frame was anchored into the sorstone walls. It was more than strong enough to stop almost anyone, but not nearly strong enough to stop her. She decided that subtlety was no longer necessary. She concentrated, and her first five levels of constrains popped open. Her Cellstructs flowed throughout her body reinforcing her bones and muscles until they were strong enough to survive using super human strength. She put her back against the opposite wall. She put her feet against the door with her back braced against the wall. She straightened her legs, and there was a sound of screeching metal as the door buckled. It was quickly followed with the awful sound of tearing stone as the door frame ripped away from the wall. It fell into the room, and Ales dropped to the ground.

She wasted no time darting through the opening she had made. The room inside was dark, but she opened her Vision a little wider. The darkness receded revealing a room of middling size with two massive doors on the other side of the room. It was an obvious last line of defense, and there was no way she was getting through it without breaking the lock. As she was working out how to do that a feeling built inside of her head. It was the feeling she got when a psionic handshake completed.

{This One thanks the gods. This One didn't know if This One would ever get the chance to speak to the Tier ever again. You are Alessandra, Family Katane.}

{Kiltik the Tier are gone. I have little time, and many many questions. I will free you from this confinement, and then we can talk.} Ales said. The response was a sharp negative.

{You cannot open the door. There is something trapped in here with This One, something that This One was creating was corrupted beyond This One's control. How much space do you have Alessandra, Family Katane? Can This One simply transfer This One's memories to your cerebral storage?}

{Kiltik we do not have time for this. If I am here too long I will be forced to kill a large number of people.}

{This One apologizes profusely. However This One cannot allow you to open the door. Please allow This One to transfer This One's memories to you. Everything will become clear once you know what This One knows.}

{Please be precise. How long will the transfer take?}

{This One calculates that at the current rate the transfer would take slightly longer than one hour.}

Ales shook her head, and sent strong negation across the connection.

{This One begs you to reconsider.}

Ales considered for a moment. Tieran Minds were always very concerned with preserving life. It would not harm her to know what Kiltik knew.

{How long would it take to transfer to me the memories that pertain to why I cannot open this door?} she asked.

{Considerably less time. This One can transfer those memories in thirty five seconds.} Ales sent an affirmative.

She quickly sat down on the floor, and braced herself. Suddenly she was assaulted with images, sounds, and thousands of other tiny pieces of information. She did her best to simply not pay attention to the information and let her mind absorb it. She didn't tip over but it was a close run thing. Finally it stopped, and she let her Cellstructs access the information she had just gained. Then she understood.

Kiltik had been found after almost thirteen hundred cycles of isolation. He had helped the native people to build the kingdom of Vilhena. Then as time passed Kiltik had slowly started to teach them about Tieran technology. It had taken Intervals to impart the concepts necessary to help him build a bondstruct manufactory. Once that had been done Kiltik had become interested in being able to do more to help them. So the Mind had built itself a body. A body made of Bondstructs. A body with super strength, and self-repairing capabilities. A body that replicated many powers of the Tier. Then as Ales had surmised from what they had found in the archives. Gifts had arrived from distant kingdoms. Gifts made of Bondstructs. Gifts with an energetic infection. Like a black cloud it flowed into every bit of bondstructed techonology in the entire kingdom. Kiltik had been able to protect himself from infection, but his body had not been so fortunate. So he had used the remaining Bondstructs to build a container that he knew even his body could never breach. The infection though that was what Ales was most interested in. She gasped in a deep breath as she emerged from the memories.

{Gods, it is everywhere isn't it? That is where those crude Cellstructs came from.}

{This One estimates that at least eighty precent of all Tieran Structures that are not self-aware have been infected. This One postulates that properly emitted elementary energy bursts could remove the infection, but leave the structures intact. However immediate reinfection is a definite possibility if all of the structures in the vicinity are not affected by the discharge.}

Kiltik's explanation was dizzying. In her time such a pronouncement would put the entire planet in immediate jeopardy.

{Kiltik how much Tieran technology did not follow the self-containment protocols?} she asked, afraid to hear the answer.

{This One estimates that sixty-one percent of all Tieran structures were destroyed in the Cataclysm that claimed the Homeland. But logical models suggest that other Minds have attempted to rebuild just as this one has. Therefore it is impossible to postulate the current percentage of surviving structures that exist.}

{Is there no safe place from which we can base our operations?}

{Apologies Alessandra, Family Katane. Logical models indicate that no sufficiently advanced area is free of the infection. Though all self-aware technologies will be immune.} Kiltik responded.

{I suppose the idea that it cannot access Antistructs or other Minds is something of a comfort. I need you to come with us, but not right now. I will find a way to free you, and your body from this taint.} Ales said.

{This One thanks you Alessandra, Family Katane.}

{Is there anything I can do to expand your telepathic range so that we can contact you more easily?}

{This One suggests a psionic wave repetition device.} The Mind said.

{Schematics?} Ales asked.

A few images, and instructions flowed across the telepathic link with the Mind causing her to blink in confusion for a long moment as she absorbed the information, and requested that her Cellstructs process the information.

{Alessandra, Family Katane. This one senses that Liassa, Family Katane is in grave danger. She attempts to contact This One, and through This One to contact you. The chamber prevents This One from reaching outside, and thus This One can determine no more than the origin and destination of the signal. Please go to her Alessandra, Family Katane.} Kiltik's mindvoice was wrought with concern.

{One last question Kiltik. Do you know Verdant's current location?} Ales asked.

{This One's calculations indicate that Verdant's trajectory would place that One here.}

A bit more information flowed across the telepathic link. It momentarily unbalanced Ales. She groaned, and waited for the sensation to fade. She stood, and turned back towards the destroyed door.

{Alessandra, Family Katane. Please return for This One? This One fears for This One's continued existence.} Kiltik's mindvoice was filled with despair.

{I will.}

62

Lia pulled her eyes open. The last of the blackhorn venom had been cleaned from her system, but when she tried to move her body wouldn't respond. Her Cellstructs informed her that she had taken two more wounds to the spine. Someone had shoved something metal into her wounds to keep her spine from healing. They must have noticed while she was unconscious that she was healing, and decided to make sure she was helpless. Still they had bound her paws with some sort of bondstructed shackles. She queried her Cellstructs for how long it would take for them to remove whatever had been shoved into her body. She was having trouble breathing, which meant they likely had nicked some of the nerves in her autonomic system. They quickly replied that whatever had been inserted into her spinal wounds they were made of Bondstructs. They were defending themselves against attempts to remove them. Her Cellstructs estimated that they would overcome the Bondstructs in roughly two days at the current pace.

Lia lowered her head to the floor. She would be dead long before that if she was any judge of the situation. Ilsa was lying close by. She was similarly bound. Her eyes were open, and she looked more angry than scared. She had been bound with her arms behind her back, and it appeared that her ankles had been tethered to her wrists. But she was determinedly working her way closer to Lia. She inch-wormed her way across the floor on her stomach. She finally got her face about a tick away from Lia's.

"Can I pull those things out of you?" She whispered.

"I don't think that would be a good idea. They might attack you. Also the one closest to my neck was inexpertly inserted if they were attempting to keep me alive. They have damaged my ability to breath. My Cellstructs are assisting me, but if you yank that out it could be very unpleasant for me." Lia whispered back.

"Then what do we do?" Ilsa asked. Tears started leaking from Lia's eyes. She tried to hold them back, but there was no point anymore.

"We hope Ilsa. It is all there is left to do." Lia said.

"It will do no good for your Night Lady to come. We have had three thousand cycles to prepare for this. You cannot prevail." The King came through a set of doors behind the throne. His voice was that of the creature, but it sounded even more stressed and insane.

"I am glad you are confident in your abilities. My sister is nothing like me, and if you are what I think you are you know that. If you think you can use us against her you are sorely mistaken. She will break you just as she broke you once before."

The King's face twisted into a snarl. "We destroyed your entire race animal. You are nothing more than the dregs of an extinct species. You are nothing!" The King screamed in rage.

"And what are you? Your nothing but bits of data shoved into our technology. You have done well to hide yourself, but that is over now. The Tier have returned, and we can see you no matter where you hide."

The King's body began to laugh then. It was a terrible sound. It was not a human sound. Nobody was ever meant to make a noise like that. It was amazing to her that the creature had managed to hide this long. It was so alien. So obviously not human once it revealed itself. She wished she could cover her ears so she didn't have to listen to that screeching, wheezing, approximation of a laugh. Ilsa actually did cover her ears. The King turned inhuman eyes down to her.

"You, and your pathetic sister are the only ones left with the power to challenge us. You cannot make more like you without one of your little Minds to help you. Like this one."

The King reached into a box beside the throne, and pulled out a shining black orb. Softly glowing green lines ran over the surface of the orb. It was Verdant. Lia's mind raced, she immediately tried to make a telepathic connection to the mind. The handshake was almost instantaneous.

{Liassa, Family Katane. Please help This One. It is attempting to infect This One. It is going to destroy This One.} Verdant's mindvoice was frantic, and filled with fear.

{I will try Verdant. I will do my best.} Lia assured her.

Information slammed into her mind, and she gasped as thousands of images poured through the link into her brain. It was too much for her to absorb, too much for her Cellstructs to process all at once. She couldn't understand any of it, but she knew who would. Verdant was giving her everything she needed to rebuild a copy of herself. She was forcing all of her memories, all of her data into Lia's mind. Lia did her best to absorb it all knowing that her Cellstructs would be able to process it all eventually. Only a Fixer would be able to use this.

She pulled herself out of the telepathic link. She was disorientated, but then she saw why Verdant was so frantic. She felt blood running out of her nose from the massive telepathic overload of having so much information shoved into her mind all at once. But the King had raised Verdant over his head.

"Don't!" Lia screamed. She frantically communicated to her Cellstructs to brace for energetic discharge. "Ilsa, cover!"

Ilsa rolled into the fetal position, and squeezed her eyes shut. The King brought Verdant down and smashed her against the floor. Lia cringed as her outer cover shattered, and clear conductive fluid spread across the floor. She had to survive this. It would take an untrained Fixer hundreds of cycles to even begin to understand the complexities of building a Mind. She couldn't help herself, she tried to force her broken body to move. If she could infuse Verdant with her Cellstructs it was possible she could be rebuilt. Minds could not be infused with Cellstructs of their own because of the high energy environment inside of their outer protective covering. Then the glow of Verdant's power source filled Lia's eyes, and she squeezed them shut.

She felt the blast, and her body was flung across the throne room. She slammed into the opposite wall, and was held there off the ground for a long moment before the discharge from Verdant's power cell gave out. Her whole body tingled from the discharge, and she could smell burning fur. When she hit the ground something in her spine shifted, and suddenly she couldn't breathe. She couldn't believe that the creature had been so stupid. Her Cellstructs worked frantically to attempt to restore her nerve connections to allow her to breathe again. It wouldn't be enough. She had perhaps a minute before she would pass into unconsciousness. Once her body started to cool her Cellstructs would no longer be able to repair her damaged body. She was astonished to see the King getting to his feet his armor completely intact. Then Ales was there, standing over Lia her eyes blazing with light.

"Lie still Sister. I have you."

Ales took Lia's head in her hands. She cupped her hands around Lia's muzzle and held her mouth closed. Ales put her mouth over Lia's nose and blew breath into her body as hard as she could.

"Take a moment to brace yourself, I am going to remove the shivs from your spine."

Ales pulled her Windblade from her jacket, and she got to her feet. She turned to the King who was pulling himself free of the rubble of the shattered throne.

"You, I will deal with in a moment. Until then out of my sight."

She lifted her Windblade, and swung it. The sound it made was a deafening crack of thunder. The King was blasted off his feet. He went through the sorestone wall of the throne room leaving a trail of crushed stone behind him. Ales gave a satisfied snort, and knelt next to Lia once again. She blew another breath into Lia's burning lungs. Ales examined the wound at the base of Lia's neck. They had slipped the shiv in between the fourth, and fifth vertebrae. Ales coated her fingers in Cellstructs, and forced them into the wound. She was doing more damage, but nothing could be done for it. She pulled the shiv free with some effort. It attempted to drive spines into her fingers, but her Cellstructs protected her. Lia groaned involuntarily.

"I'm sorry Sister."

Ales lifted her sister's head and forced another breath into her lungs. She repeated the process of removing the two remaining shivs that were lodged in her spine. By the time she had removed the second one Lia was breathing on her own.

{Be careful Ales, he is more powerful than he seems. He destroyed Verdant. His Bondstructs are shielded. They survived the discharge.} Lia said.

"I know. I received Verdant's sending when he removed the shielding. Nearly passed out when she drove that information into my mind."

Lia gasped out when Ales pulled the third shiv free.

{It is going to take me time to heal Ales. Check on Ilsa, she took some of the blast as well. She does not have Cellstructs to heal her.} Lia said.

"She has minor burns. She's not in any danger just a lot of pain. She's taking it well." Ales said.

{Praise to the Mother and Father for that.} Lia said.

"Praise to you Lia, if you had not told her to cover it would have been much worse." Ales said.

{Can you handle him?} Lia asked. Ales swallowed hard.

"It is going to be bad Lia. He's strong, and his armor took the blast of my Windblade easily. I am going to have to go farther. I can't hold back."

{Wait. These may help. Warran wasn't sure they would work.}

Lia tried to lift her front paw, but it would barely move. The nerve connections had not been restored.

{Quick, Ales, run my paw over the bag around my neck. Your Sparks are inside,} Lia said.

"Father's stones Lia this is no time for non-lethal weaponry."

"Just do it!" Lia growled.

Ales responded immediately to Lia's commanding bark. She picked up Lia's paw, and ran it over the bag. Obediently the bag spit out her Sparks. She caught them as the rolled out.

"What will these do?" Ales said immediately noticing the differences in them. She could have delved into them with her Vision but it was much easier to ask.

{What I didn't have a chance too. Like the bands around my ankles they have been adjusted to deliver a parcel of patterened energy to anything they are discharged touching. If it is made of structures that are infected the instructions contained in that data parcel will combat the infection. It may take more than one delivery to clean all of the structures.}

Lia's ears perked forward. She looked up, and saw murder in Ales' eyes. Pure black rage that she had once unleashed on the Traitor. If that got out there would be no stopping her. She would destroy everything around her including any sort of bond she had formed with the people of Vilhena. No one who brought destruction like that could be a protector.

{He's coming back. I can hear him moving through the debris. Ales be careful, he's not the only one left. We have killed two of the five. They might join him, but he must live through this. Free him Ales, free them. It is up to you to protect them.}

Ales wondered why he hadn't brought more men. If they had so many with bondarmor controlling them it would have given him the advantage. Perhaps the arrogance of whatever fel intelligence controlled him was overriding better judgment. Ales put her hands through the grips of the Sparks. They were dangerous weapons to use because they drew on the biological elementary energies that her body generated. Each discharge would make her weaker. She could use them much longer than many Arcangineers, but eventually she would tire from their use. They were a double edged sword. She gripped them tightly.

{I will try Lia.}

She turned away and walked towards the hole the King had left in the wall of the throne room.

63

Ales walked warily through the hole in the throne room wall. The King had been blasted through the wall on the opposite side of the hall, and into the observatory. Ales did something that she had only done once before. She went to one knee, and opened all seven of her Circles. Information inundated her mind. She took long breaths as her Cellstructs went into overdrive trying to help her Process all the information. The whole world slowed down like everything was moving through molasses as the Circle of Observance came into effect. Hundreds of pieces of glowing text overlayed everything she could see. Distances, materials, structural tolerances, and a thousand other little points of data helped her to understand everything she saw on a fundamental level.

She pushed her Constraints open to the sixth level, and listened. She could hear him moving. Immediately her Vision showed her exactly where he was. He was buried fifty marks ahead and to her right in the rubble of a massive black norstone column that his body had blasted through when she had hit him with her Windblade. She walked silently across the room her body taut and ready for any attack. The King flung a massive piece of the column at her when she was about ten marks away. She spun to the side as it flowed past her as if it were falling through water. She set herself, and waited for him to pull himself free of the rubble. He finally brushed dust off his armor, and folded his arms behind his back.

"Killing this man, even if you could, will not help you. We are everywhere. Your Minds have attempted to cleanse us, and failed." The King said.

"They never had tool like these."

Ales rushed forward. The King was fast. Absurdly so, but he might as well have been moving through mud. He drew a short sword from behind his back, and thrust it at her. She ducked beneath it impossibly low. Sliding on her knees she drove her fist into the King's stomach. There was a sharp buzzing sound, and part of the King's armor exploded away into what appeared to be fine black dust. The Bondstructs had lost all cohesion. The King looked down at her through the eyeslit of his helmet. That was when she saw something. It wasn't fear. It was desire. Deep seated desire for her to kill him. His eyes pleaded for her help.

She slid back out of the way of the slicing sword, and then turned her body left to let a thrust go by. He wanted this to be over. He backed her across the room, and she gave ground trying to figure it out. If she continued to punish him it would kill him, and Lia had asked her to free him. And now she had to do it. She gave ground until she was back in the throne room. The entire time she studied the armor. After a few moments she could tell it mirrored a living organism's central nervous system. It had a central brain, in the back of the armor. The way the energy flowed through it told her that it was located in the upper back. Likely between the shoulder blades. If she could hit that the armor would collapse.

Her Vision warned her immediately that there were more people in the room. The remaining members of the royal family minus the Queen, and Syle had entered. Ilsa let out a strangled grunt as Narran Roa picked her up by the back of her neck. Karan Roa stood over Lia with a sword point touching the back of her skull.

"Enough." Narran rumbled.

His words seemed to be echoing through a long pipe because her Vision distorted the speed of everything. Ales continued to calmly dodge sword thrusts. The King pulled back and held his sword at the ready. Her Cellstructs told her that if she went to the limits she could stop all three of them before they could even move. But they would be dead. There was no chance of them surviving if she hit them that hard. There was no pulling her punches if she went to that level of ability. Worse was that she knew, knew beyond any shadow of a doubt that if she killed one of them she would not stop until everything around her was destroyed. She wanted to protect them, but Lia and Ilsa ranked much higher on the scale of her protective instincts than any of the royals. If she had to kill one she would kill them all to make sure they couldn't ever hurt Lia or Ilsa again.

"It is over Antieri." The King spat the title like it was a curse.

Ales held up her hands and turned to face him squarely. Her Cellstructs reported there was someone else in the throne room. Someone that they didn't realize was there. Then the decision on whether or not to kill them was taken from her. The King lunged forward, and thrust his sword at her chest. Ales moved, dropping just slightly and to the right. The movement was so fast and small it was imperceptible. The blade slammed into her chest, and passed right through to the other side. She didn't need to fake her howl of pain as she elected to leave her pain receptors active. When he pulled the sword free, she collapsed to the ground.

A shout of dismay burst from Cole, and a much louder wordless roar from Lia. It was quickly followed by two rapid reports of a lancer. Narran dropped Ilsa, and stumbled to his right. He wobbled on his feet for a moment, but did not fall. Karan stumbled, and fell to the ground. Ales' Vision told her that he was not dead merely dazed. When Narran didn't fall Cole pulled the trigger on his Stoe again, and lancer bolts smashed into Narran's chest plate. It didn't penetrate, but it blew the giant back off his feet. Cole walked over to where Karan was stiring.

"You will never touch her." Cole snarled.

Then he emptied the entire clip into Karan's head. Ten lancer bolts smashed into Karan Roa. His helmet took most of the damage, but it would be a long time before he healed from the concussion if he ever woke up. Cole went to Narran as he dropped the clip out of one of his Lancers and replaced it with one full of bolts. He held it on Narran. He expertly slid his other lancer back into its holster. He popped the clip out of it, and slid in a full one. It was all done in less than a second without looking using only one hand. He must have practiced it hundreds of times.

"Now you are just going to stay right there, or I'm not going to miss that eye hole again. You follow me giant?"

Narran nodded his helmeted head.

"Be careful Cole. They may be able to operate without the body inside of the armor being aware."

Cole looked back to Lia. He nodded.

"Are you all right?" Cole asked.

"Not yet, but I will be soon. Pay attention there is one of them left out there." Lia said.

He nodded again and kept his lancer trained on Narran's face. The King stepped over Ales' body.

"Cole, the King!" Lia shouted.

Cole did not hesitate, and no matter how fast the King was, he would never be faster than an already drawn lancer. Cole turned the weapon and began pulling the trigger. The Stoe held thirteen bolts, and he buried every single one in the King's chestplate. In the same motion he smoothly re-drew his other iron and held it against the faceplace of Narran's helmet as he started to rise. Even the King's armor couldn't mute that much damage entirely, and he stumbled backwards. He fell to one knee.

Ales struck then. Her wound was nearly closed and didn't impair her at all. She rolled to her feet, drew back her fist, and slammed it into the King's back between the shoulder blades. She drove him face first into the floor. She hit him hard enough that it knocked him unconscious. She cringed when the floor cracked under the stress. Ales' mouth fell open with astonishment when the King's body rolled over. He had to have a severe concussion. There should be no way he was conscious. She backed away, and set herself for a fight. The Spark should have disabled the armor. It clearly had worked earlier. The King's voice was an insane warble.

"He is mine! This world is mine!" He slashed at her.

Ales turned sideways and the sword passed. She slammed a fist into the King's wrist. There was a clear snapping sound and the scaled armor exploded into black dust. The sword clattered to the floor. She backed away quickly when he lunged at her. Still she studied the armor trying to push her Vision to divine its secrets. Obviously the central core of the armor was protected somehow. Ales darted inside of his guard, and pummeled his body with a fury of blows. Then she saw it. It had tapped into his central nervous system, and in the same way her Sparks tapped into her own biological elementary forces his armor was tapping his to protect itself. When she struck it drew on him to cancel out her attack. The other armors were nothing like this one, and she knew why.

Thousands of cycles ago when the Tier were young they had begun to experiment with improving their abilities. They had been given their role by the gods, and they sought to be the best protectors for their world that they could be. As with all experimentation there were mistakes, and setbacks. The Tier erased these things from existence, but not the memory of these things. They knew it was important to remember their mistakes. One of those mistakes was a technology that had the ability to draw biological elementary energy from a body without their permission. Like her Sparks it required contact with the individual, but it worked even better in contact with blood and bone. Unlike her Sparks there were no barriers built in to keep the user safe. She had to make the decision to use the Sparks, but that old technology would simply pull energy just from being in contact with a body.

Somehow this thing, this creature, had gotten access to those old memories. It couldn't create the metal alloys necessary to build that old technology without significant resources that were very hard to come by. The knowledge of those things was hidden elsewhere. But Ales remembered two swords, forged of Black Sol alloy, hanging on the walls of the Hall of Light. Forged into swords to remind everyone how dangerous mistakes could be. Hung among hundreds of the mistakes that had brought the Tier to their place to remind the young ones who learned in the Hall of Light that even a mistake could do a good thing. That mistake had lead them to understand how to telepathically connect to their weapons. It had not only made it impossible for anyone but the Tier to use their weapons, but also protected anyone from a slow death by energetic drain.

Ales danced backed out of the King's range, and her Cellstructs warned her that she was nearing the dais that the throne had been sitting on. She was going to have to tear the armor away from his body to starve the core of energy to breech its defenses. She focused on the Circle of Breaking allowing her Cellstructs to observe the information from her other circles. She tried to prepare herself for the exhaustion she was going to feel after this. After a few more dodges red dots appeared on the King. Nerve centers on joints, the palms of his hands, the backs of his knees. A dozen locations that would disassociate the armor.

The King lunged at her again. She slid under his grasping hands, and pushed his arms up over her head. She darted inside of his guard, and struck at the points of red light overlaid on his body. She hit four in quick succession, and the part of the armor covering his legs lost all cohesion. It sloughed away from his body like a torn piece of clothing. It pooled on the floor like water or sand. The King's body posture changed completely in an instant. He was going to run, and Ales couldn't allow that. He turned, and Ales darted forward. But her Vision warned her that it was a ruse. He turned his body completely and struck at her head with the back of his fist. The armor increased the power of his blow, and Ales raised her arm just in time. She braced with her opposite hand.

She gritted her teeth when her wrist still broke. The Spark in that hand tumbled across the room and slid to a stop against the dais. Operating with nearly all of her Constraints open the bones in her wrist knitted almost immediately. She pulled the bracing hand back, and drove that Spark into the arm the King had hit her with. She hit it precisely at the weakest point at the elbow. That arm of the armor exploded into black dust. She bent backwards when he struck at her with his opposite hand, and then put her hands down flowing into a back handspring that left her standing next to the Spark he had knocked away. She bent never taking her eyes off the King. She grasped the dropped Spark, and stood.

"This is over. You are outmatched creature. Release him, or I will pry him from your grasp." Ales growled.

"You cannot have him!" The King screeched.

And then the King screamed in pain. It was not the awful screech of the creature that was working him like a puppet. It was his own scream. The creature was attempting to murder the King before she could save him. Sorstone buckled, and cracked beneath her feat. She dashed across the room in a blur. She slammed her Sparks into the weakest points of the chest piece just below the armpits. The remaining armor exploded, and the back half of the chestpiece clattered to the floor. The King immediately slouched towards the floor. Ales dropped her Sparks, and got her arms beneath the King's armpits.

She slid to the floor holding him up as all of her Constraints snapped closed. She was utterly exhausted. She had pushed far too hard trying to free him when it would have been far less taxing to simply kill him. Somehow though she knew she had done the right thing. Ales examined him with her Vision but she saw nothing that would be permanent. There were so many questions to be answered, but there were more pressing matters to attend to. The Sparks had done it, but she was utterly exhausted. Lia was still healing so she wouldn't have the energy to use the Sparks that Warran had given her. Ilsa's wounds were painful, but not life threatening. She was probably half as tired as Ales, but it had to be done. Carefully she laid Terran Roa down on the floor. She dragged herself to her feet, and made her way to where Ilsa was lying on her side struggling with her bonds. Ales knelt down next to her.

"Let me get you free."

Ales put her hands on the restraints. Her Cellstructs flowed into them. They overrode the control of the Bondstructs, and the locks snapped open. Tears of frustration ran down Ilsa cheeks. Ales wiped them away carefully. Ales closed her Vision.

"Ilsa I have to ask you to do something. I am drained and will not recover for hours. I need you to take these, and free the others of their armor." Ales gestured to the Sparks.

Ilsa lifted them. She slid them onto her hands so the bands of smooth metal covered her knuckles.

"They didn't do this to us did they? The people inside." Ilsa asked. Amazingly she had seen through what was happening. She had understood the exchanges on her own.

Ales nodded. "They are prisoners of the armor. Though be warned it may not be as simple as that. All these cycles of having no control could have damaged their minds. They were given their armor when they were very young, and they may not have been able to resist a desire to cooperate so that they could control their own bodies. They may be as evil as whatever blackness has taken control of their armor. Hurry up. We don't have much time until the guard gets back here. I don't want to have to hurt anyone else to get out of here. They are mostly innocent, and of no real danger to us. Cole be ready. Syle Roa is still out there, and she is still under the control of her armor. I haven't seen her since earlier at the banquet." Ales organized them all tidily.

"Their armors are controlled by a nerve center on the back between the shoulder blades. Strike there, and it will cleanse the entire armor." Ales explained what she had learned in her fight with the King.

Lia attempted to get up, but was unable to make her limbs function properly. She slumped back to the floor.

"I still have too much nerve damage. It'll be a time longer before I can move, Ales."

"I will carry you if I must. I cannot use my Sparks anymore this night, but in a few minutes I will be able to open my Constraints enough to carry you. We will make it out of here. We are a long way from done."

64

"That will not be necessary." An erudite voice said from the annex outside of the throne room. The Queen stood just inside the door. She had no less than a dozen guards with her. Guards that wore no bondarmor. The guards were her personal attendants, not palace guards. They had lancers drawn. Ales sagged.

"Could we not do this right now?" Ales growled. She pushed herself to her feet, and reached for her Windblade.

"How did you do this?" The Queen gestured to the King.

Ales did not lower her Windblade. The Queen made her slow way to her husband. Carefully she lowered herself to her knees. Ruinous holes pierced his arms, and legs where the armor had attached itself to him. They would leave terrible scars but he would not die from them. It took Ales a long moment to realize that the Queen had known all along.

"You knew they were being controlled." Ales said.

"Of course I did, but what could I do? I refused to wear the armor when I was brought here. I never had a hand in fighting. I was never much good at it. I was more for scholarly pursuits. The armor did not take him until I had borne our children. By then it was too late. Slowly it took them from me." The queen said, and her tone turned sorrowful.

Ales turned back to Ilsa. "Free them. We haven't much time."

"Will he recover?" Aisha asked.

"Given time, he will recover. But the infection has spread to many of the soldiers with bondarmor. We can trust no one who wears the cursed stuff. There is little time. Queen Roa, we must go. I cannot make you come with us, you must choose to go or stay." Ales said.

There was a sharp buzzing sound, and Narran Roa's armor fell away from his body into dust. The Queen looked to her son astonished. Then her eyes went wide with fear, and she covered her mouth with her hand.

"We have been giving our men new sets of bondarmor for many cycles now. Hundreds of new sets have been made, and they were given to newly minted commanding officers," Aisha said.

Ales paused, and then decided. "I have to go back for Kiltik." Her eyes began to glow again, darting around for a long moment, assessing something that no one else could see.

"Then it is true, you are of the Tier?" Aisha asked.

"We are all that is left Aisha. We cannot defend you from an army. And your daughter is still under the control of her armor. I do not know where Syle has gone, but I cannot help you get her back if we are destroyed."

"Then we must help you leave." The Queen said.

Lia finally managed to get to her feet. There was another buzzing discharge. Karan laid on the floor breathing shallowly. Blood ran from his ears. Ales examined him, but it was still too soon to say if he would recover. The level of swelling in his brain was not dangerous which was a good sign, but with a head injury like that there was no telling for sure without more time to examine him.

"I am sorry about Karan my Queen. I fear he has taken quite the blow to the head. He may not ever wake up."

Tears ran from Aisha's eyes. "I did not expect I would ever see him free of that curse. He would wail in his sleep about the things he had done. If he dies free that is a good enough end." Aisha said.

Ales nodded. She may not be a fighter, but Aisha was a hard woman.

"We can't leave them." Lia said. Aisha startled when Lia spoke.

"I am sorry to shock you My Queen, but as my sister has said there is little time. You cannot stay here. It will send those who are still in Its control, they will kill or retake everyone involved if you stay." Lia said.

Ilsa came to Ales, and held out her Sparks. Exhaustion was in ever line of her body.

"Gods how do you use those? I feel exhausted." Ilsa said.

"Cycles of practice." Ales said as she tucked them into their pouches inside of her long coat. She made an annoyed sound at the hole through the chest of her jacket.

"Lia we must make a decision. We can take them all but only if you can carry more than one." Ales said.

Lia folded her legs in series causing her body to undulate up and down. Her face twisted into a feline grimace. "I can do it, but you will have to tie them to my back." Lia said.

Ales could feel the headache coming on from using her Vision so strongly. She could not stay conscious for more than a few more hours before she would be overcome with exhaustion.

"Aisha you have to decide. I can take you all with us someplace safe for now until we can find a way to re-establish you all. It may take time, cycles before we can, but we will help you make this right. Further, your daughter, Syle, is still out there. I promise I will do what I can to track her down and free her, as well. But I can't force you." Ales said.

Aisha stayed on her knees clutching the King's hand. She did not respond, and Ales gave her a moment while she got the rest of them moving.

"Cole take Ilsa, and go down the Archive tower like you originally planned. You can protect each other. Get out of the center, and get to the clearing with Warran. Warran knows the plan, and we will catch up to you in a few days at most. More likely we will meet you there in a couple of hours. Lia might even beat you there." Ales said.

Cole nodded and turned away. Ales grabbed his arm and pulled him back.

"Cole, do not ever do this again. I am grateful for your help, and when you have come into your own as one of the Tier, you may do whatever you like. But if you disobey me again while I am responsible for you, I will be displeased. Do I make myself clear?" Ales spoke quietly.

Cole nodded, and then looked at Ilsa. He realized that she was mostly naked. Her dress was shredded in the back, and one long moment from falling right off of her. His eyes went a little wide, and Ilsa noticed. She shrugged.

"More important things to worry about than men seeing my breasts Cole. Even a man like you. Ales my parents?" Ilsa asked.

"That's one of the reasons we need to split up. I will get them out." Ales said.

"Aisha, I'm sorry but you have to decide." Ales said.

"We will go with you." Aisha said.

"I do not wish to see your children retaken, but I have to ask. Do you think they will fight us when they wake? Do you know how their time in the armor has affected them?" Lia said.

"I can't say for sure. It never controlled them as deeply as it did Terran. But I can't imagine they will be unscathed." Aisha said.

"Lia, how hard will it before you to carry them if we tie them down?" Ales said.

"I won't be jumping across roof tops, but I should be able to run fairly quickly even carrying them. We should use the Center Ales. The streets, and alleyways will act like a labyrinth."

"My Queen you will be coming with me. I assume you have something more suitable to wear?" Ales said. Aisha nodded, and rose from the King's side. Cole, and Ilsa slipped out the annex doorway.

"Will they be all right?" Aisha asked.

"I don't know right now My Queen. They are both talented if a bit young. I must believe that they will be, or else I cannot do what I must."

Ales went to Lia, who laid down next to Narran's body. Ales carefully lifted the giant man, and laid him across Lia's back. She carefully tied a harness across Lia's chest using a heavy cord she kept inside of her coat. Lia stood up lifting him easily.

"How bad?" Ales asked. Lia moved experimentally.

"It'll be fine. I can run with five times this on my back we are wasting time. Get Karan, and the King on."

Lia trotted over, and laid down next to Karan. They repeated the process stacking him on top of Narran. Then again with the King. Lia stood up, and moved slowly testing her ability to stretch without them falling off.

{*Tighten the harness around my chest Ales. It's too lose. It's going to tangle in my middle leg on the right eventually.*} Ales followed her instructions.

"Ales what is the plan?" Lia asked when Ales was done.

"I told Kiltik I would go back for him. I thought it would be once we made a place for ourselves, but the situation has changed. We have lost Verdant, and we need his help to remake her. If I don't go for him now we won't ever get another chance."

The leader of the Queen's guards stepped up. "We can help you."

"You can help me by protecting the Queen while she gets the things she needs. My Queen clothes, weapons, and travel food. Take only what you can carry. Gold will not be important. I will be back here in less than one hour. Guardsman, listen to me. If any bondarmored soldiers confront you run. Come back here, and hold them off until I can send help. I will know if you are in trouble. I will be as quick as I can." The queen grabbed Ales' arm.

"Thank you." She said.

"Thank me when we are safely away from here my Queen."

65

{*Ales?*} Lia's voice came into her mind.

{*Is everything all right?*} Ales asked. She felt the mental affirmative come across the connection.

{*What haven't you told me?*} Lia asked. Ales gave a mental sigh. It was easier to just get it out of the way. If she didn't Lia would come back for her. She kept it short.

{*Kiltik built himself a body while I was sleeping off the cataclysm. It is extremely powerful, and he is worried that I will not be able to deactivate it effectively. I'm going to attempt it now.*} She felt the mental pause that indicated that Lia was exasperated with her.

{*Do you think you can do it?*} Lia asked.

{*I'm not sure. I think with the Sparks I could disable it for a few minutes. But if I use those again tonight I don't know if I will be able to stay conscious. Kiltik does not understand how much my strength has increased with what father did to my Cellstructs.*} Ales replied. There was another pause but this one felt different. It was a feeling of worry that she had gotten from Lia many times.

{*You always do this. Right to the limits. We can come back for Kiltik. Please Ales.*} Lia pleaded with her.

{*We will never have this opportunity again, not with so many controlled by the creature coming here, and they are certainly coming, Lia. Perhaps if I can take Kiltik that creature may not even stay here any longer. But if we leave him I have no idea what the creature will do. It might destroy this entire city and everyone in it just to keep us from getting back here. I will release Ilsa's parents on the way. One of the entrances to the Citadel prison is in the Searcher's quarters.*}

Ales ran full tilt down the sorstone corridor leading to the central stairwell. It was the only one that she could jump down the center without hitting any of the floors.

{*Good Luck Sister.*}

When she got there, men in black bondarmor were storming up the stairs. She didn't bother slowing down. She pushed open the first three levels of her Constraints with some effort, and leapt over the stair well railing. She felt more than saw the swords swishing as they tried to slash at her. She fell eight floors straight down. She flipped over, and managed to land feet first. She flexed her knees to absorb the impact, and darted away down the hall towards the doors to the Searchers quarters.

The locks on the doors recognized her when she touched them, and she rushed inside. The entire Citadel was in chaos, and the Searchers quarters were no exception. Men, and women in light blue coats wearing goggles were running around like hiluk on fire. Ales simply slipped into the fray. She invoked her Vision using only the slightest pushes of Taking to make people not look at her. Even that caused the throb in her temples to increase exponentially. She thought about how stupid she had been to open all seven Circles if she didn't intend to kill someone. She could have figured out the King's armor with Breaking, and Observance alone. Hindsight she admonished herself.

When she got down the stairwell to the second door, the one she had destroyed, there were two guards at the door in black armor. She didn't waste any time. She drew her Windblade. She snapped it out in an arc, and a blast of wind roared into the enclosed space. It brutally slammed the guards against the wall. They collapsed to the ground, but began to stir immediately. She thought about doing something much more drastic, but she reminded herself that these were innocent men. She couldn't afford to kill them, but she couldn't afford to be delicate either. She was almost out of time.

Her Cellstructs had been warning her for the last half an hour that they were having trouble keeping the swelling in her brain down to normal levels. She regretted using her powers so strongly earlier more with every passing second. If she hadn't been so focused on overpowering the King she might be able to use Taking to freeze them up for long enough to get in and out of the room. Bypassing their armor without killing them was going to be difficult. Maybe though she wouldn't have to. Mentally she reached out to Kiltik. There was a surprised reply in her mind, and then she felt the handshake as Kiltik reached for her. The connection made, she spoke over Kiltik who was attempting to greet her.

{I am sorry Kiltik but there is no time. Can you deactivate the bondarmor these guards are wearing?} Ales asked immediately.

{This One cannot from this range. If you were to draw them closer to This One, This One could.}

Ales could do it herself, but it would take her long minutes, and she would kill a lot of her Cellstructs doing it. But Kiltik had dominion over all non-autonomous Bondstructs in his immediate presence. These were autonomous but only in the sense that they were under outside control. The structures themselves had no neural capacity like her Cellstructs did. Kiltik had said that was what had made them susceptible to infection. She forced her Constraints open two more levels, and found she could go no further. While using her Constraints was more a physical exertion than an energetic one they still required her bioelementary energy to power themselves. Right then she just didn't have the necessary energy to push them open further. It would have to be enough.

She slid her Windblade carefully back into its sheath, and then dashed between the two guards who had regained their feet. They made a grab for her, and they were fast, but not fast enough to catch her. She rushed across the room to the massive double doors. Then she drew out her Windblade, and lowered herself into a fighters crouch. She probably could have overridden the door without Kiltik's help but she didn't want to put any more strain on her failing body than she had too. So she waited for the soldiers to draw the lancers and fire at her. A sharp detonation sounded through the room as she swept her sword from left to right in a blur. The lancer bolts were blown out of the air.

"If you want me that bad those toys aren't going to do it." She held her sword out towards them in a taunting gesture.

{Be ready Kiltik, they are coming.} Ales said.

{This One is prepared.} Kiltik replied.

The soldiers drew their swords, and flew at her. When they got within ten paces of the door their bodies froze up, and they stumbled. They slid to the ground at her feet, and she sighed in relief.

{Thank you Kiltik.}

{This One is pleased to have helped. This One wonders why you have returned so soon?} Kiltik asked.

{Because you have to come with us now. I can deactivate your body long enough to extract you.} Ales said.

Sharp negation came across the mental connection.

{You misunderstand Alessandra, Family Katae. The only thing that keeps This One's body from escaping is This One's influence

over that body. To free This One from confinement This One's body must be cleansed.}

Ales sagged.

{What if I were to simply destroy this body Kiltik? It is not an option I wish to pursue, but I am far too exhausted to attempt a cleansing right now and I must take you with me. We will not have another chance to free you from this place in the foreseeable future.}

The Mind sent sharp feelings of displeasure and sorrow across their telepathic link.

{This One cannot survive the destruction of This One's body. The psionic link between This One, and This One's body is indelible by its nature. This One could not use This One's body without that link.} There was a long pause. Ales did not respond, because Kiltik was making a decision.

{If This One's continued existence is to be a danger to others, This One will gladly make that sacrifice Alessandra, Family Katae. But This One senses that This One can be of service to you.} Kiltik said.

Ales wracked her brain trying to find a better way.

{I will cleanse your body Kiltik, but I may not survive the encounter. I certainly will not be conscious when it is done. So I must ask if I am able to free your body will you be able to defend it from the infection?}

The response was a distinct affirmative.

{This One was interrupted when instantiating self-awareness routines for This One's body. This One was unable to respond quickly enough to defend This One's body from the infection. This One will not make the same mistake twice.}

{And your body will be strong enough to get us both out of here?} Ales already knew the answer to the question, but unlike the Mind she was human. She needed the reassurance.

{In terms of strength and speed This One's body is the equal of any of the Tier save the Newlings who are possessed of full helixical integration.} Kiltik responded.

Ales reached into her coat and removed her Sparks. She slid them over her hands, and looked around the sorstone room fixing it in her mind. There was a very real chance she would die here, so she wanted to remember it so she would have a place to start when she was reborn. She would remember nothing else but this place, but this place would lead her down the path she needed to follow.

{Before I do this, there is one more thing I need to know Kiltik. How much control do you have over what goes on in the Citadel, and the Center?}

{This One has complete access to all inert bondstructed materials in the Center. If they are not currently activated This One can take control of them. What can This One do to assist you?}

"There must be something more we can do for her."
Zezzhz said as they watched Ales through the window of the
Skyfire. Through the Skyfire they could see all of the world.

"These are the echoes of their end my love. They must be
responsible for repairing the damage. They must get their
power back. If we aid them any more than we already have
what confidence will that inspire in future generations?" She
replied.

"She will die Avaara." Zezzhz said. He always had a
better grasp on the possible futures.

"Perhaps, but I think that you may actually be surprised for
once." Avaara said a smile spread across her face. She patted
his glimmering cheek, and then made a swiping gesture with
her free hand. The view though the Skyfire changed to Lia
running through the city with three large men roped down to
her back.

"She has come a long way from the broken terrified girl we
helped to become one of the Wild." Avaara said.

"Mostly due to your tender care. She would not have
recovered were it not for you."

"Oh I think she would have, but I'm not sure she would
have recovered yet. She was so very damaged when I found
her. So very strong when she finally left us again. Trust."
Zezzhz said.

"Trust my love. Our children are strong. But perhaps a
small reminder." Avaara said, and reached out slowly and
touched the image of Liassa.

Lia slid to a stop when she sensed the sending coming on. It was not very often she felt the handshake of a long range memory transfer but that feeling was unmistakable. Only the Gods and the Core could make a connection as powerful as that.

The world vanished, and she saw a memory from rotations earlier. A memory of Avaara shedding crystal blue tears. She patted the tears from her cheeks with a perfect white square of material that looked as if it were made of moss. This she carefully folded and handed to Ales.

Lia gasped as she emerged from the memory. It was like breaking the surface of a freezing lake. She shook herself briefly making sure not to dislodge her burden. She touched her paw to the bag hanging around her neck. Ales had given her the cloth after she had gained that little hiding spot. She ran her paw along the bag, and the perfect white square of moss fell out onto her paw. She opened her Vision, and focused on the Circle of Finding. She looked at the cloth, and white lines exploded from it. They shot out in all directions as her abilities as a Finder tried to determine what was connected to the cloth. One of the white lines pulsed with an almost blinding glow. It disappeared off down the street back the way she came towards the Citadel. She couldn't go back there now, not with three men stacked on her back like cord wood.

She carefully slipped the square back into her pouch. She turned around, and opened her first two levels of Constraints nearly tripling her strength and speed. There were numerous warnings from her Cellstructs about the damage this would cause. She ignored them. She ran as fast as she could manage. It still took her a long half hour to reach the clearing. She consoled herself with the fact that she could run much faster on the way back unburdened. She trotted into the clearing, and found everyone sitting around a small neatly tended fire. It was clearly Warran's work. The stones were laid in a perfect circle, and the bottom of the pit was also lined with stones. No one else would have bothered to be that thorough. He jumped to his feet when he realized that Lia was there.

"Who are they? Where is Ales?" He asked. He skidded to a stop when he recognized the king.

"Mother's End." He cursed.

"You kidnapped the King!" He said.

"Not kidnapped. Saved Warran. Please help me get them down and I'll explain it all." Lia said.

Warran carefully began to untie the harness.

"Ales is still inside the Citadel. She is attempting to retrieve Kiltik. There are complications, and I can't explain them all now. I have to go back to help her. I have something that she is going to need." Lia laid down once Warran had the harness undone. She made sure to balance the men so they didn't fall off her back.

"Wait slow down. What happened? Did she get what she needed?"

"She got some of it, but there was no time. We were hurt badly, and Ales had to interrupt what she was doing. When we confronted the royal family we changed the rules. There will be a lot of bondarmored soldiers coming back to secure this place. We beat down the infection's strongest far too easily. It makes sense that it will attempt to secure this place with overwhelming force now."

"We have to find a better way to address this monster. Did the Sparks work?" Warran asked. Cole and Ilsa joined them. They helped Warran lift the unconscious men off of Lia's back.

"They worked, but not as well as you were hoping. But that doesn't matter right now. I can explain more later. Right now I need to go back for Ales. She needs me."

Cole knelt down next to her checking the men to see if they were alive.

"Lia, they need you more." Cole whispered.

Lia watched Warran and Ilsa carry the men closer to the fire. Kayna sat warming her tiny hands at the fire. She narrowed her eyes at him.

"Trying to be a hero now Cole?"

"I'm trying to learn how to be a person Lia. Instead of just a thief. But this is something else. I've been fighting it ever since the first time I saw you, and it was stupid of me. Give it to me Lia." Cole held out his hand.

"You can't make it back fast enough for this. I can go faster." Lia argued, but she knew that she wasn't going to win this argument.

Cole nodded. "Yes, but that isn't the point here. This is for me to do. Give them to me Lia, and I will make sure they get to Ales." Cole said.

"You knew from the start this would happen. She came to you. Gods, how could I not see it?" Lia berated herself.

It was right in front of her, and all she had to do was open her eyes. In all the world there were only ever a few hundred people that the Gods revealed themselves to outside of the Tier. They were people who had a destiny. People who had roles to play. People who would likely one day be Tier. Ales had seen it. That was why she hadn't been ready to give up. She had been determined because her Vision had shown her the touch of the Mother on him.

Lia opened her Vision, and concentrated on the Circle of Light. Only there could she see the inner light of a person. Their elementary force of life. In that light there was no mistaking someone who had been touched by the Mother, or the Father. They had an indelible mark. A suffusion of pure white light that surrounded their life force. She saw it then strong and pure surrounding Cole.

"After my family was murdered, she came to me. It was a cold night, and I had taken a soaking trying to fish my dinner out of the river. That was when she came. She saw me fed, and she told me that I had to be strong because one day I would meet people who would be a family to me. That one of them would even be a katali who could talk. I was so young, and like a child I believed. When I got older I thought that she had just been saying something to make a child feel better. When you appeared, and began speaking I knew that she hadn't been telling tales to make a young boy feel special. She had been preparing me to protect my new family. She set me on a path, and this is where it lead me. If I am to stay on that path it's time I pulled my weight."

He offered his hand to her. Lia nodded, and removed the square from her bag. She tipped her paw, and it slid into his hand.

"What exactly is this?" Cole asked. He unfolded it, and saw the aquamarine liquid still wet inside of it.

"Tears of the Mother. They can heal any wound or hurt. Rarer than the breath of a winged hyron. I don't know why

Ales would need them, but I know that she does. How are you going to find her?" Lia asked.

"I'll follow the sound of the chaos." Cole said. He refolded the square, and it disappeared into his jacket.

"Cole, all the Tier are reborn, and I swear if you don't bring yourself back to me alive I will find you again one day. You understand me yes?" Lia said.

There wasn't a single shred of mirth on that feline face. What it did promise is that when she caught up with him again the torment she had dished out thus far would seem a joy-filled romp through a room filled with gold compared to what she would do to him. He took a step back away from her because for the first time he literally felt waves of emotion emanating from her. He could feel her protective instincts, and how strong they were. He nodded to her. He turned to the woods, and disappeared into the underbrush.

68

The lock spun like a gear on its axis, and the doors slid aside. Ales slipped inside her Vision illuminating the darkness for her. The door immediately began to close as soon as she was through. The throbbing in her temples intensified with each passing moment. Her Cellstructs warned her that if she continued to operate at this level she was risking an elementary energy discharge that could take cycles to repair. Worse was that she recognized the feeling. She had felt it when she had pushed herself to destroy the Traitor, and nearly destroyed herself in the process.

The black orb that was Kiltik sat on a small sorstone plinth glowing orange lines ran across its shining surface. His body was not what she had expected. It was clearly designed after the body of the rowunalf. It was a creature whose body was an oblong spheroid with hundreds of tough flexible tentacles covering its surface, and a coat on its back that closely resembled long grass. It was an amazing imitator of other predators. It could twist its tentacles into solid limbs, and often times from a distance it was impossible to distinguish it from the animal it had chosen to imitate. Even humans. This one was lacking the grass like protrusions, and was made of burnished grey metal that looked like some form of sol alloy. Her Vision told her that it was not sol. It was some combination of elements that she had not seen before. She had never seen Bondstructs so perfectly meshed together with one another. Truly this was a masterpiece of Tieran craft. Its appendages twisted insanely, and it rose to a human shape. With Kiltik buried inside it it would be a fully synthetic life form. A synthoid. It was beautiful.

{Kiltik does it have elementary force protections?} Ales asked.

{It does. This One could not allow This One's body to be so simply breeched. You will have to bypass the limbs, and create a break in the outer layer of the core, then strike through that opening.} Kiltik responded.

It rushed her, and it was as fast as Kiltik had said. Thankfully it seemed to act entirely on instinct. It threw punches and kicks that Ales was able to avoid with fair ease. She danced backwards when it tried to dive on top of her. It missed, but its limbs disentangled and flailed wildly. She had

to back up further, or be stabbed by one of the flailing
tentacles. Each of them was needle sharp at the end. A
moment later it flowed into the six legged form of a katali.
Ales ducked, and dodged as paws swiped at her.

*{Kiltik if your body is to survive this I need the schematics. I need
to know everything. I'm going to get myself killed if I try to use
Breaking to split it off little by little, or I'm going to destroy
something vital.}* Ales said.

She slid her Sparks into the pouch inside of her jacket. She
had to be more aggressive.

*{If This One sends you that information it will severely disrupt
your ability to respond to attack.}* Kiltik protested. She could feel
the fear for her wellbeing through their link.

{I will buy the few moments we need. Be ready.}

She drew her Windblade. Kiltik's body flew at her paws
wide. Wickedly sharp claws forming from the tips of the
tentacles that made up the paws. She swung her Windblade,
and the synthoid was blasted back across the room. It
slammed into the far wall, and slid to the ground. Ales spun
turning her Windblade in a series of motions that were
designed to create a wind current that would sustain itself for
a few seconds. The synthoid picked itself up from the ground.
Before it could make another try for her a gale slammed it back
and held it where it was. Ales let her blade fall to her side.

{Now!}

Images poured into her memory like an ocean. Thousands,
upon thousands of schematics, figures, designs. The synthoid
was amazingly complex. Its Bondstructs were not metal at all,
but a form of molecularly fused gemstone. It was how Kiltik
had shielded its body from elementary force interference. It
wouldn't conduct any sort of energetic discharge. It was self-
repairing, which was good because any damage she did would
repair itself fairly quickly if she didn't continue to tear it apart.
The pattern of red Breaking indicators she had been seeing
made a lot more sense now. She emerged from the telepathic
transfer, and immediately she realized she had made an error.

The synthoid had recovered much more quickly than she
had anticipated. It had crossed the gap while her mind was
absorbing what Kiltik had sent her. It had latched onto her,
and dozens of its tentacles pierced her body. Her Cellstructs
were screaming in protest as they tried vainly to mend the
dozens of wounds. The pain was excruciating, and worse she

couldn't move. The synthoid had her pinned to the ground. Needle pointed tentacles were driving into her chest, and she howled in frustration. She had done too much damage to her body to disengage her pain reactions. She did her best to focus past the pain. She crashed through the seventh level of her Constraints. It was the only move she had left.

Her Cellstructs flowed out into her body from her reserve infusing every tissue of her to a degree she did not know was possible. Fully half of her cells were supported by her Structures. They chewed through the tentacles that pierced her body. She brought her hands across her chest when the synthoid tried to pierce her with more of its limbs. She bucked her body off the ground, and her fists slammed into the center mass of the synthoid. It was thrown across the room. Sorstone shattered where it hit, and she was up on her feet before it made the journey. She grabbed her fallen Windblade off the ground. Lightning fast she swung it. Sheering blasts of air compressed to the point of plasma peeled dozens of limbs off the creature. They were precise, perfectly placed cuts that landed exactly on the indicators the Circle of Breaking showed her. Finally one of them slid through the hull of the synthoid's main body. Ales darted forward dropping her Windblade. She drew out one of her Sparks, and smashed it into the gaping hole on the side of the synthoid's body. There was a sharp sizzling sound, and the synthoid collapsed. Ales immediately dropped to her knees, and groaned her misery.

{Alessandra, Family Katae!}

The oddly formal title combinded with the shout of dismay was so out of place in her mind. Softly she began to laugh. She couldn't help it. With a mental effort she closed her Constraints to dedicate all of her Cellstructs to healing. Finally she closed her Vision before she could pass out.

{It's all right. This One has you. This One will protect you.}

Kiltik's thoughts were soothing reassurance that Ales desperately needed. She tried to stay awake, but her Cellstructs warned her that if she did not reduce her mental activity she would damage herself. She finally relinquished control to them and slept.

69

Cole hadn't known just how accurate his idea of following the chaos would be. The Citadel square was filled with festival goers. All of them were talking about the monster that had burst from the Citadel with the body of the Night Lady on its back. Cole pulled a drunken noble aside.

"Which way did it go?" He asked.

"Let go of me peasant!" He tried to shake himself free of Cole's grip.

Cole drew one of his lancers, and pressed the barrel to the noble's temple.

"If you do not tell me what I want to know by the Father I will make your head as empty as your brain is. Which way did it go?!" Cole yelled in the fool's face.

The nobleman pointed bloomward down the street. Cole ran stopping every few blocks to get directions from the people who had seen the beast running through the streets. Using the grapple, he made his way onto the rooftops when the creature took to the alleyways. The thievesway served him well, and he finally caught up with it.

"Wait!" He shouted down into the alleyway.

The creature that was carrying her obviously understood him because it turned one orange glowing eye up towards him. It shook its head and continued to run. It was so fast he didn't think he could catch it. On the run he couldn't get a clear enough shot to slow it down without risking putting a bolt into Ales. Cole groaned as he got an idea that would probably get him killed for his trouble.

"This is going to hurt." He mumbled to himself.

He jumped between two rooftops. The alleyway ended in at a t-junction. Cole fired his grapple ahead of the creature, and then leapt off the side of the building. He hit the reel on the grapple, and it dragged him forward through the air at an alarming rate. He bent his knees, and tried to brace for the impact. He thought his legs would break when his feet slammed into the side of the creature. Amazingly it didn't fall over. It spun around perfectly balancing Ales' body on its back. Its shape was similar to a maevea, but smaller. Cole pulled his remaining lancer, since the other one had zipped off down the alleyway on the grapple line.

"What in the abyss are you?" Cole said. The creature just stared him down with baleful orange eyes.

"That doesn't matter right now. Whatever you are I think you are trying to help her, and that is why I am here. If you let me I can help."

The thing adjusted its eyes slightly until they fixed on the lancer in Coles hand. It was hard to tell because they were pupilless orbs of burning orange light, but he was positive. He held up one hand, and slowly slipped the lancer into the holster behind his back. He held up two empty hands.

"I am a friend. I want to help, but I can't help if you kill me."

After a long pause the monster folded its legs, and laid on the ground. Cole approached slowly. He reached into his coat, and the thing shook its head at him aggressively. He pulled the folded white square of moss out of his jacket.

"This will make her better."

Cole approached slowly keeping his motions small, and his body language nonthreatening. He examined Ales quickly, and found dozens of wounds. She had lost a lot of blood, and he could see small blue rivulets running down the flank of the creature. He cringed, and put a finger beneath her nose. She was breathing, but barely. He looked at the glistening aquamarine liquid, and wasn't sure what to do with it. Lia had said it would heal anything, but he had no idea how to administer it. The odd creature watched him, and then it tilted its head. It was an odd animal like gesture that he had seen Lia do a number of times. It was a question.

"I don't know what to do with this."

Cole stepped back when the creature flowed out from underneath Ales. It became a mass of writhing tendrils, which slowly lowered Ales to the ground. Its limbs twisted together again and it reformed into the small maevea. It slowly walked around Ales' body. Cole squeezed his eyes closed, and prayed that this thing would not kill him. It didn't make any sound, but he felt a soft touch on his hand. He opened one eye, and found the creature's nose touching his hand. It waited until it was sure he was watching, and then it walked to Ales. It touched its nose to her mouth. It looked up at Cole, and stepped back. It shook its head once, and waited.

"Gods I hope this works."

Cole folded the cloth slightly to create a channel for the liquid to flow down. He tipped it over Ales' mouth. The drop of liquid fell into her mouth. Ales' body shivered violently. Azure light poured out of Ales' wounds. Cole saw how many there were, and their placement told him that she should be dead several times over. The wounds slowly closed, and the light disappeared. Cole bent over her. He watched the rise and fall of her chest which was strong and steady. He shook her a little but she wouldn't wake. The creature came slowly closer, and looked her over. It looked up at him, and then tilted its head. Cole shrugged. He had no idea why she wouldn't wake up.

"Maybe Lia will know what is wrong. Can you carry her?" Cole asked tentatively.

He was fairly certain it could understand him, but he couldn't be absolutely certain. Just as he was about to bend down and carry her himself the creature flowed apart again. Its tendrils slid beneath Ales, and lifted her easily. It reformed beneath her, and looked at him. It tossed its head, and turned back down the alleyway in the direction it had been going.

70

When Cole entered the clearing Lia was pacing back and forth madly. She looked up as soon as he stepped out of the bushes. She froze when she saw the silver maevea in miniature stepping through the bushes next to him. Her eyes glowed with her Vision, and then her ears came up. A look of utter surprise went across her face. She trotted across the clearing. they stood for a long moment staring into each other's eyes.

"Lia, I gave Ales the tears, but she hasn't woken up yet."

She didn't respond, and Cole waved his hand in front of her eyes. When she still didn't respond he looked up to Ilsa and Warran who had joined them, and shrugged.

"I think they are communicating telepathically." Ilsa said.

"Indeed we are." Lia finally said.

"Apologies. Kiltik was sharing his memories of what happened to Ales. It takes all of our attention to transfer so much information between us. Kiltik's body was infected by the Invader. Ales had to spend most of her strength to remove the infection. Gods how does she do it?" Lia asked. She was speaking to herself but Cole responded anyway.

"What do you mean?" Cole asked.

Lia just shook her head. "She was always the most special of us. One day you will see just how much different she is Cole. There is no way she should have been able to fight the King and Kiltik's body all in one day. Had I attempted the same feat I would be dead. The healing forces that you introduced into her body gave her system a shock. It will take some time for that to wear off. Sufficed to say she will be fine in an hour or two. By then we have to be gone." Lia's ears twitched, and she looked off at the tree line.

"It seems like Kiltik's little series of tricks worked." Lia said, and then hurried off towards three people emerging from the tree line. Two women, and a man in traveling clothes. The man was carrying a pack that looked heavy with needful things, though the two women were also carrying a bedroll each.

"May I introduce you all to Queen Aisha Roa, and..."

"Mama, Papa!" Ilsa shouted over Lia. She ran past Lia. She dove into her Father's arms.

"How did you get out?" She asked.

"A series of unfortunate events befell the guards, and everyone else who stood in the way of us getting out of the Center. Though a few guards simply got out of the way when they saw that we were traveling with our Lady the Queen. I assume we have your new friends to thank for that?" Lerand asked.

Ilsa disentangled herself from her Father, and turned back to Lia. Lia nodded.

"You could say that." Lia replied.

"How is my family?" The Queen asked.

"Resting in relative comfort my Queen."

Kiltik carried Ales over to the fire, and flowed out from underneath her.

"I didn't think we would need to move so many unconscious people. Things never really turn out the way you expect them do they?" Lia mumbled to herself.

"I am so confused." Ellena said.

"I am sorry to have disrupted your lives so profoundly. It was never our intention to do this to anyone." Lia explained.

"What precisely have you gotten us into?" The Queen asked.

"My Queen it is more of what we have gotten you out of. I don't know everything because I've not been able to speak with my sister. Kiltik tells me that you knew that many of your soldiers, and your family were being controlled. What you likely do not know is that we believe this problem to be far more widespread. With your family free of control you are now all targets for the Invader. We came here because we hope to be able to stop this Invader. That is the short of it. The long of it is a complicated story that we will be happy to share with you on the road."

GLOSSARY

Sphere	A sphere is a weight of measure that is equivalent to 2.25 lbs on earth.
Interval	100 Cycles Equivalent of the term century in English.
Long Interval	1000 Cycles Equivalent to the term millennium in English.
Cycle	Language equivalent to a year in English. 1.51 Years Earth Time (550 Earth Days) 440 Days on Ahlysim On Ahlysim a cycle has 10 rotations.
Day	Same as the earth concept. Equivalent to 30 hours in earth time.
Rotation	Language equivalent of a month in English. A Rotation has 44 days.
Span	Language equivalent of a week in English. A span has 11 days.
Falling	English language equivalent of Afternoon, or the middle of the day. After the sun has reached its peak and is falling.

Break	English language equivalent of morning, day break. Language Equivalent Examples in the morning: at breaks morning: breaking(alt. breaks depending on phrasing)
Ends	Dusk, the end of the day. Language equivalent to evening in English. Language Equivalent Examples evening: ending (alt. ends depending on phrasing such as at dusk would be at ends)
Night	Same as night in English. The time between full dark, and morning.
Curses	Mother's End: General curse, referring to the end of the world, the death of the Mother Avaara. Father's Stones: General curse, no explanation needed. How in the howling abyss(?): The howling abyss is one of the deepest canyons on all of Ahlysim. No normal person has ever made it through the howling abyss. It is said that there are supernatural creatures in the abyss making it impossible to pass. It is a phrase used to express frustration, or impossibility of a task.
Moonward	The direction from which the moon rises on Ahlysim. English language Equivalent of East.

Sunward	The direction from which the sun rises, it is directly opposite the moon rise. English language equivalent of West.
Stoneward	Generally on Ahlysim the lands in the stoneward hemisphere tend to be more mountainous, and are generally associated with The Father. Hence Stoneward. English language equivalent of North
Bloomward	The lands in the bloomward hemisphere of Ahlysim are generally a little more temperate and covered in blue than the planet to the north and so is generally associated with The Mother. Hence Bloomward. English language equivalent of South
Peb	Unit of measure. 1/36th of 1 sphere. Or roughly 1 ounce.
Fixer	Fixer is a blanket term for anyone who repairs anything. This could be carpenters, mechanics, smiths, as well as physicians. There are different terms used but Fixer is the general term.
Mender	Mender is a specialized term for a Fixer who repairs the human body. A doctor, or physician.
Flit	Flit is a common word. It is used interchangeably with the Earth word: bird.
Streic	A heavy fabric with elastic properties used for the manufacture of clothing primarily in Vilhena.

Length	English language equivalent of a mile.
	Equivalent to 6,000 marks.
Mark	English language equivalent of a foot.
	Equivalent to 10 ticks.
Tick	English equivalent of an inch.
	Equivalent to 1.5 inches.